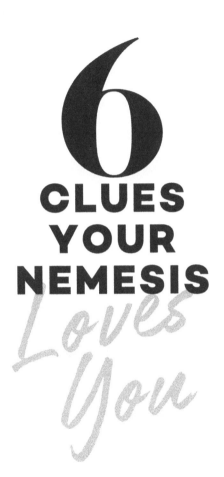

6
CLUES
YOUR
NEMESIS
Loves You

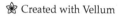 Created with Vellum

Also by Kelly Siskind

Visit Kelly's website and join her newsletter for great giveaways and never miss an update!

www.kellysiskind.com

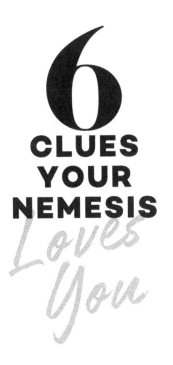

6
CLUES
YOUR
NEMESIS
Loves You

A Bower Boys Novel
Kelly Siskind

CHAPTER
One

MAGGIE EDELSTEIN WILL BE the death of me. I'm stuck in a supply closet with the door cracked open, sucking in air like I'm trapped in an oxygen-deprived elevator. I don't do elevators. Or tight spaces. Unfortunately, when it comes to Maggie, I lose all sense of self-preservation.

"The Kindness Rocks program kicks off tomorrow," Maggie says from the hallway. Her voice is as imperial as when she strutted through Windfall High, Queen Bee of her clique. "And you're telling me Allan lost the rocks?"

Mrs. Brazowski, who's worked for Windfall's Downtown Development Association since I was a teen, sighs. "He's sure he left them in the conference room, but they're not there."

I don't care where the stupid rocks are. My body has decided it's in a sweat lodge, my arms are shaking harder than when I finish a grueling rock-climb, and my heart is gunning for my throat. These ladies need to move this conversation anywhere else but here.

Maggie huffs. "Rocks don't walk away."

"No, but they do roll." Mrs. Brazowski gives a full-teeth smile.

Maggie snorts, the sound as painfully cute as I remember. "Not even your awful jokes can fix this mess."

"It's all I've got," Mrs. B. mutters.

All *I've* got is a view of Maggie's back. Her flame-red hair is shorter than it was in high school—shoulder-length now—her curvier figure hugged by a slim skirt and fitted blouse. I haven't had a good glimpse of her face since I returned to my hometown a few weeks ago, because every time she's near, I duck and hide. Or, in this awesome case, almost asphyxiate in a supply closet. Legs shaky, I lower to my knees and squint through the door crack.

Maggie tucks her stack of files tighter to her side. "Please remind Allan we have one hundred kids showing up tomorrow, and they're all expecting to get a rock so they can paint uplifting messages on them and place them around town. If he doesn't find those rocks, I'm letting the kids paint him."

Mrs. Brazowski perks up. "Can we do that even if he finds the rocks?"

"Add it to the suggestion box," Maggie says as her high heels click-clack away.

The second she's gone, I crawl out of the supply closet and splay on my back, attempting to gulp in buckets of air.

"Lennon Bower? Is that you?"

I can barely make out Mrs. Brazowski's kind face through the spots in my vision, but I wave at her. "Hey, Mrs. B. It's been a while. Great to see you."

It's been eleven years, to be precise.

Not because I left the charming hamlet of Windfall by choice. My lucky family got shoved into witness protection for a decade —thanks to my criminal father, who laundered money for a drug cartel. I'd love to say that's some kind of ironic joke about embarrassing dads and dysfunctional family feuds. But *ha-ha-ha*. Joke's on me. This madness is actually my life.

Because of dear old Dad, I spent a paranoid decade looking over my shoulder, sure a cartel hit man was hot on my heels, ready to torture me in one of those concrete basements with chains hanging from the ceiling and blood crusted into the floor. I never did meet a hit man or a blood-crusted floor. I'm also no longer in witness protection, courtesy of a vicious cartel feud. Lucky for us, bad dudes killed other bad dudes, and the bad dudes after my family are no longer alive to threaten us. Karma, I tell ya. She's one badass bitch.

My family has since left witness protection. But I'm still hiding.

From Maggie Edelstein.

"I heard you were in town," Mrs. B. says to my sprawled self. "But why were you in the supply closet?"

"Had to make a call." I mime holding a cell to my ear. "Needed privacy."

"Okay," she says slowly, not buying my nonsense. "Can I get you something? Water? You look flushed."

What I need is a world where Maggie doesn't exist.

"All good." I motion vaguely at nothing, still on my back, attempting to regulate my breathing. I refuse to tell Mrs. Brazowski my claustrophobic-self was hiding from Maggie. Gossip is this town's cryptocurrency. "I'll just be down here for a minute." Or ten. "Which way to the zoning permit people?"

Still giving me some serious side-eye, she gestures in the opposite direction Maggie went, *thank God*. "Take the hall to the end. Mr. Bajwa can help you from there. And it really is nice to see you, Lennon. I'm glad more of your family is moving back to town."

With a last quizzical glance at my reclined-in-the-middle-of-the-hallway body, she shakes her head and walks off.

"Goddamn Maggie Edelstein," I mumble.

Eleven years, and she still has the power to annihilate me.

I blink until my wooziness clears, then hop up and straighten my T-shirt. I find Mr. Bajwa easily and give him a timid "Hello, sir."

I was friends with his son Mizhir in high school. We played video games together and sometimes ate at each other's houses. There may also have been a time or seven when I coaxed Mizhir into harmless trouble. The last day I saw his father, we were sitting outside the principal's office, because I'd dared Mizhir to toss cherry bombs under the school bleachers during a football game.

Mr. Bajwa blinks at me, then grins. "Lennon Bower! How wonderful to see you."

I guess when you skip town for eleven years, some of your misdeeds are forgiven. "It's fantastic to see you too."

Mr. Bajwa helps me gather all *four* zoning applications I need. Apparently, turning an abandoned conservation camp into an activity and adventure center takes a ton of paperwork. Since I've recently joined forces with my pain-in-the-butt brother for this venture, I know exactly who'll be filling out these tedious forms.

I debate asking Mr. Bajwa how Mizhir is doing, but we drifted apart before WITSEC, mostly because I didn't pass certain high school courses. Mizhir advanced to college without me, at which point he quit returning my calls.

Papers in hand, I slough off uncomfortable thoughts of that fizzled friendship and walk down the hallway. It's nearing the end of a standard workday. I have no clue what hours Maggie keeps at her job running town events, but my lungs can't handle another closet situation.

Before I reach the central elevator area, I flatten myself along the wall and peer around the corner. An older man ambles from the opposite hallway. The elevator makes an earsplitting screech. A few people, who decided riding that death trap was smart, exit the elevator. No red hair is in sight. Keeping my eye on the prize,

I hightail it to the stairwell and jog down the three flights of stairs, busting outside into the sunshine and doing a small fist pump for making it out alive.

Yes, I am that pathetic.

The fact that Maggie reduces me to running and hiding is an embarrassment. At least in high school we didn't overtly hide from each other. We had a silent agreement—mutual invisibility. We didn't talk to each other in public. We didn't make eye contact or breathe in each other's general direction. Whatever happened between us at her family's hidden pond wasn't discussed or acknowledged, as if that section of forest existed in a different dimension, apart from social expectations and peer judgment.

Things have changed since then. Our last night at the pond was both amazing and shocking and did *not* end well. I pushed Maggie too hard, took us places neither of us expected. Then there's the whole witness-protection-ruined-my-life thing. I disappeared on her, losing the chance to apologize for crossing a boundary. I'm not sure what will happen when Maggie lays eyes on me. She could slap me. She could pepper-spray my face. There's no question she was upset the last night I saw her. I just don't know *how* upset she was.

Hence the running and hiding.

With the area outside of town hall clear of Maggie land mines, I hit a more leisurely stride. I pull a penny from my pocket and flick it into the mermaid fountain. As it plunks into the water, I make a wish. *Please let me get through the rest of the week without seeing Maggie.*

I linger a moment, watching the water stream into the pool below as another memory hits—my father and me out to get ice cream, but he detoured to the fountain. Said he loved the trickle of falling water and watching the nearby birds. He gave me a penny and said, "Wish big."

If I had any foresight, I'd have wished my father weren't a money laundering criminal.

Alas, I cannot see the future.

Shaking off that unpleasantness, I cut through the grassy square at the center of downtown. Handsewn scarecrows still decorate the surrounding lampposts from last weekend's Scarecrow Scavenger Hunt, a fun event where they hide scarecrows in stores and around town, encouraging tourists and locals to visit shops in search of them.

Trying to loosen up, I fit on a smile and spot Mrs. Jackson. She's a tall Black woman who ran Mom's quilting group before our WITSEC vanishing act. She's also the town's unofficial disciplinarian and my landlord.

I wave to her, thankful I got my rent check in on time. "Mom told me to tell you she started a new quilt."

Mrs. Jackson cringes. "Have her sewing skills improved?"

"Still abysmal. Might have even gotten worse."

She tuts with an indulgent smile. "Woman refuses to quit."

No truer words were ever spoken. Mom didn't quit when her husband's lies ruined her life. She didn't crumple when her five boys ranted and yelled and cried, furious with our father and devasted that we had to leave our old lives. Chelsea Bower is as strong as women come and as horrible at crafting and quilting as a person gets.

"She's one of a kind," Mrs. Jackson says. "And thank you for taking such good care of my property. It gives me peace of mind knowing someone responsible is living there."

"It's a special house. I'm lucky to be there." I smile, hoping she doesn't see the tension behind my grin. A responsible man wouldn't be scrounging to pay her monthly.

I walk on and nod to a couple more familiar faces as I head to Duke's Market. When Crystal Tanaka waves at me, I stop to say hi. She ran my high school's skateboarding club and doesn't look like she's aged a day.

"Wow," she says, her eyes wide as she takes me in. "So wild to see you again. All that craziness with your family." Her hands do an erratic jazz number. "Hard to believe that stuff happens in real life."

"It's as unpleasant as you'd imagine. What about you? Still a skateboard master?"

"Master?" she scoffs. "Hardly. I veered into art. Graffiti art, actually. Doing a commission in France next month, which should be really cool. Gotta run, but it's great to see you!"

Graffiti art in France is beyond cool. I wave goodbye, seriously impressed by Crystal. This part of returning to Windfall is nice. Catching up with periphery friends who didn't invoke a silent pact to ignore me in public.

I continue to the grocery store, soaking in the slower vibe I've missed. There are no traffic lights on the quaint main street. No honking horns and screeching brakes, like in densely packed Houston—our witness protection home away from home.

I walk into Duke's Market and grab a cart, less frazzled but still tense. The size of this town means a Maggie sighting can happen at any moment.

Two steps into the produce section, I finally relax. My younger brother and his better half are perusing the fruit, providing me with optimal distraction material.

"Delilah," I say, leaning my elbows onto my shopping cart, "I thought you told me you were finally ditching E. Something about him snoring loud enough to damage your eardrums."

E stares at me blandly. "What are you, five?"

I'm thirty, soon to be thirty-one in a couple of months. Any continued immaturity is from living in a witness-protection bubble for ten years, only hanging out with my idiot brothers. "I've shared a room with you. I'm well acquainted with the foghorn that is your nose."

"That's when I'm sick, asshole. But feel free to tell Delilah about the time you walked around downtown Houston for an hour and got paranoid because everyone was staring at you."

I glare at him. He knows I spent that hour terrified, sure our pictures and real names had gotten out and everyone knew the Becerra cartel wanted us dead, and it was only a matter of time before my fingers would be severed one by one. I ran around like a madman at home, yelling at my family to pack up, tossing my clothes willy-nilly, furious that they were laughing at me. Then I caught a glimpse of myself in the mirror. I had cat whiskers drawn on my face.

A couple of hours prior, E and I had gone to a park, where he'd sketched and I'd read until I'd fallen asleep on the grass. I woke up alone, unaware the asshat had doodled on my face.

I mouth *Fuck off* to E and push my cart toward the lettuce.

Delilah fondles a couple of mangoes, then puts one in their cart. "How's your rental? You don't mind being out of town?"

"The place is small but nice, and I like the quiet." Love it, actually. The hominess. The peace and simplicity. Unfortunately, I only rent the property, and paying Mrs. Jackson has been a tad challenging. "The acreage is a bonus too. Means I can booby-trap it when you guys come and visit."

E punches my arm. "We should set up trip wires with sound grenades, then invite Desmond over."

"Oh yeah." We high-five and grin like ten-year-olds who've filled our first water balloons. Desmond may be my new business partner, but nothing beats terrorizing our grouchy brother.

Delilah shakes her head. "I never know if I should encourage you two or give you time-outs."

I gesture to the apple she's feeling up. "I'm not the one giving hand jobs to fruit."

She purses her lips, then stands taller, her curly hair bouncing with the move. "How are you managing with your shopping since you've moved to Windfall?"

I narrow my eyes. It's not like Delilah to let my taunting jokes go. She's the sister I never had, dishing out jabs as fast as they come in. "I haven't starved yet," I say guardedly.

"I mean clothes shopping," she clarifies. Her nostrils flare and blue eyes sparkle, while the rest of her is steel-rod stiff, like she's trying not to laugh. "With no hipster stores here, figured shopping's hard for you."

And there we have it. "For the ten millionth time, I am not a hipster."

E steals a grape from the bundle in their cart and pops it into his mouth. "Tell that to your skinny jeans and ironic T-shirt."

My shirt does say *Ironic* on it, but I growl under my breath. The only reason my family pesters me with hipster jokes is because I react. I know it. Can't seem to control my annoyance. I mean, half the world wears jeans and printed T-shirts, and beards are everywhere these days. Yet my family loves to get under my skin.

In high school, my brothers mocked me for dressing like a hippie. Then there was my rocker phase, with my eyeliner and collection of concert T-shirts. They razzed me endlessly when I got into country music and bought cowboy boots, as if people aren't allowed to change interests and styles as they grow up.

"Last I checked," I say, "there isn't a—"

"Maggie Edelstein," E says.

My heart launches into my throat.

My back is to the entrance, so I have no clue if E is yanking my chain or if Maggie is actually here. While none of my family knows what happened between Maggie and me eleven years ago, they know her name sends me into panic mode.

Unsure if E's tormenting me for his twisted amusement or not, I do the only reasonable thing. I drop into a crouch and hide behind the apple display.

Delilah covers her mouth with her hand, doing a crap job of

hiding that she's cracking up. E full-on snorts. Yep, the mongrel's playing with me.

I start standing, when I hear, "Fancy meeting you two here."

That brazen voice is definitely Maggie Edelstein, and my heart resumes its frantic racing.

I drop back down, huddling into a tighter ball, trying to fetal-position myself into invisibility. E waves to Maggie, practically having a conniption at my expense. Delilah's even worse. Her suppressed laughter forces tears from her eyes.

I hang my head and sigh.

As a kid, I loved playing games. Tic-tac-toe, Clue, Monopoly, euchre. I got high off winning and gloating in my brothers' faces, being a total braggart about the whole thing. Truth or dare was a particular favorite. My brothers always chose dare, and coming up with horrifyingly painful tasks kept my brain busy for weeks on end.

Unfortunately, playing truth or dare was also my downfall. I should never have opened that Pandora's box with Maggie. Our secret time together was innocent-*ish* until I poked her competitive side with my provoking games. Now I'm playing a continual round of "hit the deck" whenever she's near, and it's time I grow up. Windfall is as small as towns get. I can't spend the rest of my existence hiding in supply closets and behind apple displays. What happened eleven years ago needs to be faced sooner or later.

Firming my *non*-hipster jaw, I stand and swivel to face her.

Maggie startles and presses her hand to her chest.

This is our first face-to-face meeting since I moved back to Windfall, and I can't help it. My eyes move over her hungrily, poring over her Milky Way of freckles, the sharp bite of her emerald eyes, the tiny scar on her chin from when she climbed a tree and nearly fell—one of my less-flirtatious Maggie dares. Her lips are painted ruby red, her white skin pale and smooth, and I expel a heavy breath. Seeing her stunning face this close is a sucker punch.

I expect her to adopt her Lennon-Bower-doesn't-exist expression, the one she perfected in high school. But…*no*. Color rises to her freckled cheeks. Her mesmerizing eyes do a sweep of my adult body, from my Vans, to my jeans, to my *Ironic* T-shirt, and…holy shit.

She just *bit* her lip.

Maggie doesn't bite her lip. Not around me. Certainly not in public.

Our eyes connect. Hers flare. I have no clue how I look, but I feel *intense*. Like we've been standing here staring at each other for ten days, when barely ten seconds have ticked by.

"It's been a while," I say. Not *hi*. Not *I'm sorry if I hurt you*.

She glides her fingers up and down her purse strap. "It has."

We don't say more. Just look our fill as I try to keep my emotions in check, but I'm still a lost cause this close to Maggie. All these years later, my stomach tumbles around her. My chest grows hot and tight. The way she's staring at me, seeming affected and awkward, I'm sure she feels it too—this magnetic connection. A force beyond our control. In eleven years, I've never come close to duplicating how electric she makes me feel.

Tired of pretending I don't care about her and our history, I step toward her, ready to tell her how great it is to see her in the flesh. Maybe ask her out. Work through our history and reconnect. High school was forever ago. Teenagers all over the world are known for making horrible choices.

A banker-looking guy calls, "Mags!" halting my progress. He walks over and wraps his arm around Maggie. "Sorry I'm late, babe."

Instantly, Maggie's features neutralize. Her attention darts to this guy, who must be her boyfriend, and she kisses his cheek. She doesn't acknowledge me again or introduce us. Her Lennon-

Bower-doesn't-exist expression locks into place, and she leads her boyfriend away.

The tumbling in my stomach turns into a sharp stabbing. Uncomfortable heat suffuses my face. As wary as I was about facing Maggie, having her dismiss me so obviously makes me edgier. I tear my gaze away from her and her boyfriend, grab my shopping cart, and stalk toward the beer.

CHAPTER
Two

AS MENTIONED, I love games. Anything that earns me a good-natured laugh or annoys my brothers is a particular favorite. It's day three after my Maggie Encounter, and I've recovered enough to resume my game-master throne. I'm currently hosting a staring contest with my second-oldest brother and new business partner, Desmond bad-attitude Bower, and he's about to crack.

"Why do I have to do the paperwork?" Des growls, his top lip hitting snarl territory.

"Because one of us has to do the on-site stuff, converting the cabin into our headquarters and organizing the ropes course construction. Namely, *me*." I widen my eyes, refusing to blink.

His jaw pops. "And one of us has to plan and promote the kids' camps. I don't have time for this." He shoves the stack of permit papers toward me.

Most people would be intimidated sitting across from a snarling Desmond. He has tattoos on one side of his neck and on both arms. His thick-lashed dark eyes are always intense, his frown lines permanently etched, emanating a general air of Fuck

Off. But I know how to access his inner softy and bend him to my will.

I push the forms back toward him, still refusing to blink. "You're home more than I am. You can even get Max to help you since his writing is way neater than yours. Just tell him what to write."

He passes a hand over his mouth and *blinks*. "Yeah." The guy actually smiles. "Max digs writing neatly. He'll like that."

Seriously. Desmond is this easy to manipulate. He may have earned the Most Furious at Life merit badge during our WITSEC time, but one mention of his son—the ten-year-old kid he didn't know existed until last spring—and the guy turns to mush.

He taps his thumb on the table. "I'll add the permit costs to our expense spreadsheet, and I'm working on projections for the ropes course. I'll flip that over to you soon. So far, all looks manageable financially, as long as our programs continue to grow."

"They'll grow. There's buzz around town." At least, they'd better fucking grow.

I'm not *exactly* hurting for cash. Des and I both received a chunk of WITSEC money Mom saved for us, the portion intended for schooling. Since I didn't go the academic route, I invested the money. Used the interest to build Littlewing Adventures and plan this expansion with Des—the adult component of our business, Bigwing Adventures. We've purchased the land for our home base and have huge plans. I'm excited to see where we can take this venture. But I refuse to touch the principal of my cash, even for rent. As far as I'm concerned, that's dirty money, and I want no part of it.

With today's business talk settled, I lean back in my chair and sip my green tea, enjoying another aspect of Windfall—Delilah's bakery café, Sugar and Sips. How could you not love the decorated chalkboard menus, happy pastel colors, and whimsical artwork on the walls? Plus, some members of my family are fixtures here.

E's at a table in the corner, hunched over his computer, working intently. He claims the shop's relaxing buzz is more inspiring than the quiet of Delilah's and his upstairs apartment. Considering he illustrates incredibly successful graphic novels, I should be inclined to believe him. But I know better. After spending a decade away from his first love, he works here to be close to Delilah.

The woman in question wipes down the table beside ours, then tosses her dirty cloth at Desmond's face.

He catches it with one hand. "If you want to surprise attack me, you'll have to do better than that."

"You're right." She sighs. "Your athletic prowess is simply *too impressive.*"

As is Delilah's condescending sarcasm, but she glances at me and mouths *Trip wire.* Hell yeah. We're going to have fun booby-trapping my house and inviting Desmond over. It really is a killer property.

She knocks my shoulder. "I got a new tea in stock. Special brand of organic green tea from a small farm in Sri Lanka. Very obscure. Totally hipster-approved."

I glower at her. Desmond snickers.

Whatever. There's no fighting Delilah when she's on a roll.

Pleased with her efforts to annoy me, she snatches her cloth back from Desmond and moves along to wipe another table.

I nudge Des's foot under the table. "The ropes course will be tricky. It's tough finding builders not slammed with other work."

He cracks his knuckles. "I've already sourced someone."

"Seriously?" For a guy who earned a PhD in wasting his life, Desmond's efforts with our business still surprise me.

He kicks back in his chair. "Remember Ricky? E's buddy in high school—fronted that band the Tweeds?"

I nod, thinking back to those carefree days. I wasn't what

you'd call a *studious* kid. Or organized. Or focused. I pulled enough pranks to give Principal Osorio early gray hairs. I flunked a couple of classes and did an extra year of high school, working part time at the Smash Shack—Windfall's famed burger joint—while friends like Mizhir went off to college. That was also the year of Maggie and our secret pond, and I checked out the Tweeds with E often. My dad and I fished together and hung out most weekends too. I helped him around the property, patching up the perimeter fence, going for drives to gather supplies. We laughed at Mom's horrible crafting skills and talked about movies and sports and which fishing lures were the best.

After our outings, I'd always think, *Damn, I'm lucky to have such a great dad.*

Once again, *ha-ha-ha.* Joke was on me.

I rub my chest, attempting to soothe the ache that's settled there since moving back to Windfall.

"If Ricky's into it," I tell Desmond, veering back to the task at hand, "lock him down. Once the forms are filled out and we have our permits, we need to start ASAP."

He nods as his phone rings. The second he looks at the screen, his face—no joke—*lights up.* "Hey, honey. No, no. It's fine. Just at Sugar and Sips with Lennon."

He leaves the table to talk to Sadie in private. Delilah is now sitting with E in his back corner, the two of them whispering close. He takes her hand and kisses her fingers. She leans forward and noses his neck.

Another pang hits my chest.

These lovey-dovey scenes aren't so different from my pre-WITSEC life. E had been obsessed with Delilah since the day we moved to Windfall, and Des and Sadie were a fixture for years. I'm not surprised my brothers have rekindled their old romances. What *does* surprise me is how envious I am. With my history, I should be used to feeling alone.

I drag my attention away from Delilah and E's PDA and see a white woman staring at me. She has a pointy face and an eighties-style perm and doesn't look away when I catch her ogling me. I raise my eyebrow. She stares harder. I give her my best stink eye. She doesn't blink.

I get that this town is small and everyone is in everyone else's business, but common decency dictates that when you're caught staring, you have to look away. Not this permed lady.

The bell above the front door jingles.

I break our stare-off and glance at the entrance. My limbs lock.

Maggie Edelstein.

I haven't seen her since I stalked away from her ignore-Lennon face at Duke's Market. Three blissful, Maggie-free days. Although that's not entirely accurate. I've thought about her so often since then—the lip-biting conundrum, specifically—it's like she has a front-row seat in my brain.

Once again, Maggie isn't alone. Her preppy boyfriend is kicking up the rear, blond and blue-eyed, exuding a hefty dose of Ivy League flair. I debate bolting for the door when they get in line, but I'm done being affected by this woman I didn't even date. I need to embody laid-back Lennon. The chill guy who was friendly with everyone in high school and didn't dive-bomb when girls were near.

"If it isn't Maggie Edelstein," I say in an overly chipper voice. Decidedly *not* cool. "Are you following me around town?"

My bad joke is out there, floating in the no-man's-land between us. She can't pretend she doesn't see me. I can't hit rewind and sneak out Delilah's back exit.

Maggie flicks her head in my direction but clings to her boyfriend's arm. "Why in the world would I be following you?"

"I mean, I get it. I'm sure you've missed me."

"How could I miss someone I barely knew?"

So we *are* still playing the we-don't-know-each-other game.

Except I think I'll change the rules. For four months, while I was nineteen and she was seventeen, I let Maggie lay down our parameters. I was stuck redoing my last year of high school. She was two years younger than me and miles more mature. Probably still is. But I've been a version of invisible for ten years of WITSEC and have spent my first year of freedom living in Houston, feeling disconnected. I'm thirty now, finally back in Windfall. The only person in charge of my life these days is me.

"Well." I tap my chin. "We weren't exactly besties, but we did hang out a fair bit. Spent a lot of nights together at—"

"Can we not?" she says firmly. "History is history."

She steps toward the counter, but her boyfriend wants no part of that decision. He gives her a little tug and leads them to my table, oblivious to Maggie's horror-stricken expression.

"Hi," he says and shoots out his hand. "I'm Harrison. Maggie's plus-one."

I fit my hand into his and attempt to give a firm shake, but his hand does one of those limp-fish numbers that creeps me out. "I'm Lennon. I'm sure Maggie's told you all about me."

"Not you, specifically. But your family's pretty famous around here. The whole witness-protection thing."

I release his floppy hand and make a conscious effort not to wipe my palm down my jeans. How a guy who limp-shakes can handle a firecracker like Maggie is anyone's guess. He doesn't even have a callus on his manicured hands.

"I recall something about witness protection," I say, upping my sarcasm. "There was a death threat or fifty."

My joke falls flat. Harrison drags his hand through his Ivy League hair. Maggie barely looks at me, except...no. Her eyes keep flicking toward me. If I'm not mistaken, there's *sympathy* there. Compassion in the softening by her mouth. Or I'm just reading into everything Maggie, my typical modus operandi around her.

"Harrison," she says, flashing him a stiff smile, "why don't we—"

"What brings you to Windfall?" he asks me, not picking up on Maggie's get-me-out-of-here vibes.

She seethes, her fair complexion burning red.

I do what I do best in awkward or emotional moments and fill the discomfort with humor. "Figured I'd pick up where my father left off. Work for a cartel and launder money. The usual."

Harrison's eyes dart around as he hunches toward me. "You work for a cartel?"

Wow. This limp-shaker is not only clueless to Maggie's emotional vibes, he's also painfully gullible. "Only on weekends. The rest of the time, I run outdoor programs for kids. Send them into the wilderness in *Hunger Games*-style death matches."

He blinks at me for several long beats. Maggie rolls her eyes and clenches her jaw. I can't tell if she's annoyed with my jokes or irritated that her boyfriend's IQ hovers at equator levels.

She schools her features and yanks on Harrison's arm. "My lunch hour is vanishing fast. We should order."

"Your wish is my command, Gummy Bear." He kisses her cheek.

She flinches, likely at that ridiculous nickname. What I don't understand is *why* she's dating this tumbleweed.

The Maggie I knew would've punched me in the dick for calling her *Gummy Bear*. She was fun and brash, outspoken and wild. Too smart for a guy who falls for obvious jokes. She's certainly too sexy for those smooth, limp hands. But what do I know? Ivy Leaguers like Harrison were her type in high school too. Polished presentation. Rule followers.

Guys she acknowledged *in public*.

I avert my attention from them, hating how much Maggie still affects me.

"Lennon."

I glance up, and she's back. Alone this time, while Harrison gets settled at a far table. The sympathy I thought I saw before is in ample supply, thawing her often stern expression.

My tension loosens. "Yeah?"

"I'm sorry—for your father and what you've been through. When I found out…" She closes her eyes on an exhale, then slays me with those emerald beauties. "I can't imagine what you went through. I'm really glad you're okay, but the stuff that happened between us is in the past. There's no point rehashing it, and there's no avoiding each other in this town. So, can we just agree to forget about it? Say hi and whatever, without all the awkward?"

I clasp my hands over my stomach, trying to read Maggie's mind. Hearing she worried over me has warmth invading my chest, but as far as I'm concerned, we have unfinished business. Avoiding that topic will only give it more heft.

"Depends. Does your definition of 'saying hi and whatever' include me apologizing to you for our last night together?"

Red steals across her cheeks. "You can't even last one second without bringing that up."

"Because *that* was a big deal. It was for me, at least, and I'm pretty sure it was for you. And I—"

"Hello, Maggie." Desmond returns at the absolute worst time, looking concerningly amused. My brothers have pestered me plenty about Maggie, excavating for the nitty-gritty on how we know each other. I stonewall them every time. Nothing good can come of their interference.

He grins wider at her. "Lennon talks about you all the time. You guys hung out during high school, right? When he flunked math and had to do another year."

Maggie blanches, neither confirming nor denying facts.

I jam my elbow into Desmond's thigh. "He's lying. I never talked about you."

She winces at that, then swallows hard. Like she's…*upset*?

As usual, she's as tough to read as *The Scarlet Letter*. (I also

6 CLUES YOUR NEMESIS LOVES YOU   21

flunked high school English.) Does she want to know I replayed our time together on a loop my first few years away? That I couldn't shake thoughts of her? I relived our first meeting at her pond so obsessively that every detail is etched in my brain—how I tossed and turned with insomnia that night, then headed out on an uncharacteristic midnight walk, traipsing through the forest for so long I got lost and came upon Maggie swimming in her family's pond.

Battery-powered fairy lights had decorated the surrounding trees, their glow and the moonlight turning her red hair into waves of muted fire. Water sparkled on her pale skin, making her look like an angel or a siren or a whimsical mermaid.

And she was humming the soundtrack to *Jaws*.

Up until then, I only knew Maggie vaguely from school. She was a couple of years younger than me and best friends with Delilah, but she kept her circle of friends contained. She didn't talk to the stoners or rockers or skateboarders. She was always prim and put together. I never paid her much mind, until I stood at the edge of her pond, entranced, watching her swim around, humming *Jaws*, doing somersaults in the water, then karate-chopping the waves. It was hilarious.

She jumped when she saw me, splashing in the water. "Who's there?"

"Lennon Bower. E's brother. Didn't mean to scare you."

She swam toward the edge of the pond until she could stand on the bottom, her yellow bikini top slipping above the surface. "Do you make a habit of sneaking up on girls in the dark?"

"Only pretty redheads who pretend to be sharks."

Her lips were pressed tight, but the corners twitched. "Make a wrong move, and you'll see how hard I bite."

I was curious about her bite. About this silly girl who played demure at school. "Is standing here to enjoy your beautiful pond the wrong move?"

She folded her arms over her wet bikini top. "It's definitely creepy since I'm at a disadvantage, being in the water down here."

Without thinking twice, I walked into her pond, shoes and socks and sweatpants and all, getting completely drenched. Just walked right in, right up to Maggie, and matched her pose, crossing my arms over my chest. "How about now?"

A slow smile lit her face, full of wonder and mischief. "Who are you, Lennon Bower?"

Maggie's not smiling at me now. She has no clue how many hours I've spent reliving our secret nights and endless discussions, our blunt honesty as we swam around each other with only the stars and trees to witness our growing attraction. She actually thinks I went into WITSEC and didn't give her a second thought.

"I don't share personal details with my family," I say for both her and Desmond's benefit, choosing my words carefully. "Not when they can take my *favorite* ones and use them to torment me."

She bites her lip. *Again.* This woman lives to discombobulate me.

"Magdalene," E says, popping up beside my table, getting in my business too. "Remind me again how you know Lennon."

She faces E, serene and haughty. "Remind *me* again why a grown man draws doodles all day?"

I snicker. Seems Maggie excels at busting E's balls, and I now have another reason to like her too much.

E lifts his chin. "I illustrate best-selling graphic novels, as you well know."

"Glorified scribbles. And you can both move along." She gives my brothers a hard look. So challenging, even Desmond has the wherewithal to lean back. "Take your gossip-sniffing noses elsewhere."

Shockingly, they do as they're told, slinking away and leaving me alone with the World's Most Confusing Woman.

To me, she says, "Your family's a pain in the ass."

I smile, because yeah. They're awful, and I love them. "Back to my eleven-year-late apology. Our last night together—"

She holds up her hand. "I wasn't joking before. I need to leave the past in the past. I'm happy and in a good relationship. So can we just drop it?"

"You're happy with Harry?"

"*Harrison.*"

"The name's not the issue." I glance in his direction. He's facing away from us, sipping his coffee and eating a muffin while playing what looks like Candy Crush on his phone. "Have you ever shaken hands with the guy?"

Maggie glares at me. "We've progressed past shaking hands. But back to us."

"So you admit there is an *us.*" My gaze slips down her body, remembering that freckle-covered skin, all her smooth curves bared to me, before she'd run into the pond screeching.

She touches her neck, then fists her hand and drops it to her side. "There is no us, and I'd appreciate it if you'd quit the bedroom eyes around me. You don't need to apologize for anything, and I don't want to discuss those days."

Between Maggie's lip-biting, her dejection when she thought I didn't think about her during WITSEC, and this vehemence now, I'm inclined to think there is an *us.* I could push, ask why she's hell-bent on denying our intense connection. But really, what's the point? I'm tired of living a stalled life. Chasing Maggie has always been a one-way ticket to nowhere.

"No problemo," I say, going for unaffected. "Consider our history forgotten."

I lean casually into my chair, like I'm immune to Maggie's whims, but my weight tips the chair back. I have one of those *oh-shit* moments where my chair teeters and my balance wavers. I slam forward and grip the table. "See? I'm super cool with our arrangement."

She snorts but quickly schools her expression, like she's not allowed to laugh near me. I'd bet she doesn't laugh around Ivy League, either. Unless she's laughing at his expense.

She swivels away and joins her boyfriend. The eighties-permed stare champ is still intent on me, but I don't have the energy to stare back. I slump forward and rub my eyes.

Kicking my Maggie attraction won't be easy. I don't know much about the woman she's become, but she still gets under my skin like no one else. Except there hasn't really been anyone else, has there? No one of substance, at least.

Maybe that's the issue.

Too overwhelmed with the changes in my life, I haven't dated the past year. During WITSEC, I had to use my alias, Logan. I wasn't allowed to talk about my past, leaving years zero to nineteen off-limits. But I no longer need to hide my history. I can actually use my real name. Without a vault of secrets, I might hit it off with someone new. A woman who doesn't confuse me and ignore me on a whim.

I push my chair back and walk behind the coffee counter, heading for the swinging doors that lead to the kitchen and hopefully to Delilah.

"You can't be here," a skinny barista says, stepping in my way. "Employees only."

"I work for Delilah," I tell the kid. "I help her make fun of E." I scoot around his puckered face and find Delilah in the back, putting together sandwiches.

She glances at me and abruptly strikes a nonchalant pose, leaning on the stainless-steel counter. "So, you and Maggie, huh? She told me all about high school."

I call bullshit. Maggie hasn't said a word to anyone about us. Delilah's working on behalf of E, drilling for dirt. "Pathetic effort," I say. "And what's with the permed woman who doesn't know how to blink?"

Delilah smirks, resuming her sandwich artistry. "That's

Sandra. She was a secretary at a security firm, but she's retired now and works as the town busybody. She eavesdrops in the café all the time and volunteers at local businesses, helping out when staff are sick or on holidays. Mainly to gather gossip. She also loves driving E batty."

If she riles my brother, maybe I judged her too harshly. "I should introduce myself."

"She'd love that, and I heard your father's book might have early copies ready soon." Worry lines bracket her mouth. "You holding up okay?"

"Guy just can't let us get on with our lives," I say bitterly.

Her face darkens. "I didn't think it was possible to hate someone as much as I hate him."

I grunt the affirmative and feel a twinge of guilt for the happy memories that have weaseled into my mind as of late. But yeah. That stupid book of his isn't helping. It wasn't enough that our father's criminal activities ripped us away from Windfall. He had to go and write a tell-all biography, chronicling his cartel exploits and working with the FBI, who gave him immunity and witness protection in exchange for his testimony. He'll probably make it sound like he orchestrated the ruse to help authorities bring justice to the world.

All the more reason not to touch the principal of my investments. His grubby fingerprints are all over that cash.

"Do you have any single friends?" I ask Delilah, focusing on why I invaded her kitchen.

She cocks her head, searching my face. "Yeah, actually. A couple women in my knitting group."

"Would you do me the kindness of setting me up?"

Instead of replying with an easy *yes*, she dips her knife into a huge jug of mayo and slathers some on a thick slice of delicious-looking grain bread. "One of the women, Sloan, is probably a good match. Moved here a few years ago. She's into hiking and biking."

"Great. Sounds perfect. So, just…you know. Do it up. Give her my number. Or give me hers. Whatever works in today's world of dating."

What isn't working is that I can't keep from glancing at the swinging doors—a magnetic pull to look for Maggie, even though I don't have X-ray vision and can't see through drywall and Delilah's barista bouncers. I snap my focus back to Delilah, whose expression is worryingly smug.

"Sloan's sweet," she says, "but she's on the quiet side."

"Quiet is fine. I like quiet." I glance at the wall clock, trying to move Delilah along. How hard is it to set someone up on a date?

"She doesn't sass people."

"Even better."

"And she doesn't have red hair." She bats her lashes, as though the picture of innocence.

Even though we're not blood related, she's as meddlesome as my brothers. "Last I checked, the redhead you're referring to is in a relationship, and I'm not into swinging or cheating. Sloan sounds nice. Absolutely perfect. I'd appreciate it if you'd hook us up."

I nod once, sharp and final. Delilah's blue eyes twinkle in a concerning way, but whatever. She's a means to an end. One where I finally move forward with my life. Maggie has decreed our history banished. According to her, it never happened. As of this moment, I barely know Maggie Edelstein exists.

CHAPTER
Three

IT'S impossible to pretend Maggie Edelstein doesn't exist when she's everywhere. I just walked into the Barrel House and —*surprise, surprise*—there's Maggie, in a booth toward the back, talking with someone over beers. Probably her limp handshake of a boyfriend.

Before she notices me, I swivel and push back out of the entrance, growling at the sky.

Windfall's minuscule size isn't news. The slower pace and friendliness of this small town are some of the reasons I returned here. Unfortunately, flying under the radar is tough when you live in a snow globe. It's even worse when you're hoping for a modicum of privacy.

Tonight is my date with Sloan. The Barrel House is one of the new businesses to pop up in Windfall during my eleven-year hiatus. Based on my reconnaissance, I've heard that the Barrel's the go-to spot for casual drinks. They host trivia nights and movie nights and hit-the-dance-floor nights on Saturdays. Twice a month, they have a Pride Night that supposedly blows the roof off the place. The bar is away from the main square, near a string of art galleries and my former place of employment, the Smash

Shack. It sounded like the perfect first-date spot, especially on a quieter Tuesday evening. I got here early to get settled and make sure Sloan didn't have an uncomfortable wait for me.

Alas, Maggie Edelstein.

I pace a tight line outside, debating texting Sloan and canceling. Having a first date is nerve-racking enough. Having a first date while Maggie's in plain view has trouble written all over it. I search the lamppost-lit parking area, looking for a sign, any hint of how to manage this curve ball. The fall leaves blowing across the pavement give me nothing.

My attention veers to a man standing beside his Volvo, helping a young boy out of the back. They hold hands, wait to cross the street, then head for the Smash Shack.

A sharp pang hits me.

My dad and I used to do food runs together for the family, anything to alleviate cooking for Mom. Along with a defunct crafting gene, Mom hates cooking. Cal helped on occasion. Otherwise, it was grilled meat and some form of potato or frozen pasta dishes. Easy and filling enough for her five hungry boys. Dad's contribution was Friday night takeout, and I was his wingman. Smash Shack for burgers. The Curly Tail for ribs and barbeque.

We'd drive to our destination, and he'd let me choose the music, my ever-changing interests keeping things fun—rocker, country, rap, acoustic jams. Dad would pretend to sing along, not caring that he was messing up the lyrics. Then he'd knock my shoulder and say something stupid like, "I should've done Broadway."

I snap my focus to a weed pushing up through the asphalt and rub my sternum. I didn't expect memories of him to bombard me like this. I mean, yeah. Moving back to Windfall was bound to unearth a mess of feelings. There's no emerging unscathed from my sordid history, but I haven't seen or spoken with my father in a decade. Six months into WITSEC, he left us.

Never got in touch again, and everyone was relieved. *I* was relieved. Now, for some reason, good memories are creeping back, and this fondness is throwing me for a loop—how much I suddenly miss this asshole who ruined our lives.

An asshole who thought it was a swell idea to write a tell-all book.

Jaw painfully clenched, I blow out a rough breath. There's no changing the past. My father did what he did. Our lives are what they are. Maggie is whoever the heck Maggie is on any given day, and I need to banish both of them from my thoughts.

Kicking my own butt, I push the doors to the Barrel House back open. Sloan should be here in fifteen minutes or so. I count a slow exhale and walk casually up to the bar, refusing to glance Maggie's way.

When Jolene Daniels turns around, I actually grin. "Jo. Wow. You look amazing."

She does a little jump, her brown eyes going soft. "Lennon, look at *you*." She hurries around to my side and drags me into a fierce hug.

I sag into her, surprised at how much I need the comfort.

Jolene was always an exceptional hugger. She was best friends with Callahan growing up, the second-oldest Bower boy, before she fell in love with the oldest of us, Jake. She dated Jake for a couple of years, until they broke up a month or so before our WITSEC bomb. Before that, Jolene was a fixture around our house, hanging out with Cal and flirting with Jake, a rough-and-tumble girl who played football with us and never complained when she skinned a knee or got dirty. Seeing her is a breath of much-needed fresh air.

I rub her back and kiss the top of her head. "So, you're a bar wench now."

Jolene shoves me off with a playful punch. "Bar owner, actually."

"No shit." Not that I should be surprised. Jolene was always a take-charge girl.

"Yep," she says, a little less perky. "This joint's all mine. Along with endless paperwork."

She glances toward the two pool tables at the back, seeming tired as she surveys the wooden booths and tables. A few of them are filled with smiling and chatting patrons, and yes, I *do* look toward Maggie's booth. I have eyeballs after all, and it's only natural to follow Jolene's line of sight. Plus, Maggie is sitting *right there*. What I don't expect is for our eyes to clash.

My skin prickles. Abruptly, she looks away.

The move is predictable, but guess who's sharing a booth with her? Not her loser boyfriend, as I expected. Of all the people in all of Windfall, the one and only Delilah Moon is on the opposite side of their booth. The same Delilah who set me up on my impending date. The woman who might even have known I was coming here, if Sloan gave her the lowdown.

"You okay?" Jolene is staring at me, head cocked, like she's waiting for an answer to a question I didn't hear.

"I'm great. Fine." I'm not great or fine. I don't like that Delilah's here. Nothing about this feels like a coincidence.

"Are Jake and Callahan okay?" Jolene asks, lines settling between her brows. "I haven't seen or heard from either of them since everything came out. Not that I'm a priority. There's just…"

"A lot of history," I say, finishing her trailing sentence. These are the messes my father created, hurting countless people with his actions. When we left town, Jolene lost Jake—her ex-boyfriend but still a friend—*and* she lost Callahan, her partner in crime. "Jake's good enough. Still lives in Houston, working as a carpenter with Cal. Bosses us all around. And you know Cal. The guy can find a silver lining in a tsunami."

She smiles but also sniffles. "God, I've missed him. And Jake," she adds. "I tried to get their numbers from E, but E passed mine along to them instead. At least, he said he did. Neither of them has called."

Since Jake is her ex, his silence isn't surprising, but hearing Callahan hasn't reached out to his former best friend has me frowning. Now that I think about it, Cal has communicated less with *me* since we left WITSEC. Like, a lot less. I've been so busy building my business and moving, I haven't given his silence much thought. An oversight that isn't cool. Continued silence from any of us Bower boys is never a good sign. I'll need to reach out soon.

"I'm glad they're good," Jolene says quietly. "I can't imagine how hard this has been on all of you. But…" Her eyes get glassy. She blinks a bunch. "I really miss them."

I give her shoulder a squeeze. "Reconnecting's been hard for all of us. Jake and Cal even more so, I think. They seem hesitant to associate with people from their pasts, deal with the memories it brings back. I'm sure they'll reach out soon."

She nods, giving me a watery smile, then makes her way back behind the bar. "Consider your drinks on me. Grab a stool. I have a craft hipster beer that's perfect for you."

"Ha-ha," I say, already planning ways to piss off my brothers. I have no doubt E or Des told Jolene how best to annoy me. They love nothing more than getting under my *non*-hipster skin. "While I appreciate the jab, and the beer, I'm actually here to meet a date. So I'll be taking the *craft* beer, which lots of people like because craft beers are made with love in smaller batches, to a table where I can sit without seeing your irritating smirk."

"What?" She grins wider, not even pretending my annoyance doesn't amuse the shit out of her. "I've missed you so much."

She's missed razzing me is what she's missed.

Laughter carries from my right, a high-pitched cackling that is definitely Delilah. The cute sound is followed by another familiar chuckle—Maggie's husky laugh. Gritting my teeth, I thank Jo for my beer, then find a table as far away from those laughing women as possible, but my attention is stuck on their distant voices.

Before I sit, I steal a glance their way. Maggie's no longer on her side of the booth. She's heading toward the bathrooms, but Delilah the Meddler sticks her head out of her side of the booth and, I shit you not, *flutters her fingers at me*. She presses her lips tight, then disappears back inside the safety of her booth.

Unbelievable.

I sit facing her booth, hoping she sees my glare when she inevitably pops back out. I plunk down my beer and pull out my phone to shoot off an angry text.

> Me: What the hell?

Seconds later, my phone lights up with her reply.

> Delilah: What the hell what?

> Me: Did you know I was coming here?

> Delilah: Have you seen the size of this town? This is the coolest bar. Who's to say meeting here isn't a coincidence?

> Me: Your horrible poker face says so, that's who.

> Delilah: Fine. Yes. Sue me. I knew you'd be here.

I fucking knew it.

> Me: And you thought bringing Maggie here would help me on my blind date?

Delilah: No. I came to make sure your date went well. Maggie's with me cuz I need to convince her to break up with her loser boyfriend.

At least I'm not the only one who sees how awful those two are together.

> Me: Have you shaken his hand?

Delilah: THE LIMPEST OF THE LIMP FISH

I snort out a laugh.

> Me: Pretty sure he also believes the world is flat.

Delilah: See? He's all wrong for Maggie. And I maybe thought bringing her here would make her jealous and she'd finally admit she likes you, not him.

My stomach swoops. My breaths come hard and fast. Maggie doesn't "like" me. Maggie Edelstein avoids me. She *told* me she wanted to forget our time together happened. She also bit her lip around me and seemed oddly emotional at Sugar and Sips, suggesting Delilah's not completely off base, but Maggie made her stance clear.

> Me: News flash. Maggie wants nothing to do with me.

> Delilah: News flash. Maggie wants everything to do with you. She's just scared of you for some reason.

Honestly. One hint that Maggie has feelings for me and I'm flustered, searching the bathroom entrance for any sight of her infuriatingly beautiful face. The same face that made the parameters of our relationship, or lack thereof, crystal clear.

> Delilah: Things with Maggie are more complicated than you realize. Give her a chance.

A chance? I gave her a lifetime of chances in high school. I tried to apologize and reconnect the other day. All I ever get from Maggie is stonewalled.

Delilah pokes her curly head out of her booth again, her expression soft and patient, like she's explaining basic math to a child.

"Lennon?"

I snap my head up. A pretty brunette in a flowery blue dress, who matches my date's description, is standing by my table, setting me further off-kilter.

"You must be Sloan," I say loudly, my voice sounding strained.

I hit mute on my phone and flip it over, cutting off Delilah from tossing more confusing insinuations my way, but I'm already distracted. I stand abruptly to greet Sloan and knock over my chair. Ten seconds of me wrestling the upturned furniture into place and nearly spilling my beer, I lean not so smoothly with my hand on the back of my chair and go for suave. "Glad you found me."

Sloan holds her purse against her stomach, smiling shyly. "The beard gave you away. And Delilah said you usually wear plaid or printed T-shirts."

I *might* be wearing a light blue plaid button-down that brings out the blue in my blue-gray eyes, but honestly. I cut a hard glance toward Delilah's booth, sure she made a hipster joke about me to Sloan. Instead of seeing Delilah creeping us, Maggie's there, back in her side of the booth. And guess what? She's staring at me.

Her eyes dart to Sloan, then back to me, then back to Sloan. Her cheeks seem to redden, but it's tough to tell from this distance. Not that my pulse cares. It punches my neck insistently. My face flushes hot. Just as quickly, Maggie's attention cements back on Delilah.

I don't know what those darting eyes mean, or how I'm supposed to focus when Delilah's hinting that Maggie secretly likes me.

I hold out my hand to Sloan. "I wear other things besides plaid and printed T-shirts, but glad Delilah's intel helped."

She shakes my hand, giving me a way firmer grip than

Harrison's limp fish. I laugh, thinking of Delilah's shared horror on the matter.

Sloan slides into her seat and crosses her legs. "What's so funny?"

"I was just texting with a friend, and we were discussing limp handshakes." Sloan frowns. "*You* weren't limp," I add. "You gave a great shake. We were making fun of someone else who shakes like he has no bones in his hand." I flop my hand around for effect. "Highly unpleasant."

She laughs and relaxes more. "My father was in the army. He drilled into us the importance of eye contact and firm handshakes to exude confidence."

My father drilled into me that people lie and cheat as easily as they breathe. "Sounds like a good man."

A waiter comes by to take Sloan's order. I sip my beer as they discuss the wine list, and I try not to look Maggie's way, but my traitorous eyes have apparently cut off communication with my brain. Maggie is still focused on Delilah. A second later, her attention shifts to me. I expect her to break the connection. Instead, our eyes lock and load. We stare at each other, intense and heated, the electric energy I always feel around her sparking to life.

"So," Sloan says, drawing me back. "Delilah mentioned a business you're starting—an adventure camp for kids."

"Right. Yeah." I give myself a mental slap and smile at my blind date. "The business isn't exactly new," I tell Sloan. "I started it in Houston but struggled to grow it. With Windfall's hiking and biking trails, figured I'd have lots of terrain here, and my brother and I are adding adult components. Corporate packages to build teamwork and party events revolving around a high ropes course."

She lights up. "Like the ones where you wear a harness to climb really high and do crazy jumps?"

"Exactly like that, but we're also adding games to the

courses. Scavenger hunts where they use the courses to find clues and solve a puzzle or supposed crime."

"That's a really cool idea."

"Hopefully other people will agree." I lean my elbows on the table and spin my beer. "Can't take all the credit, though. My brother came up with the scavenger hunt part. What about you? Delilah mentioned you take a knitting class with her. Is that a hobby, or do you plan to put Windfall on the map by knitting the world's largest scarf?"

She gives a cute snort. "At the rate I'm learning, that might take a century, but it's fun to hang out with the women in the group. My day job revolves more around rodents and bugs."

"So *you're* the one running the illegal rodent-racing ring."

She laughs politely at my joke as the waiter delivers her red wine. She swirls her glass, gives it a sip, then smiles at me. "My family has a pest control business. I opened a branch here a few years ago."

We talk more about her work and my work. We discuss how great the weather is in Windfall—not too hot in the summer, the winter season shorter and milder than other areas of North Carolina. She broaches the subject of witness protection and my years spent living in hiding as Logan Baker, but she doesn't push when I keep things vague.

Sloan is pretty and nice and easy enough to talk to. Fantastic on paper, but there's no zing with her. That undefinable connection that leads to stomach acrobatics and racing hearts. Yet every time I glance at Maggie's booth for half a second, my stomach decides it's in a circus act.

Eventually, our conversation thins. I'm not sure how Sloan is feeling about me, if she's also ready to say goodnight and pull the plug on this date, but she checks her phone and cringes. "I need to head out, but this was nice."

"It was," I agree. Unfortunately, nice isn't exciting. Nice isn't connection and attraction and the hope of a goodnight kiss. Nice isn't the redhead who's held a larger portion of my attention all evening.

Sloan and I stand. We have a typical end-of-date awkward moment, unsure if we should hug or wave or give cheek kisses. The upfront woman she is, she cuts through my floundering by holding out her hand. "How about a non-limp shake to end the night?"

I laugh. "Excellent plan."

We shake, neither of us lingering or holding eye contact to show interest. I'm pretty sure Sloan found this date as neutral as I did.

The second she leaves my table, I flip my phone back over, ready to text Delilah and tell her to quit meddling with my love life. There's one text notification, for sure from her. I tap on the icon, preparing a snarky reply, and damn near drop my phone.

> Lennon, it's your father. I'd really like us to talk. Thought a text might be easier. Give you time to think about it. Please reach out when you can.

My hands turn clammy. My saliva dries up. I search the bar, as though he's here, stalking me so I can't delete this message and pretend I didn't get it. All I see is Maggie—shock of shocks —who's watching me more intently. Her concerned expression reminds me of the pond night when she convinced me to get into an underground hideout she'd built. My claustrophobia sent me into a panic back then. "It's okay," she said, over and over as she smoothed my damp hair from face. "You're okay. I've got you."

My face probably reflects similar abject fear now. Or more like fury. Why would my asshole father suddenly reach out after a decade of silence? What the hell could he possibly want? Without replying to him, I shove my phone into my pocket and storm out of the bar.

CHAPTER
Four

I LIFT my weight off my mountain bike, letting my arms and legs absorb the bumps and ruts of the forest trail. I blank my mind to everything but *this*. The path. Momentum. Not getting creamed by a fall. The second the terrain smooths out, I focus on pedaling and navigating the muddier sections. A log up ahead has me pulling up on the handlebars, shifting my weight back. On cue, my front wheel lifts. And *shit*.

For a split second, my back wheel skids, almost sending me flying. I pedal harder, my heart and lungs pumping, until I stabilize. I hop over the log, pitch my body low. Lift my ass and squeeze my seat with my thighs, readying for the steeper section on the home stretch. The rush downhill is as exhilarating as I hoped.

I read about the biking trail on my favorite Get Outside North Carolina website. As touted, it was fun and challenging. Intricate enough to force focus and build skill. I have five kids signed up for this afternoon's intermediate program. Pretty decent, considering I only advertised a month ago. Desmond's hiking sessions are almost at capacity, and I'm stoked about introducing the high ropes course and adult sessions next spring.

Unfortunately, I'm not stoked enough to forget the unanswered text burning a hole in my phone. Or the fact that I feel like a traitor.

I kick off my bike and hang my helmet from the handlebar. I walk in circles, catching my breath. As invigorating as that ride was, my nerves are still shot.

I'm not sure how my father got my number, not that it's tough. In the early years of WITSEC, Mom mentioned he kept tabs on us, and I have the same cell for personal and business use. Regardless of how he found me, my family's views on Raymond S. Bower are no secret. If he comes up, the words *scumbag* and *fucking-asshole-shithead* are often tossed around. I may not have reached out to him, but this connection gives me Judas vibes, as though I've betrayed my family. Precisely why I've avoided speaking with any of them the past week.

Around them, I'm not a good liar or hider of secrets. If they see me or hear my voice, they'll know something's up and will force the information out of me. If my brothers learn Dad reached out, they'll go nuclear and play target practice with my phone. As they should.

As *I* should. But I haven't. No fucking clue why.

I scowl at my phone for several painful seconds, silently cursing it for being a conduit between my father and me. Getting nowhere, I tuck it away, load up my truck, and drive to town. I'm sure there are errands I can run. Staying busy is the best thing for me right now.

By the time I slip into a parking spot on Main Street, I'm slightly less agitated. A quick scan of the area doesn't show signs of my family, whom I'd have to avoid, but I do spot the other person who's consumed my thoughts this week—Maggie confuses-the-fuck-out-of-me Edelstein.

Surprisingly, this is my first sighting of her since my date with Sloan. She's standing by a lamppost, pointing to an affixed scarecrow from the recent Scarecrow Scavenger Hunt festival, gesturing as she talks to someone. Her tight knee-length skirt does exceptional things to her curvy figure. As do her high heels. Predictably, I blow out a gusty sigh.

I've reread Delilah's texts a few times, mulling over the possibility that Maggie's as intrigued by me as I am by her. She may have a boyfriend, but according to Delilah, Harry the Limp-Shaker is nothing but a placeholder. Whatever the deal is with them, complying with Maggie's "let's ignore our history" mandate has started to feel like the wrong move. Agreeing with her was the easy choice. The coward's way out of our complicated past. Truth is, I won't be relaxed and happy in this town until we hash out our last night together at the pond. Also, dealing with her is an excellent distraction from dealing with my father.

Now seems like the perfect time to hook Maggie into a fresh round of truth or dare.

Even though I'm wearing ragged cargo shorts and a threadbare T-shirt, I hop out of my truck, determination propelling me forward. But I spot Sandra of the Eighties Perm, along with a piece of paper escaping her purse as she hurries by.

I hop into action and chase the page before it floats away. A few steps later, I snatch the escaped paper and jog to Sandra. "Looks like you dropped this."

She blinks at the page, then at me, then over my shoulder like we're being watched. She finally accepts the paper, carefully folding it into four. "Thank you."

She gives me a sharp nod and resumes her hurrying. According to Delilah, Sandra is the town busybody—the type of woman you want on your side. Hopefully this accidental run-in earned me points.

Feeling like luck is on my side, I strut toward Maggie, focusing on her gorgeous face and bonfire hair. When I'm closer, she whips her head my way, as though she senses my presence. She watches me, eyes narrowing. Probably wondering why I'm on a direct path toward her, my determined strides eating up the space between us. Before I reach my goal, she gives me her back and hurries toward town hall.

Gotta give it to her, she's fast in those high heels. Not only do they make her shapely legs look amazing, they seem to give her speed-walking superpowers. She hits the town hall's front doors seconds before me and breaks into a dainty sprint.

Run all you want, Little Shark. Your moment of reckoning has come.

I nip inside behind her, expecting her to be stuck with me, but someone walks off the elevator and she zips inside.

Dammit all to hell.

Why does every obstacle in my life come with its own obstacles?

That supply closet I nearly asphyxiated in at least had a door cracked open. I debate giving up, saving this talk for another day. I mean, it's an elevator in an old building, and it made that terrifying grinding sound last time I was here. My lungs might explode the second I walk on, but town hall only has four floors. I've suffered through elevators in the past. I hate them, but I can survive them.

When Maggie peeks my way and bites her lip, the decision is made for me.

I jog forward and squeeze into the elevator right before the doors slide shut.

"I thought you were afraid of elevators," she says, sounding annoyed I followed her in here.

I'm too freaked out to care. Panic slithers through me.

This was a bad decision. Like hugely, incredibly bad.

I hit the Open button. When that doesn't work, I jab it violently and maybe hit a few other buttons, or all of them. I don't know. The air in here is depleting fast. My dried sweat decides to rehydrate and flow. I jam the Open button over and over, but the elevator starts rising. I keep jamming. Maggie is saying something I can't decipher. The elevator emits an ear-piercing screech, or maybe that's just me whining.

The death trap jerks. We stumble. Stillness follows.

"Um." I freeze. The outside of me does, at least. My insides are trapped in a violent cyclone. "This isn't happening. I'm not in here. We are not stuck in an elevator."

Maggie clasps my upper arms and gives me a shake. "Get a grip."

I look at her, trying to focus on the freckles decorating her nose. "We're gonna die."

"We're not gonna die."

"I can't breathe."

"You can and you are. What you won't do is keep hitting those buttons. This elevator is ancient. You stalled the damn thing."

I glance around wildly. I swear the walls are closer. "We're stuck."

"Yeah, Sherlock." Her voice gentles, her grip on my arms loosening. "But it won't be long. Happens occasionally. I hit the alarm. Assuming Doug isn't on lunch, we should be out of here in five minutes."

"Doug might be on lunch?" Yep, I'm whining.

"It's a possibility."

"We're gonna die in here," I murmur again, gulping in breaths.

My body turns heavy. I have no choice but to lower to the floor. I start on all fours, then push back into child's pose. (Yes, I've taken yoga. *No*, that doesn't make me a hipster.) I cradle my head with my shaky hands, focus on filling my lungs. I'm aware enough to know I'm embarrassing the shit out of myself. Any hope I had of convincing Maggie I'm cooler than her wet-noodle boyfriend leaks out with each of my wheezy exhales.

A loud sigh carries from above me. Next thing I know, Maggie's tugging at my shoulders, guiding me to move. She's on the floor, her high heels kicked off, her legs folded under her. Gently, she pulls my head down to her lap. Her fingers slip into my hair, stroking the sweaty strands from my forehead. My tension unwinds a fraction. She digs her fingers deeper, tunneling through my wavy hair, dragging her nails over my scalp, trailing them down my neck and starting over.

Now I have a hard-on.

Seriously. My body doesn't know which way is up. I'm at death's door, struggling to breathe and turned on at the same time.

I open my eyes, unsure if this is a nightmare or a fantasy.

The compassion on Maggie's face indicates somewhere in between. "If you're still scared of tight spaces, why did you come in here?"

I could lie. Take the easy path. Get through this torture and deal with my Maggie history another day, but I followed her for a reason.

She keeps stroking my hair. I nuzzle into her lap, letting her fingers soothe me. "I came in here because you were in here."

Her hand stills. Just a beat. Then she's stroking again, slower this time. When she traces my ear, I shiver. "Only you, Lennon Bower."

"Only me, what?"

When her fingers graze my beard, my hard-on gets harder. "Nothing."

Nope. Not okay. This elevator stalled for a reason. I may have been jabbing the buttons like a coked-up lab monkey, but for the first time in eleven years, I have Maggie alone.

"Our last night together," I say, keeping my focus on her. Not the walls. Not our situation. Maggie and her gorgeous green eyes. "I did something you didn't like, and I've been upset about it ever since."

"No." She shakes her head vehemently. "I—"

"Maggie, can you please just let me apologize? I mean, I've

never crossed a boundary with a woman. I've never pushed if they said no. I would never do that. We were just so in the moment and you were so gorgeous out there, and I..." I give my head a shake, not getting my words out right.

"Lennon." She gives my neck a light pinch. "When I said *no* just now, I wasn't trying to shut you up. I meant *no,* you didn't do anything I didn't like. Whatever you've been stressing about the past eleven years, you have it wrong."

I blink and frown. Her words don't make sense. I've replayed that night ad nauseam. All our nights, reliving them in hopes of remembering how alive I once felt, always finishing on our last evening together. The sharp ache in my chest as Maggie ran away from me, furious and upset. Or did I get it all wrong?

CHAPTER
Five

AFTER MY FIRST night with Maggie, walking into the water fully clothed, I *wanted* her. It's a deep emotion, wanting. Wanting consumes your thoughts, wiggles into the cracks of time where you normally hum or walk or move without thought. Suddenly, I was thinking all the time, curious, wanting more of Maggie. More time. More glimpses of her mischievous smile. I wanted to shock her again and again, put that indignant blush on her cheeks.

I began showing up at her pond most evenings, wearing a bathing suit, ready to take a running leap into the water. Maggie didn't disappoint. She'd already be there, clad in her tiny bikini, doing lazy strokes on her back, lit by her twinkle lights above.

A few weeks into our secret meetings, she looked up at me as I stepped into view and beamed so brightly my heart squeezed. "There's my favorite creep."

I ripped off my T-shirt and tossed it onto the ground, grinning. "There's my favorite shark."

I jumped in, swam down, grabbed one of her ankles, and gave it a teasing bite. She kicked at me, her bubbling laugh drifting through the water. I popped up, and we resumed our usual spots, floating side by side.

I licked my wet lips, watching her. "How'd the science test go?"

We'd seen each other at school that morning. As usual, Maggie had walked by me without glancing my way. I could've broken our silent agreement. Called her name, asked her about her test then, but I was out of sorts those days. A grazer who flitted between social groups, friendly with everyone, not close with anyone. Mizhir and my other buddies were off at college, having new experiences, meeting new people. I'd call Mizhir and wouldn't hear back for days. When he *did* call, he was cold and distant. Talking to Maggie at school would have broken our we-don't-talk-in-public rule, and I didn't want to lose her too.

At night, though, I could talk to her. Ask her how school went.

Instead of groaning about her science test, she swam a circle around me, then swiveled and gave me her back. "Do you ever feel like you're watching yourself from above? Like you're doing and saying things and can't stop yourself from being a certain way?"

Her shoulders had tensed. She didn't glance at me, but I liked this—Maggie opening up in tiny increments. I dove under the water and swam away from her, coming up farther down the pond. I flipped to my back and gave her space. The more space Maggie had, the more she shared.

"I don't know about the out-of-body thing," I said, "but I often feel alone, even when I'm around people. Like, they see me, but they wouldn't care if I disappeared." The close-but-not-close friendships I collected. A hoarder of acquaintances. "Except my dad. I always feel seen around him. Do you have anyone like that? Someone who makes you feel grounded? Like you can be your true self?"

We swam past each other, swapping positions under the

partly obscured stars. "I feel like that out here with you," she whispered but hesitated a beat. "You make me feel things I've never felt before."

"Good things?"

"Scary things." She drifted below the water. Disappeared for two, three, four long seconds as I digested her admission.

She feels seen with me. She maybe likes me as much as I like her.

I didn't know if Maggie was becoming my nemesis—a challenging temptress who'd always be out of reach—or if her distance was born of insecurities she hadn't shared. I certainly knew I wasn't good for her. I'd had more detentions during high school than the trees had leaves: cherry bomb incidents, spitballs to make people laugh, outbursts in the middle of class—singing or reciting movie lines—when I was bored. I was stuck redoing classes I'd flunked. I wasn't anyone's idea of a guy going places, but I was addicted to Maggie.

She breached the surface and sucked in a breath. Flipped to her back again, eyes on the sky. "I feel this pressure to be someone else at school—stay friends with the right people, work insanely hard to keep up my grades—all to make my parents proud. They gave up so much for me, and I'm so thankful. But I can't shake this feeling that I'm locked inside, playing a never-ending game of make-believe."

"I get what it's like to pretend," I said, thinking over her confession and understanding her public persona a bit better. "I'm closer with my father than my brothers are. We have a similar sense of humor, and it's always been easy with him, but this year's been different. We still hang out and go fishing, but... I don't know. He's more distant. Disappointed in me for flunking math and English, for sure, but it feels bigger than that. When I think about it, I get this hollow in my gut. Like I'm not good enough, so I act goofier. Louder. Try to pretend everything's okay."

She made a disgruntled sound. "If your father doesn't know

you're smart and hilarious and one of the nicest guys around, he's the one who's not good enough."

Happiness puffed up my chest. "You think I'm smart and incredibly handsome?"

She laughed and splashed my face. "I didn't say handsome."

"It was implied, and my father *should* be disappointed in me. I suck at school, and I have no clue what I want to do after this year. I basically have no real friends," I went on, voicing worries I'd only ever stewed over privately. But there, under those fairy lights, everything burbled up. "They've all moved on, and the idea of heading to college is painful. I'm not the school type, but I'm worried if I don't go, they'll drift further away and this weird distance between my father and me will get bigger. So yeah, I get that feeling of wanting to play a role to appease your family, pretend you're happy when you're not, but the Maggie I've gotten to know here is special. She's carefree and fun and has this confidence I totally admire."

Our upper bodies drifted apart, our calves and feet mingling. Nervous energy filled my stomach, along with a shot of desire.

"I'm not confident," she said on a sigh. "I live my life scared. You're the effortless one. This easy guy who doesn't show off at school to look cool and who walks into a pond fully clothed, just because he feels like it. You do what you want, when you want, and you don't apologize for it." She pushed upright, treading water until I did the same. "If anyone's worth admiring, it's you."

No. She was wrong, but there was a shift between us. A deeper understanding of our fears and secrets. The tough stuff you only shared with your inner circle. I wasn't sure when Maggie had become my circle. A tiny ring of two. But I knew it then, to my core. I also didn't want to linger on this heavier conversation. I wanted to make Maggie smile.

I dove under the water, pinched her waist as I swam by, and popped up where I could stand. "I really am admiration-worthy.

I mean, look at this body." I pushed my wet hair back and struck a body-builder pose, arms up, biceps flexed. I was fit and lean, but not jock bulky—Maggie's typical taste. Still, I hammed up my performance, earning a headshake and sputtering laugh.

"You're hopeless, Lennon Bower," she called as she did a back flip in the water.

Hopelessly into her, yeah.

After that more personal night, we rarely skipped evenings together. I'd hurry to the pond after work at the Smash Shack. Maggie would always be there, swimming and splashing, sometimes doing her shark imitation because she knew it cracked me up. For four months, I had Maggie Edelstein all to myself. I'd swim around her as we'd talk and talk and talk, our subtle touches getting more brazen. I'd let my hand graze her hip, even push her wet hair off her face, my fingers lingering on her neck or ear. She'd kick me lightly, shove at my shoulders, but yeah. Her hands would linger too.

We were two lingerers, testing boundaries, never fully crossing them, until I arrived one night, stood on the pond's edge, and said, "Let's play truth or dare."

"Okay." Even in the moonlight, trouble sparkled in Maggie's eyes. "Dare it is."

"Okay," I agreed, already knowing I was either taking us somewhere new or ending what we'd started—my reckless effort to push us that final distance, because I *wanted*. So much with this complicated girl, who had infiltrated my waking dreams. "I dare you to skinny-dip."

She was already in the water, neck-deep, but she didn't hesitate. Keeping her eyes locked on me, she undid the strings of her bikini top and let them drop. Even though I couldn't see her bared breasts, I licked my drying lips. She ducked underwater, and next thing I knew, she tossed her bottom and top on the shore, right at my feet.

A hot pulse of desire throbbed through me.

"Truth or dare," she said, her voice huskier, reflecting my *wanting* back at me.

I winked at her. "Dare, of course."

She treaded water, her arms drawing lazy circles, the tops of her breasts teasing the surface. "I dare *you* to skinny-dip."

Like the first night I walked into the water fully clothed, I decided to shock Maggie. All or nothing. Reckless for the win. Instead of making her comfortable by getting in the water and tossing my swim trunks next to hers, I dropped my shorts right there. Got buck naked on the pond's edge, not bothering to hide my erection. Proof of how much I wanted her.

Maggie's eyes widened then grew heavy, drawing a torturous path down my chest, past my tensing navel, landing on my cock, which twitched in response. Knowing I'd start jacking off if I didn't move, I walked into the water, swam right up to her, and splashed her face. "See something you like?"

Her face flushed a deep red, her nostrils flaring wide. "Just a pest who likes to play dangerous games."

"You think I'm dangerous?"

"I *know* you're dangerous."

Nothing else happened that night. We talked as usual, laughed and splashed and shared, but our awareness was heightened. She kept shooting heated glances at my chest and lower, even though the water covered my goods. I was very aware of Maggie's pale breasts bobbing close to the surface, of her bare skin so near to mine. But we didn't touch.

The next night, I dared her to streak naked around the pond. Laughing, she shrieked and ran the perimeter, complete with a cannonball at the end. She dared me to do a naked belly flop. Being the good sport I am, I complied but held my junk so as not to crush the family jewels. She howled with laughter.

The night after that, I dared her to stand and stare at me for one full minute. We were naked in the water, as had become our habit, our bodies covered by the pond's glassy surface. We stood toe to toe, not touching, never once grazing each other, but *holy shit*. I'd never been so turned on. She retaliated by daring me to cover myself in mud.

The next week, I was desperate. I hadn't even kissed Maggie yet, but I was consumed with her. Her demeanor at school still frustrated me. I had a vague sense of why she wouldn't acknowledge me there, our talks about family pressure and expectations shining a light on the issue. I was an underachieving delinquent, the opposite of what her parents wanted for her—the opposite of what she *deserved*—but I was in too deep to walk away.

I got to the pond earlier than usual that night, stripped naked and jumped in, beating her for the first time. When she arrived, she seemed lost in thought, frowning to herself, her stormy gaze distant.

The second she saw me swimming, she startled, then broke into a wide smile. "Fancy meeting you here."

I treaded water and winked at her. "I'll meet you anywhere, anytime."

She laughed, but her smile dipped. She knew I wanted more from her. A kiss. More than a kiss. Her acceptance in public. Her hands pulling at my skin. My hungry hands all over her.

When she stayed quiet, I said, "Truth or dare."

She glanced behind her, toward the direction of her home. She fiddled with a rip in her jean shorts, seeming indecisive, which was odd. Out here, Maggie didn't hesitate with me. Out here, she didn't play roles or put on airs. But she fidgeted and hesitated, then blinked hard and faced me. "Dare, of course."

My heartbeat picked up. I didn't know why she was suddenly hesitant. All that mattered was her reply. I knew what I was doing, where I was leading us. I couldn't keep pretending I didn't *want* everything from Maggie, so I walked to the water's edge, slowly emerging from the pond until she could see all of me—fully naked, how turned on I was. One look at her was all it ever took.

Her bottom lip fell open, her eyes raking over me and settling on my flushed erection.

"I dare you to touch yourself," I said, sounding like I'd swallowed sand. "Here, in front of me," I added, in case my meaning wasn't clear.

She had on a yellow tank top, no bikini poking out. The absent swimsuit was odd, but there was no missing how wide her chest swelled, the slight shaking of her hands. "That's a bold dare."

"You can say no. You can always say no."

Her eyes flicked up to mine as her hands found the hem of her top. She yanked it off, revealing a black lace bra. "Dare accepted, but I dare you to do the same."

Wow. Okay. *Yeah.* As intense as our flirtations had gotten, I mostly expected Maggie to turn me down. Call it quits. Put me and my misguided hope out of our misery.

"Yeah," I said, nodding like an idiot. "I'll accept your dare."

"You can't touch me, though," she said quickly. "You can only look."

I nodded again and wrapped my palm around my aching shaft, already feeling like I was seconds from blowing. She undressed quickly, stood stark naked before me. The last light of day gave me a better view of her rounded hips, those heavy breasts I pictured every time I closed my eyes. She had freckles everywhere. A flood of freckles, cascading over her hills and valleys, along the secret places in between. I'd never been this close to her out of the water, and I hated not exploring those freckles. Not kissing them or kissing *her*. Not running my hands through her blazing hair, down her back, over her hips and ass. I hated the distance between us, but I wouldn't break her rules. Not when she was giving me this gift.

Slowly, she lay down on the ground, her intense eyes fastened on me.

Unsure what to do, I knelt in front of her. She seemed hesitant then, resting her hand on her belly, not moving it lower. My body verged on haywire. Just looking at her this close, naked, was enough for me to combust. Unable to wait or think clearly, I licked my hand and palmed my length, groaning as I gave myself a rough tug.

Maggie made a needy sound, then she was moving too, spreading her thighs, dipping her fingers lower, and *dammit*. I could see how wet she was. How turned on. She moved her fingers slowly at first, squirming her hips, her eyes locked on my hand pumping up and down my throbbing shaft. I was lost. Totally, completely entranced and addicted to Maggie Edelstein.

More than entranced, I realized in a rush. *Love.*

I was in love with this confusing girl who kept me at arm's length, but she also lifted me up when I felt down. She listened to my stresses, made me feel smart and funny and worthwhile—in private, at least. I was pretty sure there was more going on with her than she'd admitted. Other reasons for her different behavior at school. In time, I was sure she'd trust me enough to open up. I'd one day know the joy of kissing Maggie, touching her skin, holding her hand in public.

That night, though, we weren't allowed to touch. And I didn't break my word. I fought all my base instincts to kiss her and line up our bodies. Not so we could have sex. Just to feel the hot rush of my skin against hers, my heart beating against hers. I fought those frenzied instincts, but the second she came, arching her back, her legs trembling as she grabbed her breast with her free hand, I came too. Not on the ground as I'd planned. As I should have. I came in a blinding rush all over her moonlit skin, my thighs flexing, her name on my lips—rough, broken, unchecked.

When my soul returned to my body and I opened my eyes,

there was no missing how stiff she was. Her gaze was locked on her body, because *fuck*. My release decorated her skin from her neck down to the intimate red curls I wanted to bury my face in. The sight was beyond erotic, but she'd told me I wasn't allowed to touch her. She'd set up sexual boundaries, and when a woman sets up sexual boundaries, you do *not* break them.

I may not have touched her physically, with my hands or body, but I came all over her, which I was pretty sure was miles worse.

She kept looking down at herself, breathing hard. For half a second, I thought I saw desire there. Eroticism in her heavy-lidded gaze, then she blinked. She frowned. A look of sheer panic crossed her face, then she was grabbing her clothes and running off, disappearing into the woods before I could gather myself enough to apologize.

Then lucky me went into witness protection.

Talk about piss-poor timing.

CHAPTER
Six

FOCUSING on that amazing yet upsetting memory has somehow slowed my erratic pulse. I'm still trapped in this stalled coffin with the woman I hurt. Doug must have flown to Paris for lunch, because five minutes (or five years) have come and gone. I should be hyperventilating, but my head is on Maggie's lap. She's stroking my hair, silence lingering between us as I try to understand what she said. The admission that doesn't line up with my memory of our last night together. *No, you didn't do anything I didn't like. Whatever you've been stressing about the past eleven years, you have it wrong.*

I force a swallow and look up at her, forever confounded by this woman. "You told me not to touch you, and I came all over you. Then you ran off without a word. Of course I've been upset over that. I hurt you, Maggie. And hurting you was the last thing I ever wanted."

Her shoulders drop, her fingers gliding more slowly through my hair. "Lennon..." She trails off and closes her eyes. When she opens them again, there's fire there—the shark impressionist and dare-taker I fell in love with at nineteen. "To this day, that is the single hottest thing I've ever done with anyone. I wanted you so badly back then. You have no idea."

A hot flush fills my stomach, driving lower. She's right. I had no idea. I mean, I knew she was attracted to me, enjoyed flirting with me. But this? "Then why'd you run?"

"Do we really need to rehash this?"

"We definitely need to rehash this."

"I disagree."

"That's nice for you, but we're not teenagers anymore." I try to look serious, like I mean business, but I'm lying on her lap. I'm pretty sure my sweaty hair is standing up in every direction. "You don't get to dictate how or when I speak to you any longer."

She glances at my head, and her lips twitch. Yeah, I for sure look like I've stuck my finger in a light socket—pretty much how Maggie makes me feel—but I don't back down or blink.

She plunks the back of her head against the elevator wall. "I'm sorry about high school. I feel horrible about the way I treated you."

I would've traded my prized mountain bike for that apology in high school. Today, the admission has me feeling edgier. Annoyed, almost. My claustrophobia has clearly usurped my brain. "While I appreciate the apology, you're deflecting. If you weren't upset about what happened between us, why'd you run?"

"It's complicated."

"As complicated as the time I couldn't figure out why you were laughing at me, until I discovered a huge booger hanging out of my nose?"

She barks out a laugh, her face overflowing with delight, then she slaps her hand over her mouth.

"That was rude, by the way," I add, basking in Maggie's laughter. "Real friends tell friends when they have boogers on their faces."

She stares up at the elevator ceiling, her lower body softening under my head. "You should've seen your face when you realized. Like you thought you were covered in leeches."

"I was horrifyingly embarrassed. Didn't want my crush thinking I was unattractive."

She twirls a strand of my hair around her finger in tantalizing slow spins. "Nothing about you was unattractive to me."

Well, then. I'll take more of those truths, thank you very much. More of her fingers playing with my hair, but we need to stay on topic. "I appreciate the compliment, but I've gotten better at figuring out complicated things. So, I'll ask again, if what happened that night didn't upset you, why'd you run?"

She releases my hair and rolls the hem of her skirt between her fingers.

"Maggie," I say softly, no longer joking around. "*Please.*"

An eternity later, she whispers, "Because I liked it too much." Her eyes meet mine, the force of their intensity nearly blowing me through the floor. "Because falling for you scared the shit out of me, and I wasn't supposed to be there that night. I came to tell you I couldn't hang out. I was supposed to pick up my sister from her dance class, then you offered that dare, and it was you and I couldn't leave, and bad shit happened because of me. Bad shit always happens when I'm not careful."

"What do you mean, not careful? And what happened to Emma?"

The elevator jolts. My *heart* jolts. I need those doors open and air and space, but I need this too. Maggie's confession. Her finally being open with me.

The elevator starts moving up. We're staring at each other, still sitting on the floor, her partial admission confusing me even more. *She's scared of you.* Delilah had written that when texting me at the Barrel House. It didn't make sense then, and it doesn't now.

At a loss, I reach up and cup Maggie's cheek. A bold move

toward a woman with a boyfriend. Desperation has me acting reckless. "Can we go somewhere? We need to talk this out."

She places her hand over mine, her fingers tender and soft. "I have to work, but—"

We quit moving. The doors slide open.

Doug, who has more white hair in his thick eyebrows than on his head, stands with a cloth draped over his coveralls. "Sorry for the wait, folks. Darn machine gets finicky when I'm not around. Does it to mess with me," he mutters.

Maggie's hand yanks off mine. I go from staring into her stunning eyes to staring at her calves. She's standing, slipping her feet into those sexy high heels. I push to all fours and crawl out, doing zero to increase my cool factor, but I'm light-headed from my near-death experience and that disconcerting conversation. A man leans over me, asks if I'm okay. I take several steadying breaths as he grabs my arm and helps me stand.

When I'm sure I won't pass out, I turn to talk to Maggie. Find a time to meet and finish this life-changing talk. But Maggie's gone.

CHAPTER
Seven

"MAKE sure my muscles look bigger in this one." I strike a pose, sitting on the grass in town square, one leg bent, my elbow resting on my knee. "My forearms should have that corded look."

"I draw what I see," Max says. "And I don't see big muscles."

"Oh, I definitely have big muscles." I roll my T-shirt sleeve above my shoulder and flex. "Look at these guns."

He gives a cute snort. "My dad has big guns. Those are just arms."

Yeah, Desmond is more cut than me. He's also often moody, except for this morning when I picked up my nephew so Des could have "alone time" with Sadie, otherwise known as loud-sex-with-no-kid-in-the-house time. "Your dad's a meathead gym rat who grunts more than he talks. His arms don't count."

"I'll tell him you said that," Max says on a laugh. He pokes his tongue out of his mouth, stealing glances at me as he sketches.

Kid is an insanely talented artist, like his uncle E. His brash cockiness comes from his father. The tattling threat, though—that's all me.

Growing up, I forced my brothers to play truth or dare by threatening I'd narc on them to Mom. Attuned to everyone's rule-breaking, I knew Jake had a party in the house and someone broke Mom's favorite blue vase that mysteriously went "missing." I knew Callahan stole Dad's bottle of vodka and replaced half of it with water. I knew E snuck out at night to visit Delilah, and that Des stole money from Mom's wallet to buy Sadie concert tickets. I lorded my extortion over my brothers with glee, which actually sounds like something my criminal father would do.

Puffing air out my nose, I try to forget his still-unanswered text on my phone and relax into my role of Best Bower Uncle. "You can tattle on me," I tell Max, "but then I'll have no one to share milkshakes with at the Smash Shack later."

His thick-lashed eyes shoot to me. "We're going to the Smash Shack?"

"Depends on how handsome I look in that sketch."

He rolls his eyes, resuming his drawing. I bop my shoulders, then my head, holding time to the acoustic tunes drifting from a lounging guy's phone.

"Quit moving," he says, laughing. "You're distracting me."

I'm about to dance harder in my seated position—anything to get a snort-cackle from Max—but my attention snags on a new couple setting up a blanket.

Maggie and Harrison the Limp-Shaker.

I freeze as Max requested, but not by choice. Seeing Maggie has this effect on me—locking me in place while my insides decide they're in a bouncy castle.

Maggie gets comfortable with Harrison, tucking her legs under her as she pulls a book from her bag. She's wearing light-green pants and a white tank top speckled with what look like tiny ladybugs. *So damn cute.* A fifties-style bandanna is tied over her head, holding back her hair. *So damn sexy.* Harrison sits with his phone in his hand, probably playing

Candy Crush or maybe Googling *Is the* Hunger Games *based on a true story?*

I grind my teeth.

Seeing them here isn't odd. It's a Saturday. Windfall's central grassy square is always filled with loungers and readers and play-with-their-doggers on sunny Saturdays. Or in my case, uncles who pose for their art-obsessed nephews so their parents can bang. While Maggie has every right to enjoy Windfall's popular park, seeing her irks me, as it has every time I've glimpsed her since our near-death elevator incident.

During the past four days, we've acknowledged each other on the street or in Duke's Market, trading tentative smiles and waves, but we haven't spoken directly.

I blame her relationship status.

While petrifying, our time in that elevator kicked my Maggie interest into overdrive. I want to know the nitty-gritty on why she's afraid of me and apparently of herself. I'm worried about whatever happened with her sister that fateful night. I also get the feeling she's hiding deeper truths from me, like she seemed to be during high school. Aside from those mysteries, I keep replaying Maggie's important confession about us getting off together, that it was the hottest thing she'd ever done.

I have to agree with that statement.

Not only was the act itself mind-blowing, the sensual moment was the result of months of flirting, teasing, wondering. I've been with women since her. Actually kissed and touched them and had penetrative sex, but that night was the most erotic experience of my life. But Maggie's in a committed relationship. Her choice of boyfriend confounds me. Not even Delilah thinks the limp-shaker is good for her, but this is Maggie's life, and I'm not a cheater or a relationship-ruiner. So I've kept my distance.

Doesn't mean I like their relationship shoved in my face.

She pauses from reading her book, glances at Harrison, and gives him the polite smile she perfected in high school. Collected and distant. Painfully serene. At our pond, her smiles were wild and brimming. The few times I've made her laugh since returning to Windfall, she unleashed her electric smile, followed quickly by schooled features or a hand covering the unabashed reaction. All Harrison gets is a veneer.

Max is still intent on my portrait. I try to focus on him, but yeah. Five guesses on how that's going. Maggie's attention leaves Harrison, roaming the groups dotting the square. Her lazy gaze passes a doodle-something dog chewing a bone and the yo-yo player knocking out cool tricks, then her eyes land on me.

A small hitch of her shoulders.

A slight parting of her lips, which she then *bites.*

Honestly. Forget confusing. Maggie's more complicated than twelfth-grade calculus. How can she be so affected by me, bite her lip like that, while lounging with Mr. The World is Flat?

I tear my gaze away and heave out a sigh. I remind myself Maggie's decisions are hers to make, even if they suck. I force my attention on a boring lamppost, but the posts aren't mundane. The straw-stuffed dolls from the Scarecrow Scavenger Hunt have been replaced by ghouls and skeletons for this year's inaugural Blood and Guts Festival—Windfall quirkiness at its finest.

Aside from its vibrant arts scene, equestrian facilities, and picture-book charm, Windfall is known for fun festivals and for growing exceptional beets. Ruby Queens, in particular, are widely cultivated, deep red in color, and bursting with flavor. They're also excellent at staining things blood red.

If I had to guess, I'd say Maggie's responsible for next week's Blood and Guts Festival, where townsfolk will try their hands at using ground-up beets and beet juice to create grisly scenes and half-dead bodies. She had a secret love of B-horror movies in high school. It's a clever way to ring in Halloween while promoting area farmers. Another feather in her cap as one of the town's event coordinators. I, however, am not supposed to know she loves B-horror movies. I'm supposed to pretend we never whispered secrets to each other while swimming in the dark.

I haven't given the festival much thought. My waking moments have been consumed with work and my father's unanswered text. But taking part in the ghoulish festivities could be a fun distraction. Maggie will no doubt be at the event she planned, but I can't let her appearances stop me from participating in an awesomely gory spectacle.

I nod to Max. "How do you feel about intestines?"

He scrunches his adorable face. "What?"

I gesture to the bloody skeleton. "The Blood and Guts Festival. First prize for the best beet-inspired bloody tableau is an all-you-can-eat dinner at Smash Shack. Which means bottomless milkshakes, and I have a killer idea."

"*Yes.*" He clutches his pencil, his eyes wide with excitement. "Can Dad help too? And Uncle E? And I wanna be bloodied, but I wanna do the art for it too."

"Well, *I'm* the lead designer. You'll have to fill out an application."

The tips of his ears burn red, mischief sparking in his dark eyes. "Is it a..." He presses his lips tighter, his whole face twinkling. "A *hipster* application?" A giggle slips out, rolling into a full-blown laugh attack.

My fucking family. They for sure put him up to this, told him to slip in a hipster crack when opportunity struck.

I try to give him my stern face, but he's too cute, doubled over in hysterics. "Just for that, I'm taking you to the vegan restaurant for lunch instead of the Smash Shack. You'll be having brussels sprouts."

He laughs harder, hugging his stomach, barely squeaking out the words, "Vegan...is...hipster."

Goddamn it. I tug out a handful of grass and attack, getting him in a good headlock and shoving grass down his shirt as he cracks up and squeals and flails. When I'm worried he'll pee his pants, I kiss his head and release him.

I glance at Maggie, forever tuned-in to Ms. Confounding, and guess who's watching me win Uncle of the Year? She's beaming her vivacious grin at me, the one full of joy and laughter. Quickly, she frowns and shoves her book in front of her face, but her eyes betray her. She peeks at me again, the corner of her lips twitching.

Goddamn, this woman.

"I am *not* a hipster," I tell Max sternly, "but we are going to create an awesome gory scene for the festival."

"What if we…" He trails off as he grabs his sketchbook and starts drawing on a new page, his artistic brain already in hyperdrive.

My phone pings as I smile at him. One glance at the name on my screen has my stomach hardening. When I saved my father's contact information, I didn't go with the name Dad or Raymond. I chose a more apt moniker.

Life Wrecker: I hope not hearing from you is a good sign. That you're still considering meeting with me. I know how hard this must be for you, but it's important.

I nearly crush my phone in a death grip. My pulse strikes my neck. A second later, my cell rings. I make a weird squeaking noise and drop the damn thing, hunching lower, sure my Benedict Arnold of a father is out here spying on me. Thankfully the flashing name on my phone is *Desmond*, but hearing from him ups my already tweaked anxiety.

I'm supposed to have Max for another hour, minimum. Des

should be locked in his bedroom with Sadie right now, not calling me. Unless he somehow bugged my phone and knows our traitorous father is reaching out, and he's calling to warn me that he launched a nuclear missile at my cell.

I answer and say, "If you're having trouble getting it up, it's probably because you're masturbating too much." The joke comes out high-pitched and shaky.

"Fuck you," he mutters. Then, "The advanced copies of Dad's tell-all are out. Family meeting here tomorrow."

"Isn't that earlier than expected?"

"It is."

This can't be a coincidence. The Life Wrecker reaching out at the same time as his tell-all biography hits early readers is alarmingly concerning. Maybe I should meet him. Find out what this is all about, get the lowdown before more shocks blindside my family, but the thought has my phone turning slippery in my grip. I'm also still not sure I should tell my family about the texts yet. They'll explode and demand action—blocking Dad from my life—when I don't know what I want to do.

"I'll be there," I tell Des. "And seriously. Less masturbating."

He growls and hangs up.

Feeling like the ground is tipping sideways, I look up and try to focus on anything but my phone. My eyes dart to Maggie, like the sight of her will stop the sinkhole in my stomach from deepening. She's watching me intently, concern in her pinched brow.

Are you okay? she mouths.

I could mime drinking, pretend my likely panicked expression is a hangover, but I'm too overwrought to even joke. I shake my head and mouth *No.*

I don't bother watching her for a reaction. Not when I have to see the limp-shaker beside her. I get Max up and hurry us to my truck, hoping a Smash Shack strawberry shake will cure what ails me, like it did when I was a kid.

CHAPTER
Eight

BOWER FAMILY MEETINGS never end on a high note. The tense discussions have revolved around a plethora of fun debates, such as which fake names we should choose for the fake lives we didn't want. That particular chat ended with Jake punching the wall. When we needed to stage an intervention for fear E would chain himself to his computer and wither away as he scoured the internet, searching for news of his lost love, Delilah, the night culminated with E in a heap on the floor, bawling into his knees.

The meeting Mom called, where we learned Dad hadn't started laundering money recently, as we'd assumed, but that he'd been lying to us for *eight fucking years*, we debated hiring a private eye to find him so we could light his house on fire. Cal talked us off the ledge, but Des threw a lamp across the room in a glorious, shattering mess.

Today, we've gathered to discuss Dad's upcoming tell-all book—the biography he wrote to earn more cash from his devastating betrayal—and the energy in Des and Sadie's home is shocking, to say the least. Everyone is actually *smiling*.

Delilah's on the floor with Max and her two dogs, Candy

Cane and Macaroon, playing tug-of-war with them. Mom is watching Desmond with a small smile on her face as he whispers something to Sadie. Sadie blushes and swats his stomach. Desmond, no lie, *grins* like he's swallowed a bowl of Christmas cheer. He kisses her temple, his hand splayed on her waist in a possessive hold—his usual stance with his future wife.

Jake and Callahan are here too. It's their first time visiting Windfall since we left WITSEC. While they're more subdued, they're listening to some story E's telling, looking entertained. E gestures wildly and mimes slapping the air, then not-so-subtly nods to Delilah.

She levels him with a baleful squint. "If you're telling the story I think you're telling, I'll be changing our apartment lock."

"What story? There's no story." E does an abysmal job of hiding his amusement.

Cal quickly shakes his head. "No story here. Just reminiscing about the time E tried to play tennis and kept tossing his racket at the ball to hit it."

"That was one time," E says.

Cal pats his shoulder. "Keep telling yourself that. So there's no story," he reassures Delilah, but his lips are compressed to keep from laughing.

She huffs. "You're all liars."

"Nope." Jake stands in his usual crossed-arm pose. "We're definitely not talking about the fact that you approached a stranger bent over the open hood of his truck, smacked his butt, and said 'nice booty.'"

She huffs out an irritated breath and covers Max's ears. "Assholes, every single one of you." She releases Max's head and sharpens her glare. "The guy was wearing the same shorts as E and driving the same truck, and I didn't know E had moved *his* truck so the guy could pump gas."

"I'm sure the guy wanted to pump something after being groped," Jake says on a laugh.

"Hey. Hello. Hi." Sadie waves at the group, then points to Max. "Child in the room."

"I am *not* a child," Max says in full exasperation mode. "I know what pumping is."

Everyone freezes. Mom's eyes widen.

"Dad lets me pump the gas in his car," he says emphatically. "*Pumping.*"

"Right." Des claps his hands for no apparent reason. "Pumping gas. The pump through which the gas flows. That is what pumping is."

Delilah picks up a dog toy and beans E in the head. "See what your loud-mouthing caused?"

E shrugs, sheepish. "But it's such a good story."

"If you want a good story," Delilah says, sitting straighter, her eyes alight, "you should ask E about the time he tripped going up the stairs and—"

"Don't you dare," he warns.

"But it's such a good story," she mimics in a high-pitched voice, her grin pure evil.

Jake shoves E out of the way to give Delilah his full attention, but E bounds back to intercept them. Cal gets in on the action, holding E's arms in an iron grip, all of them laughing as E struggles to break free—a useless effort. E may be the tallest of us, fit and lean like me, but he's smaller than our muscled gym-rat brothers. As predicted, E can't escape. He goes limp, nearly dragging Cal to the floor. Max cracks up. The dogs bark and jump.

Delilah starts shouting about E going commando one day and that he tripped on the stairs. "And his jeans ripped…" She howls as the words stutter out. "His butt was totally hanging out, and"—laughing, she backs away from my brawling brothers—"he gave snooty Mrs. Wiser a view of his *butt crack.*"

E escapes the guys and tackles Delilah, trying to cover her mouth. The dogs join the melee. Mom releases the keening laugh that sends us all into hysterics, even though it's complete bedlam.

Unfortunately, I'm not partaking in my family's jokes. All I've done this morning is bounce my heel fast enough to dislocate my knee. I've barely said three words since walking in here. My father's infuriating texts are to blame. Mentioning them would mean dealing with them, when I still haven't decided how to handle the Life Wrecker. So it feels like I'm sitting on a massive secret. One wrong move and I'll blurt it before I'm ready.

My family's laughter and teasing gradually mellows. Mom, Delilah, and Sadie take Max and the dogs out back, where my nephew will sketch and dog-sit, and where he can't hear our impending discussion. When we talk about Dad, the Bower boys tend to drop a lot of "fucks."

I burrow deeper into my seat, attempting to fly under the radar, but Cal sidles up to me. "You not feeling well?"

"I'm all good." I go for nonchalant, letting my body sink into this cushy couch, but my twitching eyelid foils my efforts. "Just, you know, dreading this conversation."

"Yeah, I hear you." He nods, his eyes full of sympathy, but he's also watchful. Of all of us, Cal is the most rational and calm, always eager to offer advice and keep the peace, but I don't like how intently he's observing me. "Whatever Dad's tell-all unearths," he goes on, "we'll get through it. We always do. But…"

He zeroes in on my face. My eyelid spasms.

He tilts his way-too-intelligent head. "Something's up with you."

"Nothing's up."

"Right." He cranes his neck forward, analyzing my general self. "Except we were making fun of Delilah and E, and you didn't jump in to take either of them down with an obnoxious joke."

"Is that a crime? And my jokes aren't obnoxious."

"They most certainly are, and from you, it's a federal offense. There's also the issue of your eyelid." He narrows his deep brown eyes at me until it feels like I'm being hypnotized, then he faces my brothers. "Lennon's eyelid is twitching, and he's plastered to the sofa."

Guess Max and I aren't the only Bower boys who are tattletales.

"It's a chaise lounge," Des says, walking over.

"It's pronounced *longue* not lounge," Cal says. He studies the piece of furniture I'm trying to disappear into. "But I thought it was more of a divan."

My four brothers gather around me, not looking at my face, just analyzing the stupid sofa as though it's an archaeological find.

"Tough call," E says. "It's a lounger and has arms on both sides, but one arm is shorter. My vote is divan."

"Agreed." Cal gestures to the sides. "The shorter arm on the left means it can't be a chaise."

Des offers a derisive grunt. "You assholes are wrong. It's a chaise...*longue*."

"Definitely a chaise," Jake agrees, assuming his crossed-arm pose. He diverts his attention to me and skewers me with an intense stare.

I stare back, annoyed with my brothers for being my brothers. I mean, I get what they're doing. Making me sweat, waiting on me to crack, but the conversation is almost amusing enough to forget the land mine I'm sitting on. I assume E knows a *divan* from a *chaise longue* because he's an artist who examines the beauty and quirkiness of his surroundings. Jake's and Cal's construction work must lead to interactions with designers. Des is the shock factor here.

When we lived in Houston, all our apartments were decorated in a style I like to call bland-on-bland. IKEA essentials.

Garage sale finds. None of us wanted to give our fake identities the homey permanence that came with choosing stylish accents and vibrant colors.

Now Desmond's living with Sadie, engaged to be married, their Victorian home painted a cheerful yellow, with gorgeous artwork on the walls, while he waxes on about his *chaise longue*, because my brothers know I'm hiding something.

"Regardless what the chair is," Jake says, still winning our staring contest as he points at me, "this is a lying Bower."

Their oppressive circle shrinks around me. A pack of wolves, waiting to pounce.

"I'm not lying." *Twitch, twitch, twitch* goes my eyelid. "How can I lie if I didn't say anything?"

E presses his fingers to either side of my spasming eyelid and holds it open. "Yeah. He's hiding something."

I swat him off me and keep my mouth shut.

"It might be nothing," Cal says, resuming his role of Bower Tension Defuser. "He's probably just stressed."

Des nudges my shoulder with his fist. "Spill it."

"Nothing to spill. Cal's right. I'm just stressed about Dad's book." When my treasonous eyelid tremors again, I smack my hand over my eye and sigh. My brothers haven't budged. They're a ring of brown-headed interferers watching me with mixed expressions of concern and wariness.

Except E, who smirks. "I bet it's Maggie. I heard the two of them got stuck in an elevator together. She probably freaked out when she realized he isn't packing much between his legs and—"

I kick his shin, eliciting a grunt and laugh from him. There's no point evading this truth grenade. These assholes will only get more irritating.

Sitting more firmly in this exceptionally comfortable divan-chaise-longue-*whatever*, I scratch my beard and say, "Dad texted me."

"He *what*?" Desmond's barked tone matches his rabid expression.

Jake's face looks ready to erupt. "The asshole has no fucking right."

"Always a fucking angle with him," E says, his words quiet but deadly.

"Maybe there's a good reason." Cal's make-the-peace words are barely out when our three brothers round on him with "No fucking way" and "The guy's a fucking virus" and "Shut the fuck up with your glass-half-full bullshit."

Good thing the girls have Max outside.

Jake paces, then spears his hand through his hair. "What does he want?"

I deflate and rub my eyes. "To meet with me, but I don't know why."

"And you *agreed*?" Desmond gets in my face, looking like a bloodthirsty Viking.

I flinch and shove him away. "Exhaling your noxious breath on me isn't helping. Ever heard of toothpaste?"

"Swear to God," he mutters, his thunderous expression verging on scary. "I will kill that man."

Of all of us, I get Desmond's hatred of our father most. Being forced to leave Sadie broke him. Losing her sucked out his drive and determination, leaving behind a mad-at-life grunter with a collection of horrible tattoos and an even worse temper. Eleven years later, when he found out Sadie had been pregnant at the time and they had a son, he fell to pieces.

Des missed ten years of Max's life, a decade he can never get back. He and Sadie may have reconciled, the two of them finally living as the family they were meant to be with Max, but there's no galaxy in which Desmond doesn't want to murder our father for what was taken from him.

That same hatred has kept me awake most nights since getting the Life Wrecker's texts. Unfortunately, so have the happier memories I shared with my father. The latter is what concerns me most.

"You can't meet him." Jake stands taller, assuming his bossy oldest brother pose. "Don't give him the satisfaction. I know you guys had a different relationship than the rest of us, closer or whatever, but he doesn't deserve to see you. He'll lie. Infect you with some bullshit. Try to make you feel bad for him, or ask for help with something in his fucking book to make him look better. So tell the asshole to fuck off, then block his number."

"That." E hooks his thumb to Jake, nodding his agreement.

Des curls his lip. "Or we could trace the number, find his house, and blow it up."

"What are we blowing up?" Mom walks in with Sadie and Delilah, the three of them eyeing us with concern.

The rest of us trade here-we-go looks, hating when we have to blindside Mom with unexpected news. She's dealt with ten lifetimes of heartache.

As expected, Jake steps forward. The leader of our ramshackle platoon. "Dad texted Lennon and wants to meet with him."

"What? Why?" She clutches her chest, eyes darting to me. "What could he possibly want?"

I chew the inside of my cheek, hating how tired Mom looks. Her gray-streaked brown hair is long and loose. She's wearing makeup and a cheerful pink top, but there's no missing the darker circles under her eyes, the sag in her shoulders.

Maybe we *should* blow up Dad's house.

"I don't know what he wants," I say. "He asked to meet. Said he has something he wants to discuss. With the timing of the early copies of his book being out, I'd guess it has to do with that."

"Hasn't that man done enough?" Sadie is breathing hard, her skin mottled. "Why can't he leave you all alone?" She looks to Desmond, worry plain on her face.

He instantly softens and opens his arms for her. She hurries to his side, wrapping herself around him.

"Don't worry," Cal says gently. "Lennon's not going. Jake told him to block the number."

Mom's face tightens, her attention moving from Desmond and Sadie, to Jake's stern stoicism, to E now tucked close with Delilah, to Cal's patient head tilt.

The lines around her mouth soften. "What Lennon does or doesn't do isn't our choice." Her eyes settle on me, filled with compassion. "You had a close relationship with your father. As far as I know, you never confronted him, told him how much his deception hurt you. You certainly didn't forgive him."

Des growls, and Mom shoots him a look. He glares at us both, then folds in closer to Sadie, their heads bent in quiet conversation.

Mom sits on the end of my divan-chaise-longue-*whatever* and launches another series of mind-your-own-business looks at my remaining brothers until they give us space.

"You need to do what's right for you," she tells me gently. "Your father's betrayal was brutal and deep and left scars on us all. If you need to meet him for whatever reason, I'll support you and your decision. The price of closure can be steep, but the price of avoidance is steeper."

I don't know if closure is possible with that man, but I'm still having Dad memories—good flashes that remind me how much I loved him *before*. But also how much he hurt us after. Maybe confronting him about it all will break that cycle and let me get on with my life. Or it'll make me feel worse.

"I'll think about it," I tell Mom.

She nods and pats my shin, then gets up and faces our broody clan. "I don't want any of you pestering Lennon about those texts. If he has something to share with us, he'll share when he's ready."

My brothers stare at me and give their heads minuscule no-fucking-way shakes. Except E, who mouths *Nope*. I huff out a strained laugh. My family's impossible, but yeah. They won't leave this alone because they're worried about me, which is fine. I'll do what I need to do, whenever I figure out what that is, and deal with them after.

"On to more pressing matters." Mom stands taller. "The publisher of your father's book emailed me and asked if we want to read it early, while also subtly suggesting we could add a quote for the final print, if any of us feels inclined."

"Oh, I'll add a quote." Desmond's back to fuming. "Raymond S. Bower is a lying piece-of-shit asshole who doesn't deserve to make money off our misery."

Jake's cheekbones sharpen. "How about, Raymond S. Bower is a low-life traitor who ruins lives?"

The conversation devolves quickly, swears tossed around, one-liners shot out, getting kind of funny as they go. In the end, they agree Mom alone will read the book first. She'll prepare us for any shocking reveals. Then they're back to calling Dad names and grumbling about his stupid book.

Still stuck on his text and not knowing what to do, I head to the kitchen and pour myself a glass of water. Midsip, Callahan corners me, but I'm tired of discussing Dad. Since there's only one way to get Cal off my case, I say, "I saw Jolene."

He clamps his mouth shut.

"She owns a new bar in town," I go on, poking his apparent weak spot. "Cool place called the Barrel House. Being your former best friend, she asked about you, said she passed her number to you through E, but you haven't called her."

"Right, yeah." He scuffs his toe over the hardwood floor and rubs the back of his neck. When his gaze slides to mine, there's tension there. "How is she? Doing well?"

"Well, there was the amputation and the leprosy, and I'm pretty sure the gangrene was tough for her."

Cal tries to skewer me with a dirty look, but he's not

Desmond. His scowl is more of a kind stare. "Can you be serious for five seconds?".

"Can you explain why you're avoiding Jolene?" When he continues his polite staring, I huff. "She was your best friend, Cal. If you want to know how she is, call her. Don't you want to hear her voice?"

"Whose voice?" Jake plants himself beside Cal and me.

"Jolene's," I say. "Pretty sure she asked you to call her too."

At the mention of his ex, Jake's posture snaps straight. "You've seen her? How is she?"

"Of course I've seen her. Windfall's the size of a pincushion. She's great, but she doesn't understand why neither of you will call her. I don't understand it either."

"Just brings up bad memories," Cal says quickly, his attention cemented to his shoes. "Dad stuff."

"I should reach out." Jake's usual commanding presence gets as twitchy as my eyelid when I lie. "When we broke up, it sent me for a spin. Got in my head a lot during WITSEC. But yeah... maybe I will."

I knock his arm. "It would mean a lot to her. Whatever happened between you two, it's in the past."

I have no clue why Jake and Jolene actually broke up. There were rumors that Jake cheated, but I know my brother. That gossip was the legendary Windfall rumor mill and nothing more. Plus, he and Jolene stayed friendly afterward. Whatever the dirt, he's acting odd. And Callahan looks like he's holding his breath, his face reddening and eyes watering as he continues studying the floor.

I kick Cal's boot. "Suppressing your feelings will give you an ulcer. What the hell is up with you?"

He looks at me blandly, his expression schooled. "Have you finally told Maggie you're obsessed with her? Pretending you don't want her will give you an incurable case of regret-itis."

"Speaking of beets," I blurt, dodging his stealth attack. "The beet festival is coming up."

"I hate beets," Jake says, looking like I pissed in his mouth. "And no one mentioned them."

"I mentioned them just now, and you two should come back for the Blood and Guts Festival next weekend. We're planning a killer tableau. Could use your carpentry skills to make it extra gory."

"Littlewing could use your skills too," Des says, joining our circle. He slaps Jake's back. "We hired Ricky to build our ropes course, but he needs help and is struggling to find workers."

"Last I checked," Jake says, "we live in Houston. Definitely can't make the festival, and we can't work here."

"Last I checked with Cal—" Des elbows our introverting, breath-holding brother "—you're almost finished a job. Nothing's keeping you in Houston long-term. It would be great if you two moved back here. Max would love it."

Cal and Jake keep their mouths shut, like they've both developed sudden-onset laryngitis. I'm not sure if their hesitancy to move back is because of their own Dad memories or if Jolene is the issue. Either way, Des is right. Having the family together would be awesome.

"I agree with Des," I say. "You two should quit pretending you don't miss Windfall. If you come back, Mom will come too. I know she misses this place and her friends here, hates not being around Max more. You two moving would give her the push she needs."

We all look at the Bower matriarch, who's chatting and laughing with E and Delilah, reminding me of her younger self. In her youth, she quit teaching science to raise us boys, gave us all her love and attention. When her life got turned upside down, she didn't return to work. I think being with people was hard for her—the lying we had to do, her trust issues. She took up tutoring instead, quiet one-on-one work with kids, slowly building herself back up. I still think she'd be miles happier in Windfall, with us and closer to Max.

Jake and Cal continue their laryngitis routine, but there's no denying the tenderness in their gazes as they watch Mom. My bet is they'll cave. Do what's best for Mom. I think they miss having us close too. We may be a dysfunctional family, who lives to torment and tease one another, throwing out tantrums and glares on a whim, but we're five fucked-up boys who love one another fiercely in our own aggressive ways.

Regardless of their choices, I have my own dysfunction to handle. I need to decide how to deal with the Life Wrecker sooner rather than later. And then there's Maggie.

Callahan's retaliation to my Jolene taunt wasn't off the mark. I thought avoiding Maggie since the elevator incident was the mature choice. Letting her get on with her life and gullible boyfriend felt responsible and level-headed. But I still can't quit thinking about her. As teens, I never told her how much I cared about her—that I fucking *loved* her. I never risked asking her on a proper date, and I stewed over my cowardice for years afterward. If I don't try harder now and offer more honesty, that case of regret-itis will definitely bite me in the ass.

I'll be seeing Maggie next weekend at the Blood and Guts Festival, and I think we need to make a change to our family's planned tableau. A bolder scene to remind Maggie of our secret pond nights and special connection. Let her know there's another man who thinks about her and would love the chance to take her out. The change would take a ton of work, but something tells me my shark-imitating nemesis is worth it.

CHAPTER
Nine

I SHIFT my hips in a minuscule move. Enough that a one-inch tooth jabs my abdomen. "Could we not have made the mouth larger? This was built for a ballet dancer."

"You *are* slender," Sadie says, snickering as she looks through her phone at us.

I used to think she was Desmond's better half. I was wrong. "I am not *slender*. I have lean muscle."

"He's more petite than slender," Delilah adds, earning herself a scowl from me.

"He prefers the term *slight*," E offers loudly from behind me.

"Fudge you all," I say since Max is here. "I have more muscle than E."

"Maybe," E admits. "But it's too bad you don't still have those braces. Your face was terrifying back then. Scarier than our gory tableau."

Unable to give him the finger, I growl. Our *Jaws*-inspired Blood and Guts tableau is perfectly scary as is. He also knows having braces in my early teens was no picnic. Being the only one of my brothers to have braces was equivalent to walking around with a "kick me" sign on my back. E would regularly shade his eyes at dinner and shout, "The glare off those fuckers is intense. I can't sit across from him."

Then Des would make a crack like, "He'll never get kissed with those train tracks. Guy's gonna die a virgin."

The assholes can suck on my straight teeth now.

"Sadie, babe." Des grunts from his spot in front of me. "Can you pause riling Lennon and take the picture? My arm might fall off."

His arm falling off would actually be a plus. Our gory tableau would go from grotesque to monstrous.

"But riling Lennon is so fun," Sadie says, earning an eyebrow raise from me.

Laughing, she stands back, intensely focused as she snaps some shots with her phone.

Max wiggles in his spot. "Does it look gross from there?"

She lowers her cell, grinning her face off. "The grossest. We'll for sure win."

"Let's see it." I nod to her since my head's the only thing I can move without ruining my makeup, although it's more of a stiff twitch. It's a chilly afternoon, and I'm wearing a bathing suit.

She comes over and holds up her phone, and hell yeah. My homage to Maggie—the little shark who hummed the theme to *Jaws* and stole my heart at nineteen—is hideous perfection.

Behind us is the outline of a wooden boat, which Des cut out and Max and E painted. They also painted the drop cloth in layers of blue for the water. Max is lying on his side, in a wetsuit to keep warmer than us grown-ups, with his bottom leg folded behind him at the knee. There's beet pulp, chunky beets, and beet juice covering the joint, as though his lower leg was bitten off. E is behind me, his bottom half covered by a painted blue tarp to simulate treading water. His hand is wrapped up and gooped to look like it was bitten off at the wrist.

I'm the centerpiece, standing in the mouth of a ferocious

great white shark created in papier-mâché by E, Max, and Sadie, with beets oozing from my abdomen. An intestine built from panty hose is hanging out of me for effect. Then there's Desmond. He's wrestling the shark with his knife lodged in the mighty fish's throat. His savage expression suggests he's either a surprisingly good actor, or he's picturing the shark as our father.

"It looks great," Delilah says, hugging a bucket filled with beet goop. "Judging starts in a few minutes, so nobody move. But Max needs a bit more gore on his knee."

She takes her bucket to him, wearing plastic gloves that are doing nothing. Beet juice is up to her elbows and inside the gloves. Her hands will be blood red for a week.

From my position, I scan the other seven tableaux setup in the town square. All of them did some version of a zombie apocalypse, except for a creepy clown scene inspired by *It* that might give me nightmares. Smartly, they fenced off this event and set up a bouncer at the entrance, ensuring only people ages fourteen and up can enter, unless they're accompanied by an adult.

Along Main Street, local farmers have set up booths, promoting their beets with beet baked goods, beet savory delights, beet sauces, beat marinades, and the like. All beets all day, thanks to Maggie's ingenuity.

"Showtime," Sadie calls with a little clap and full-teeth smile. "Maggie's on her way."

Sadie and Delilah skedaddle to the side, hitting play on the *Jaws* soundtrack as they go. Max starts moaning and flailing on the ground. E's making a sound that's a cross between a yowl and a crazed laugh. Guy can't even get into character. Des still looks murderous. He definitely pictures the shark as Dad, which has me thinking about the two texts on my phone I *still* haven't answered. I'm waiting for a sign to tell me if I should block his number, or text him to go fuck off, or agree to talk. So far, the sign gods have given me zilch.

Getting bitten in half by a wooden shark is an excellent diversion.

I amp up my performance, going for the shocked victim—frantic face, silent screams.

Then I see Maggie.

I break character. Just for a second, but *damn*. She's wearing skintight dark jeans and a throwback green sweater that matches her eyes. Her straight hair flirts with her shoulders, those bonfire strands glinting in the late-afternoon sun. She's with two other judges, assessing the tableau beside us, all of them writing on their clipboards. Maggie tells the participants how great they are. She's lying. It's a subpar effort compared to our masterpiece, and I can't wait to see her reaction to our creation.

I resume my silent screaming.

She steps in front of us and jolts. Her emerald eyes dart from Max to E to Des, her grin growing as she takes in the gore-tastic scene I created for her. When her sights lock on me, fondness bursts from her gaze. I wink at her and amp up my acting, groaning in fake pain. She snorts, then laughs fully—so hard she has to walk around and catch her breath.

Good-natured shrieks and laughs drift from other displays. A headshake later, Maggie jots notes on her clipboard and sneaks another look at me. Pretty sure there's heat in her steady perusal.

As per the rules, we're supposed to hold form for another half hour, letting townsfolk tour our grotesque works of art, so I don't corner Maggie like I crave.

Desmond's buddy Kyle Jackson walks by with his wife. Kyle is a former jock from their football days—a big Black man with an infectious smile and a rock-hard build. Cearra is a local tattoo artist, sporting a cool collection of ink. Instead of looking appropriately scared, they glance at Des and laugh.

"Dude," Kyle says, pointing at him, "your butt crack's showing."

Max giggles.

Des startles and glances over his shoulder. "Crap. Man, you gotta fix it."

Kyle guffaws. "And ruin that view? Not a chance." He walks off, laughing harder.

Des fumes. "Someone call for Sadie."

"Nope," I say. Like there's any chance I'd miss the opportunity to humiliate Des.

Snarling at me, he breaks character and yanks up his swim shorts, while E and Max almost die of hysterics. We resume our roles, and I take in this amazing festival—how much work Maggie must have done to pull it all together, celebrating Halloween and Windfall's farmers in a wacky, fun event.

A piercing scream cuts through my enjoyment.

This isn't an actor-in-character scream. This is a child screaming, as though being tortured. Another shriek follows, of the B-movie variety, loud and shrill, followed by pandemonium. Young kids—younger than the fourteen-plus age limit—are suddenly everywhere. They're running past the gory tableaux, trying to escape the fenced area of horrors.

Terrified cries of "Mommy!" ring out.

Zombies jump into action, attempting to corral the screeching children, no doubt scarring them for life. The *It* clown is roaming with its terrifying teeth exposed.

The only person *not* moving is Maggie.

Instead of busting into damage-control mode, she's off to the side, frozen, her eyes wide and face pale, watching with abject horror as things go south fast. Instantly, I move. I bust out of the shark mouth and weave through the madness, jogging toward the entrance. Whoever they hired to keep kids out must have died or left their post. Best way to stop a flood of screaming children is at the source.

Partway there, a cute girl with pigtails blocks my way. She takes one look at me and wails so loud my eardrums ring. Guess the beet goop and falling-out-intestine is as realistic as I hoped.

"I'm not scary," I tell her. She screams louder. Guess that's that.

I race to the entrance and find it abandoned. An A-frame sign is tipped over—the one warning people of the gore in the fenced area. A family wanders over, drawn by the shrieks and shouts.

I barricade the entrance. "Sorry. This area's being used as a set for a student film. No entrance at this time."

They frown and move along.

When Desmond's friend Kyle and his wife try to leave the war zone, I block their way. His huge muscles are exactly what I need. "You two can't leave."

"It's worse than *The Evil Dead* in there," Kyle says, hooking his thumb toward the mayhem.

"Exactly. I need bouncers. Guard this entrance with your lives. No one gets in."

Cearra salutes me. "We're on it." Hopefully her ink and piercings will up their intimidation factor.

I race back inside, tearing off my hanging intestine as I go. I help a few zombies herd crying kids toward their parents. A yellow Labrador retriever has gotten loose and is covered in beet gore. I nab his leash and tug him back to his owner. I spot Kyle's grandmother, Mrs. Jackson—one of the few people who doesn't look like a horror movie extra—and ask her to help clear out the last few children.

As the pandemonium settles, I find Maggie at my shark display, staring blankly at the empty tableau.

"The area has been contained," I tell her, my adrenaline ebbing. "Just cleared out the last of the traumatized children. Kyle and Cearra are guarding the entrance." I stop at her side, a cool breeze reminding me I'm in a bathing suit on this brisk fall afternoon. I cross my arms over my beet-dyed chest.

Maggie picks a bit of beet goop from her jeans and flicks it on the ground. "This was the first event that was all mine—my idea, I led the team. My boss fought me on the concept at first, worried it would be too scary for kids, but I convinced her I had it under control."

I hate the defeat in her voice. Nowhere in there is the Maggie who dared me to belly flop naked.

I move in front of her and tilt up her chin, letting my thumb linger on the thin scar almost hidden under her freckles. "This is just one section. Out there—" I gesture to the booths of farmers and food, the happy townsfolk mingling and shopping "—that's a raging success. The kids are learning about our local agriculture. People are sharing fun pictures on social media. They'll be talking about this event for months."

"Because zombies were in here chasing children."

"Most of the zombies were lame. Barely looked dead." But I picture the one with its heart outside of its chest, her arms outstretched as she chased after a wailing child. I press my lips together, attempting not to smile.

This is *not* funny. I will not laugh at Maggie's expense.

She narrows her eyes at me. "Don't you dare laugh."

"I'm not laughing." An uncontained squeak slips out.

"*Lennon.*"

I full-on laugh. "Sorry. I can't..." I cover my face and let it out. When I get my shit together, she's at least smirking. "Who'd you hire to watch the entrance anyway? That's who screwed this up, not you."

Fury burns up her cheeks. "Doug."

"The same Doug who went to Tokyo for lunch when we were stuck in the elevator and he took seventy-nine years to rescue us?"

Her glare could cut glass. "The one and only."

"Doug is the worst."

"He really is." Her attention drops to my bare abdomen, then ever so slowly meanders up my chest. She clears her throat. "Thanks for flying into action and taking charge. I've never frozen like that."

Checking that the beet dye on my hand is dry, I graze my fingers down her sweater-clad forearm. "I'm sorry, Mags. Everything about this was amazing, until Doug screwed up."

She watches my fingers on her arm, as do I. A slight shiver courses through her. "I loved your tableau," she whispers. Her eyes flick up to mine. "It was perfect."

Since I'm done avoiding my feelings for Maggie, I let my fingers drift lower until they're covering hers. "I did it for you."

Her breath catches. A rush of warmth invades my chest.

It's time to lay it out for Maggie. Get answers from her and tell her what I want. Let her know our business isn't finished. "In the elevator, you said I scared you when we were teens. That I still do." I dip my head to catch her eye. "What did you mean?"

Her next swallow seems to last an eternity. Just when I worry she'll shut me down, she sets her jaw. "You make me feel carefree, like I want to set the world on fire and be wild."

"And that's a bad thing?"

She sways forward, as though drawn toward me. "Everything about you makes me feel electric, and when I feel that way, I get reckless. I make bad—"

"Oh my God, there you are." Delilah, of the worst-timing-ever Delilahs, runs over to us and pulls Maggie into a hug. "I'm so sorry about the event. I found Doug and gave him shit. Made sure to do it in front of your boss, so hopefully that helps."

"Thanks, hon." Maggie rubs Delilah's back, but her attention is still on me, lingering on my eyes. Her focus drops to my lips, which are suddenly very parched.

Delilah pulls back and cringes. "I got beet on you."

Yep. Delilah is a beet monster. Maggie's green sweater is now smeared red in spots. Instead of getting annoyed, Maggie shrugs. "The outfit better reflects my mood now."

I gesture to my chest. "At least you don't look like your nipples are bleeding."

The girls laugh, even Maggie, her eyes crinkling with fondness.

Delilah gives her a compassionate pout. "Some of us are heading to the Barrel House. You should come and decompress."

Maggie nods while straightening her clothes. "I need to do damage control here, make sure the clean-up crew's all good. I'll meet you after."

Maggie steals another glance at me, quick but intense, then trudges off to do her work.

I watch her longer than is decent, hating that our talk was cut short. *I make her feel electric. I make her feel wild.* The feeling's mutual, but she's worried she'll lose control around me, that I'll bring out something bad in her. Guess my new job is to prove otherwise.

"Someone's got your attention," Delilah says, always in my business.

"Someone lives to confuse me and keep me guessing."

Delilah rocks on her heels, her face pensive. "Maggie's life is nothing like people think. She hides a lot."

Her veneer in high school. Her placid smiles with her Ivy League boyfriend. The insight is similar to Delilah's texting when I had that date with Sloan, suggesting Maggie's life is more complicated than anyone realizes, but I'm still in the dark. "Quit with the vagaries. If you have something to say about Maggie, spit it out."

"Not my story to tell."

"Right. You just enjoy tormenting me with cryptic clues."

"I do." She picks a blob of beet out of her curly hair, cringing as she flicks it on the ground. "But I will tell you this—whatever went on with you two in high school, I think Maggie was in love with you back then."

My brain goes on the fritz. "She told you that?"

"Not in so many words. But we were out a few years back, drinking our weight in tequila, and I was nagging her about the latest guy she was dating—a selfish prick who dicked her around. I told her to ditch him, but she said he was nice enough. So I told her she didn't know from nice, because all the guys she dated were losers or jerks."

"Wow. If that's how you talk to your friends, remind not to get on your bad side."

Delilah rolls her eyes. "I obviously said it nicer than that. But then *she* said, and I quote, 'I was in love once, and the guy was nice and sweet and really fucking great, and he still broke my heart. I'll stick with the jerks and losers.' " Delilah's expression softens. "She said I didn't know the guy. Claimed he was some art student from her college dorm, but with how she's acted since you've been home, I'm pretty sure she was talking about you."

My brain's no longer on the fritz. I can barely swallow. "Because I broke her heart by disappeared into WITSEC?"

"I mean, it makes sense. As far as I know, you're the only guy from her past she never talked about with me, and her relationships since then have all been short-lived. To this day, Maggie only dates guys if she knows it won't get serious. And if anything *does* get serious, she ends it. But there's more to that pattern than your disappearance. Like I said before, her history is complicated. I think she wants to open up to you about it all. It's just hard for her. Give her time."

I blink at the grass, attempting to rearrange more of my Maggie history. For over a decade, I assumed Maggie moved on easily after I disappeared. Maybe missed me a little, but I was the guy she ignored in public. Our final night ended with her running away from me. I was sure I'd hurt the girl *I'd* loved. But Maggie recently admitted our last erotic night had been the hottest sexual encounter she'd ever had. Now Delilah's telling me Maggie might have been in love with me too.

Or Delilah's wrong and Maggie was upset over some other guy.

Either way, my feelings for her aren't fading. I want to give Maggie time to open up to me. Talk with her more, understand the woman she's become, the fears that seem to guide her life. The complicated past Delilah keeps hinting at.

Compared to my past, I highly doubt hers is shocking. Maggie had loving parents growing up, a cute little sister. As far as I know, they're still close. Her father didn't launder money for a drug cartel and destroy his family, but something's up with her. And her commitment issues are a red flag. I'm not looking for casual. I've had eleven years of meaningless flings, and nothing about Maggie is meaningless to me.

I should quit pushing, let her continue dating losers who don't make her happy. Save myself from getting hurt. But the thought of walking away from Maggie, not kissing her and teasing out her husky laugh, has my stomach twisting into knots. Regret-itis.

Guess that means I have to make tonight's meetup at the Barrel House count. Somehow convince Maggie to ditch her boyfriend and share her secrets with me, then hope like hell the choice doesn't bite me in the ass.

CHAPTER
Ten

THERE'S a lot of red at the Barrel House this evening. Red hands. Red arms. Red stains on clothes and faces. Beet juice has seeped into the town, but my favorite shade of red hasn't appeared at the bar yet. The DJ is playing upbeat country tunes. People mingle as they gossip and laugh about the zombie incident. I hate that the event wasn't a success for Maggie, but she certainly created buzz. Maybe more so than if it had gone according to plan.

I leave Delilah and E's circle of friends, sidling up to the bar for another beer.

Jolene has joined her bartenders, nodding to me as she pulls a bottle from the fridge below. "One hipster beer coming right up."

I lift my middle finger.

Laughing, she slides the beer my way and grabs my money. "Whatever you said to Jake, thanks. He called this week."

"Just told him you were dying of a rare venereal disease. Probably wanted to pay his last respects."

"Pest." She mock scowls. "But yeah, it was great to hear from him. He said he might be moving back with Cal. We'll hopefully meet up soon."

I hadn't heard confirmation of that intel, but I'll be thrilled if it happens. Having my family split apart doesn't feel right. "Des and I need help building our ropes course, and I think Des reached out. Seems they have time and probably miss the people here."

"Not sure about Cal on that last one." A customer lifts his hand to get Jolene's attention. She waves him off, staying intent on me. "He still hasn't called me."

The same Cal who seemed to hold his breath when we discussed Jolene, then studied his shoes like they held a treasure map. The odd behavior, especially in relation to his former best friend, has my Bower intuition shifting into a higher gear. "Did you and Cal have a fight before we left?"

"No." Jolene shakes her head so emphatically I'm worried she'll pull a neck muscle. "I mean, not really."

"Not really?"

She laughs haltingly, even though I didn't crack a joke. "Just a few off weeks. Things were strained between us, and we didn't get the chance to talk it out, but it was no big deal. Anyway..." She wipes her forehead. "Look how busy we are. We've been kinda slow lately, so busy is great, and I *really* need to get back to work."

With an awkward wave, she zips away, not giving me a second look.

I drum my fingers on my beer. Something clearly happened between her and Callahan, a man who has a tendency to go overboard when faced with problems.

I'm not sure the rest of my family knows Callahan Bower is a secret wheeler and dealer—a schemer, if you will—but the guy lives to fix problems, no matter the method.

When I was fourteen, I found him sliding money *into* Dad's wallet, as though replacing something he'd stolen. The move was uncharacteristic, and Dad was in a foul mood that week, doling out harsh punishments like cleaning the attic if we stepped out of line. Being the blackmailer I was, I cornered Cal and accused him of stealing the cash then returning it. He confessed quickly. Almost too quickly, with a hint of a smile. I then bribed him to do my math homework for a month or I'd snitch on him. He agreed, but I caught Des running around shortly afterward with a new cell phone I knew our folks had refused to buy him.

That's when the puzzle pieces snapped into place.

Cal hadn't swiped the cash, but he knew Desmond had stolen it, and he hadn't wanted Des to get caught in Dad's crosshairs.

There were other instances of his conniving over the years, more diabolical in nature. Freddie Lorimer turned up with a mysterious broken finger after picking on E, but Des—the usual Bower bully punisher—was away playing football. At the end of high school, I received a B on an English essay. No big deal for most people, but I needed a B to pass my second attempt at the class. I'd rushed my essay on Shakespeare's *Othello*. Kept mixing up Othello and Iago and should've flunked the paper, but miraculously…I got a B. That same day, I saw Callahan leaving school property, even though he had long since graduated.

I don't have proof Cal schemed to our benefits, but I always found him afterward in an extra-chipper mood, smiling that half smile of his, like he had secretly won the lottery. All this to say, Callahan's need to keep those he cares about happy goes beyond kind words and nice gestures. He'll do dark deeds to avenge his family or help those he loves, and Jolene used to be his best friend. It's possible a scheme of his went awry.

"Maggie!" someone shouts.

I whip around, and there's my old nemesis still looking defeated as she nears the group…and she's not alone. Her tumbleweed of a boyfriend is in tow.

I grit my teeth, silently cursing my luck.

I didn't see the limp-shaker at the festival, figured he wouldn't be here tonight. His appearance ruins my plan to convince her to ditch the guy...unless I can get her alone.

Another upbeat song kicks in. The people on the dance floor hoot and jump. I scowl at Maggie's plus-one, trying to figure out how best to separate them. When I spot a few of Delilah and E's friends, an idea sparks.

Avoiding Maggie's eye, I tug Delilah to the side and whisper my plan in her ear. I don't need Maggie alone for long. I have a million things I want to discuss with her, but only one of them needs to be said tonight.

"I'm so in," Delilah says, sparkling with intent.

"Don't do it until I'm dancing beside her."

"Roger that."

We discreetly bump fists.

I nod to Maggie and Harrison and succeed in not grimacing at him. "First round's on me. What's your poison?"

"Tequila with a shot of tequila," Maggie says.

"Tequila overdose. Got it. And you?" I try to smile at Harrison. I think I resemble the vengeful clown from the creepy *It* tableau.

Bopping to the tunes, he says, "I'll have a strawberry daiquiri."

Of course he orders a slushy for a cocktail. "I'll get you an extra straw."

Halfway to the bar, a man knocks into me, sloshing his drink on my shoes. "Shit, sorry."

"No biggie. The rest of me is dyed red with beet juice." I glance up from my shoes and startle. "Mizhir?"

"Lennon?"

I take in my former friend's thicker frame, the contacts he's wearing instead of glasses. He's gained a bit of weight and has shorter hair, but I still see the guy I dared to light cherry bombs under the bleachers. The friend who got too busy at college to connect with me. "Great to see you, man."

"Yeah, yeah. I mean, I heard you were back, but…" He shrugs and rubs his jaw. "Just been crazy busy."

A jab of aggravation strikes. It's a subpar excuse for not reaching out, not that I've been any better. I didn't exactly go out of my way to find him when I moved home. Too many bygones and years under that rickety bridge. "I'm on a bar run, but I'm sure I'll see you around."

"Yeah, sure."

We nod our goodbyes, neither of us making a concrete effort to meet up later. I have more pressing concerns than pretending Mizhir and I might reconnect.

By the time I return with the beverages, Maggie seems more relaxed. She's chatting with Delilah and E and their friends Avett and Naomi. Harrison is standing to the side, talking with some other Ivy League-looking guy.

I shove his slurpy at him, then present Maggie with her first tequila shot like a servant bowing to royalty. "Your liquid amnesia, ma'am."

She rolls her eyes. "It'll take more than a shot to forget today."

"That's why there are two." I hold up the second.

She slams back the first, barely pausing before she snags the second. Two shots down, she hands me the glasses, and our fingers brush. Except they don't just *brush*. There's definite lingering. She flexes her fingers, dragging her nail lightly along my skin. My nerve endings decide they're live wires. She licks her lips while eyeing mine, but she misses a droplet of tequila. It takes all my willpower not to lean in and lick the alcohol clinging to her top lip.

Swallowing a groan, I deposit the glasses on a high-top table and focus on the conversation.

"I need to buy a red shirt." Delilah holds up her stained hands. "Something to accessorize with my skin."

Maggie huffs. "You and the rest of the town."

"I have skunk shampoo that's pretty strong," Avett offers. He was best friends with E before we disappeared into WITSEC. He's a vet now and a solid guy, with a trim beard and a bright smile, except the mischief on his face matches E's too well. "It might get out the stains, but I'd have to spray everyone with skunk first. Make sure using it is legit."

E high-fives him. "Killer plan."

"Or," I say brightly, "we could pretend we're dying from some rare skin disease. Get the media involved. Think of how much attention it would bring Windfall."

Maggie raises an unimpressed eyebrow. "Because everyone would be evacuating the town and the businesses would tank and I'd officially lose my job?"

As usual, she makes an excellent point. "Maybe we won't do that. On a more serious note, the farmers' booths were super busy."

"I bought beet-dyed yarn for my knitting group," Delilah says. "I'm planning to knit dog sweaters."

"I bought beets to pickle." Naomi nudges Avett. "We'll make that goat cheese salad you like."

Harrison butts into our circle and slips his arm around Maggie. "See? No reason to stress over the festival, Gummy Bear. Everyone had fun."

Her face pinches like she wants to throat-punch him, then a curtain seems to fall—actress Maggie offering him an amiable smile. "I'll stress if I want to, *sweetheart*."

Yep. Maggie's not into her boyfriend. It doesn't take a genius to read the signs, and she'll be getting an earful from me.

The song blasting from the speakers changes. I recognize Lee Brice's "Love Like Crazy" from my cowboy-boot-wearing phase. A rocking song that has the crowd cheering.

I plant my hand on Avett's shoulder. "Might I steal your wife for a dance?"

Naomi lights up. "Yes, please."

"You'd be doing me a favor," Avett says, stepping aside. "Dance floors and I don't get along."

"I promise to return her before your car turns into a pumpkin." I lead the way to the dance floor, not before I give Delilah intense eyes, silently telling her Operation Corner Maggie has commenced.

She winks at me, then grabs Harrison and Maggie by their arms, not-so-subtly shoving them toward the dance floor. "You two need to unwind! Shake a leg! Dance the day off!"

Her over-the-top enthusiasm is pitiful, but her antics force Maggie and Harrison to the dance floor. We all get into the groove. Naomi and I dance a few feet away from them. Unsurprisingly, Harrison's more of an arm-waver than a dancer, while Maggie's hips hit every beat, riling me up without even trying. Naomi and I have fun in our little bubble of two, dancing and jumping to the music. By the middle of the song, I spot Delilah beside the DJ, whispering into his ear. My accomplice doing her duty.

I grab Naomi's hand and twirl her, maneuvering us toward the sexy redhead who puts every dancer out here to shame.

"I'm your wingwoman," Naomi says in my ear, her eyes darting to Maggie and back to me.

I grin. "That you are, and I apologize in advance."

"For what?"

"It's time to switch things up!" the DJ calls as the song hits a gentler but still upbeat country vibe. "Grab the dancer beside you for a spin. Make a new friend!"

Smooth, Naomi mouths as she shoves me toward Maggie and gets stuck dancing with the human windmill, otherwise known as Harrison.

Maggie glares at me, barely moving, like she knows I put this plan into motion. I don't pay her annoyed expression any mind. I move us into a sort of waltz, while other people take a more modern dancing approach. "Fancy meeting you here."

She stiffens a moment, then softens against me. "It's a small town."

"You can say that again. And while we see each other plenty, we never seem to have time to finish our conversations."

She follows my footwork, the two of us moving to the music. I realize suddenly that this is the closest I've ever been to Maggie. I've seen her naked. I've had my head on her lap and have come all over her skin, but we never so much as hugged in high school. Not gonna lie, she feels fucking amazing. I love having my arm locked around her back, my chin pressed to the side of her head. I love feeling her soft breasts against the hard wall of my chest.

In seconds, there's a situation in my jeans.

"Talking," I say again. There's a reason I put this scheme into action—forced time with Maggie. "We need to do that."

"You're right," she says, confounding me as usual. I expected more pushback. Avoidance from the Avoidance Queen. Instead, she looks up at me, compassion softening her expression. "The day in the town square, when you were with Max, something happened before you left. And when you had that date with Sloan here, you got a similar pained look on your face. Is everything okay?"

"No, not really." There's no hesitation in my reply. I still haven't dealt with my father's texts, and I'm not sure why. I can't talk to my family about it. They have too much skin in this game. I sequestered Maggie to discuss her and us. Specifically, her relationship that's hampering what I really want—to take Maggie on a date. But I'm suddenly clinging to her more firmly, veering off topic. "My dad texted me. First time I've heard from him in over a decade."

"Holy shit."

"Yeah."

"What the hell does he want?"

Isn't that the million-dollar question? "To meet and talk to me. Probably about the book coming out. Not exactly sure why. And the worst part is, since moving back, I get walloped by these intense memories. Like, I find myself missing him. The guy he *was*, obviously. And I don't want to give him the satisfaction of getting to me. Of pulling my strings, because he knows how much he affects me."

Maggie splays her fingers wider on my back. "When's the last time you saw him?"

I try to piece through my memories—the awful time in our first Safesite, then later in our new Houston home. "Around the six-month mark into WITSEC. We were settled in Houston, all of us walking around like we were rigged with dynamite, ready to blow. My dad was still around, but I avoided him. Didn't punch walls like Des or break down like E. I just…shut down."

"Because you worried you'd lash out at him?"

"I think it was more about anxiety," I say, moving with Maggie, the slow sway easing out my words. "When I was around him, panic would start to mount, kind of like when I'm in a tight space—that awful shaky and trapped feeling. My family was dealing with so much, and I didn't want to fall apart in front of them and make it worse. So, I pushed it all down. Ignored my father, left a room if he walked in. Ate at different times. Then one day, he was gone."

"*Gone?*" Her sharp tone could cut glass. "Like, he just disappeared on you guys?"

I almost smile at her defensiveness. "Mom said she kicked him out and he didn't put up a fuss. He moved somewhere else and never got in touch. Maybe he realized his presence was slowly killing us, or he was tired of being stonewalled by his family. I don't know. She apologized to us for not making him leave sooner, said she was going through her own hell, trying to get through each day. But yeah, I don't remember the last time I actually saw him." I fist and unclench my hands, discomfort edging my dance moves.

Maggie strokes her hand down my lower back, softening deeper into me. "In high school, you talked about your dad a lot, how he singled you out from your brothers. Spent more time with you but had gotten distant in those last months. You put a lot of blame on yourself, thought failing your classes and doing another year of high school was the reason, which it clearly wasn't. From what you just said, it sounds like you never confronted him about that or any of it."

"Confrontation isn't the answer to everything. For me, it leads to more stress. A huge fight with him would've made everything worse for everyone."

"Avoiding conflict isn't the answer either," she says, her voice firmer. "It grows into suppressed anger that festers and infects."

I spin us in a quick circle, finishing with what I hope is a dashing smile. "Do I seem angry to you?"

She gives her head a rueful shake. "Maybe in your case, conflict avoidance leads to bad jokes and awkward dance moves." She turns her head toward mine, her nose brushing my jaw. "Your father's intentions don't matter. If you reply to his messages, you're not doing it for him. You're doing it for you. To say the things you left unsaid, or maybe to forgive yourself for loving him."

That nugget of wisdom sinks like a rock in my stomach. Maybe that's the crux of my ambivalence. Not my anger at my father, but the possibility that I still love him—*present* tense, not past. That I'll *miss* him when I see him and feel a bigger surge of fondness.

The thought fills me with more shame.

She doesn't say more, and my mind is too tangled to pull at the knotted threads. Also, I didn't orchestrate this dance to talk about my father. The song's almost over, and along with it, my time with Maggie.

I refuse to leave here without saying my piece, especially after this unexpected talk. My honesty with her proves what I've suspected all along—even after so long apart, she knows me better than anyone. We still affect each other in inexplicable ways, and if I *am* the guy she once loved, she might be fighting these same feelings.

I slow my steps and lean toward her ear. "Thanks for listening. It means more than you know, but I have some advice for you too." I run my tongue over my teeth, teetering on the edge of this cliff. "You should break up with your boyfriend."

She tenses. "That is none of your—"

"You don't love him," I go on, making it clear the floor's mine. "I'm not even sure you like him. And I'm right here—a man who knows when your smiles are real or forced. A man who unleashes all this wild energy you keep contained, and I want to unleash it. I want to spend time with you, figure you out again. Figure *us* out. And I'm not reckless, Maggie. I won't hurt you. I just know what I want."

I've never heard my voice this deep and shadowy. *Possessive.*

Maggie's chest swells, her soft breasts pushing harder against me, and heat blasts up my thighs. Her eyes are beyond intense, darker and searching. My body is rigid enough to snap. I'm dying to kiss her. Lick into her mouth and steal my first taste of Maggie. The way she's looking at me, her face flushed and eyelids heavy, I'm pretty sure she's equally as hot for me.

But she's in a relationship.

I dip my lips to her ear again and exhale against the delicate shell, eliciting a lovely tremble from her. "It's time you quit living for everyone else and start living for yourself. When you're ready to ditch your boyfriend and finally explore our connection, come find me."

The second I finish, I tear myself away from her and stalk

toward the exit. My blood's thrumming too fast. My throat burns with desire. And Maggie isn't single.

When I get outside, I'm shaky but also exhilarated. Whatever happens from here, I was honest and gave it my all. My heart's firmly in her court, and our talk about my father made something else inside me click. Missing and loving my dad is tied to the past, not the present. Waiting to reply to him has only given my memories more power over me. If I want to move past this ongoing angst, I need to meet with him. Allow myself to feel whatever it is I'll feel, then banish him from my life forever.

Before finding my truck, I pull out my phone and thumb to the Life Wrecker's messages. I type before I can overthink it. Simple and to the point.

> Me: I'll meet you as long as I choose the place.

CHAPTER
Eleven

I PUT my screwdriver down and maneuver the cupboard door, checking the new hinge I installed. Swings like a well-lubed charm. It's barely nine a.m., but I've been working since the crack of dawn. I cross item number three off my to-do list, right between *Fix leaky faucet* and *Replace cracked tile in upstairs bathroom*.

Most of Mrs. Jackson's farmhouse is worn-down, but there's history in the trodden-on floorboards. Evidence of family dinners on the scuffed dining room table. It's the style of no-frills house you'd see in a period ranching movie, but I love the realness of it, its humble bones and groaning creaks. The type of home where a person grows old.

Preferring not to test Mrs. Jackson's kindness and lose this place, I open my laptop and check my investments. The bulk of my money is sitting pretty as always, untouched by me. The rest is disappearing faster than is comfortable on painting supplies, deposits for Littlewing's construction work, my day-to-day needs, and upkeep on this farmhouse, even though I could ask Mrs. Jackson to cover the work. But I *like* doing the work. I like feeling as though this place is mine, even if it isn't. The first real home I've had in eleven years.

I debate accessing a chunk of principal to take the financial edge off, but my fingers stiffen on the mouse. *No can do.* I move some money around instead and set up next month's rent payment, mentally reviewing my upcoming earnings. Tight, but I'll get by.

Time for a well-earned cup of tea.

I drive to town and head toward Delilah's coffee shop, smiling at everyone I pass. I'm proud of my crack-of-dawn work and pleased I faced two big stresses last night—Maggie's boyfriend issue and my father's text. I'm looking forward to today's group hike, but two steps inside Sugar and Sips, as the delicious smells of roasting coffee and melting sugar assault me, Sandra of the Eighties Perm blocks my way.

"Maggie broke up with her boyfriend last night."

I discreetly fist-pump, my good mood improving exponentially.

She gives me a quick nod, like we're in cahoots, then hurries off. Probably to go on a stakeout somewhere else, but I give myself a mental pat on the back. Seems grabbing that floating paper of hers earned me points. Having the town busybody on my side is an excellent resource.

As luck would have it, Maggie's here, huddled with Delilah at a small table. Thanks to Sandra, I don't have to wonder how my confession last night affected her or worry she's going to shut me out. If she broke up with the limp-shaker, she must be as into me as I am into her. She's finally ready to date a guy she actually likes.

I saunter to her table with an extra swagger in my step.

When she notices me, she startles, then frowns. I *frown*, unsure why she's frowning. Basically, there's a lot of frowning going on when we should be sharing sexy winks and come-hither smiles.

"Oh, wow. Would you look at the time?" Delilah resumes her role as worst actress ever, jumping up from her seat and doing an awkward shoulder shimmy. "I have to get back to work. So much work to be done with all the work in here. Feel free to take my seat, Lennon." She gives Maggie an intense look and scuttles away.

I gesture to the now-empty seat. "May I?"

Her long-suffering sigh is a concern. "If you must."

"I definitely must. Rumor has it you're single."

"This fucking town," she grumbles.

Don't I know it. I love how small and quaint Windfall is, broken-telephone gossip train included. What I don't love is Maggie's tense features and formal demeanor. "I'm sorry about your breakup."

She stares at me blandly. "No, you're not."

Accurate. "Harrold wasn't right for you."

"*Harrison.*"

"Once again, name's not the point. But you're right. I'm not sorry about your split. Now I can ask you out to dinner for tonight."

She crosses her legs and sits straighter. "I'm busy tonight."

"How about tomorrow?"

"Also busy."

"Does Tuesday work, or any other calendar day that ends with a 'Y'?"

She crosses her arms too, all of her crossed and barred to me. "I'm washing my hair those days."

I squint at her, unsure why she took my advice to ditch her loser boyfriend but isn't taking my advice to go out with me. Then I remember Delilah's clues. *Maggie's afraid of you. She doesn't do commitment.* "Remind me again why I scare you?"

"I already told you."

"Right, yeah. I'm too exciting and too much fun. I sound *horrible*," I say with exaggerated disgust.

A laugh slips past her stony expression. Her worried eyes dart over my shoulder. I turn to see what she's looking at. Delilah, of course, who's mouthing something to her. I'm not an expert lip-reader, but I think she's saying, *Tell him.* Or maybe she's saying, *Sell shrimp.* I don't know.

When I look back at Maggie, she's fiddling with the handle of her empty coffee mug. "I know you think I'm acting weird. I mean, I *am* acting weird. And trust me when I say I don't like being this way—dating guys I think I like, but not feeling what I want to feel. What I *should* feel. Then you come along and you're so"—her agitated fiddling increases—"*you.* You're all I think about, but jumping into anything with you means opening up and being honest." She dips her head, her voice quieting. "There's just a lot to wade through, stuff I never talk about. Most of it sets off my tendencies to dislike myself, which can get really ugly."

Delilah was right. There's more under the surface pulling Maggie's strings. Upsetting truths that seem to be stressing her, but she just said I'm all she thinks about. Coincidentally, she occupies a large portion of my mind. Guess that leaves me one option.

"If that's the case, let's uncomplicate things. Forget the date. Let's be friends, nothing more. But real friends this time, spending time together, hanging out, even if it's in public. Let's get to know each other properly, no expectations of anything more."

The last part's a lie. I have ginormous expectations, but I don't like seeing Maggie upset. I'd rather be friends than nothing at all.

She taps her fingers on her mug. "No expectations?"

"You can expect to have fun with me, but it won't be sexy fun."

"It better not be." Her glare would be intimidating, if it weren't for the tiny lift of her lips.

"There will be no skinny-dipping or salacious dares," I promise.

A blush descends to her neck, her pale skin always a direct conduit to her emotions. I give myself mental props. I have no intention of putting the moves on Maggie unless she says she's ready. Never again will I cross a stated barrier with her. I am, however, not opposed to reminding her of my last dare, hoping she pictures the two of us flushed and panting, my release streaking her stomach.

"We can be friends," she says, her tone laced with huskiness, "but no flirting."

"Got it. And now that we're best friends, I have a favor to ask."

She purses her lips. "It better not have anything to do with my family's pond."

"Jesus, Maggie. I just agreed to no flirting, and there you go bringing up *the pond*."

She rolls her eyes.

I settle into my seat and this new banter. My newfound freedom to joke and tease Maggie, without worries over her relationship status. "Des and I purchased the abandoned conservation camp at Huntington Pass. It's home base for our business, and the cabin's a wee bit of a disaster. At least, it was. I've cleared out the dead animals." And the live ones. "Bleached the shit out of the place. I'm starting to paint it this afternoon and could use some help."

"Why, pray tell, would I spend my Sunday afternoon doing manual labor?"

"Because that's what friends do. They help each other. I mean, we're already off to a roaring start, bettering each other's lives. Thanks to you, I texted my father and actually slept through the night for the first time in a while. Got up early and did a ton of stuff around my place."

"Wow." Her rigid posture relaxes, her crossed arms slipping

free of their stubborn hold. "That's so great. Are you meeting him soon?"

"Apparently, he's busy for a few weeks and will be in touch." I shake my head, still confused by his reply.

I'm so happy to hear from you, he wrote. *I'll meet anywhere you want. Just can't do it for a few weeks. I'll be in touch.*

I expected him to be down my throat, hurrying up our father-son reunion. He was the one who pleaded to see *me*. Not that the timing matters. I've set the meeting in motion. Soon, I'll be able to torch any lingering affection for him. See the man he truly is now—the betrayer and wrecker of lives. Quit building up our history in my head like some little kid whose worth is tied to his father's affections.

"I'm glad you at least replied," Maggie says. "And slept through night."

"And I'm glad you took my advice and broke up with Harvey."

"*Harrison.*"

I smile wider. "Like I said, you and I are good for each other. And now you owe me."

"What we are, Lennon, is even. And friendships aren't tit for tat."

"Maggie." I lean toward her and drop my voice. "Are you offering me *tit*?"

Her nostrils flare. "What did I say about the flirting?"

"Whatever you said, it got canceled when you brought up the pond."

The indignant noise she makes pleases me more than it should. "Fine, I'll help you. Just to shut you up."

"Perfect." We'll be in a small cabin together, no malfunctioning elevators or annoying boyfriends to interrupt us. The perfect place to build the foundation of our renewed friendship—and hopefully our eventual courtship. *Ginormous*

Expectation Land. "I'm running a Littlewing hike today with Des. The loop starts and ends at the cabin, so we'll meet after."

We trade numbers and enter them into our phones. It takes me a second to decide what name to list her under. *Maggie* is too obvious and mundane. When the perfect description hits, I chuckle while typing.

She narrows those gorgeous green eyes at me. "What's so funny?"

I flip my phone toward her, letting her read the name I wrote: *Nemesis.*

A laugh bursts from her. She flips her phone toward me, but she's laughing so hard the screen's shaking. Once she gets herself under control, I grin at my description: *Bane of My Existence.*

CHAPTER
Twelve

THERE ARE two reasons I'm teaming up with Des to lead today's Littlewing Adventures hike.

First and foremost, we have a handful of kids who wanted to try out the fall program with their eyes on winter camps. As a growing business in this area, we decided to designate one day of the fall camp to single-day testers, adding them to our already full Sunday roster. The influx of kids meant we needed a second adult to lead the troops. I could've asked our one employee, Aanya, to work a Sunday, but that would've meant missing out on the other reason why I'm on this lovely hike: one of the regular kids in Desmond's group—his self-proclaimed hiking assistant, Olivia—torments the living hell out of him. She's a thirteen-year-old Black girl who wears shockingly bright clothes and is frighteningly smart.

The two of them are kicking up the rear, Desmond grimacing as he keeps pace with her. I'm too far to hear what she says, but he stops a moment, squeezes his eyes shut, then curls his lip. She beams her know-it-all smile. He wipes his forehead and wags a finger at her.

Anyone who can unravel Des into a disgruntled finger-wagger is gold in my books.

The rest of our kids are at the trail's end, drinking water and chatting about the hognose snake we saw, while others compare the leaves each of them gathered from the ground. They've been leaf hunting the whole hike, identifying species and growing their collections. The one with the widest variety of leaves wins a woven bracelet Desmond actually made. For some bizarre reason, the kids love those things.

I meander over to him and his mini-tormentor, just as Olivia says, "I suggest using stronger deodorant next time. You nearly asphyxiated me out there."

Seriously. How great is this kid?

Desmond's teeth clack together. "I suggest talking less. According to science, silence allows new brain cells to develop. Since humans lose brain cells as they age, you're gunning for zero."

"I disagree," I pipe in. "Talking is the key to development. It allows you to question your world in a meaningful way."

Des huffs. "You'll be questioning your world in a meaningful way when these kids are gone," he grumbles quietly to me.

I smile wider and give Olivia a thumbs-up. *Keep up the good work annoying my brother.*

Instead of smiling back at me, she gives my face an unnerving perusal. "Did you know beards carry more bacteria than dog fur and a used toilet seat?"

My grin slips. Des snickers.

Maybe she's not so great.

"Also." She shares a worryingly amused glance with Des. "American Apparel called. They want their hipster clothes back."

My fume starts from my toes, curling a path up my spine as I growl at Des. "What the fudge?" I say, forcing the non-swear.

He punches my shoulder, way too pleased with himself. "Don't look at me. Look in the mirror."

The two of them walk off and high-five each other.

Note to self: next time this group needs a second adult, put Aanya on the job.

The group gathers at the picnic tables outside our work-in-progress cabin. Everyone is abuzz, talking about leaves and nature as they wait eagerly to hear who won the bracelet. I'm always amazed at how keen the kids in this area are. Windfall and neighboring Ruby Grove seem to draw like-minded people, many of them active, their love of outdoor activities bleeding down to their kids. I struggled building my business during WITSEC, barely tapping into Houston's outdoor-activity market. Here, thanks in large part to Des, everything's been easier.

The parents show up in their car caravan, and I do my thing with them, chatting and buttering them up, waving off the kids as they carpool home. Except Olivia, who gets a hard stare from me. Des and I do a quick cleanup afterward, then step back like we usually do when we're here alone.

"Cal and Jake agreed to work on the ropes course with Ricky," Des says, surveying the forested section of our property.

"I heard. We'll need to hire more group leaders when it's done."

He nods. "Means we're growing. It's a good thing."

An investment paying off. A web of trails fans out from the property we purchased. The small section of forest we actually own will soon be our high ropes course. The fire pit and surrounding logs will be used for Desmond's planned evening adventure walks. He's got creepy ghost stories on the agenda, along with s'mores galore. I plan to hide and jump out of nowhere to scare the bejesus out of him.

All in all, as I take in what we're doing here, I feel a rush of pride. And a bit of anger.

See this? I want to tell my father when I face him. *See what I've done with my life, no thanks to you?*

"You reply to Dad yet?"

I startle, wondering if Des can read my mind, but this is the first alone time we've had since our family meeting. He was bound to ask about our sperm donor eventually.

I shove my hands in my pockets and kick my hiking boot over the grass. "I agreed to meet him. Time and day to be determined."

I brace, waiting for Des to launch a series of snarled reasons why meeting Dad is a horrible idea.

His silence is surprising, as is his pensive expression. "You do what you need to do. I know I went off at my place, but your relationship with him was different from the rest of us. But if he says one thing about me, one fucking word of apology if he knows about Max and what I missed with my son, I will fucking murder him. And he doesn't get to meet his grandson. Ever. If that's why he's reaching out, the answer is *fuck no.*"

I hadn't thought about Max being the reason Dad wanted to meet, but it makes sense. If he got my number, he might have been keeping tabs on us without our knowing. Maybe he thinks I'm his in. His gateway back to his family. Maybe he's getting older, nursing regrets, and he learned about Max and wants to make amends.

Not on my watch. "He'll get nothing from me where you or anyone else is concerned. I'm going for myself, and that's it. He doesn't deserve Max."

Des drops his head and rubs the corner of his eye, because he's actually tearing up. My rock-hard brother, who grunted and growled his way through WITSEC, is still a mess over what he lost. I mean, he's head over heels in love with Sadie and living his best life with his son, but those lost years still clobber him.

The next time I have a happy memory of Raymond S. Bower, I need to lobotomize myself.

"I've revised our numbers," Des says, back to staring at our property. "The ropes course will cost more than we first thought. Sadie has savings she'd like to use to help on my end. If you need a loan, she's open to chatting with you about it."

This morning's financial numbers do a dizzying tango through my head.

Des crosses his arms, assessing me. "You okay financially?"

I tuck my hands into my pockets and shift on my feet. "Yes and no."

"Please explain."

"Wow." I gawk dramatically at him. "Did you just say *please*?"

"Tell me what the fuck is up," he growls.

There's the brother I know and love. "With your WITSEC cash, did you use the principal for our business or just the interest Mom earned when it was invested?"

"Both, since I didn't have much to start." He squints at me. "Why?"

"Never touched mine—the principal portion. I've gotten lucky on some of my investments, mostly with Cal's help. Earned enough to get by without touching the original amount."

He stares at me for a few slow blinks. "Because it makes you feel complicit? Like you'd be using dirty money?"

"The only reason we have it is because Dad laundered money for a drug cartel. So yeah, I've steered clear of using it. Only spent the stuff I've earned off investments, which I guess is still drug money, but it doesn't feel as shitty."

"I get it." He drags his hand up the back of his hair. "But the money came from the government, not him. We didn't get it because he laundered money. We got it because our hellish experience helped put a dangerous criminal behind bars."

That's one way to look at it. The rational way, maybe. I swallow, trying to rearrange my thoughts on the matter. It's not easy changing an eleven-year habit.

For over a decade, I've resented that money. Only used what was needed. This business, though. It's as important for Des as it is for me. Growth of any sort takes an influx of cash. If the ropes course costs a lot more than we projected, I won't be able to dig much deeper without hitting the principal. Banks don't like loaning cash to self-employed people. If my options are taking a loan from Sadie or using my WITSEC cash, I might have to use that chunk I've avoided until now.

"I'll think on it, and thank Sadie for the offer. Not sure how you landed such a sweet woman."

"You and me both," he mumbles with a smile.

Crunching gravel has us both turning around. A Jeep pulls into our parking lot, sparkling white and clean, speeding my heart. Maggie steps from the driver's side in cute pink overalls, her ripped T-shirt revealing the tease of a red bra strap. Cute *and* sexy. Her hair's tied up in a bun, loose pieces cascading around her freckled face. I have no control over the gusty sigh that leaves my chest.

"Well, well, well," Des says, perking up. "Who do we have here?"

I spin and grip the front of his shirt. "We're on shaky ground. Friend zone for the foreseeable future. Do not embarrass me."

"*Me?* Embarrass *you*?" He shoves me aside and saunters up to Maggie. "You know Lennon has a habit of picking gum off the sidewalk and eating it, right?"

My fucking family. "That was one time, and you dared me."

Maggie tips her head back, laughing. "I bet he was a dirt-eater as a kid too."

"You have no idea." Des whispers something to her, which pisses me off to no end, then spins to face her as he walks backward toward his car. "Make sure he mouthwashes before kissing you."

"There will be no kissing," Maggie says quickly, her cheeks flaming their signature cherry blush.

I wave at Des with my middle finger.

She fusses with her overalls, then lifts her head and joins me by the cabin. "Am I early, or are you ready for me?"

I've been ready for Maggie for eleven long years. "You're right on time. Let's get painting."

CHAPTER
Thirteen

A COUPLE OF HOURS LATER, two and a half walls in the cabin's main room are painted Island Getaway green, with the rest taped and ready for our brushes and rollers. Maggie pours more paint into her tray as she fills me in on some town gossip I missed.

"You're pulling my leg," I say, pointing my brush at her. "Never in a million years would prissy Melanie Campbell turn her parents' farm into a grow op."

"Ten acres or something, and her parents had no clue. Until the cops showed up and arrested them."

"No fucking way."

"Right?" She rolls her roller in the paint tray. "They actually *arrested* Mrs. Campbell."

I'm full-on gawking now. Mrs. Campbell was the PTA president, poised, polished, and put together. She wore pearls with every outfit. "Is she covered in tattoos now? Has she joined a biker gang?"

Maggie laughs. "Maybe. They moved not long after, so you never know."

"At least I'm not the only Windfallian tied to drugs. What other shockers did I miss?"

"Well." She climbs her ladder and finishes the top corner of her wall. "Crystal Tanaka's a celebrity graffiti artist. Like, world-famous. And Rylee Polat is transgender—he's now Ryan Polat. Lana Young got knocked up and married Blake Robinson. Pretty sure they're miserable. Oh, and E's buddy Ricky Spears came out as gay a couple years after you left, but you probably know that since he's building your ropes course."

I mumble a vague agreement, no longer able to form actual words. Maggie's on her tiptoes on the ladder, reaching up, causing a rip in her T-shirt to flash the side of her bra.

"He got married last year," she goes on. "Remember Aaron Rothman?"

She turns to look at me, and yeah. I'm busted, doing nothing but staring at her curves, my paint-soaked roller dripping on the drop cloth. "Sorry. Rothman what?"

She quirks an eyebrow. "Am I painting the room by myself?"

"Well, you are neater than me. I could just direct you where to paint. Coordinate and delegate."

"Or you could organize a painting party and pay your friends with pizza."

"In order for that to work, I'd actually have to have friends."

I've chitchatted with plenty of old acquaintances since returning to Windfall. Quick catch-ups and salutations traded while grocery shopping or walking through town. It's nice seeing most of the people from my past, hearing about the stories and events I missed from Maggie, but none of my old buddies has specifically reached out, asked to get together. Running into Mizhir was nothing but stilted. Everyone's busy with their lives. Which is fine. I have other relationships that need tending, the most important one standing in this room.

Maggie climbs off her ladder and saunters toward me.

As a rule, Maggie Edelstein doesn't walk. She sashays or

saunters or swishes, those curves of hers doing seductive figure eights. Knocking me senseless with each tantalizing swivel. I don't know if she knows she does it. If she tries to exude sex appeal in her every move. Accidental or on purpose, my pulse seems to be connected to her hips, tapping out a hungry beat to her swishy moves.

She stops in front of me. "You said the same thing in high school once, at the pond, that you didn't have friends."

Freckles. All I see are freckles, a swell of tiny dots decorating her pale skin. They outline her feline eyes, cover her nose and cheeks and chin. The tantalizing dip between her collarbones and cleavage. "You're distractingly beautiful."

A tiny sound escapes her. "What happened to no flirting and no expectations?"

"You're the one who brought up *the pond* again."

The sound she makes is distinctly more disgruntled. "You were friends with everyone in high school," she says, ignoring my uncontrollable urge to tell her how stunning she is. "The cliques didn't matter. You liked everyone, and everyone liked you. But when your friends went to college, you didn't stay in touch."

"Sure, I did. I called them, tried to connect. They were always too busy." Hitting up parties, meeting new people, studying while I flipped burgers at the Smash Shack and redid English and math.

Maggie sasses out her hip. "Calling to say *hey* isn't trying."

"What was I supposed to do? Send out a SWAT team to bring them back to Windfall so we could hang out?"

"Keeping friendships takes more than a few calls."

Paint drips from my roller, splatting beside my boot. She stares at me blandly.

When she doesn't budge or talk, I sigh. "Am I supposed to ask what a real friendship takes?"

"Bane of my existence," she mumbles and purses her lips.

"Like anything else in life, friendships take work, and you didn't put in the work. You didn't have an honest conversation with Mizhir or any of them. You never asked why they didn't return your calls or tell them getting brushed off hurt. You bowed out of the friendships as much as they did."

No, I didn't wax on to my buddies about my feelings of inadequacy, that I felt left behind and lonely. There was no point. Their dismissal wasn't personal. Life moved forward for them, and it was stagnant for me. Plain and simple. Telling them I was in a weird place wouldn't have changed anything.

Instead of explaining myself to Maggie, I take my paint roller and do the next best thing.

I roll it up her stomach.

"Oh my God." She freezes, staring down at the streak of Island Getaway green on her overalls like it's a zombie from her Blood and Guts Festival. "What the hell?"

"You said something about a painting party."

"And you thought ruining my clothes would make my forced labor here more fun?"

I scrunch my face into an exaggerated pensive pose. "I mean, *I'm* definitely having more fun."

Her expression turns *The Exorcist* scary. "You are so dead."

She moves quickly, eyes on my stomach, intent on exacting retribution, but the move is predictable. I jump back in the nick of time, saving my favorite hiking T-shirt—the slogan across the front says *Take a Hike*—but Maggie doesn't give up. She lunges forward, a sharp move with her arm flung out and roller reaching. She rolls paint right over my crotch.

I gesture to my lower half. "I thought you said there was no flirting."

"The last thing this is, Lennon Bower, is flirting."

I point to my groin, like I'm a game show host showing off a prize. "You painted my dick."

She makes a weird half-choked, half-snorting sound.

Taking advantage of her distracted amusement, I roll a paint streak down her leg. She fumes and hits my T-shirt, right over the slogan I love.

Woman has no sense of self-preservation.

I pretend I'm the Hulk, trying to tear off my shirt with an incensed growl. All I manage to do is to rip the neck. Maggie barks out a laugh, allowing me to swoop in and retaliate with a shot across her breasts.

Her mouth gapes open. "I seriously might have to murder you."

"But that's the *tit* part of our 'tit for tat.'"

She mouths what I believe is *Die motherfucker*.

Things devolve quickly after that. She grabs the paintbrush, dunks it in her can, and chases me around until I have paint dripping down the back of my shirt. Cracking up, I give up on tools and use my hands, finger-paint style, turning her hair Island Getaway green. My beard gets drenched. Paint zigzags across our arms and legs. We're growling and groaning and grinning like mad, getting tangled up in each other until we're a heap on the floor, lying side by side and breathing hard. Then Maggie laughs. An uncontrollable belly laugh—bright, light, and carefree, rainbows shooting from her eyes. I clutch my stomach, losing it too.

When my laughter subsides, I starfish beside her. "Best ab workout I've had in ages."

"I can't believe we just did that." She lifts up on her elbows and surveys the wreckage. Her attention pauses on the wall facing the forest. "Have you thought of doing an accent wall? Something fun where the kids can participate?"

"I have not." But I can almost see the wheels spinning in her clever head.

"You could do a map of the area on the wall," she says, talking quickly as though keeping up with her thoughts. "Use a projector and trace the image so it's accurate. Then you can let the program kids trace hiking or biking routes they've done and sign their names. Make them feel like they're part of this space."

"Maggie Edelstein, that is a fantastic idea." The type of fun activity that kids might boast about to their friends. Those friends might want to join Littlewing themselves, get in on the wall-writing action. "I totally get why they hired you to run town events. You're a natural at this."

"When I'm not scaring children with running zombies, maybe." She slumps back to the floor. "I'm dreading facing my boss tomorrow. Shannon does not take mistakes in stride."

"All you can do is apologize. Tell her how well the rest of the event went. Delilah and Naomi weren't the only ones buying from vendors. I scrolled through social media last night. People had a great time, all because of your planning."

"That's sweet of you to say, but I'm not sure she'll agree." She knocks her toe into mine. "At least your career is soaring— buying this property, growing the business the way you are. How'd you end up starting it?"

"I can thank Coldplay and Callahan."

"Because Callahan is secretly pals with Chris Martin, and they took you on a crazy hike in the Himalayas?"

"As cool as that sounds, it was because I played 'Fix You' on repeat while I wallowed in my room for days, refusing to talk."

Her attention lingers on my profile. "At the start of witness protection?"

I nod. "It was after six or so months. Callahan invaded my miserable fortress, shoved a newspaper in my hand, and told me to get a job. He'd circled an ad for camp counselors needed."

"And the rest is history," she says, fanning her hand at the room.

It sure is something. Eleven years later, I'm expanding my own business with Desmond, planning outdoor activities, fostering confidence and leadership skills in kids and adults, all because Cal circled that ad in the paper and shoved it in my face.

"Still don't know why he thought I'd be good at teaching and leading programs, considering I sucked at school. Probably just wanted to save his eardrums from Coldplay hell."

"I bet he hated seeing you so sad. *I* hate that you were so sad," she says tenderly.

We turn our heads at the same time, smiling fond smiles at each other. The gift of easy companionship—sharing stories, even when some of them are tough.

The moment lingers, the tender mood tipping into something more intense. We're on our backs, staring at each other, our smiles transforming into parted lips and heavier breaths, and I'm at a loss. I don't know where to look when it comes to Maggie. Everything about her is too much—her striking cheekbones and petite nose, those sensual lips, her mass of freckles, here there and everywhere. Those mesmerizing emerald eyes that seem to absorb and memorize my face too.

Her tongue traces the luscious curve of her top lip. I bite my cheek, the zip of pain an attempt to contain myself. *Do not grab her. Do not devour her sassy mouth.*

Awareness drags south, down to my abdomen—a hot tug that has me flexing. "I lied before."

Her pupils blow wider. "About what?"

"I do have friends. I have Delilah and my brothers, who are annoying but awesome. And…" I pause, hoping she reads the sincerity in the weighted beat. "I have you."

Her expression shifts, hints of desire tumbling into what looks like longing. Or maybe that wistful look is quiet affection, her tender gaze and paint-splattered face proving how much fun we have together. "I didn't realize how much I missed you," she whispers.

"Told you I bring the fun."

"You certainly do." Hesitantly, she touches my beard, dragging her fingers over my jaw.

Electricity sizzles through me, so intensely I want to close my eyes and soak in the sensation, but I don't. I can't miss a moment of Maggie.

Something fervent flashes across her face. Just as quickly, she grins. "You're gonna have paint in your beard for weeks."

"All thanks to you. Might have to shave it."

"No," she says, then clams up.

"No?"

She shrugs a shoulder. "I like the beard."

It's a bashful admission, the sentiment hitting me in the chest. She presses her fingers harder into my beard. I turn my head, enough that my lips hit the tips of her fingers. I give them a soft kiss—the tender gesture of a friend, who would like to be more one day.

She doesn't reprimand me for breaking her no-flirting rule. She curls her fingers into a fist. Not angry or defensive. Just folds her fingers delicately like she's holding my kiss in her hand.

CHAPTER
Fourteen

THE NEXT MORNING, I'm once again hiding from Maggie Edelstein. This time, instead of asphyxiating in a supply closet, I'm wedged behind a large tree, waiting for her to leave her house. As per our conversation yesterday, my nemesis is nervous about seeing her boss today. She probably didn't sleep well last night. I can't help her with her work issues, but I can give her morning a boost.

I'm on one of Windfall's quaint streets, colorful Victorian homes stretching in both directions. Rows of hickories cast shade over the asphalt and grass...and the tombstones dotting the lawns. Windfall clearly still loves Halloween. The town has done an exceptional job creeping itself out for tonight's trick-or-treating. Maggie rents the basement in that cute yellow house covered in spider webs and skeletons. Based on when I've seen her at Sugar and Sips, I've concluded she leaves her home on weekdays around 8:30 a.m.

As expected, she appears on time.

She swishes from the back of her house, her high heels clicking on the paved driveway. Her hair is pinned back in a neat ponytail, her slim skirt emphasizing every sway of her hypnotizing hips. I bite back a groan and hide more firmly behind my tree.

Her white Jeep is parked across the street from her home. She doesn't seem to notice the white paper I stuck under her windshield wipers. Her lips and brow are pinched, her strut gaining speed. Her focused expression hints at a loud internal monologue.

Everything about her reads, I'm Stressed about What Today Will Bring.

That's where my note comes in.

Unfortunately, she swishes to the driver's side of her Jeep, without so much as a glance at her windshield. *Dammit.* She opens her door with zero reaction. Turns the ignition. She starts pulling onto the street, but she quickly brakes.

I perk up.

She shoves out of her car, looking incredibly annoyed. She tears off the paper and frowns. I wait impatiently, recalling the note I wrote as she reads it.

YOU'RE STRONG. YOU'RE SMART. YOU'RE INCREDIBLY CREATIVE. FROM THE FIRST DAY I MET YOU AT [REDACTED], I WAS AMAZED BY YOU. TODAY IS JUST A BLIP ON YOUR RISE TO SUCCESS.

PS: YOU'LL NOTICE I DIDN'T BREAK OUR NO-FLIRTING RULES AS FLIPPANTLY AS YOU BY MENTIONING [REDACTED]. YOU'LL ALSO NOTICE I DIDN'T SAY I THINK YOU'RE [REDACTED] AND [REDACTED] AND PARTICULARLY [REDACTED]. I'LL ONLY SHARE THOSE SPECIFICS IF OUR RULES CHANGE.

Maggie's head whips up, and she scans the street. I stay hidden, my body abuzz, waiting on her reaction. A second later...she bites her lip.

Warmth fizzes through me, and I almost step out to show myself, bask in her reaction. But I don't. Writing that note wasn't about me. There may have been some low-level flirting, but her lifted mood is all I need.

She reads the note again, presses her hand over her heart. More lip-biting ensues as she unleashes a gorgeous grin and carefully folds the note, like it's a precious thing.

I blow out a gusty breath as she drives away.

I spend the rest of my morning at Sugar and Sips with Desmond and Ricky, going over the specifics for our high ropes course. We'll be building three levels of difficulty: easy (green), intermediate (blue), and advanced (red). Participants will test their balance and agility by negotiating high-strung beams, tires, swings, and climbing nets, all hanging thirty feet above the ground. Desmond suggests we also build a low ropes course for kids. Something easier and fun to get little ones involved.

Once again, I'm impressed by his creative thinking. "That's actually a great idea."

He glowers at me. "Don't sound so surprised."

"Don't be such a grunting scowler, and I won't be so surprised."

Ricky snickers, pushing back his chair and standing. "I know enough to start plans and get you more exact costing. I'll connect with Cal and Jake, then we'll reconvene when I have drawings and an estimate."

I cross my fingers it won't be as high as Des projected. Ricky leaves and joins a guy in line, who's dressed for Halloween as an old-school sailor. When they kiss, I deduce that the sailor is Ricky's husband, Aaron. "They're cute together."

"They're a lot of fun. We sometimes see them for dinner." He kicks my foot under the table. "You thought more about your finances? What you'll do if you don't have enough cash?"

"I'll use the WITSEC money," I say, even though it pains me. But desperate times and all that. "Everything you said the other day made sense. It wasn't drug money, and it's mine to use. I won't like doing it, but it is what it is."

He nods. "Glad you—"

Both our phones buzz, cutting him off. We share a frown, then grab our respective phones, where we're greeted by a Bower boys group chat helmed by Jake.

Jake: I went by Mom's and could tell she'd been crying. She won't tell me why, but she was reading the fucking asshole's stupid fucking book.

Callahan: Maybe she was just having a bad day.

Jake: Are you fucking serious right now?

E: Someone tell Cal that nice guys finish last.

Callahan: There's no point assuming the worst.

Desmond: When Dad's involved, there's only the worst.

Desmond's eyes flick up to mine. He doesn't say anything about my plan to meet our father. He doesn't need to. The hardness in his steely gaze translates clearly—*You still sure meeting that asshole is a good idea?*

Nope. Not even a little. I focus on my phone and tap out a text.

Me: Did she say if she's almost done the book?

Jake: She said she's taking a break from reading. We'll convene in a few weeks or whenever she's done.

Des: If this sends Mom into a spiral, I will fucking kill him.

Jake: Not if I get to him first.

E: You'll have to fight me for the knife.

Des: I was thinking flamethrower.

Jake: Explosives. We strap them to his chest.

Callahan: I'll bail you idiots out of jail.

Normally, I'd be right in there, suggesting gruesome torture with terrifying spiders or fire ants, or force-feeding our lactose-intolerant father nothing but dairy. Instead, I keep quiet.

Only Des knows I plan to meet Dad. My other brothers have shockingly kept quiet on the subject, and this news isn't good. I need to meet with the Life Wrecker before Mom calls our next Bower family meeting. Deal with him and get past this weird angst knotting me up, so the next time my brothers gang up to plan his homicide, I'm front and center egging them on.

"Gotta head out," I tell Des, not wanting to discuss the book or Mom's reaction.

He gives me another hard stare.

Ignoring his silent judgment, I hurry outside and squint at the thick clouds. Rain is coming, and the downpour will be fierce. I hightail it to my truck and seal myself inside. I pull up the Life Wrecker's last message and type with hard taps of my thumbs.

> Me: If you want to meet, it needs to be in the next few weeks.

Bouncing my heel, I send the text. I hate how unraveled he makes me feel. The most mundane communication, not even in person, and I'm starting to sweat.

I immediately pull up *Nemesis* from my contact list and write her.

> Me: I hope work's going okay.

No reply comes in, which isn't a surprise. My job allows me a tremendous amount of freedom. Maggie works a steady nine-to-five, including some weekends for events. Still, texting her steadies my frantic pulse. My bouncing heel slows. I reach to press my truck's ignition, but my phone pings.

Grinning, I grab my cell...and there goes my smile.

> Life Wrecker: I'm busy for the next few weeks. I can meet you November 22. Please don't say no.

I should say no. I should pull up my family's group chat and tell them I'm meeting Dad so I can strap him with dynamite. Instead, I reply to him with one word.

Me: Fine.

Eyes closed, I lean into my seat. The first drops of rain hit my roof, a steady *pat, pat, pat* that mimics my short breaths. My fucking life, I tell you. When my phone pings again, I groan. The sight of *Nemesis* lighting up my screen has me sitting straighter.

Nemesis: Work is predictably painful. Boss is unimpressed. But

Me: But?

Nemesis: I had a wonderful drive this morning.

Warmth unfurls behind my navel.

Me: Is that so?

Nemesis: Couldn't quit smiling for some reason.

I rub my chest, unsure how I can shift so quickly from uncomfortably agitated to puffed with pleasure. I start typing that I miss her already and want to take her out on a proper date, but it's too soon. We've only been best friends for a day. Maggie was visibly upset when vaguely discussing her commitment issues, and all this stuff with my father is messing with my head. I delete and rethink. Settle on a different kind of honesty.

> Me: Desmond agreed to your accent wall in the cabin. Can you help me with it this weekend?

> Nemesis: Why would I subject myself to another paint fight?

Instead of reminding her that she's the one who painted my dick, I switch topics. Sort of.

> Me: My father and I booked our reunion date. November 22.

> Nemesis: Wow. How are you feeling about it?

> Me: I'd really love for you to paint the wall with me this weekend.

Asking for her support is easier this way. Driving the scenic route around the stress that is my life. I resume bouncing my heel, waiting on her reply.

> Nemesis: Count me in. And maybe we can get out on a hike too. I'd love to see the area from your perspective.

Or she knows getting me out in the wilderness is my ideal distraction. As is slowly wooing Maggie, and I know just how to continue.

———

The next morning, I leave Maggie another note. I don't hide and watch for her reaction this time. I leave the folded paper under her windshield and drive away, smiling to myself. This message reads:

Roses are red
Violets are blue
I failed English
So this is all I've got

Wednesday's note is a simple:

I dare you to have a fabulous day.

Thursday's note is one word:

[REDACTED]

Friday's note is more for me than for her:

THIS TICKET ENTITLES YOU TO ONE FREE FRIEND HUG.
LENGTH OF HUG: UNTIL IT GETS WEIRD.
VALUE: PRICELESS.

ONE FRIEND HUG
(NO FUNNY BUSINESS)

Saturday's note is particularly fun. Honoring Maggie's love of horror movies, I bought a magazine and spent Thursday night cutting out letters, serial-killer style. The creepy note reads, I KNOW WHERE YOU LIVE.

I hurry to her Jeep, ducking and diving around the parked cars, like a neurotic, not-very-good burglar. I tuck the note under the wiper, laughing while picturing her reading it. The visual's so amusing I decide I need to witness her reaction.

Resuming my hiding spot behind my tree, I wait, but I didn't plan this well. I'm not sure of Maggie's schedule on Saturdays and could be here for hours. I reach for my phone to scroll through social media and maybe send Delilah the message: THE KILLER IS IN YOUR HOUSE. I've been bitten by the horror-line bug. But Maggie appears surprisingly early.

Not only does she seem sprightly this Saturday morning, she doesn't do her usual swish-sway-saunter. She *dashes* to her Jeep, nearly tripping in her rush to get there, the upward twist of her lips slaying me. She looks like a kid at Christmas. Or in her case, a kid at Chanukah. She yanks the letter out from under the wiper, takes one look at it, then doubles over, leaning on her Jeep while she cracks up.

Point in the Wooing column for me.

CHAPTER
Fifteen

"I TOLD you I wanted to go hiking," Maggie says, clinging to the rock wall at our left, "not plummet to my death, where wild animals will tear me apart before rescuers can extricate my mangled body."

"At least you're not dramatic." I keep one hand protectively on her hip, in case she slips on the ledge.

"This isn't dramatic." Her body is rigid, but she glances at me over her shoulder. "If we get off here alive, I will scream at you so loud your head will explode. *That's* dramatic."

I chuckle. "Noted. But I promise, where we're going is worth it."

She mumbles something unintelligible. I smile at her back.

As per Maggie's request to see this area from my perspective, I planned this outing for us. The scenery around Windfall and Ruby Grove is always breathtaking—the majesty of the Rough Ridge Mountains, expansive forests, and cascading creeks—but I wanted to take Maggie somewhere special. And maybe romantic. Granted, we're only out here as friends, but there are no rules that friends can't visit a stunning waterfall together. If the scenery happens to be laden with romance, that's just nature doing nature's thing.

Following Maggie, I move slowly along the narrow cliff path. She quits threatening me, but her legs shake slightly as she walks. Normally I'm loose and carefree on a hike, but my body is tense, my focus zeroed in on her steps. I watch her for any falter, ready to grab her if she stumbles. The fact that she's out here, scaring herself on this challenging trail, adds more pressure to my straining chest. The only reason she's here is to help me get my mind off my father.

She wavers on a step.

In seconds, my arm is latched around her waist, her body safely tucked against my chest. "Careful there."

I feel how hard she's breathing. She clutches my forearm, giving it a surprising squeeze. "This thing could double as a steel bar."

If I keep her pressed this close, so could the situation in my hiking pants. "Nothing will happen to you while we're out here."

She shifts her head, nudges her nose against my beard. "I'm not so sure about that."

There seems to be more meaning infused in those breathy words. I don't care to decipher her intent at this juncture. "I've got you, Mags. Trust me to look after you."

She nods, and her nose brushes my cheek again. Just her goddamn nose, barely grazing my beard, and tingling spreads along my scalp. I ease her forward. Her next step is steadier. Two more, and her legs are no longer shaking. She's steadier because she knows I won't let her fall, and a chuff of pleasure fills me.

At the end of the narrow cliff trail, we breach the forest edge. She doesn't yell at me as she threatened. I breathe easier, no longer worried about her stumbling. Fall has painted the remaining leaves in a kaleidoscope of color, those on the ground crunching under our boots as we hike.

Maggie slows her stride until we're side by side. "That was scary but maybe fun." Her cheeks are rosy, kissed by the pleasantly cool air. There's pride in her lifted chin.

"*You're* scary at times," I say, mesmerized by her beauty as usual, "but maybe a bit fun."

She laughs. "Not as scary as your serial killer note."

"No clue what you're talking about. I left no such note."

"Right." She gives me a saucy wink. "And you had nothing to do with the other thirteen notes on my windshield."

"That's a specific number. Have you been counting?"

"I don't know," she says quickly. "It was just a guess." She's wearing a cute green woolen hat. Although I can't see her ears, I'd bet the tips are burning red.

Enjoying flustering Miss Maggie Edelstein, I move behind her and lean toward the side of her head. "Are those mysterious notes saved in a special shoebox?"

Her jaw firms. "You're gunning for a silent treatment."

"Did you put them in an album with pressed dried flowers and doodled hearts?"

She swivels and jabs a finger at my chest. "Quit it with the flirting, Lennon."

"I'm not the one who falls asleep after pressing lipstick kisses to random notes."

She makes a *grrrrr* sound and stomps ahead of me. I laugh under my breath, hoping no bears are around to hear her growl at me. They might think she's part of their pack.

"I love writing those notes," I tell her as we resume hiking. There's no point lying to Maggie. I actually love being honest with her. About my life. My desires. Using my real name instead of my alias. All I want from here on out is honesty in my life. "I think about you all day, wondering if they made you smile."

She darts a quick glance at me, questioning, like she's not sure if I'm still teasing her. Her expression softens. "They always make me smile. Because we're friends," she adds.

"Definitely because we're friends," I say, more contented than teasing now. Being friends with Maggie feels good.

She glances up at the trees, her attention moving from their imposing height, down to the large crevasse cutting through the rock at our right. Her footfalls slow. "Not sure why I never go hiking. It's gorgeous out here."

"This is my favorite thing in the world."

"Which part?"

"All of it." I suck in a big breath, inhaling the loamy scents permeating the fresh air. "How old and real these lands are. Remembering that I'm a guest in this world. That if I'm kind to Mother Nature, she will provide."

"Yeah." Maggie takes in the stretch of trees above us again. "I'm really glad we did this."

"Me too. And if you never explore Windfall's natural playground, what do you do in your free time? What is Maggie Edelstein's favorite hobby?"

"Reading."

"Stephen King and all things horror?"

She shakes her head. "As much as I love cheesy horror flicks, I don't do gore in my books. Suspense is good, though. Dark romances and romantic comedies. Oh, and I love sweeping historical novels and young adult fantasies."

"Variety is the spice of life."

"Variety is great, but..." She walks more slowly, as though she's thinking too hard to focus on her steps. "Reading is also an escape for me. The characters are my avatars. I get to explore the world, be wild, make daring escapes, battle beasts, solve crimes, fall madly in love. I get to live extravagant lives in far-flung places whenever I want. Reading a good book is like being reincarnated in whatever body I choose."

"When you describe it like that, makes me want to set up camp in a library."

"Or bring a pile of books out here." She drags her hand along

the gnarled trunk of an old tree. "The best of both worlds—
reading while surrounded by nature."

"I'm sold," I say, picturing just that. Maggie and me, cuddled
in a tent, reading through a storm. Emerging later to sweet, post-
rain smells and the humbling sweep of a mountain range.

We hike another half hour, chatting periodically, letting
nature speak at other times. Companionable quiet. I'm so used to
doing hikes alone or with a gaggle of kids. Being out here with
Maggie is different. I love learning more about her and sharing a
vital piece of myself with someone. In all my years hiking in
Houston, I never once took a woman into the wilderness with
me. Maybe because this is my place to be real and honest. Feel
the weight of my thoughts. Lying about my name and my life
while accepting nature's gifts made me tense.

We hear the waterfall before we see it. Maggie stops
suddenly and cocks her head. "Is that what I think it is?"

I shrug a shoulder. "Quit walking so slowly and you'll find
out."

She squints at me, like she's annoyed. Her dancing eyes tell
another story. I follow close behind her, my heart picking up
speed. Not from exertion. I can't wait to see Maggie's expression
when we break through the trees.

She hikes faster, boots crunching over more fallen leaves. She
hops over a branch, practically running to the forest edge.

One step onto the rocks she gasps. "It's stunning."

"It is," I say, coming to her side. My eyes are locked on her
mesmerized profile, the wonder in her slightly opened mouth.

She glances at me, catches my meaning, and blushes.
"Stop it."

"Stop what?"

"You know."

"Just enjoying the view."

The irritated noise she makes suggests she knows what game
I'm playing, but I didn't create the romance of Elder Falls. I

haven't magically made the water spill over 120 feet of rock into a sparkling pond. I didn't blanket the surrounding stone in a tapestry of fall leaves or turn the sky a gorgeous shade of picture-perfect blue.

Maggie tucks her arm through mine, pulling me closer. "Thanks for bringing me out here."

"Thanks for suggesting it."

The water crashes in front of us, powerful and invigorating. A hawk rides a current high in the sky. We breathe in tandem, like we're human versions of the bird, thriving on each other's air.

"If you ever need to talk," she says softly, "about your father or anything. I'm here for you."

I nod and latch my hand over hers. I don't want to talk about my father right now. The moment's too perfect to let him in. Being out here with Maggie feels too good. I don't want to do much besides revel in nature's beauty and Maggie's companionship. The way her proximity makes my ribs cinch and pull, like they're belaying ropes tightening as my heart trips into a free fall.

CHAPTER
Sixteen

ASIDE FROM MY looming Life Wrecker meeting, the past two weeks have been the best two weeks I can remember. My continued notes to Maggie have been a blast to write. We've been on a couple more hikes. She and I have finished painting the cabin's interior, including the map accent wall. If we run into each other in town, she actually grins when she sees me. Lights up like a Chanukah menorah, making time to linger and chat, even sharing a tea with me if we're at Sugar and Sips.

Tonight, she called me out of the blue and said, "You're coming to karaoke night."

At which point, I froze in terror.

At the tender age of twelve, my mouth full of braces, I was invited to Melanie Campbell's birthday party, where they had a karaoke contest. I had zero intention of getting on their makeshift stage and drawing attention to the fact that my puberty-stricken voice cracked more than a shattered mirror. Alas, peer pressure. Everyone egged me on until I was in front of the crowd, heart thumping wildly, belting out Kelly Clarkson's "Since U Been Gone." (I did *not* choose the song.) My screeching voice scared every man, woman, child, and animal in the vicinity. I was then called Screech for the rest of the school year.

Good times.

But here I am, walking into the Barrel House, where I'll have to relive the horror of my puberty-afflicted days, because when Maggie wants to see me, I'm powerless to refuse.

Unfortunately, she's not here yet, but my brother is.

"There's the man of the hour!" E shouts when he spots me. "Screech in all his karaoke glory."

If Maggie only knew what I endured to see her.

"Edgar Eugene Bower," I reply and receive a dirty look for my efforts. His full name is always a direct hit. "I hope you've taken singing lessons since your horrible performance in *Oliver!*"

"I was great in *Oliver!*"

So bad, Delilah mouths to me, then she says loudly, "You were fantastic, babe."

They were both atrocious in Windfall High's production of the famed musical. I doubt their karaoke is much better, but it's likely superior to mine. Not that it matters. There's no chance I'll be singing anywhere near that stage tonight.

I join the gathered group of Ricky and Aaron, Delilah and E, Avett Lewis and his wife—my wingwoman Naomi—all of them intent on me with nods and handshakes, while a big biker dude sings "Sweet Caroline."

Avett raises his beer in salute. "I remember the Screech thing. Something about your voice."

My brother will pay for this betrayal. "There is no Screech thing. Nothing happened."

"He's a karaoke legend," E says, butting in like the pest he is. "His voice cracked so hard while singing Mariah Carey—"

"Whitney Houston," Delilah says. "It was Whitney."

"No, no." Ricky grins around his beer bottle. "You're both wrong. It was Kelly Clarkson."

I drag my hand through my hair. "Did any of you read the recent climate-change report?"

This topic needs to be killed faster than our ozone layer. Maggie will be here any minute.

"Kelly Clarkson." E points at me, ignoring my attempt to squash this subject. "He sang 'Since U Been Gone,' and that woman has some serious pipes. Unfortunately, Lennon's pipes were rusted and squeaky, thanks to his friend puberty."

I rub my forehead. "Does any of this really matter?"

"Does what matter?" Maggie appears at my side. Worst timing ever. "What did I miss?"

"Nothing in the slightest." I debate covering her ears or yelling *There's a bomb!* "Let's head to the bar for a drink, shall we?"

E speedily blocks our path. "We were just reminiscing about the time Lennon sang Kelly Clarkson, but he sounded like a cat being tortured, and everyone called him Screech for half a year."

Maggie's gorgeous face erupts with glee. "I need more details."

"You need nothing." I hook my arm through hers and forcibly direct her toward the bar, as our friends laugh at my expense.

If I could time travel, I'd find whoever invented karaoke and spike their meatloaf with poison. That wouldn't be my first time-travel stop, though. I'd be remiss not to spike Dad's meatloaf first. Except I don't want my father dead. I just want him... different. And I really don't want to think about him or our impending reunion in two days.

We haven't gotten any more news on his book or Mom's mental state. Our family tête-à-tête hasn't been called yet. Normally, I'd have phoned to check up on Mom, but she'll ask me about meeting him. If she sounds rough or sad, my guilt over this choice will worsen. So, not only am I growing more stressed and anxiety-ridden by the day, I'm being a shit son.

Heavy sigh.

Maggie and I find a spot at the bar. We wait for the bartender, while I attempt to drop-kick thoughts of my family drama. A few more patrons belly up to order drinks, pressing Maggie and me closer together. She leans her side into me, the graze of her soft body making me sigh. I place my hand on her back, angling toward her. Heat builds where we touch, glowing sunshine that burns off more of my morose thoughts. I'm not sure if she means to rub against me slightly, but her hips move until her pelvis is notched against my thigh.

Forget glowing sunshine. This is a solar flare, building so bright I groan.

She glances up at me, pressing even closer. "If you hate karaoke, why'd you come tonight?"

It's a simple question, but it isn't. This is the elevator all over again, facing my fears for one reason and one reason only—to be near Maggie. And she's so damn close, practically flush against me.

I splay my hand wider on her back. "Because you're here."

She makes a tiny noise and shifts her hips. I tug her firmer against me.

"What can I getcha?" the bartender asks, being the opposite of my wingman. When you want their attention, you're invisible. When you don't want them, they're in your face.

"He'll have a craft hipster beer," Maggie says, and I can't even be annoyed. Her mischievous smile is too cute. "I'll have a gin and tonic."

She disentangles our legs but stays close. "Do you want to leave after our drinks?"

"Not really." My other option is sitting at home stressing about dear old Dad.

"We'll have fun." She squeezes my upper arm, the small move relaxing me.

We return to our group of friends. They've thankfully

dropped the Screech jokes and have moved on to teasing Avett. During high school, he accidentally locked himself inside the science lab and had to pee so badly he used a beaker. That famed moment occurred at the exact instant Mrs. Luong let in her next class.

A vein in Avett's forehead throbs. "Can we talk again about how Lennon's singing can shatter eardrums?"

"Nope," I say. "Whipping out your junk in front of your teacher is way more interesting than the basics of my puberty."

"You don't even know," Ricky says, laughing as he talks. "I was walking by when Mrs. Luong opened the door. Her scream could be heard on Mars."

"He chose a flask," E says, the master of ceremonies for everyone's teenage embarrassment, "because it was the only item thin enough to fit his tiny penis."

Ricky doubles over, leaning into Aaron as he loses it. Delilah cracks up so hard tears leak from her eyes. Maggie snorts and kind of falls into me, the two of us laughing at Avett's expense. Better than laughing at mine.

Avett points at E, scowling. "You're an asshole. And she—" he wraps his arm around his wife "—knows you're full of shit. So, fuck you all."

Naomi cuddles closer and rubs her hand down his abs. "My man is packing. The rest of you are just jealous."

Actually, I am jealous. Not of what Avett's packing. I have no issues in the size department. We're all hanging out as a group, but there are subgroups. Couple groups. Three in-love pairs, plus Maggie and me, and I want what they have. To know she's coming home with me tonight, where we can laugh again about Avett's humiliation and gawk over how the chick singing could pass for Lady Gaga. Joke about how relentless E can be. Rehash our evening the way couples do, making everything brighter. Full-color nights. Then I'd peel off that sexy sweater of hers— coral pink slipping over her head—dig my thumbs into the sides of her painted-on jeans, drag them down, lick a path up her shapely thighs, drown in those soft red curls I've been salivating over for years.

Sadly, we're not there yet, but I hoard moments like this when she leans into me instead of away. The brightness in her smile that makes it feel as if someone's lit fireworks in my chest.

Ricky's name is called to sing next. We all cheer except Aaron, who gets up on his chair and wolf whistles. "These people don't even know they're gonna be serenaded by rock royalty," he says when he's on the floor. "My man, the rock star."

Ricky may have been the front man for his rock band, the Tweeds, but he chooses a slow song for tonight's performance. He locks eyes with Aaron as he belts out Tina Turner's "Simply the Best." It's the romantic version immortalized on *Schitt's Creek* and has the small crowd swooning their faces off, including Maggie, who's clutching her chest. For some reason, my heart mimics the move, seeming to contract in on itself, unwilling to let a drop of this overwhelming feeling escape.

She glances at me, catching me staring. Instead of lowering her gaze or looking away, her attention lingers. Those emerald eyes glint with fondness, and I need to lean against the booth beside me before I hit the floor.

Cheers erupt when Ricky's done. All I can do is watch Maggie holler and grin and clap, so damn into her and thankful she invited me out tonight.

Until the karaoke MC calls, "Lennon Bower! You're up next."

Panic grips me by the balls and squeezes. "I didn't sign up."

"I know, but..." Maggie's in my space, looking apologetic and suspiciously excited. "I maybe asked E to put your name down. And I possibly chose a song for you?"

"Please tell me this is a joke."

"I thought singing would be fun for you. You love making an ass of yourself."

"When I *choose* to make an ass of myself. No part of me chose this." I may be past puberty, but singing is not my forte. E will call me worse names than Screech.

The sparse crowd is clapping and chanting my name. My feet have become cement blocks.

Maggie slips her hand in mine, linking our fingers. "You don't have to sing. I didn't realize you'd been this traumatized by karaoke. I really thought it would be fun."

I'm not sure what happens to me. If I'm having some kind of upright seizure, or maybe this whole evening's been a dream, one of those vivid alternate realities where you do and say the opposite of what you're thinking.

My mind right now: *No fucking way am I getting up there to sing.*

My voice: "Whatever. It's no biggie. Of course I'll sing."

Because Maggie organized this. Because Maggie thinks getting up there will be a good time. Because standing here, with her hand in mine, all I can think is *yes*.

She squeaks and pushes at me. "You'll do great. So good. I'll have a shot waiting for you when you're done."

The only shot I want is a taste of her, but I move toward my doom, my feet dragging over the sticky bar floor. Cheers echo. Whistles ring. Chants of my name turn this into my own personal Colosseum of hell. I'm in ancient Rome, about to battle to the death. Or in my case, until I achieve utter humiliation. I have no clue what song Maggie chose, but I'd bet my "Ironic" T-shirt it will be painful. If it's Kelly Clarkson, I'll just keep walking and hurl myself out the back emergency exit and run home.

I get up onstage, squinting through the bright lights. All saliva vacates my mouth as I read the song title and artist on the screen, then I start to cough. A hacking attack as I choke on nothing because, really? Eminem's "The Real Slim Shady"?

Maggie certainly outdid herself with this choice. But I can do this. I'm the Bower Jokester. I thrive on laughter and uncomfortable awkwardness, *when* I'm the one in control of the narrative. At age twelve, my changing voice and I were shoved into the spotlight without our consent. Maggie pulled the strings to put me here tonight. For fun, but also to embarrass me, because that's what we do. Push each other's buttons. Tease and torment, all for a laugh or a smile. But I'm in control now. There are no karaoke rules saying I have to sing the lyrics on the screen. Mizhir and I used to listen to rap in his basement all the time, making up riffs on our own, rhyming stupid shit to make each other laugh.

Maggie has no clue what she just unleashed.

I strike a confident pose, hand on my hip, chest thrust forward, mic at my mouth. "Let's do this."

The room is only a quarter full, but wolf whistles sail from our friends.

"Screech is in the house!" E shouts.

I attempt not to grind my teeth. Maggie has one hand partially in front of her face, her expression all scrunched, like she's watching a horror movie through her fingers.

Just you wait, Miss Mischief.

The music starts. I follow the first verse, but Eminem's quickfire lyrics are a freight train barreling away from me. That's when I start to improvise.

"Y'all don't know Maggie Edelstein
Jaws impersonator and cold-shoulder queen
She's a horror movie addict
Lover of screams and overlording
She's a secret super villain
Who gets a monthly Brazilian."

I don't know her waxing regimen, but it rhymes, and the sparse crowd erupts with shouts and laughter. Maggie's face burns you're-so-dead red. I wink at her as I hit the chorus.

She's Maggie Edelstein, the real Maggie Edelstein
But she loves being called Gingersnap

So won't you call her Gingersnap
Just shout out the nickname and slap her back
'Cause she's a fiery redhead with sass
You other Gingersnaps are just impostors
So won't the real Gingersnap give us a wave
Please wave at your adoring fans

A chorus of *Gingersnap!* catcalls follows. Maggie gives me the universal fuck-you finger as I continue messing up lyrics and teasing the heck out of her. By the time I'm done, the small crowd goes wild. I'm vindicated. The newly crowned karaoke king, leaving embarrassed twelve-year-old me in his dust.

I hop off the stage and strut toward one very uppity woman.

She crosses her arms. "Proud of yourself, are you?"

"Unbelievably. Where's my shot?"

The biker dude who sang "Sweet Caroline" waves in her face. "Gingersnap! Hey, Tommy! It's Gingersnap!"

She grimaces a half sneer at him, then her green eyes transform into twin lasers, burrowing holes into my forehead. "The only shot you're getting is a shot to the head."

I close the distance between us, practically pressing my cheek to hers as I whisper, "If that means your hands are on me, you won't hear me complaining."

"No flirting, *Lennon*." She shoves me away, but there's huskiness in her voice. "You're incorrigible."

"I'm a shitty singer who did my best to turn the tables in my favor. And since you're the one who orchestrated my doom, you're buying me a drink."

She huffs out a sigh and hooks our arms together. "If I must."

Two hours later, I'm tipsy. My throat is chafed from heckling our friends and cheering on their performances. We're all crammed into a booth, teasing Aaron for his horrible singing, which rivals mine. Maggie is next to me, looking sleepy, her eyelids lowered and her body soft.

"I had fun tonight," I tell her quietly.

She shifts, blinks at me, and smiles. "Figured getting out would be better than sitting at home, stewing about your dad. That's why I invited you."

She doesn't say more. Just leans her head on my shoulder, not caring what our friends think. Acting like her comment was no big deal.

But I never told her I was in a funk tonight.

Two weeks ago, she asked me to take her hiking. Not because she's an outdoorsy woman who was dying to get out. She was hoping the outing would calm my ongoing worries. Tonight, she insisted I leave my house, knowing it would get me out of my head. Aside from the start of the evening, I didn't brood over my father once. Her nudge to socialize reminded me there's more to my life than my past. Tonight's antics even pushed me to obliterate my fear of karaoke.

I'm not sure when Maggie truly became my best friend, but she's usurped the role. There's no understudy. She's the leading lady in my life. And I think I fill the same void for her—alleviate her stress with silly notes, lift her spirits when she's down, wrangle zombies for her when her work plans explode. I'm still on a mission to literally woo the pants off her, but being here for each other and having fun is even more important, breaking down each other's walls. Whatever secrets lurk in her mysterious, complicated past, the foundation we're building will surely make us indestructible.

CHAPTER
Seventeen

DAD and I are finally meeting tomorrow. Maggie's karaoke ambush shoved the meeting to the recesses of my mind last night. The effort's been more challenging today. Not only has my anxiety been resuscitated, but Des and I got Ricky's construction quote this morning. Looks like I'll officially need to dig into my WITSEC money, which annoys me even more. So here I am, waiting for Maggie outside town hall. The one person who eases the tension I can't otherwise seem to shake.

She pushes out of the building doors and scans the area intently. I don't often meet her after work, but I've surprised her on a few occasions. The fact that she's scanning the square, her expression expectant, suggests she's searching for me, hoping I'll meet her.

The awareness unwinds a knot in my chest.

"If you take any longer to spot me," I call, "I'll turn to stone like them." I hook my thumb to the mermaid fountain.

Happiness seems to flush her cheeks. "If you turned into a Lennon fountain, your brothers would stumble here at night, wasted, and pee on you."

It's true. As teens, they'd often get drunk and pee on the mermaids. "Would you toss a penny into my pool?"

She swish-sway-saunters up to me, putting an extra swing into her step. "I'd toss all my pennies at you."

Her slinkier tone adds a layer of innuendo that has me dropping my voice too. "And what would you wish for with all those pennies?"

"Wouldn't you like to know?"

"I would."

She's in my personal space, the edges of our coats brushing. We're couple close. Nearly kissing with tongue close. She tips her face up to mine, and I'm not prepared for the sadness swimming in her eyes. "Wishes are for delusional kids. They don't come true."

She tries to walk past me, but I clasp her arm. "Everything okay?"

Keeping her focus away from me, she shrugs. "Just a weird day. Wanna grocery shop with me?"

What I want is to fuck her brains out. I also want to ask her what *weird* means, but my time with Maggie is a balancing act. Pushing too hard, too fast might scare her off. With the intensity of my life, I'm not sure I can handle losing her right now.

Taking her lead, I start walking. "Duke's Market, here we come."

Neither of us speaks as we stroll. Maggie and I can talk or not talk and it never feels awkward, but she still seems distant, stuck in her head. I'd normally crack a joke to make her laugh. Tomorrow's agenda has sucked my humor dry.

Inside the market, I grab us a cart to share. "Front half is yours. Back half is mine. No intermingling."

She stops and raises an eyebrow. "What if I want the back half?"

I make a show of checking out *my* back half. "So, you're an ass woman?"

Okay, maybe not *all* my humor has evaporated.

She rolls her eyes. "Is your mind always in the gutter?"

"Around you, one hundred percent."

Instead of telling me to grow up—her usual reaction to my antics—she laughs and actually checks out my ass. My butt cheeks clench in response. Since I'm a believer in equality for women, I give her a lingering once-over too, barely refraining from biting my fist. Those high boots with her slim red jacket are doing *things* to me.

Needing to cool my rushing blood, I start bagging some brussels sprouts. There's nothing sexy about brussels sprouts. We stroll the aisles together, grabbing vegetables and groceries, discussing tonight's respective meal plans—a burger and roasted veggies for me, a quesadilla for her.

At the beer and wine aisle, I consider the offerings. "Maybe if I drink for the next twenty-four hours, I'll be wasted enough I won't remember my meeting with my father tomorrow."

Maggie joins me at my side. "Are you freaking out?"

"I believe I am." My sleeping has gone to shit. My stomach thinks it's a contortionist, folding in on itself. "Either that or I've contracted a terminal disease."

Customers push their carts around us, many of them studying our intimate pose. Kindling for the gossip junkies in this town, but I don't care.

Maggie doesn't step away or continue shopping. She weaves her fingers with mine in view of everyone. "I think you're doing the right thing. If you didn't meet him, you'd always wonder what he wanted. This might be more upsetting, but at least you'll have closure."

"Yeah." My tone's noncommittal. I can only hope she's right.

She runs her thumb over my hand. "You'll see. The buildup is often way worse than the main event."

"I don't know." Taking a cue from her affection, I drag my

nail down the side of her palm. "Recent experience is teaching me the buildup can be as much fun as the main event."

She blushes but doesn't reprimand me for crossing her flirting boundary.

I angle my body, bringing us closer. Maggie's tall enough that she comes to my nose. As teens, I somehow used to feel smaller than her, always trying to get her to notice me. I'm fuller now, broader and stronger. If I wrapped my arms around her, I'm pretty sure she'd feel safe. "Thanks for the pep talk."

"You have to call me right after. Tell me how it went."

"I will."

"You better." She chews her lip, then her eyes flick up to mine, hesitant and bashful.

I'm not used to Maggie being anything but brash and upfront. The sudden change has nerves tunneling through my gut. "What is it?"

Her palm turns damp, pressed to mine. "Will you go out to dinner with me? On a date tonight, instead of us both cooking alone?"

Everything in me freezes. Just a second, then my stomach does a celebratory spin. I almost do a victory *lap* around the store, but I rein myself in. I never expected Maggie to make the first move with us. I knew she loved my notes and enjoyed spending time with me, but distant moments like when she first left work interfered with my woman radar.

Now she's asking me out.

As quickly as my adrenaline spikes, it starts to ebb.

I desperately want to say yes. Begin the next stage of our relationship. But a second ago, I was feeling out of sorts. I need to deal with my father before I go out with Maggie. Move past the stress knotting me up. Once I'm free and clear, I'll be relaxed enough to give her the undivided attention she deserves.

"It's fine," she says quickly. "We don't have to. I just

6 CLUES YOUR NEMESIS LOVES YOU   155

thought… Anyway, it doesn't matter." She tries to pull her hand from mine.

I firm my grip, keeping her close. "You thought right, and it does matter. My answer is *hell yes*, but not tonight or tomorrow. I'd love to go out Wednesday night, if that works. Meeting my dad tomorrow will be rough. I'll need to decompress. In order to woo you properly, I have to be at my best."

Her bashfulness returns. "That sounds perfect."

It does, and I hate my father a little more for delaying my Maggie gratification. I lift her hand and give the backs of her fingers a lingering kiss, then grab a bottle of wine. "This should get me adequately sloshed for tomorrow."

"Oh shit."

I swivel at Maggie's worried tone. "What?"

"Wednesday is my sister's birthday. We're doing a small family dinner with my folks."

I shrug. "That's fine. I'll just come."

I expect Maggie to freak out at my suggestion—meeting the family is undoubtedly a massive step forward into committed territory—but I'm surprised her face actually pales. Even worse, her eyes widen, like she just opened a real serial killer letter. "That's ridiculous. Why would you want to come to my sister's birthday?"

"Because you'll be there."

"It'll be boring."

"Good thing I bring the party with me. I'll even do Eminem karaoke."

Her next swallow takes an eternity. "Nobody spends their first date with family."

"Is this really a first date, though?" I tap my chin thoughtfully. "Technically, those pond nights were dates. I think we had, like, a hundred of those. And paint fights definitely classify as dates."

She huffs. "A friend doing a favor painting doesn't classify as a date."

"Do I need to remind you that you painted my dick Island Getaway green?"

A nearby woman gasps and hurries her shopping cart away.

Maggie's panic morphs into her Die Motherfucker Face. "It's a good thing we've been *dating* so long. You won't be blindsided when you get dumped in one minute."

"I'm not getting dumped. Don't you think it's high time I meet my future mother-in-law?" There's no eye roll or dirty look this time. Her face falls so spectacularly, I'm worried it'll slide right off and hit the floor. "Maggie, I was joking. Just messing around. We can go out this weekend. I don't need to meet your family."

But she's studying the linoleum floor so intently I worry my knee-jerk humor has hurt her somehow. Or my future talk hit her commitment-phobic button, which I knew was an issue, but *ha-ha-ha*. There goes my unchecked humor again, usurping my brain.

I lower my head and try to catch her eye. "Mags?"

"No."

Something inside me atrophies. "No, what?"

"No, I don't want to wait." She stands taller and clenches her jaw. "It's fine. It'll be fun. You'll come to my sister's birthday."

While I appreciate her quick turnaround, there's a veneer to her expression, as though she's morphed into the Maggie who puts on airs in public. A presentation to appease.

She grabs the cart and marches ahead of me, as I scratch behind my ear and wonder if I've just set us back another eleven years. Even worse, I have to get through my Life Wrecker meeting tomorrow before I approach that land mine.

CHAPTER
Eighteen

I'M OFFICIALLY A MESS. Thanks to a suggestion from Desmond, I arranged to meet my father at a casual diner in Ruby Grove, an hour outside of Windfall. Thanks to a suggestion from my anxiety, I'm sitting in my parked truck, glued to the seat. I was supposed to meet the Life Wrecker ten minutes ago. Several times, I've attempted to open my door and get out. All I've managed to do is stare into space, pretending to be a Lennon statue that my brothers will urinate on. If they knew I was here, they would most definitely pee on me.

At a loss, I text Maggie.

> Me: SOS

Instead of getting a text back, my phone rings. I answer swiftly. "If I die here, will you move my body so my family doesn't know what I was doing?"

"Always so dramatic, and Des already knows."

"I was counting on him to stop me. The asshole didn't."

"Lennon."

"Yeah?"

"You can do this," she says, her voice gentling.

I rub my eyes until they hurt. "I hate feeling like this."

"I know, babe."

Her compassion means everything, as does that last word. "Are we calling each other cute names now?"

"What do you think?" Her snark is a clear *no*.

"But I have so many for you."

"Do *not*," she warns.

"Come on, *Gingersnap*. You know you love that one. Or I was thinking Frostbite for when you're all cold and calculating. Or how about Dollface?"

"I should hang up on you."

"I know. I'm sorry." I roll the back of my head side to side along the headrest, wanting to slide to the floor. "Jokes usually calm me."

"The longer you drag this out, the more stressed you'll get. Go in and get it over with, then call me after."

I nod several times, even though she can't see me. "Thank you. You're the best. *Sugar Beet*," I add and hang up.

I let out a nervous laugh, give my upper body a shake, then open my door.

Once I'm on my feet, I don't delay. I march toward the diner entrance, arms swinging with purpose, eyes on the prize. My father can't hurt me now. I'm here for me, not for him, even though I have no clue what I want to say to the guy, or what I'm hoping he'll say. What I want is to go in there and feel nothing for him. No affection or love. I want this meeting to be over yesterday.

I push the door open, and a bell above me jingles. My heart decides it's a jackhammer as a hostess walks up to me and smiles. She says something, but her words barely register.

I search the red vinyl booths, sweat gathering everywhere sweat gathers.

Then I spot the Life Wrecker.

Eleven years have added weight to Raymond S. Bower. He's still handsome, resembling Des the most of us boys, with his square jaw and thickly lashed eyes. But Dad's face is fuller now, his once-thick hair thinner. Even from here, the strands look dyed, dark through and through, which kind of fits—a fake facade for the world to see.

When he spots me, he stands and wipes his hands down his jeans.

I nod to the hostess, who's just staring at me now. "I'm meeting someone."

My asshole father, I don't add.

Feeling like an observer out of my body, I walk toward him, my insides vibrating with a slew of emotions I can't name. When I reach him, I fist my hands.

"Lennon." That's it. That's all he says.

My eyes burn, like I'm sad and I miss this asshole. The absolute last thing I want to feel. Forcing a harsh swallow, I slide into the bench seat.

He sits too, neither of us holding eye contact for long. My attention keeps snagging on his too-dark hair and the stains at his scalp, like he dyed it recently. The urge to grab a cloth strikes. The vicious need to rub his scalp until I see the gray.

"Thanks." He clears his throat. "For coming. It means a lot."

"Sure." I drum my fingers on the table, my attention hopping around the diner. A few patrons sit at the counter reading newspapers. Half of the booths are occupied by eating and chatting family or friends. We no longer classify as either.

A server comes by and asks what we want. *An escape hatch.* "Just water for me."

The Life Wrecker asks for a refill on his coffee.

When she leaves, I resume looking anywhere but at my father.

"I'm sorry," he says, his voice stronger this time. I whip my attention to him. "I never told you I'm sorry, but I am."

"What exactly are you sorry for?"

"For putting all of you at risk. For making a string of bad decisions. When you read the book, you'll understand more, but I wanted to tell you to your face. Shame is the reason I never explained back then or apologized, but I want to explain now."

I have nothing for this man. No words of encouragement or anger or compassion. I don't understand what he wants. Why I'm here. All I manage is a stiff nod.

He leans his elbows on the table, slumping forward. "When you kids were young, I did some creative accounting for a longtime client. Nothing drastic, just used some loopholes for her gain. It wasn't a big deal. Accountants do it all the time, but I also…"

He glances down, scrubs a hand over his mouth. "I also had an affair with her. Short-lived and meaningless, but I did it. Turned out the client was tied to the cartel, and they'd been tailing me. They used the transgression against me, demanded I work for them or they'd tell your mother what I did. I couldn't risk losing her or you kids, so I did it. Laundered money and got in deeper until I knew too much. They made it clear if I tried to quit or leave town, you'd all be in danger. So I was basically a prisoner, until the FBI got to me and showed me a way out for all of us."

For all of us. As if we ever had a choice in the matter.

After Dad left, many of our early Bower meetings revolved around the why of his betrayal. *Why* did he launder money? *Why* would he risk our lives? Mom said she had no clue about his motives, which means my mother is reading about his affair now, learning about it for the first time on the pages of his salacious tell-all, and I want to punch my father's face. Break bone. Draw blood. Explode like Desmond used to in a mess of growls and broken glass.

Alas, I'm me. I opt for a hard stare. "Am I supposed to feel bad for you?"

"No, no. This isn't about that. I never told any of you or your mother what I did, out of disgust for myself. I didn't want to see the hurt and disappointment on your faces, so I just kept digging myself deeper. I took your anger and hatred as my sentence, didn't want to offer excuses. If any of you asked me why I worked for the cartel, I refused to explain that I was protecting you. That's not how it started, but that's why it continued. I didn't think I deserved your forgiveness."

E told me about a conversation they once had—E lashing out, demanding to know why Dad risked our lives to work for a cartel. The Life Wrecker said, "I had an opportunity and I took it."

If that was his way of punishing himself, he sure didn't consider how his cavalier comment sucker-punched his kids.

"So, what is all this? This meeting we *just had to have*? You think you deserve our forgiveness now?"

"Of course not. I know we're beyond that. I've been seeing a therapist recently, realized I need to own my truth. I'm here to face what I should've faced a long time ago. I wanted you to hear the truth from me, before you read it. I also wanted to give you this."

He slides a folded paper across the table, but I don't touch it. My jaw aches from the pressure of clamping my molars. My heart hurts for my mother and my family and all we're still going through.

I flick my fingers at the page. "What the fuck is this?"

"Read it and you'll see."

Wanting to get this over with and get out of here, I open the page and scan the writing. Details for some bank account. "I don't understand."

"I opened the account in your name. That's why I needed time before meeting you. Organizing the account with my old name wasn't easy, but it's done. It's just waiting for your signature. It holds the advance money for my book, the foreign deals, and any royalties I eventually earn. It will all be deposited there. The money is for the family. All of you. I know it doesn't undo the past, but it's all I have."

All he has? *All he fucking has?* "So...what? You're trying to buy us off with your drug money? Beg for forgiveness with cash?"

Maybe this is his way of worming into his grandson's life after all, getting to Max through money since he clearly doesn't have a heart. There's no fucking way in hell I'd touch a drop of this dirty money.

"The money isn't linked to the cartel or drugs. It's honest money earned through book sales. And—"

"Honest money?" I whisper-hiss, barely keeping my volume in check. "The only reason you have a book deal is because you're a lying criminal who ruined our lives."

"You're clearly still upset, which is fine," he says evenly. "Like I said, I don't expect forgiveness. I needed to do this for myself."

Everything in me goes eerily still.

All this time I've been stressing about this meeting, I thought I was worried seeing my father would remind me of our good times. He'd maybe apologize to me with tears in his eyes, tell me how much he loves me. That hurting *me* destroyed *him*, and he wants to rebuild the father-son bond we lost. I was worried I'd have trouble cutting him off the way I knew I should and ultimately would, and I'd live with that shame.

But I was wrong about the root of my stress. I was actually worried about *this*—that he *wouldn't* break down and tell me he loves me. I was scared to learn he hasn't been reliving our happy memories like me.

This money and apology aren't born of our once-close relationship. This is his twelve-step recovery program to free himself of his guilt, burying it under his perceived martyrdom.

"Why me?" I ask, still seeking. *Hoping.* The little boy who misguidedly loved his dad wanting a sign I'm wrong. "Why give this to me?"

Eyes dry. Face blank. "I knew you were the only one who'd accept it."

My anger roars back, vicious words clawing at my throat. *Bastard. Asshole. Narcissistic egomaniac. Careless. Reckless. Cruel.* I want to rail and demand to know how he could dismiss me with cash like this. Why he hasn't asked one thing about me and my life, or about his other sons. Why he doesn't lament our relationship and what we lost. I have so many questions, enough anger to have my stomach turning over, and nothing comes out. Not one word. The ugliness twists and contorts, churning my nausea, and I can't look at him and his dyed hair a second longer.

I snatch the bank paper from the table and give him a placid smile. "So great to see you. Consider yourself forgiven in perpetuity. A lifetime of forgiveness for anything else you ever do, as long as you never contact me again."

"Lennon, wait. Don't go. There's still something—"

I'm gone before he can finish talking, storming then jogging until I'm out the door and safely inside my truck. My rasping breaths come in gulps. My arms shake. I'm no longer out of my body, observing myself from afar. I'm strapped into this vibrating contraption of skin and bones, barely able to hit my truck's ignition, but I do. I gun it out of there, no destination in mind except *get the fuck away.*

I drive blindly. The kind of mindless push where you can't remember if you stop at stoplights or slow down to make turns. Backroads blur by. My throat burns. Gravel crunches under my tires as my mind churns over that sorry excuse for a reunion. I debate stopping to light those bank account details on fire, but that money isn't just about me. If my family wants it, that's their choice.

My dashboard flashes with a Bluetooth text from Des. I jam the Read button on the screen. The creepy robot voice says, *"Mom finished the book and called a meeting. She has extra tutoring booked for the end of the semester, so it's in three weeks."*

Immediately, I fumble with my phone and power it off.

My brothers will no doubt organize another group chat. If they start bantering about the myriad of ways they'll kill our father, I will turn this truck around and run Raymond S. Bower off the road. Gut him like the lying fish he is.

Instead of ending up in jail, I take a left and head to Hood Rock Provincial Park. The calming expanse of cliffs and forest is my safe place. A temporary escape. When all else fails, and the Smash Shack's milkshakes are too far, nature and climbing are the things that cure me.

———

An hour later, I'm at the top of Hood Rock, wearing the warmer vest and cargo pants I keep handy in my truck. I rig my anchor and rope for a self-belay. Once it's all set, I return to the bottom, hook myself up with my belay, and focus on my breathing.

Slowly, I start to climb.

I don't know why I can deal with heights, but not cramped spaces. I don't know how my father can work so hard to forgive himself, but not to know or understand me. Did I fabricate our relationship in my head? Did he actually find our time together tiresome and not fun? Is there something inherently wrong with me that makes me unlovable? Maggie refused to acknowledge me in high school. Mizhir and my high school buddies didn't keep in touch at college. My father distanced himself at the end of our time together and doesn't miss our bond.

Inadequacy. That's the feeling propelling me up this rock face. *Unworthiness.*

Acquaintance to many, close friend to none.

Toes. Fingers. Grip. Pull.

I move up the climb, pausing to take the slack out of my rope, using leverage and handholds to propel me. Gradually, the cool rock chills the heat rushing in my veins. The burn in my forearms and calves takes over the busyness in my head. I'm nothing but a body in motion in moments like this, defying gravity, leaning on Mother Nature. She's always here for me. Unconditional acceptance in her sprawling arms.

I sit at the top for a while, the late-November air turning my sweat clammy. I do nothing but breathe and listen. Absorb the stillness and quiet forest chatter, the steady pound of my pulse, but I'm not as relaxed as I hoped. The closure I expected from this meeting feels out of reach. Maybe it was my parting words. Telling my father he's forgiven in perpetuity wasn't my strongest comeback. And I hate the money he offered—the temptation of it and how dirty it makes me feel. Not that it matters. What's done is done. I won't use that cash, and I never have to miss him again or wonder if he cares.

In a day or two, this gnawing unease will fade.

Once I'm down, I load my truck and hit the road. The sun starts to lower on my drive. By the time I turn down the long drive to my rented farmhouse, I'm exhausted, emotionally and physically. I'll nuke some frozen pizza. Stuff my face, then pass out early and hopefully sleep like the dead.

Just thinking about hitting the hay has me yawning, until I notice a white Jeep in front of my house. I clamp my mouth shut and search my property. It doesn't take long for me to see red. Specifically, Maggie's red jacket, her fire-red hair, and her beet-red Die Motherfucker Face as she tries to murder me with her eyes.

CHAPTER
Nineteen

"DID I MISS OUR DATE?" I ask once I'm out of my truck. I've never seen Maggie this livid. Her usual haughty annoyance at my jokes is more of an amused irritation than a bonfire of fury. "Was your sister's party tonight?"

"Where the hell have you been?"

"Rock-climbing?"

Her glare hits Medusa levels. "*Rock-climbing.*"

"Yes?" I hedge again. I'm so taken aback by her vicious sarcasm I'm starting to wonder if I actually went to Hood Rock. I mean, I'm pretty sure I went climbing. My muscles are sore. I'm wearing the outdoor clothes I keep stashed in my truck, but she's so incensed, I can only imagine I actually blacked out after meeting my father, went on some kind of killing rampage, and I *will* end up in jail. Maybe I drove back and ran my father over after all.

I glance at my truck. No blood on the tires.

"Did you drop your phone while *rock-climbing*?" she asks.

I replay the climb I *think* I took and shake my head. "My phone's in the truck."

"And is there a reason you didn't call me when you said you would after meeting with your father? Is there a reason you didn't answer when I called fifty times? Is there a reason you dropped off the face of the earth and worried me silly?"

Oh.

Oh.

"Fuck, Mags. I'm so sorry. I wasn't thinking. I didn't think."

"No, you didn't think. God, I've been so worried. I called everyone. No one knew where you were. Desmond's freaking out now too, so thanks for that. Excuse me while I text him and tell him you're not in jail or dead somewhere." She gives me another lethal look, then turns while she jabs at her phone, presumably texting Des.

I should feel awful about worrying her. Ashamed I only thought of myself while processing that awful reunion. But I'm too stuck on the intensity of her reaction, the way her shoulders are shaking with barely contained fury. There's only one reason she's this upset, and that road sign points exactly where I want it to—toward Maggie's heart.

I approach her back and gently place my hands on her upper arms. She startles. Only for a beat. "I'm sorry I didn't call. I was upset and needed a breather. Then I got a text from Des about Mom finishing Dad's book and couldn't handle more family stuff, so I turned off my phone. It was thoughtless. *I* was thoughtless. I hate seeing you this upset, but I'm so happy you're here."

She curves forward and wavers on her feet. "I kept imagining the worst—you doing something reckless or being so upset you got in an accident."

I press my chin to the side of her head. "The only reckless thing I did was not call you. I'm so sorry."

She nods and sniffles. Discarded leaves blow around our feet. My old porch swing creaks in the wind. Maggie's got on tall boots over her jeans and is wearing a warm jacket, but she shivers.

"Mags?" I whisper in her ear.

"Yeah?" Her voice is breathy—careful and quiet.

"Do you want to cash in your ticket for your free friend hug?"

She lets out a watery laugh and rubs her face. "I would love to cash in my ticket."

I turn her around and grip her shoulders. "There are rules."

She rolls her eyes. "Of course there are."

I make my face as somber as possible. "This is a full-contact hug, but no funny business. As mentioned on the ticket, the hug lasts until it gets weird. Keep your hands where I can see 'em."

"If my arms go around your waist, you won't see my hands."

She's always one step ahead of me. "Rule amendment—you can put your hands around my waist, and one ass grab is allowed."

"You're a pest."

"Just play by the rules, *Magpie*."

"Call me a cutesy name again," she huffs, "and I will tie you down and force you to drink non-craft beers."

"I'd like to see you try. Now get over here."

I tug her to me and instantly realize I was wrong earlier. I thought Mother Nature was my cure-all. My happy place. But *this*—feeling Maggie's arms slide around my waist, her hands splayed on my back, the whole front of her pressed to the whole front of me—is the definition of comfort. A sigh pushes out with my next breath. Angry thoughts of my father still linger, but the longer we hug, the more they fade. She burrows her face into the crook of my neck. I cup the back of her head, letting my fingers sink into the soft silk of her hair as I inhale this amazing woman who cares so much she was worried into a tizzy.

"Thank you," I whisper.

"For what?"

"For being a good friend."

She hugs me tighter. "How did it go?"

"Not good."

"Do you want to talk about it?"

"Yeah, but not right now." I move my nose through her hair, trying to define the tantalizing scents teasing me—strawberries and almonds. A shot of amaretto in a strawberry milkshake.

Maybe that's why she's so comforting. She smells like a souped-up version of my favorite Smash Shack shakes. Except, no. Maggie's the only person outside of my family who knows all my fears and insecurities, eleven years ago and now.

True comfort is not having to pretend you're fine.

I inhale deeper, move my hand up and down her back until all of me is moving, a subtle rocking with Maggie in my arms. She glides her hands on my back too, drawing random patterns, each drag of her fingers guiding this friend hug into a non-friend zone. We move to the rhythm of our deepening breaths. The wind swirls around us while we stay warm pressed together.

There's no fighting my body's reaction when it deepens. The hot pulse up my thighs, the sharp tug on my abdomen, the way my thickening cock presses into Maggie. She makes the tiniest sound, a soft moan that heightens everything. And her hips? The way they just rolled toward me? I am desperately close to losing my composure.

"Is this getting weird?" I ask, my voice roughened with pent-up longing.

"No." Her reply is so quick, followed by a desperate pull of her hands on my back.

I take her at her word, but I need more. I move us more fully, escalating this early evening dance of ours, testing how close we can get. Our warming bodies are separated by my vest, her jacket, our clothes. So many layers, like the woman in my arms. My nemesis and best friend, who comforts and worries after me, but she hasn't shared her truth. She hasn't opened up with me yet.

Not that my body seems to care.

Even after this upsetting day, I've gone from half hard to pumped full of lead, everything in me tightening with desire. I should create distance, get more answers before this goes further. Tell her it's time for her to explain the fears that drive her artificial veneers and wariness of me.

Unfortunately, the theory that men often think with the head between their thighs is sometimes true.

I press my hand to the small of her back, anchoring her to me while pushing my thigh between her legs. She responds with a hip swivel, her mouth opening at my neck. My grunt is pure animal, and she gasps. *Fucking hell.* We're heading way past friend hug, rushing into rubbing-bodies-desperate-for-release territory.

"Mags?"

She whimpers a sort-of reply, her nose and lips coasting up my neck.

My hands get more aggressive. "Can I kiss you?"

She moves without a word, tilts her face up to me, the final rays of sun painting her hair in shades of burnished gold. When her eyelids flutter closed, I don't wait. But I don't dive in. This excruciating wait to taste Maggie Edelstein has been too long to rush.

Our noses brush. She tugs at my back, asking for more, but I don't crush my lips to hers. I'm digging the barely there graze of our parted lips. Hot breath slipping in. Chests swelling faster. Tingles spreading each time our mouths skim until I can't take the suspense a second longer.

I kiss her on a groan, diving deep with a clutch of my hands on her full curves. Our tongues slide and curl. I swallow her gasp with a possessive grunt. Our lips slant and move, fused together, then I'm dropping wet kisses on the tiny scar on her jaw, her neck, catching as many freckles on my tongue as possible. I chart a return path to her addictive lips, greedy and hungry for her. She trembles in my grip, writhing against me.

"Come inside," I say with a nip to her ear. "I need you naked."

"Yes." It's a desperate pant, followed by her hands in my hair. A fistful gripped and tugged.

I start walking us toward the house, but neither of us wants to part. Somehow, we end up on the cool ground outside. And by *somehow*, I mean I lift her up and lower her down on top of me, because I'm an impatient motherfucker. I need Maggie now. This moment. Her consent means everything, and I don't want to stop and think about what she hasn't told me, or her habit of ending relationships that get serious. I don't want to pause and remember how upset and angry I was today. I need this. Her. To show this woman how good we are together.

She straddles my hips willingly, grinding down on my cock like it's her job. I'll pay her overtime in friend hugs if she keeps moving her hips like that. Leave her extra love notes on her Jeep if she keeps looking at me with that intoxicating rush of absolute desire.

I yank her coat open, help her shrug it off, then cup her breast over her soft sweater. "You're so fucking sexy. I can't take it."

She runs her hand over the ridge of my erection, gripping me through my cargo pants. I growl or grunt or maybe swear a few times. "You have no idea," she says, her words dripping with seduction, "how much I've fantasized about finally touching you."

"Tell me."

"Since the first time you stripped at the pond, any time I've touched myself it's been to thoughts of you."

Jesus fucking Christ.

I thrust upward, the two of us grinding mercilessly. I want her clothes off. *Our* clothes off. I'm not sure I have the patience, and it's cold outside. "I'm passing a new bylaw on our friend hug." I grip her hips and hold her down. "It includes dry humping until completion."

Maggie freezes. Abject fear passes over her face. "*Shit.*"

"What? What's wrong?"

She moves, scrambling off me, eyes wide and worried.

For the record, I am not okay. The last time Maggie and I got frisky, it ended with a similar expression of fear on her face as she gathered her clothes and ran away from me.

There will be no repeats.

The second we're on our feet, she starts hurrying toward her Jeep. I jog ahead and block her way, gripping her arms. "What just happened?"

"I forgot."

"Forgot what?"

"My meeting. I left work early to look for you, and I have a presentation tomorrow. A really important one for my next event, and I asked my coworker Stacey to meet me at my place to go over everything, including a bylaw hiccup, and I totally forgot."

"Okay." I rub my hands up and down her arms. "Call her and apologize. Explain that it's my fault. I'm sure she'll understand."

"That's just it. It isn't your fault." She's heaving now, her tone getting louder, angrier. "*I* got too focused on you and carried away and totally fucked this up, and I'm on thin ice at work. If this next event doesn't go well, I could get fired. So no, it's not your fault. It's mine for being thoughtless and reckless and irresponsible."

She resumes her fierce scowl, but there's devastation under her anger, and I don't fully understand why she's this upset. I get being frustrated, kicking yourself for forgetting a meeting, but she's verging on breaking into tears.

"Tell me what to do. Tell me what you need right now."

Her wild eyes lock on mine, a whirlwind of emotions behind them I can't begin to decipher. "I'm sorry," she whispers. "I'm not sure I can do this."

She pulls out of my grip and runs to her Jeep. She's inside it in seconds, driving away, leaving me staring after her in a dusty cloud of gloom, wondering what the hell just happened.

CHAPTER
Twenty

SOME PEOPLE APPROACH conflict head on. They take a bull-rider approach, strapping themselves to the issue, shouting reprimands or challenging questions to provoke a response, hoping they don't get thrown by the replies. Some people never get in the ring, choosing flight over an angry bull bucking them off. I'm the rodeo clown who knows there's a problem but chooses to dance around, waving my hands, acting a fool, intent on saving the rider over myself.

Instead of calling Maggie this morning, asking to meet and talk about last night, or telling her I won't let her push me away, I keep my text light.

> Me: What can I bring to your sister's birthday party tonight?

I have no intention of ignoring Maggie's "*I don't think I can do this*" brush-off, but there's no shortcut to understanding her. For whatever reason, earning her trust will take more time and patience. I need to buy myself that time. After last night's more than friendly "friend hug" burned me up, I'm more committed than ever to painting my face and flailing around like the rodeo clown I am. Anything so she can escape her demons long enough to share them with me. Hopefully I don't get charged by her inner bull in the process.

She doesn't reply to my text right away. Today's a big day for her at work, so I don't take it personally. No reply is better than a quick *You're no longer invited tonight.*

I deal with an expected angry call from Des and a group text from my brothers. I put them off by replying: **Yes, I met with Dad. I'd rather discuss it when we're all together.**

My edginess from that awful meeting persists, the closure I expected still dancing out of reach. My best guess is I'm stressed about showing my family Dad's guilt money. Or maybe "blood money" is a better term. Over $250,000 at this point, with more to come. The idea of any of us using it pisses me off, but it's not my call to make. Unfortunately, the account is in my name, which means I'll be the one doling it out as needed. Tied forever to my father's withered heart. So, yeah. I'm dreading telling my family about the meeting and dealing with the cash.

For now, I have Littlewing work to do and a woman to woo.

Because of my horrible meeting, Aanya ran yesterday's mountain biking session for me. Today, I'm running her hike. The fresh air helps clear my mind, the group of kids easy to excite and engage. The littlest ones are always a blast. We link hands around the largest trees to test how many of us can cover their girth, then we discuss how old the trees are. I let them bury me under dead leaves, then I chase them around like a leaf monster, growling and earning a torrent of giggles. In a clearing near the end, they each get rope and learn to tie knots, at which point my phone vibrates in my pocket.

"I need a moment," I tell the group. "Keep practicing. If you have questions, ask Tonell. He has mastered his knots."

Tonell beams. I give him a thumbs-up, then strut to the side and pull out my phone.

Maggie. *Finally.*

> Nemesis: I think it's better if you don't come tonight.

I think it would be better if Maggie quit fighting the undeniability that is us.

> Me: Wrong answer.

> Nemesis: Don't make this harder than it needs to be.

> Me: The only one making this harder than it needs to be is you.

> Nemesis: Bye, Lennon.

Nope. No way. This is not how this goes down. I didn't survive a decade of witness protection to lose Maggie now. I search the forest, looking for inspiration. Any clue for how to get through to her that I'm a safe place and she doesn't have to hide from me. All I see are trees and rocks and a group of fun kids tugging at rope.

Which gives me an idea.

"Gabriela!" I smile and wave at her. "Can I borrow you for a moment?"

Gabriela is adorable personified. She's seven, with long brown hair, light brown skin, and a button nose. She has a tiny mouse voice, and thanks to her missing two front teeth, her lisp pushes her cute factor over the edge.

She runs her little legs over to me and looks up expectantly. "Yes, Mr. Lennon?" But it sounds like *Yeth, Mithter Lennon*.

Seriously. This level of cute should be illegal. I hold up my phone. "I'm going to call someone who only likes speaking with little girls, even though she pretends she doesn't. If I tell you what to say, will you talk to her for me?"

It's a sneaky move. If I call Maggie, she'll either curse or shout or hang up on me, none of which she can do to this adorable seven-year-old. With Gabriela in on my plan, I hit dial and wait for Maggie to pick up.

The second she does, she unleashes her most exasperated tone. "Lennon, I told you—"

"I have someone who wants to speak to you, and you better be nice."

"Maggie?" Gabriela says when she takes the phone from me. "I'm Gabriela." She looks up at me with wide brown eyes. I nod my encouragement. "Mr. Lennon is sad. He says you won't talk to him."

I cross my toes, hoping Maggie says something to the effect of *"Can you please put Mr. Lennon back on the phone,"* since that's what I told Gabriela she'd say.

Gabriela grins, clearly pleased with Maggie's reply. "He can't talk now. He's busy. But he asked me to ask you if he can see you at the party tonight. Please," she adds, that lisp and her tiny voice impossibly sweet.

Gabriela does an excited bounce as she listens to Maggie's answer, then she hands me my phone. "She said yes. And then she said you should bring..." She squints a moment. "A bulletproof vest."

I laugh. That sounds about right.

———

Three hours later, I pull up to Maggie's childhood home. The classic white farmhouse has a wraparound porch and inviting mahogany door. The property around is clean and well tended. While I've never been inside her parents' home, I know the back property intimately. Specifically, the pond nestled in the forest, under a sweep of twinkle lights, where Maggie and I swam circles around each other.

I grab the small wrapped birthday gift from my passenger seat and attempt to maneuver out of my truck. Unfortunately, it's not easy getting through the door wearing Desmond's old football gear—the closest thing I could find to a bulletproof vest.

Maggie's standing on her porch before I'm on my feet. Her Die Motherfucker Face is alive and well, but when she sees me strapped in shoulder pads, wearing a protective cup over my jeans, she cracks up.

"Oh my God." She laughs harder, wiping at her eyes. "Only you, Lennon Bower."

"If it's easier, I can spend the night outside. Eat on the porch and watch you all through the window."

Her face glows with amusement. "Get that stupid stuff off and get inside. No clue why I thought I could shake you."

She can try all she likes, but I'm here to stay.

I thankfully divest myself of the football gear and meet Maggie on the porch, standing over her. "Hi," I say quietly.

"Hi," she replies, equally as soft.

"Thanks for inviting me."

"You didn't leave me much choice."

"Do you really think we're a choice?"

Her eyes flare, the heat of them radiating in my chest. Her hair is pulled back in my favorite fifties-style wrap, exposing the long line of her neck. Unable to resist, I lean down and nose her ear. "I think we're inevitable."

I drop a tender kiss to her cheek, loving how she shivers, then walk past her into her home.

"Lennon! So great to have you." Maggie's mother pulls me inside with a hug, tutting over me as though we're long-lost friends. Her eyes and hair are clones of Maggie's, or the other way around, but where Maggie's features are more angular, Dana Edelstein is rounder and softer. She beckons me to follow her to the kitchen, toward the delicious, savory smells.

I walk more slowly, because lo and behold, I've been presented with Maggie's childhood in the form of a Family Wall of Fame. Her life, captured in pictures.

Maggie grinning, no front teeth in sight.

Maggie holding up a track-and-field ribbon.

Maggie in her prom dress, next to some tall guy I ignore.

Maggie and her sister in matching hot-dog outfits, a yellow line of "mustard" flowing up to their chins, taking the Halloween costume from cute to adorkulous.

I gesture to the splendid piece of embarrassment. "Can I please get this blown up for my wall?"

"Sure," Maggie says, her tone flat. "As long as you're not upset when your house burns down."

"Maybe I'll pass." But I will find a way to make that picture my phone screensaver.

We join the others in their farm-style kitchen, drinks handed out as we perch on stools and chairs. Jason Edelstein is a knee-slapper of a man, big and broad with a booming laugh that suits him perfectly.

"Love the plants in here," I say, taking in the burst of greenery. The natural world brought inside.

"The lovely plants are my wife's doing." Jason surveys the

plethora of pots livening up the kitchen. "But it's gone a bit overboard. I'm worried if I fall asleep with my mouth open, she'll plant something in me."

Dana tosses a dishcloth at him, earning laughs from us all. The move barely breaks her stride. She appears to be a master chef, flitting around effortlessly, stirring and chopping and sautéing.

"Careful," Emma tells her father, "or it'll be poison ivy."

I chuckle, enjoying her sass. She's the most like Maggie, in personality more than looks. Her red hair is a shade darker, and she has fewer freckles and a longer face, but they share the same strong personality. The girls tease their father's jokes and how their mother pronounces "schedule" with a soft *sh*, everything about this warm family scene so normal. So perfectly inviting and happy, I can't for the life of me understand why Maggie was worried about bringing me here.

Unless it wasn't her "difficult" family that had her freaking out. Maybe it was *me* she didn't think would fit in with them. Or she was worried this was too much, too soon—me meeting the Edelstein clan like the boyfriend I want to be. Both options have me getting quieter, observing more than participating.

Dinner is as entertaining as our pre-meal hang out. We pass around roast chicken, blistered green beans, and a sweet potato casserole that has me going back for seconds—all Emma's favorite foods. Maggie's parents ask me briefly about witness protection and my years in Houston, deftly switching the subject to my move here and Littlewing Adventures. Tact and kindness in abundance. Birthday cake follows the delicious meal, candles and wishes and claps filling the dining room with warmth.

"I bet my office would be keen on those high ropes activities," Jason says, placing his napkin on the table. "The team-building programs for Bigwing Adventures sound great."

The compliment has me flushing, but also feeling heavy. My

father didn't ask about my work or life. He won't be boasting about me to his friends and coworkers, if he has any of those.

"I'll contact you when it's ready," I say, swallowing the hit of jealousy that has no place here. I'm thrilled Maggie has such a great dad. Such a loving family. "We're hoping to launch the adult programs next year in the early spring."

"What about you, Mags?" Dana focuses on her eldest daughter. "How's work? I was worried after the last festival."

"Fantastic," she says quickly, her placid veneer sliding into place.

The move is so abrupt that I squint at her. Maggie's been surprisingly relaxed since my football-gear stunt, sharing smiles with me and joking with her family. Now she's sitting ramrod straight, her hands clasped neatly on her lap.

"The zombie thing was just blip," she says, overly bright. "And the team's great. We're working on a seniors event I'm organizing, busing men and women from different retirement homes to Windfall. We have a full day planned for them. Gallery tours. Lunch at the cidery. A trip to the agriculture museum, with plenty of time to peruse the shops and spend money in the town."

"That's my girl." Jason beams at her, then nods at me. "Maggie always has an angle. Creates amazing events while finding ways to boost the town's economy."

"She's as clever as they come," I confirm, watching the interaction with interest. I know for a fact that Maggie's zombie apocalypse event wasn't a blip. She's worried about her job. Yet she's sitting here, lying to her family without batting an eye.

"If only I could live up to my sister's high standards," Emma laments in dramatic fashion. More good-natured teasing. "Goody-Two-Shoes never steps a foot out of line," she mock whispers to me. "I have to do the extra-hard work of pissing off our folks on my own."

We laugh at the joke, but Maggie's smile is strangely thin.

"Keep calling your sister names," Dana says, "and Lennon might not come back for dinner."

I wink at Emma. "I encourage the name-calling." Maggie groans, finally relaxing. Her parents laugh, and I can't help the nostalgia that settles over me. "This has been really nice—being part of a normal family dinner. It's been, well…" I stare at my empty plate a beat. "It's been a while."

"You're welcome anytime," Dana says gently. "Just pop on by."

"The more, the merrier," Jason adds.

Their kindness means more than they know, but it's Maggie who draws my full attention. She's staring at me intently, a whirlwind in her eyes, like she's both happy and sad at once. I want to ask her what's wrong. I want to know why she was worried about bringing me here and why she lied to her family about her job. I want a lot from Maggie, as per usual, but I settle on being happy she invited me tonight.

I'm about to offer to help clean up, when she abruptly stands. "Is it okay if I take Lennon for a walk on the property?"

"Of course. You two have fun." Dana gives us a knowing look I'd love to run with.

Yes, I'll be defiling your daughter if she lets me.

Judging by Maggie's still-intense expression, I'm not sure fun is on the table.

Hugs and more birthday wishes later, Maggie and I are bundled in our coats, strolling down the path behind their house. It's just wide enough for us to walk side by side, but we're not holding hands like I want. Our arms brush occasionally, the chilly air almost cool enough to turn our breath into mist.

She slows her pace. "Tell me about your father."

Right. That fiasco, which I haven't yet aired out loud. I tuck my hands into my pockets and kick at the ground as I walk. "He didn't care about meeting me. He just wanted to give me banking information so we could have his book money. A way for him to feel less guilty, I think."

She stops, looking livid. "Did he apologize to you?"

"Sort of. I mean, *yeah*—he said the words, but it was like he was following a checklist: if I say this thing like I'm supposed to, I will be absolved. He didn't ask once about me or my brothers. Just wanted to get what he did off his chest, which, by the way, is shit. He cheated on my mother, and she's now reading about it in his tell-all. As per usual, it's all a fucking mess."

I grit my teeth and count to five, attempting not to punch a tree.

Maggie takes my clenched hand and weaves our fingers together. "Will you accept the money?"

"No way. It took me eleven years to touch the principal from my WITSEC school money, which I'm only using now because I want to grow my business and am short on choices. And this cash is worse. He earned that by blasting our pain into the world without our consent." I shake my head angrily. "If my family wants their share, that's up to them."

"Don't you think it's your due? You might need more for your business, or you could use the money to buy your first home. Grow something good out of his deception."

"And know the house I'm living in has his dirty fingerprints all over it? Thanks, but no thanks."

Maggie nods, running her thumb over my knuckles. "I hope you at least tore him a new asshole."

I shrug, staying quiet, and thread our fingers more firmly together. Her cool skin is a balm to my rising temperature.

She sighs. "You didn't tell him off, did you?"

"Doesn't matter. I'm over it and over him. He doesn't deserve any emotion from me."

"No, he doesn't. But you always do this."

It's dark out. Most stars are hidden by the clouds, but my

eyes have adjusted enough to make out her judgmental expression. "I always do what?"

"You don't stand up for yourself."

"Wow, okay." I separate our hands and cross my arms. "Tell me how you really feel."

"I didn't mean it like that. It's just…" She drops her head back and studies the dark sky. "You're this amazing guy, so fun and sweet, but as teens, you didn't yell at me for ignoring you at school. You didn't tell Mizhir his brush-offs hurt after he left for college. You didn't ask your dad why he quit spending time with you that last year, although it's clear it's because he's a scumbag. You refused to yell or tell someone off, and you're still doing it. But I don't know why."

"What's so good about yelling?" I keep my voice even, unwilling to let this escalate, even though my temper is rising. There's also no point denying Maggie's claims. I hate fights. I just don't get the big deal. "Isn't forgiveness the path of righteousness? I see it all the time in documentaries—people who've suffered grave losses go out of their way to forgive the perpetrator for closure. Even some prisoners of war forgive their captors. Forgiving my father is nothing compared to that."

"This isn't about forgiveness. This is about you burying your pain. You need to face your father."

"I met with him, didn't I?" Listened to the jerk as he tried to free himself of his guilt.

Her jaw bunches. "*Yes*, but you didn't tell him how much his actions hurt you. You didn't give him shit for ruining all your lives. If you don't let out your true emotions, you won't heal."

"I'm healing just fine." But my voice comes out stilted. A muscle in my jaw throbs. "Also, speaking of not letting out your true emotions, I just sat through dinner with your amazing family, can't believe how lucky you are to have them, but you lied to them about work. You were freaked out about me even meeting them, and you keep hinting that there's some trauma in your past that's made you all messed up. If there's a burying feelings contest going on, pretty sure you'd win."

Maggie flinches, and her eyes go glassy.

A hot poker of guilt jabs at me. No one should be pushed to air personal issues before they're ready. Now Maggie looks upset, and I feel like shit. This is why I don't engage in conflict. I may have kept my tone in check, but what I said was insensitive.

"I'm sorry, Mags. You don't have to share anything with me."

"Actually—" she drops her arms to her sides and stands taller "—you have nothing to apologize for, and I do have to share my story with you. You deserve the truth." She blinks rapidly and her chest pumps faster. "Yes, my family is amazing and loving. I couldn't ask for better parents. But…my mom and dad aren't actually my mom and dad. They aren't my birth parents."

CHAPTER

Twenty~One

MY MOM *and dad aren't actually my mom and dad.* I stare at Maggie, struggling to comprehend her words. She has the same hair and smile as her mother. There's a striking family resemblance that's impossible to miss. "I don't understand."

She wraps her arms around her middle and holds her elbows. "Jason and Dana are my aunt and uncle. Dana's my mom's sister, and they look a lot alike. They adopted me when I was little."

"I had no idea." I close the distance between us and run the backs of my fingers down her cheek. This is clearly a hard topic for her, which means the reasons behind the adoption aren't straightforward. "Is your mom still alive?"

She nods, leaning into my touch.

"Will you tell me about her? About what happened?"

She closes her eyes, fiddles with the bottom edge of my jacket. Finally, she nods again. "Can we walk?"

"Of course."

I take her hand this time, tuck our linked palms close to my side. I don't push or prod or make a joke. We hit a slow stride. I listen to our steady footfalls and a hooting owl. Rustling leaves whisper to one another.

Maggie's attention moves from the trees above us to the sticks and stones at our feet. "The best way to describe my mother is that she's a loose cannon. A wild child who never grew up. She's a junkie, but not with drugs. She's an irresponsible and reckless pleasure-seeker, who acts before she thinks. Everything for her is about living in the moment."

Sadly, I can relate to having an irresponsible and reckless parent, but hearing Maggie's mother might have harmed her, emotionally or otherwise, has my vision turning spotty. "Please tell me she didn't hurt you."

"Not physically, no. But I sometimes wonder if physical pain would have been easier in some ways. Visible scrapes and cuts that heal, although I know that's bullshit." Her voice doesn't waver, but she sounds resigned.

I squeeze her hand gently. "How old were you when you went to live with your aunt and uncle?"

"Two. After a particularly disturbing call, Dana went chasing after my mother and found me left behind in a motel room. She and Jason had plans to travel and work abroad, but they gave it all up to raise me."

During our pond nights, when Maggie admitted she felt locked inside herself, playing a constant game of make-believe, she said something about working to make her parents proud. Mentioned that they gave up so much for her, as though their sacrifices weighed her down with guilt. "If they didn't want and love you, they wouldn't have taken you into their home and lives."

She gives a noncommittal shrug. "Family duty is big with them, and they didn't tell me about her. When I was little, as far as I knew, they were my mother and father. Nicki—my birth mother—didn't fight the adoption, and they decided I was better off not knowing about her."

"Why wouldn't they tell you?"

She unwinds our hands and fits hers into her pockets, making herself smaller. "My mother's volatility is a black hole that can suck you in. They were worried if I got curious and reached out to her, she'd hurt me."

We breach the forest, entering into a clearing that shoots me back in time.

Our magical pond.

The area looks smaller than I remember. No twinkle lights illuminate the water with fascination. There's no crimson-haired siren calling me to her with her mischievous eyes and shark impressions, but I instantly relax, soothed by the memories here. My place of safety. Refuge during my tough last year of high school. Rounds of truth or dare. The tender ache of first love. Hours upon hours with this complex woman, who hides so much of herself.

"I missed this place," I say into the crisp night.

Her sigh is thick with meaning. Loss? Nostalgia? The vividness of history out of reach? "I loved meeting you here. Couldn't wish the daytime hours to race by fast enough."

I smile. "I might have tripped a few times, eating dirt, running to meet you." We stand beside each other, a world of memories filling the darkness. Maggie's honesty fills a hollow in my chest. "Truth or dare," I whisper.

One corner of her lips kicks up. "Dare, of course."

"I dare you to let me hold you."

She looks up at me sharply, her freckles nearly hidden in the blue-tinged darkness, but there's no missing how her lips part on a near-silent intake of breath. "Your dares are getting weak in your old age."

"Or more meaningful." We're standing close enough to feel each other's heat, for her to hopefully understand my intentions. *Let me be here for you. Let me absorb some of your sadness.* "Do you accept the dare?"

She studies the stillness of the pond, the seconds elongating, then she opens her arms to me. Instead of going in slow, hugging her with quiet affection, I pick her up and swoop her into the air.

She shrieks. "Oh my God. Put me down."

I toss her over my shoulder, firefighter-style, earning a few back-pounds. "This is the dare. I am officially allowed to hold you in any position I deem fit. Now let's hear the rest of this story."

"The only story I'll be telling after this is the sad tale about the night you drowned in the Edelstein pond." She pinches my sides, but my jacket saves me from her revenge-seeking fingers.

I smack her ass and howl at the moon while she snorts and squirms. She gets her hands up my shirt, finding skin after all, and turns herself into a human lobster claw. She pinches my side. I yowl and almost drop her, the two of us ending in a heap on the ground.

"You pinched me," I say when I catch my breath, lying flat on my back.

"You are a menace." She's on her elbow, looking down at me, fondness in her tender gaze.

I trace the line of her black-and-white hair wrap. "I love these on you. You slay the fifties vibe."

She traces my jaw, drags her fingertips over my beard. "I love this on you."

"You just want to know how it'll feel on your inner thighs."

Her nostrils flare, but her mouth stays firmly shut. She doesn't deny her desire. There's no hiding the slash of color on her cheeks, even in the dim light.

I tug her down, fit us together so we're a human puzzle, arms and legs intertwined with her head on my chest. "Do you know your birth father?"

She shakes her head, her hair wrap rubbing my beard. "My mother claims she doesn't know who he is, but it's hard to know with her. She'll lie and cheat if it gets her what she wants.

If I had to guess, she knows but wants nothing to do with the man."

"And how'd you learn you were adopted?"

"By accident."

When she doesn't go on, I kiss the top of her head, glad we're here for this talk. At our pond. The secret world where the story of Maggie and Lennon began.

She flattens her hand on my chest, silhouettes of trees guarding us from outside ears. "Emma calls me Goody-Two-Shoes because that's who I am now—who I became. When I was young, I was wild. An adrenaline chaser, like my mother. At twelve, I hid all night in the forest because I thought it would be fun to freak out my parents. At thirteen, I took my friend's father's car for a joyride and crashed it into a telephone pole. That same year, I climbed to the roof of my house, determined to jump to the large oak in the backyard. I broke my leg in the process. A month later, I caused a fire at a friend's home by setting off fireworks."

I try picturing the polished Maggie I know flouting rules, causing damage and chaos. My mind rebels at first, but I recall her at the pond, lighting up when I'd dare her to do something crazy and fun. Those were the moments when she seemed most alive. "There's nothing wrong with having a wild streak. I'm sure you gave your parents early gray hairs, but it sounds like no one got hurt in the process."

"Luckily, no one did. But after the fireworks night, I couldn't sleep and got up to get some water. I overheard my parents talking in their room. Not yelling or getting mad the way they sometimes would when I messed up. They sounded scared, and I'll never forget it—my mom's exact words." Maggie's next inhale feels unbearably weighted. "'*She's too much like her. I don't know what to do with her anymore. If she doesn't hurt herself, she'll hurt someone else. She's going to break my heart, just like Nicki. Maybe we shouldn't have adopted her.*'"

"Jesus, Mags." I wrap my leg over her and cup the back of her head, trying to shield her from the hurt she's lived with for so long.

"Yeah," she says quietly. "Worst words a kid could hear, and I gasped. Couldn't contain the reaction. Ran back to my room and hid under the covers, hoping they didn't hear me, wishing I hadn't heard them. But they rushed into my room, apologized, and hugged me. Wiped away my tears. That's when they told me about Nicki—what she was like and why they took me in. My mom apologized over and over for what she said, explained she was just scared, but I heard what I heard. I believed they didn't want me, and I lashed out. Demanded to meet my birth mother until they agreed."

I smooth my hand down her back. "What was she like?"

"Larger-than-life. So much fun. Nicki swept into my small-town world with fast car rides in her convertible and all the junk food I wanted. Dared me to jump off the cliff into Bear Lake. I was thirteen and she spent one week with me that summer, and I was hooked on her. Wanted to be her. Scoffed at my parents for their rules and thinking I was damaged. Then Nicki stole sunglasses and booze from a gas station and told me to stand watch inside while she left."

Maggie fiddles with my jacket zipper, her voice getting smaller. "By the time I got outside, she was gone. She left me there like trash, off to chase another of her dreams. An easier life without a kid."

I have no words. No jokes to lighten the mood. I pull Maggie up higher and kiss her forehead, her closed eyelids, her cheeks and jaw. Cover her with as much affection as I can, finishing with a soft kiss on her lips. "I'm so sorry."

She sighs and presses another kiss to my lips. "As you can imagine, I changed after that. Refused to be like her. Worked my ass off to prove to my *real* parents who took me in that I was worth keeping. I made new friends, focused on school. Ms.

Goody-Two-Shoes to the core, terrified I'd wake up one morning and find my parents had left me like Nicki, stranded with no one. I was determined not to be like my mother."

So much about Maggie snaps into better focus: her facades in high school, always careful and poised, choosing boys back then and the limp-shaker recently who offered her easy predictability, even if mundane. The opposite of the guy I was back then, pulling pranks, landing in detention. A high school flunky causing trouble for a laugh. "That's why I scared you."

"You were everything I wanted, Lennon. Everything I tried to deny about myself. You were exciting and a little wild. You made life feel fun and unpredictable again, and fun unpredictability was a gateway for me."

"But you didn't go off the rails with me. We were wild and silly out here, but it didn't affect your life."

"Actually, it did."

I freeze, everything in me going still. "What do you mean?"

A soft breeze cools the tip of my nose. Branches scritch and scratch in the stretching silence.

"I ditched a lot of schoolwork to hang out with you," she finally says. "Failed a few tests and blew off curfew. My folks started getting nervous again. They had no clue what I was doing or who I was seeing, but I sensed how on edge they were."

"I didn't know."

"I didn't *want* you to know. I wanted you to think I was as free and fun as you."

"The last thing I would've wanted you to be back then was like me, flunking classes, watching your friends leave for school. Enduring parental disappointment and disapproval is no fun."

She shrugs, and my awareness of the negative part I played in her troubled youth grows. Maybe my father's betrayal and WITSEC have a silver lining after all. Maybe the best thing I did for Maggie was leave. "Guess things went back to normal after I left town."

"Lennon." Her voice sharpens. "I fell apart after you left."

I slowly shift to sitting, not liking the sound of that. "What do you mean *fell apart*?"

She sits up too, presses her hand to my thigh. "You were the center of my world back then. I knew I liked you, but I didn't realize how much until you were gone. And it was like my mother all over again. Finding this person who shone brighter than the sun, who lit me up and I adored, then you left me without a word. Discarded me like I was worthless."

A razor scrapes along my throat. The backs of my eyes burn. Delilah must have been right, assuming I was the guy who broke Maggie's heart, but hearing it from Maggie—the larger extent of the damage I caused—hurts in new, painful ways.

"You're the opposite of worthless. Leaving you gutted me. Like, fucking *wrecked* me. If it was up to me, I'd never have left."

She cups my cheek, a sad smile tipping her lips. "I know that now, but I didn't know that then. I ended up failing English and had to take a summer course. I withdrew from my family and friends, didn't know how to explain what was wrong with me when no one even knew we were friends."

"Fuck." I rub at my eyes and shake my head. "I'm so fucking sorry."

"It wasn't your fault."

True, but I hate my father that much more. All the tragedy he caused. The pain.

She touches my hair, tunnels her fingers through the messy strands. "I eventually got my shit together, mostly because of Delilah."

"But you never told her about me."

"Not specifically, no, but I eventually noticed what rough shape *she* was in. Losing E was like losing a limb for Delilah, and I was so stuck in my own spiral I didn't notice at first." She blinks quickly, sudden emotion shining in her eyes. "When I realized she was in trouble, verging on major self-destruction, I had no choice but to gather myself. Be there for my best friend. So yeah. We both came through, talking a lot about E leaving and my issues with my mother, which brings me back to us."

Us. Such a small word, wrapped with life-altering implications. This whole night is wrapped with nothing but monumental ramifications. Thanks to E's recent graphic novel, telling his life story in a fictional world, I know what devastation Delilah endured after he left her. Pain I can't think about without getting choked up. Maggie's turmoil doesn't sound as devastating, but that time has left scars. *I've* left her with scars. "I wouldn't have chased you so hard for a date if I'd known I'd hurt you that much."

She raises an eyebrow. "Yes, you would've."

I huff out a sad laugh. "Fine, I would've. But I'd have been subtler about my flirting."

She traces random shapes on my thigh. "I didn't tell you all this to push you away. I just want you to understand why being with you now is hard for me. You're tied to a lot of painful memories, and I still feel that electricity with you. Like I'm one step away from turning into my mother, ditching the world for a moment of recklessness, and that always leads to trouble."

I shake my head and capture her hand with mine. "I agree, we're electric together. When I'm with you, I feel wild and on the edge of something big. And yeah, the intensity scares me too. I imagine it terrifies you. But the difference here is we're doing this together. I'm no longer a stupid kid getting in trouble for the hell of it. We're not failing classes. We both have jobs we love. I won't let you hurt yourself or anyone else, and I will *not* disappear on you again. Plus, I have it on good authority sharing similar tendencies to a parent doesn't mean you'll repeat their mistakes. None of us boys are running around half-cocked, breaking laws."

"Right, but this is different. *I'm* different. You make me lose my head, in the best and worst way. Like, when I'm with you,

I'm cemented in the moment and block out the rest of the world. That last night at the pond, I was supposed to pick Emma up from dance class, but I decided to fool around with you instead, couldn't resist the pull to finally be with you, and some stranger almost picked her up in a van."

I flinch. "Jesus."

"I know. And thankfully she knew enough to run and yell for help, but I was selfish. And when I'm selfish, bad things happen. Even the other night, I got caught up in you and forgot about my work meeting. I'm not great at multitasking and remembering commitments, especially when I'm hopped up on adrenaline. It makes me feel like I'm one step away from being like my mother, and I don't know what to do with that."

Except she's finally opening up to me. Her trust has to mean something. "Do you want to be with me, Mags?"

Her chin trembles. "I want to try."

"And do you realize that your fears—and I say this with the utmost affection—lean toward irrational? You've grown up and changed, but you're talking like you don't have any control. One wrong move and you'll end up like your mother, when all I've seen from you is responsibility and control."

"I know." She hangs her head and rubs her brow. "I feel how overboard I go with it all—dating the wrong guys on purpose, pushing you away. Ignoring you in high school so we wouldn't get too close, thinking your wild nature would bring out the worst in me. Delilah gets on my case about it, saying I'm being too hard on myself. There's just this fear deep down I can't seem to shake. Like you," she says, her head whipping up. "Like your claustrophobia. Rationally, you know you won't die in an elevator, but your adrenaline takes over and you can't shake the fear."

"True." I cup the back of her neck and give her my softest smile. "I'm terrified of elevators and tight spaces. It's an irrational fear beyond my control, but I still walked into that death trap, because you were inside it. I faced that fear to be with you, and I'm asking you to do the same." The creases between her brows lessen. I press my forehead to hers. "Will you do that for me, Mags? Face your fears to be with me?"

She grips my shoulders. "You can't ever leave me like that again. You can't disappear."

"Never." My undying promise. I would rather sever a limb. "I will never make you feel discarded or left behind again."

"Okay." Her quiet agreement is watery. One word drenched with emotion.

"Okay?"

"Yes, we can try this."

I exhale years of pent-up pining for this woman. "Was it the football gear I was wearing? The cup? It made you hot for me?"

She punches my arm, dragging us back to lying down together. "You are such an idiot."

"Maybe, but I have a stipulation. If we're doing whatever we're doing, you have to tell me when you get nervous. When something starts to set off your tendencies to pull back, you have to speak up before you freak out."

She kisses my neck, rubs her nose along the sensitive spot below my ear. "Okay. But I need to take this slow."

"Right." Except that could mean a lot of things. "What's your definition of slow?"

"Can we just not label what this is? Take it one day at a time?"

A spot behind my ribs hardens. Vagueness like that could end badly. "In this unlabeled situation, will you be dating other people? Because that's not okay with me."

Her body stiffens. "God, no."

"Okay." I massage the tension radiating up my neck. "Then we're dating."

"Except there's no need to call it *dating*, is there? You're the first guy I've shared my history with. My anxiety needs time to catch up."

A tamp down the rebuttal that wants to rise. *Cool, calm, and collected.* That's what Maggie needs, no matter how badly I want to crow that she's mine. "So you're saying I *shouldn't* have our names skywritten over Windfall, letting everyone know we're together?"

She gives my shin a light kick. "You're a pest."

"What about my planned public service announcement on the radio?"

She snorts and doesn't bother answering.

"Fine." I sigh dramatically. "We'll take this slow. How do you feel about having our first official date tomorrow night?"

"That would be nice," she says softly.

"And just so we're on the same page, I'll allow second base, but not a step further."

She presses her fingers into my beard, getting all up in my business. "I mean slow emotionally, not physically. When we do get naked together, Lennon Bower, I want this beard of yours all over me, and I plan to suck your cock so hard you see stars."

Jesus Christ.

I suddenly realize Maggie's fears are the least of our problems. I'm not sure I'll survive her wicked mouth. Except I feel lighter than I have in weeks. Sad after learning what she went through with her mother and with me, but also clearer. Nothing's worse than dealing with the unknown and building worst-case scenarios in your head.

I'll work to make Maggie feel safe with me. Together, we'll conquer our irrational tendencies and eventually take the town of Windfall by storm.

"Anything else I can do to make you feel comfortable with me?" I ask.

She cuddles her head into my neck. "I need more of your notes. All the redacted parts."

A happy hum moves through my chest. "That can be arranged, as long as I get the hot-dog picture of you. That beauty's going on my phone."

She laughs and tries to tickle me, but I'm wearing too many layers. I roll her fully on top of me and hold her close, thinking of all the ways I'll prove we're meant to be.

CHAPTER
Twenty-Two

I WAKE up before the sun, eager to face the day. I can't wait to take Maggie out tonight, and I love my new morning routine—tackling an item on my house to-do list, then strolling through the property as the sun brightens.

I grab my tools and head to the front porch, pausing to let the tranquility of this land settle on me. I can hardly believe I lived in the rush of Houston as long as I did. I nearly didn't return to Windfall, worrying over facing my past. Living here has righted a part of me that's been off-kilter too long.

Eventually, I get to work replacing a portion of the rotting wood on my front deck. I enjoy every *thwack* of my hammer, every jolt of my body. Hard work that feels purposeful and good. I brew my tea afterward and walk across the property as the morning sun paints the wild grasses gold. Contentment fills me, along with a yearning. The wish to call this place *mine*, even though I rent it. Own the land that's finally given me a real sense of home. Maybe Littlewing will be successful enough that I can buy the place from Mrs. Jackson one day.

I stop at the large maple by the tree line. It's imposing and beautiful, and an idea hits me. A surprise for Maggie I bet she'll love. I mentally add it to my to-do list and smile at the sprawling property as I head back.

My good mood continues with my day. I tackle my bills, feeling less annoyed about using my WITSEC principal. Maggie's advice to grow something good out of my father's deception is starting to hit home. The afternoon's mountain biking program is a blast. I even convince a participant's brother to join next week.

Now I'm hurrying toward the flower shop, hopped up on adrenaline and anticipation. My first date with Maggie needs to be flawless. Flowers to liven up her home. A special gift and note to add a personal touch. Attentiveness and quiet romance for my favorite nemesis.

A few steps from the flower shop, I see Sandra.

She stops directly in front of me, invading my space. Sandra is a bit of a close talker. "When you take Maggie to Carlino's Trattoria tonight," she says, practically breathing on me, "do not order the calamari."

Without waiting for me to reply, she pushes past me, disappearing down the street.

I stand there blinking, downright impressed by Sandra's ability know things I don't even know. I mean, *yes*, I'm taking Maggie to Carlino's Trattoria. The restaurant is romantic and charming, and the food is supposed to be great. Sandra must have learned this intel because this town loves gossip as much as it loves beets, but how she knew I'd read the menu and was intrigued by the calamari is anyone's guess.

A shower and change later, I show up at Maggie's front door with a bouquet in shades of red and what looks like a box of chocolates, but it's actually a pretty box holding a copy of the B-horror movie *The Blob*. The perfect gifts to woo my nemesis, including the letter in my hand.

I crouch and shove the envelope under her door, then stand and knock.

The clack of high heels indicates she's on her way. The clacking stops, but she doesn't open the door. Hopefully she's picking up and reading the letter I wrote. It's similar to my first note to her, but all the "redacted" parts are filled in and some lines are changed.

YOU'RE STRONG. YOU'RE SMART. YOU'RE INCREDIBLY CREATIVE. FROM THE FIRST DAY I MET YOU AT [THE POND], I WAS AMAZED BY YOU. YOU STILL AMAZE ME, EVEN IF YOU HAVEN'T HANDED OVER THE HOT-DOG PICTURE YET.

PS: CONSIDER YOUR NO-FLIRTING RULES OBLITERATED. I PLAN TO TELL YOU OFTEN AND LOUDLY THAT I THINK YOU'RE [BREATHTAKING] AND [SO DAMN SEXY] AND PARTICULARLY [HOT WHEN YOU CALL ME THE BANE OF YOUR EXISTENCE]. I CAN'T WAIT FOR OUR DATE TONIGHT.

A few seconds pass, then a few more. I stare at her closed door, suddenly nervous. Maybe the note was too much. Maggie made it clear she needs to take this slow. Yet here I am, blurting my obvious feelings before she even opens her door. I should've left the letter on her Jeep this morning, as she would've expected. Given her time and space to feel the complicated emotions I inspire.

Great first move, idiot.

Finally, the door opens.

Maggie is decked out in a polka-dot hair wrap and a white dress covered in tiny cherries, upping her fifties sexpot status to pass-out levels. Her neutral expression is tough to read, but my reaction to her is undeniable.

I sway to the side and lean on the doorframe. "How do you expect a man to function when you're wearing that?"

"How do you expect a woman to function when you write her notes like this?" She holds up the letter, her voice a bit shaky.

"Too much?"

She doesn't answer. Her attention drifts to the flowers and gift I brought. "What's all this?"

Yep. I went overboard. "Just something for the friend I'm taking on a date."

She rubs her red lips together. Instead of taking my tokens of affection, she gives me a flirty once-over. "You look edible."

I glance down at my tucked in blue-and-white plaid shirt and worn jeans. "E and Delilah say everything I own is hipster. Best I could do was try for non-sloppy hipster."

"First." She runs her hand down the front of my shirt, ending by tucking her fingers inside the waist of my jeans. "This shirt makes the blue in your blue-gray eyes brighter, and your eyes always do me in. I also know what's going on under these clothes, all those hard, lean muscles from your rock-climbing and outdoor work. You could wear a velour sweatsuit, and I'd still be undressing you in my mind all night."

She seems to be ignoring the gifts I brought, but the muscles in question flex and preen. "Noted on the velour sweatsuit. I'll make sure I wear one next time we go out."

She snatches her hand back. "I was joking, explaining how hot you are with the use of *theoretical* ugly clothes."

"No, no. I think, deep down, purple velour gets you *ready*."

Her face pales. She knows I'll do it. Embarrass the hell out of myself, if it means garnering a laugh from her and others. "Please don't," she pleads.

"You prefer pink?"

Glowering my favorite glower, she finally yanks the flowers and box from me, accidentally popping off the box's lid in the process. One look at the movie inside and she bites her lip.

"I went out on a limb," I say, "assuming you still have that old VHS player."

"I do, and thank you." Her voice is quiet, but she doesn't meet my eyes. Abruptly, she turns and walks toward what must be her kitchen. "I'll just put the flowers in water," she calls. "Then we can go."

A moment later, she's sashaying back to me, her posture straighter, a calculated gleam in her eyes. She locks her door and leads me down her front steps. "I didn't get you a physical gift, but I thought you might want to know I'm on the pill, and I've been tested since dating Harrison."

I nearly stumble over my feet. "Are you trying to get me in a car accident?"

She gives me a cheeky look over her shoulder. "We're not even in your truck yet."

"But I've been tested too and have never slept with a woman without a condom, which I'm pretty sure is what you're suggesting and, FYI, might be the *best* idea you've ever had." As is the fact that she was serious about not taking the physical aspects of us slowly. "Now I'll be thinking about sinking into you bare as we drive and will for sure ram into the first moving object that passes my truck."

Except my steps slow.

I'm beyond ready to consummate my feelings with Maggie. I'm thrilled she feels the same, but that's twice she's diverted to flirting and sex talk when we've veered toward emotional moments. Protection tactics, likely. She's using the physical aspect of our attraction to avoid the deeper feelings she's not ready to explore.

I frown, unsure if tonight's date is too soon. But she was open about wanting to push her boundaries with me. If she didn't want a proper date with dinner and romance, she would have said no.

I drive us to Carlino's Trattoria and am not disappointed by the atmosphere. Intimate lighting. White tablecloths. Soft music. There's even a red rose laid over Maggie's plate.

The second we sit, I take her hand in mine. "You look gorgeous."

"Thank you, but all these flowers are too much."

"That one wasn't me. The restaurant must just believe in romance." We glance at another couple walking in. The table they're seated at doesn't have a flower. Odd. "And anyway, you deserve a field of flowers."

Her eyelashes flutter, and she glances down sharply. I run my thumb over her wrist, feel the fast race of her pulse.

A few swallows later, she slays me with a seductive look. "Maybe we should skip ahead to the after-date part. Do dinner another time?"

"Nope. I can't wait to get you home, but I love this too much to miss it." This marrow-deep *wanting*. The hot pulse that travels through me every time I picture her pretty dress sliding to the floor. I lift her hand and kiss her knuckles. "I want to enjoy all of you."

Her shoulders soften. "When did you get so charming?"

"One second ago. Also, order anything you want, but not the calamari."

She frowns. "I like calamari."

"As do I, but I ran into Sandra today."

"Sandra of the nosier-than-a-bloodhound Sandras?"

She nailed that one. "The woman's pulse on the town is creepy. She somehow knew about this date and where I was taking you, then she warned me away from the calamari."

Maggie shudders. "Consider it not ordered. That woman once told Delilah she needed to hire a new barista, even though Delilah was fully staffed. The next day, her lead barista quit."

Once again, I'm more than pleased Sandra and I are on the same side.

After more light conversation, we peruse the menu and

decide to share everything we order. We ask our server for his wine recommendations. By the time he's back, placing a glass of white in front of Maggie and a glass of red in front of me, we're deep in discussion on the hot topic of senior citizens.

"The event sounds amazing," I say, running my fingers over her palm and wrist. I can't stop touching her smooth skin. Even better, she's flirting back in a softer, less overt way, dragging her nails over my palm. "I have no doubt you'll rock those seniors' worlds and reinstate your good name at work."

"I better. Shannon keeps questioning me, asking if I triple-checked venue accommodations, timing, and logistics. She has me so frazzled I keep thinking I've forgotten something important."

"Nonsense. You're a planning queen. And you have until mid-December to figure it all out. The event will be a showstopper." I twine my ankle with hers under the table. More places on Maggie for me to touch. "If you need to liven things up with them, I don't mind jumping out of a cake."

She laughs. "Only if you wear assless chaps."

"Are there any other kinds of chaps?"

We laugh and talk and touch, ankles mingling under the table, her fingers playing with the hairs on my forearms. We taste each other's wine and eat off each other's plates, getting quiet at times, simply staring into each other's eyes, slow swallows dragging with intent.

She always breaks eye contact first, but she's been present this whole night. Engaged and showing affection with her light touches. I've never felt so in tune with another person. So aware of someone's mannerisms, from the uptilt of her right shoulder before she laughs, to the way she rubs her thumb and middle finger together when she's thinking. And the romance at this restaurant is second to none. Not only was there a special red rose upon our arrival, but our server brings us a complimentary slice of chocolate cake for dessert.

I don't see other tables getting this sort of treatment. Maybe they confused us with someone's special anniversary dinner, and I don't bother correcting them. Maggie digs in greedily, moaning and licking her lips.

I wish I could slather her in that cake and lick it off her with thorough strokes of my tongue. "Seems you love chocolate."

She hums. "Better than sex."

"Only because you haven't had sex with me."

She moves her tongue sensually over her fork, eyeing me like I'm her next bite. "We should leave."

"Agreed." But I'm not done with our date yet.

I pay for our meal, refusing her offer to share the cost. I whisk her to my truck after and plant my hands on her door, caging her before I let her inside.

"Are you ready?" I palm the dip of her waist and kiss her neck.

"Yes," she says, breathy.

I chuckle. "That was easy."

She hooks her fingers into my belt loops and tugs my hips forward. "What did I just agree to?"

I pull back and grin. "We're going dancing."

"No, we're not. We're going to my house. Or your house. Or any house in any part of the world, as long as that house has a bed. Actually, there doesn't even have to be a house or a bed. I have it on good authority there's a patch of grass in this parking area we can use."

"In good time, Magpie." I run my thumb over the soft fabric of her dress. "Wait until you see where we're going."

She groans. "There's only one bar for dancing in this town, and it's the Barrel House. I've been there, like, a million times. We should be at the naked part."

"Shush, you." I tap the tip of her nose, not ready to end this portion of our date—Maggie showing me her softer sides. "It's

Pride Night, and Ricky says it's a blast. It'll be fun, and I promised you a fun date."

I open her door for her, loving her cute pout as she steps into my truck.

I get in my side and reach for the ignition, but Maggie is staring intently at me. I study her furrowed brow. "You okay?"

"Thank you," she says softly.

"For what?"

"For being patient with me. For pushing me to take a chance on us. I had an amazing time tonight."

I cup her cheek and blow out a rough breath. She may have focused on our sexual chemistry to distance me emotionally at times earlier, but her effort with me at dinner and now shows how hard she's trying to open up. We've both fantasized about each other for eleven long years. Delaying having sex would be cruel to us both.

I drop a kiss on her gorgeous mouth, murmuring the one word that defines us, "Inevitable."

Instead of driving us to the Barrel, I hit the gas and head to my place.

CHAPTER
Twenty-Three

"THIS IS BETTER THAN DANCING," Maggie says on a moan.

My mouth is on her neck, my hands squeezing her glorious ass as we dry fuck in my hallway. I'm hopped up on adrenaline and pheromones, aching for Maggie, her strawberry-amaretto scent driving me wild. I'm dying to fast-forward to the part where I thrust hard and deep into her, but she's pulling at my clothes, not giving us a chance to appreciate the beauty of this moment—the two of us finally, gloriously together. Her frenzied hands are everywhere, yanking at my belt, fumbling in her hurry.

I wrench away, stumbling back. "Truth or dare," I say.

She's panting, looking as ravenous as I feel, but her lips quirk. "Dare, of course."

It's our usual repartee, but I don't want usual. I want more from Maggie. "I dare you to kiss me without touching me."

A spark of surprise lights her face. "Dare accepted."

This is how I slow us down. Take us to the next level. Show her how much more we are than this blazing attraction, our deeper connection always hovering under the surface.

I crowd her, walking forward until I have her cornered against my hallway wall. Unlike Maggie's childhood home, my rented farmhouse doesn't have a Family Wall of Fame. The place came furnished with worked-in couches, white curtains, and simple wooden furniture. Nondescript but nice.

I suddenly crave splashes of color. A red accent wall the same color as Maggie's fiery hair. Framed photos of her bright smile. A room decorated with her fifties flair and my *non*-hipster style. More permanence in this comforting space I love.

I want a million more nights with Maggie, the two of us building a life together, and that starts here.

I plant my hands on the wall, caging her in, but I keep my body at a distance.

She knocks her head back and licks her lips. "Are you trying to torture me?"

"I'm trying to *show* you," I say as I brush our lips together.

I slant my mouth over hers, sharing her breath, ghosting our lips then pressing harder. So slow but thorough. I want her to feel my devotion, my absolute dedication to her pleasure and happiness. The kiss goes on and on, air sipped between deeper passes. My body is electric. On fire with wanting her, but I don't let us touch.

An eternity later, our lips slowly part. "You're amazing," I murmur.

Her lips are puffy, her sensitive skin pink from my beard. Marks that stoke the primitive man in me, who wants to growl, stake his claim, and call her *mine*.

Her eyelids flutter as she touches her lips. "That was...unexpected."

"In a good or bad way?"

She seems to press herself harder into the wall, her shoulders hitching higher. "Feeling what you make me feel terrifies me."

"Letting go is scary. *Falling* is scary, but I'm great with ropes and a belay. I'll always catch you."

"What if I can't do this?" She searches my face, her wide eyes darting. "What if I freak out and hurt you?"

I shrug as though the possibility is a nonissue. Total lie. Truth is, everything Maggie does affects me, good and bad. "It's a chance I'm willing to take."

Simple math. One plus one equals two. Maggie plus me is an equation I'm willing to gamble on.

I pick her up and swing her into my arms. She squeals, tossing her head back with an unabashed grin. I cradle her against my chest and walk us upstairs, toward my room, loving how she relaxes into me. She kisses my neck, that moment of intensity melting into something sweeter. The truth of us. We can be real together—intense, fun, honest, and everything in between.

I drop her at the foot of my bed, then start undoing the buttons on my shirt. "Race you to nakedness."

She quickly reaches for her back zipper. "You have a head start."

"I have more clothes."

Grinning at each other, we unlatch and untuck and unzip, hopping and stumbling in tandem. My shirt hits my dresser. Her heels get kicked off somewhere. My belt flings against the wall as I nearly trip on my jeans and briefs. Her dress and bra and sexy underwear wind up strewn all over my room, and Jesus *fuck*. Freckles. All of them. A galaxy of stars, decorating the full moons of her breasts, the crest of her belly, the womanly lines of her thighs and calves. A constellation of freckles I'd like to name *home*.

I grip my shaft, give it a squeeze. "You're a fucking fantasy."

She rolls back her shoulders, the confident move shredding what's left of my sense. There's nothing sexier than a woman comfortable in her own skin. "What do we do in this fantasy of yours?" she asks.

"You touch me. Everywhere. All at once. Or part of me. I

don't care. I just need your skin on mine." Now. Yesterday. Eleven years ago.

We move at the same time, meeting in a crushing embrace, and *yeah*. I knew feeling Maggie skin against skin would short-circuit my brain, but this smooth slide? Her soft breasts rubbing against my hard chest, the porcelain planes of her back and waist under my roving hands, our legs and hips meeting as my erection presses against her abdomen?

I was not prepared for *this*.

"I thought you were hot in high school." She charts my back, her palms sliding down to my ass. "But now? You're so fucking sexy, Lennon. And sweet and funny. You're…" She trembles as she trails off.

Everything in me clenches, including my heart.

I kiss her and move us to my bed. We fall together onto the mattress as her hands bump down the lines of my abs. My fingers dance on a swirl of freckles at her hip, then I toy with the delicate curls between her thighs, my mouth and tongue busy on her full breasts. I can't touch enough of her. Can't believe she's opening herself up to me, but it's a battle of wills. Maggie's hands are everywhere too. On my shoulders, my hips, my ass. She flicks her tongue over my nipple—a move that rips a gusty *Jesus* from me—while we touch and slide and slip against each other.

When her soft hand wraps around my length, my hips buck. She gives my shaft a few pumps, then she drags her thumb over the swollen head.

I hiss. "Fucking hell, Mags."

I'm so hard it hurts. A dribble of come escapes, and she pushes her finger through the wetness, branding me with fire. I move her hand off, can't take this much pleasure. "When I come, baby, it's gonna be inside you. But I think I'll taste you first. Lick that pretty pussy of yours."

Her eyes flare. "Someone's a dirty talker."

"Consider yourself my muse." I bite and lick her ear.

I move down her body, charting a course to my nirvana, and we both moan. My first lick up her slit has her bowing off the mattress. My teasing strokes have her clutching my hair. Enthralled, I go harder, flicking her swollen nub while marking her hips with my fingers.

She yanks my hair. "God, that feels *good*."

"It's about to get better." I go slower and make her curse. Rub my beard over her inner thighs, then go back for more. I want her desperate for her release. Desperate for *me* and more mind-blowing nights like this. When she bucks up and whimpers, I give her what she wants, sucking harder, flicking faster, until she shakes against my face, shouting *Fuck* and *Yes* and *Oh my fucking God*.

My Maggie fantasies didn't do her justice.

I rise over her and drag my forearm over my mouth, loving the taste of her on my tongue. "That was so fucking hot."

She reaches for my aching cock and gives it a squeeze. "I need you in me."

"You and me both." I fit myself between her thighs, but I pause. My dick is on fire, desperate to sink into her. But my heart's beating faster, swelling so large it jams up my throat. "You're sure you want me inside you bare?"

The question is quiet but serious. If she freaks out for any reason after this, I will not be okay. This quick-witted, complex woman, who undoes me with a flash of her smile, has embedded herself under my skin.

She runs her hands down my chest, along the V of my hips, until she has my length in her grip. "I'm sure."

Clearly, I did something right in my lifetime.

We shift together, my hips nudging forward as she places me at her opening. She doesn't move her hand like I expect. She leaves her fingers there, feeling me as my length pushes slowly inside her, a ridiculously hot move that has me nearly blacking out. She's a vision in shades of bliss. So damn sexy, squeezing me with her inner walls, touching my flushed cock as a rosy blush decorates her breasts.

Unable to keep still, I push in farther, the heat and pressure while bare blazing across my skin. The intensity is more than I expected. Everything about Maggie has always been more than I expected. The posh snob during the day, acting like a silly shark at night. The girl who ignored me in school, telling me her secrets at our pond. The woman who's done nothing but fight our connection, inviting me into her body.

I'm not sure how I got lucky enough to have Maggie Edelstein in my bed. I'm not sure how I'll sleep in here again without drowning in fantasies of her.

"Fuck, Mags." I thrust deep, bringing us flush. "How do you feel this *unreal*?"

She shifts under me, moving her hand away from where we're joined. She sighs as her body softens, giving me more access. "How can *you* feel this unreal?"

"I promise, your tight pussy feels better." Always a game with us, one-upping each other.

I pull my hips back, kiss her as I sink in deeper, rolling my body with the move. We set a rhythm, parting and joining, my hand on her breast, hers on my ass, both of us still touching our fill. When I pause and keep us flush but rock my hips forward, rubbing her deep, she arches her back with a throaty "*Yes.*"

My inner sex-savant takes a bow.

I give her more of that—long, dragging thrusts, followed by deep pushes that shake my bed and her body. She digs her knees into my waist, rocking against me, getting louder, moving more frantically. I pump harder, no longer able to hold on. I'm close, my legs on fire, a volcano of energy rolling at the base of my spine and tightening my balls. I push up quickly, needing her eyes. Those green beauties on me when we fall apart.

The second we connect, her eyes flare, turn watery and red.

My eyes and throat burn with all I'm not saying. The love I felt for her as a teen expands so fast, I can't imagine my chest won't burst from the pressure.

Abruptly, she closes her eyes, clenches her body tighter. I'm too far gone to force her eyes back on mine, plunging so fast and deep stars spark in my periphery, obliterating any other thoughts but this moment. *Maggie. Yes. Finally.*

She comes first, moving faster, tugging my hips as she contracts and calls my name. I tip over after her, coming with her name on my tongue, an ache in my chest, and my body spasming with a release so intense I'm shaking.

She pushes her hands through my hair after, rubs her cheek against my beard. "That was amazing."

Aftershocks continue stealing my sense, as does the hot rush of my release coating us both. I move my hips, getting off on all that wet heat, refusing to slip out of her. "We need to do that again."

"Are all hipsters this good at sex?"

Laughing, I bury my face into her neck. "Nope. Just me. Not that you'll ever find out, since you'll only be having sex with me for the rest of your life."

She stills under me, and I give myself a mental slap.

Way to go, idiot me. Delving into future talk when Maggie can't even hold eye contact for more than a second during sex is a winner of a move.

I slip out of her, hating losing the connection. "Let's pretend I didn't say that, shall we? Except the part where I'm the best at sex. Because I am."

She twines her arms around my neck, bringing our faces so close I can't read her expression. "I'm so happy we did this. I want to try to make this work—to get over my issues and trust these intense feelings. You're worth stepping out of my comfort zone, but like I said last night, I need to take the emotional side of us more slowly. Which means I should probably go."

I frown. "Go?"

"I'm not ready to sleep over yet."

My stomach sinks. As does the rest of me, deeper into the mattress. "Yeah, sure. Okay." Continued patience on my end is needed, which makes sense. She went through more than I realized after I left. She has to learn to trust herself with me and believe I won't inadvertently hurt her again. "I get it. We'll go at your speed."

"Physically, though, I'm all for pushing ahead." A hint of bashfulness threads into her voice. "There's actually something I kind of want."

I rub our noses together. "Do tell."

"I want to do what we did together that last night at the pond. Not now. Just…eventually. I want you to come on me like that."

Yep, I definitely did something good in a past life. "I'll think about it. I'm quite shy."

She snorts, eyes shining with amusement. "I love how much you make me laugh."

I love you, I almost say. But I'm not that big of a moron. I kiss her instead. Try to keep her with me a little longer. And plan for more time together. "There's an exhibit at the Yard Goat Gallery in a couple weeks. Art from local kids, and Max has some stuff up. Care to join me as my date?"

She slinks out of bed and starts getting dressed, but she shoots me a warm smile. "I'd love that. And I can cook you dinner tomorrow night, if you're free?"

"Count me in."

I pull on my jeans and shirt and walk Maggie to my truck. We don't talk much on the drive to her home, but the quiet is comfortable.

I park on her street and kiss her softly. "Sleep well."

She smiles against me. "Thanks for a great night."

She doesn't pause or glance back after she leaves. I watch her sashay to her front door, feeling mostly happy. I want Maggie back in my bed, cuddled up to my chest, but tonight felt like the start of something deeper between us, and I'm good with that.

A buzz startles me. One glance at my phone has me wishing I hadn't brought it tonight.

> Life Wrecker: I know you don't want to hear from me, but you left before I finished. There's something else you need to know.

A flash of anger blinds me.

How does he not understand how hard hearing from him is? Why can't he just let me go so I can get on with my life? I also want to throttle him for inadvertently hurting Maggie all those years ago. But I won't reply. I am nothing to that man, and he is nothing to me. As far as I'm concerned, Raymond S. Bower doesn't exist.

I move my thumb to power down my phone, but an email notification pops up. I frown at Mrs. Jackson's name.

I start reading her message. By the time I get to the end, my father's text is the least of my worries.

> *I'm sorry to do this, but I'm making some personal changes, and I've decided to sell the property. I have a buyer interested. It's in the very early stages of discussion, but if it goes through, she wants a short closing date. I'll give you as much notice as possible. Whatever happens, thank you for taking such good care of my family's home. It's been a joy having you as a tenant.*

I close my eyes, picture my morning working on the porch, walking the land, planning a fun surprise for Maggie, basking in the quiet of the serene area. I knew the property wasn't mine. I knew my rented home wasn't permanent. Still, the weight of my disappointment feels crushing.

CHAPTER
Twenty~Four

THE YARD GOAT Gallery is an artist co-op built into Windfall's old train station. The historic building has been lovingly restored to its original red brick walls and worn wooden floors. Big windows let in loads of natural light, and a number of artists share the vibrant space. This afternoon, they're hosting an exhibit to showcase talent from the local schools. You better believe my nephew is one of those exceptional kids.

Desmond is standing near a wall adorned with several framed drawings, his arms crossed and legs planted wide. Everything about his body language reads "stay away," but the guy is *grinning*. Full teeth, hearts practically exploding from his eyes. He's with Sadie, and Max is nearby, chatting to a young girl.

Since Maggie's meeting me here after she's done work, I head toward them. "Did you slip Ecstasy into his Metamucil this morning?" I ask Sadie.

She laughs and pulls me into a hug. "I can always count on you to keep Des humble. Thanks for coming."

I kiss her cheek.

Desmond's expression flips from heart-eyes to *fuck you*. "With comments like that, consider yourself uninvited to this event."

"I don't recall you buying ownership in this lovely gallery, so it's not your call."

Sadie shakes her head at us. "I'll let you two continue antagonizing each other. I need to chat with Jasmine's mom."

Des watches her leave, his smitten smile returning.

I nudge his arm. "Anything I should know about? What's with the moony grin?"

Sadie's probably home for longer than usual from traveling for work. Or they've made specific wedding plans. Or honeymoon plans.

He shrugs a shoulder. "Just had a good morning. And I love seeing Max's art up."

Huh. I expected something splashier to put the extra wattage in his grin, but after the life we've led, this makes sense too. Simple stuff can hit hardest. "You should be damn proud of Max. Which ones are his?"

Beaming—swear to God, the guy could double as a glow stick—he gestures to the two frames closest to us. One sketch is of a classic airplane, but half of it is transformed into a mythical bird, as though it's flying into another dimension, where it exists in a different corporeal form. The other is a winter landscape beside a pond, but the image reflected is more fantastical. The trees and rocks and flowers are dripping with jewels and grandeur.

"These are amazing. He'll be better than E soon."

Des grunts and lifts his chin.

"You scored in the kid department."

Another guttural sound, definitely in the chuffed neighborhood. My brother excels at nonverbal communication.

"As well as the fiancée department," I add.

This low rumble is accompanied by a long perusal of Sadie. Then he faces me. "You met with Dad."

It's a statement, not a question, and it's my turn to make a nonverbal sound. Mine hovers in snarl territory. Since Mrs. Jackson's unpleasant email, I'm more pissed than ever about Dad's book money. I've reached out to her about her property. Her sale price is fair. Her buyer is a friend of a friend of hers who might not be able to get financing, so nothing is set in stone. I, however, have money in a bank account ready to be used, and I'm pretty sure I could convince Mrs. Jackson to sell me her property. But every time I debate making the move, the words *blood money* swim through my head.

Des stares at my face, so intently I start to overheat. I expect him to launch barked questions, digging for dirt on why the Life Wrecker asked to meet. Why I shut the family out afterward, rock-climbing instead. The last thing I want to do right now is rehash that meeting. I'll just obsess more over Dad's dirty book money and his latest text I've studiously ignored. *There's something else you need to know.* Today is supposed to be a proud, happy day for Desmond.

A muscle worms in his jaw as he studies me. "Maggie still giving you a hard time?" he asks.

The question is a sharp U-turn, but I relax ten notches. I guess Des doesn't want to ruin today either. "Yes and no. We went on our first official date a few weeks ago, and we've seen each other a bunch since. Dinner at her place or mine." *With naked calisthenics before and after*, I don't add. "But she puts on the brakes when emotions run high. Won't do sleepovers or admit I'm her boyfriend."

He runs his tongue over his teeth. "Be patient. She'll come around."

She comes *around* me plenty. It's the idea of opening up more fully that's the issue. "Do you think she'd be pissed if I pulled the spark plugs on her Jeep? Stranded her so she has to sleep over?"

"Considering she seems like the type of woman who'd gather

your favorite hipster clothes and light them on fire for a stunt like that, I say go for it." He slaps my back. "I'll bring over marshmallows to roast."

Maggie wouldn't stop at lighting my clothes ablaze. She'd include my mountain bike and climbing gear. Rightfully so. "Guess I just need to be extra charming."

Des nods and stretches his neck, then his posture straightens. "Or I could help."

He struts toward the entrance, where Maggie just walked in. She looks stunning in her high boots and a green wrap dress, but I don't have time to appreciate her breath-stealing beauty. Not when my brother's about to do something that will no doubt embarrass the shit out of me.

Des walks right up to her. She startles briefly, then smiles at him. He smirks and leans closer to her, saying something quietly in her ear. I hurry over, but she already has a hand over her mouth and she's cracking up.

"Have a great night," Des tells me and punches my shoulder. The betrayer returns to his family.

I pull Maggie to a quieter end of the gallery. "How badly do I have to hurt him? Bruises, a break, or until he needs his jaw wired shut?"

Still laughing, she says, "Probably just a break."

I drop my head back and scrub my hand down my face. "What did he tell you?"

"Nothing bad. Just that you're a great cuddler."

"Okay…" I say slowly.

"From the time you got into bed with him," she adds, beaming. "He said you excel at spooning."

Honest to God. My fucking brother. "I was drunk. Totally shit-faced, and his room was right next to mine. Did he also mention he broke my rib when he sent me flying out of his bed?"

She presses her forehead to my shoulder, shaking as she laughs. "He did not."

"Whatever," I grumble and run my hand down her back. "I *am* an excellent cuddler, by the way. If there was a spooning competition, I'd win gold. It would be my honor to show you later."

Maggie's laughter trails off. She straightens and tightens the tie on her wrap dress. "Which pieces are by Max?"

Right. Max. *Art*. Topics such as cuddling and spooning still give Maggie hives.

I hold out my arm to her. "His are the best ones, obviously. Shall we tour the show, milady?"

"We shall." She takes my arm and relaxes.

Together, we tour the gallery. We praise Max and his amazing pieces. Maggie goes gaga over a miniature merry-go-round one kid made. I get lost looking at an exquisite painting of Elder Falls, remembering how special it was being out there with Maggie. I also tell Sadie that Desmond once drank too much Gatorade, and Jake jumped out of the bathroom to scare him, at which point Des peed his pants. His answering glare is worth the price of admission.

Maggie and I gather our coats and leave together, hands held on this brisk but bright evening. "Let's take a walk," I suggest. "It's too nice to be inside."

She gives my hand a squeeze. "Let's."

The sun has started to dip, painting the distant Rough Ridge Mountains a lighter gold. We stroll toward Corner Creek and the path behind the gallery, swinging our hands as the water gurgles steadily. A stretch of forest on the opposite side adds a hit of tranquility only nature can provide.

"I really missed this town," I say. "Doubt there's a prettier place in the world."

She makes a soft *mmhmm* sound. "Being with you in and around town is like being with a little kid."

Um, yeah. Not the comparison a man shoots for. "Maggie, I'm strong and masculine. I eat little kids for breakfast."

She snorts, leading us toward the small bridge ahead. "Of course you do. But you know that feeling kids give off—pure excitement over small things adults take for granted? When I'm around them, I look at the world through their eyes. See things in a fresh way. You do that for me with Windfall." We walk into the middle of the bridge, lean on the railing, and stare down into the burbling stream. "Everything's prettier when I'm with you. You remind me how lucky I am to live in this amazing slice of paradise."

Everything's prettier when I'm with you. Says the woman who thinks she can't handle the intimacy of commitment.

Unwilling to let those special words go unappreciated, I cup the back of her neck and tilt her face up to mine. "You're part of what makes this place so special for me. *You* make it shine."

Her pupils blow wider. There's a swirl of fear in their depths but also a hint of…wonder?

I turn us back to standing side by side, giving her a moment to let my words settle. We watch the water, practically leaning on each other as we rest our forearms on the railing.

"Reading," I say after a beat. "You mentioned a while back that you read lots."

"Every night before I go to sleep."

"Your nightly vacation to far-flung locations?"

She smiles. "Yeah."

I run my tongue over my teeth, wanting to dig deeper. Understand what makes her tick. Gentling my words, I say, "Is it because of your past? Your way to be wild and reckless without actually *being* wild and reckless? Living through an avatar, like you said."

She stares intently at the running water. "I've never analyzed it, really, but I bet that's part of it. Probably a big part, actually."

I rotate toward her, brush her hair behind her ear. "Is that why you won't sleep over too? Why you need to take things slow emotionally?"

"Because I like living wildly in my head?"

"Well, I *know* you don't need to read erotic romances these days. No avatar is needed when I'm in your life."

She presses two fingers to my abdomen and walks them up my chest. "Overconfident much?"

I grab her fingers and give them a kiss. "Am I wrong?"

She lifts her shoulder in a cheeky shrug. "When's the last time you tied me to a bed and brought out a whip?"

Jesus. My body heats, but only for half of that fantasy. "Do you want that?"

"No. Pain isn't my kink."

"Thank Christ, because I would not get off on hurting you." Although tying her up would be fun. A naked Maggie at my mercy.

"Would you have, though?" she pushes, studying my face. "If BDSM were something I wanted, would you have tried it?"

"I guess, yeah. Once to see if I could handle it." I lean into her ear and whisper, "My safeword would be Gingersnap."

She tips her head back and laughs. "That would cause me to inflict more pain on you, not less."

"So I'm the submissive in this fantasy of yours?"

"I don't have BDSM fantasies, babe. I love our sex life as it is."

"But you don't sleep over because of your past, right?" I ask gently. "Like reading is a way to deal with the wild side you don't want to unleash, keeping distance is your way of protecting yourself too. Not putting yourself in a position to be hurt or abandoned, like with your mom." *And like with me*, I don't add. Disappearing on her without a word.

She focuses on the wooden railing, picks at a loose splinter. "I'm practically a poster child for abandonment issues, aren't I?"

I wrap my arm around her, tug her into my side. "Sorry to push. I just want to understand you better."

She leans her head on my chest. "I don't mind talking about

it. I mean, it's not easy. Admitting weakness is hard, especially when it feels irrational. But it's nice being honest for a change."

"Amen to that. Ten years of lying was no picnic."

"It must have been brutal," she says, her voice tinged with sadness.

"It wasn't awesome, but I had fun at times. Invented wild stories to entertain myself."

"Of course you did." She wraps her arms around my waist in a comforting hug. "What was one of the best?"

"Definitely the time I told a coworker I grew up on a farm and lost my left foot to a tractor accident. I limped around a bunch, and he did half my work for me."

"Such a manipulator."

"I learned from the best," I say, less amused.

"You're nothing like your father, Lennon. You're kind and caring. You love your family fiercely and have been incredibly sweet and patient with me."

"Thank you," I murmur into her hair, breathing in Maggie and her words. The truth that I'm nothing like the betraying man who raised me.

Maybe that's part of why I hate the idea of using his book money. Profiting off our family's pain would make me more like him, even though I love my family more than my own life. I'd never choose cash over them. *You could use the money to buy your first home. Grow something good out of his deception.* Maggie's advice from weeks ago is even more apt now, and maybe she was right. Maybe turning that money into something good—a home, a real life in this town I love—would make me feel better about myself and my choices, not worse. Proof I'm nothing like that man.

I kiss her temple, brush my lips back and forth over her skin. When that's not enough, I dip my head down to taste her lips and this deeper honesty she's shared.

She sighs, tunneling her fingers through the curly ends of my hair. We share slow and gentle kisses—soft swipes of her tongue, a nudge of my nose against hers—like we're making small promises with every intimate touch.

Normally, this is when I'd ask her to come back to my place. Hope she takes a chance and sleeps over, while preparing myself for her rejection. After tonight's talk, I hold back. In time, she'll feel secure in us—*in herself*—to take that leap.

"I'll walk you to your car," I say instead.

She cuddles into my side as we meander along the path. Laughter echoes from outside the gallery, the cool November air tickling my nose. I hum the notes to "Can't Help Falling in Love."

Maggie stops. So suddenly, I stumble and nearly trip us both.

"You okay?" I ask, steadying her.

"Yeah, just…" She swallows and rocks on her heels. "Is it okay if I call you my boyfriend? I mean, only if people ask. I won't shout it randomly on the street."

A hot flare lights up my chest. "You want to claim me as yours, Mags?"

She nods, looking adorably shy. "I'm still not ready for sleepovers. Something about having my space in that way makes me feel safer. Which maybe doesn't make sense, but I was talking about you to a coworker today, and it felt weird calling you a friend when you're so much more."

Who needs sleepovers when I get tender vulnerability in addictive doses?

"I'd be honored to be your official boyfriend. But just so you know, you've been my girlfriend since your sister's birthday party. You have catching up to do."

She laughs and latches herself around my side again. I release a happy sigh, thankful for her trust and this step forward. Building a foundation on friendship, laughter, and amazing sex can only help us. When she's ready to be all in, everything we have will be heightened tenfold.

I walk her to her Jeep and pause by her door. "If you're free tomorrow, I have something on my property I'd like to show you."

She quirks her eyebrow. "If you're practicing trip wires and booby traps for your brothers, I'll pass."

"As entertaining as that would be," I say, feeling strangely self-conscious, "this is a specific surprise just for you."

Her expression softens. "I'd love to come."

I kiss her softly and watch as she gets in her Jeep and drives away. I turn to head to my truck, but I spot Mrs. Jackson walking toward the gallery with her grandson Kyle, his tattooed wife, Cearra, and their cute daughter.

Before I think too much, I jog up to them. "You guys heading to the gallery?"

They stop and Kyle smirks. "Excellent deduction skills, Sherlock."

"Ha, yeah. Sorry." The Yard Goat Gallery is the only building on this quiet end of the street. My sudden nerves are stealing my cool. "It's a great exhibit. You'll enjoy it."

"You seem to be enjoying yourself as well." Cearra gives me a knowing look. "Saw you chatting with Maggie by her Jeep."

"We're dating," I say, pleased I can share that fact with Maggie's blessing. But I face Mrs. Jackson, a tangle of jitters gathering in my stomach. "I'd actually like to talk with you for a minute, if you don't mind."

Holding her purse close to her plentiful stomach, she pats Kyle's arm. "Head on in without me. I'll meet you inside."

When we're alone, she smiles kindly at me. "This is about the property."

"It is," I say, barreling ahead. Not thinking. Not worrying. Just doing. "I love that house—the land and everything about it. Ever since you told me you wanted to sell, it's been eating me up. And I actually might have the funds to get a mortgage and buy it from you. Enough to match your other offer, and I swear

I'd take good care of the place. Not bulldoze it and turn into some fancy sterile house with no heart. I'd keep the integrity of what you and your family created, but I realize you've also made other commitments with that other deal."

"Lennon." Her full cheeks round with kindness. "I would love nothing more than to see you in that house. You've been doing work on the place, even when it wasn't your responsibility. With everything you and your family have been through, I'd be honored to be part of this new chapter of your life. The other buyer has been slow to move forward. If you can match the price, consider the house yours."

I nod as an overwhelmed flush moves up my neck. "Can you give me a couple weeks to figure this out? And if your buyer makes a move earlier, let me know."

"Absolutely." She dips her head, then walks toward the gallery.

I don't move, shocked I took this leap. Uneasy about actually using that money. Unsure I can handle the resulting guilt. But if I do this, if I get past my hang-ups, that land will be mine, including the surprise I'll be showing Maggie tomorrow night.

CHAPTER
Twenty-Five

"THIS PLACE IS AMAZING," Maggie says as we traipse through my large backyard, surveying the forest at our left and the rolling hills ahead. "I could sing to my heart's content, and no one would hear me."

"I do that all the time. I've perfected my modified Eminem song."

She grabs me by the front of my jacket. "If I ever hear that song again, I will smother you in your sleep."

God, I love her passion-fueled temper. The rise of color to her cheeks on this chillier night. "If you smother me with your tits, I'm all in."

"Imbecile," she mutters and walks on, tucking her hands into her coat pockets. "Tell me again where we're going?"

"It's a surprise. And do you really love this property?" It's dark out, but the moon and stars are shining, my eyes gradually adjusting to the blue-black intensity blanketing the land.

Maggie slows her pace to match mine. "Why would I lie about loving this property?"

"You wouldn't. I'm just extra-sensitive about it right now."

"No part of you is extra-sensitive. And don't you dare make

a dick joke."

The dick jokes are plentiful, but I don't cling to my usual method of deflection. Or the grin I usually sport around Maggie. I inhale a lungful of cold air, hold it a beat, then let it seep out. "I haven't mentioned it, but Mrs. Jackson is planning on selling the property, and I asked if she'd consider selling it to me."

"Oh wow." She stops walking, her usual wildfire expression more tender. "I had no idea you were thinking of buying it."

"I love the house. It's old but has great bones, and I'd work on it slowly over time. Renovate the smaller, outdated rooms, fix the falling-down barn, cut more trails through the trees. She's keen. Sounds like it'll actually work out, but..." I heave out a sigh.

"Why is there a but? Buying this place would be amazing. A house of your own."

"It *would* be amazing. I'm thrilled it's happening. I just don't love that my father's book money would be helping with the purchase."

"Oh." She studies her tall boots, then moves to stand in front of me. "I know I've said this before, but if you actually told that asshole off for being a supreme asshole, you might feel better about accepting his money."

"Ugh." I drop my head back, upping my dramatics. "Why do you keep harping on that?"

"Because he deserves to hear what you really think, and you deserve the closure that comes with getting it off your chest."

I still don't feel like I have closure, but she's wrong. Telling him off would only up my anxiety. Which is why I haven't told Maggie about his last text—the mysterious "thing" he still needs to tell me. Awareness of that message is a sliver burrowing under my skin, a sharp pinch I've studiously ignored. If I tell Maggie, she'll just push harder, when what I need is to forget that man.

"While we're on the subject of parents, have you mentioned

to yours that they put too much pressure on you to be perfect?"
Deflection for the win.

It's her turn to sigh and slump. "They don't put the pressure on me. I put it on myself."

"Sure, but it's all linked. You won't be able to change your inner dialogue until you change the dialogue with them."

"Maybe," she says, but I can tell she's brushing me off.

I'll push her more another day, the same way she'll keep urging me to confront my father. Nudging each other because we care.

I take her hand and twirl her away from me, drawing her back in an impromptu dance, finishing with a filthy kiss.

She hums against my lips. "What was that for?"

"For being you." And getting us to happier topics. "Have I mentioned I have a surprise for you?"

Her eyes reflect the twinkling sky above. "Have I mentioned I love surprises?"

"If you quit making out with me, we'll get there faster."

"Me? You're the one who—"

I steal another kiss, shutting her up in my favorite way. Soft, pliable lips. Seductive moans. A sensual swirl of our tongues, as the evening blankets us with privacy.

Slightly freaked about how hard I've fallen for her, I pull back and tug her through the property's winding trail. I can't help picturing the two of us living here together one day, strolling through the tall grasses at night, building a tree house in the forest, lying in the broad field, searching the sky for falling stars, painting the walls in our new home while also painting each other. A Maybe One Day fantasy.

When we crest the last rolling hill, Maggie gasps. "Lennon."

The large maple near the tree line is dripping with fairy lights, sparkling in the darkness—a reminder of our early days, swimming under a twinkle of lights.

"It's not a pond," I say, "but it's the closest I've got."

"I love it," she breathes.

Thank goodness for that. "Race you?"

"It's dark out. Do you want me to trip on a rock and maim myself?"

"Guess this is the only option." I swing her into my arms and jog toward our tree.

"You're crazy." She clings to me, nearly cutting off my airflow. "Put me down."

"I'll put you down when I'm good and ready." Which is basically never. I have a thing for holding Maggie in my arms. "Actually, there's a funky bog by the old barn. I'll drop you in there."

"Child," she mutters.

Slightly out of breath, I release her at the tree, making sure she drags down my chest achingly slowly. "Was that so bad?"

"You're a pest." But she can't hide the fondness in her tender gaze, or the way she's clutching my shoulders and flexing her fingers like she doesn't want to let me go either. "This is beautiful."

"*You're* beautiful. The lights only reflect what they see."

She bites her lip.

I rub our cold noses together. "Tell me." I stroke her hair back, keeping our eyes locked. "Where do you see yourself in five years? Professionally," I add, curious about her ambitions. Being under the twinkle lights is like being in that pond all those years ago, the two of us sharing our hopes and worries. "What does Maggie Edelstein want to be when she grows up? Besides a professional hot-dog mascot."

She steps out of my reach, does a slow walk around the tree trunk, dragging her fingers along the bark. A circling shark stuck on land. "I want to run the Downtown Development Association."

I whistle. "Queen of Windfall."

"Minus the crown."

"Oh no. There would be a crown made of zombie teeth and dentures to commemorate all your clever events." The Blood and Guts Festival. Her upcoming seniors day. Maggie's endless creativity and smarts putting Windfall on the map. "You'll do it. I have no doubt."

She leans into the trunk and shrugs. "Maybe."

"Maggie, you took one look at the wall in the cabin we painted, *after* you painted my dick, and turned it into a fun activity that kids will splash all over social media. One second, and you improved my business. You're smart and innovative and can do anything you put your mind to."

Something changes in her expression. Not quite the openness I see in small doses. More like an energy shift that slams into me, waves of appreciation pouring off her.

"Thank you," she says quietly.

"I only speak the truth."

"What about you?" She leans into the tree, pinning me with curiosity. "What does grown-up Lennon want to be?"

"Aside from a karaoke champion?"

She glowers. "If I ever hear that song again—"

"I get smothered by your tits." I wink at her. "I know."

"You truly have a death wish."

Her breasts are just that wonderful. Can't think of a better way to go. "Roots," I tell her.

"What?"

"Grown-up Lennon wants roots." I survey the grass and trees and rolling hills. The abundance of nature's bounty. "I also want world domination and a lifetime supply of Oreos, and I'm excited to expand my business. Building the adult component has so much potential, but this…" I pick up a rock and spin it in my hand. "The idea of having a real home seemed so impossible for so long. Aside from buying a silly movie poster, I never decorated my Houston apartment. Hated the idea of being there forever, but I was scared to leave. For safety reasons, obviously, and I worried about my family. So, I got on with my life. Built a business and experienced moments of success, but it all felt muted. I never felt like I belonged anywhere."

"That's a long time to feel adrift," she says, her voice tinged with sadness.

Eleven-plus years of feeling unmoored and unsettled.

I toss the rock and approach her, caught in her tractor beam, unable to resist her pull. "It was, but everything's different now. This house and the land—maybe buying it and being back in Windfall." I place my hands on the tree's huge trunk, caging her in. "You."

Her trembling breaths brush my neck. "Lennon."

"Shh." I don't want her to say she's not ready for more from me. Don't want her to reiterate her fears that I'm linked to the bad memories of her childhood self, or that her fear of losing me one day is bigger than our connection. All I want is for her to *feel*.

I graze my lips over hers, sultry and slow. Kiss her deeper, showing her how much she's adored. Confession in motion. She's part of the permanence I crave. Bursting sunshine in her sauciness, a windstorm of creative energy, lightning strikes of righteous indignation, a rainbow of laughter—that's the Maggie I want. All her seasons. The wild unpredictability of nature, beautiful and fearsome.

Her hands flex on my neck, sift through my hair. Ever so slowly, she opens her eyes and...fuck. *There.* That's what I've been missing. A bottomless well of affection beaming up at me. "Can I sleep over tonight?" she whispers.

I guess fairy lights are magic after all. "Only if you promise not to hog all the covers."

She smiles. "I'll promise that, if you promise to sleep naked."

"Maggie." I give her my sternest face. "I told you. I'm quite shy."

She tips her head back, laughing, and I swear to God the lights above wink down at me.

CHAPTER
Twenty-Six

MAGGIE STIRS BESIDE ME, a tiny shift and stretch that makes me smile. She half groans and half sighs, the pout of her lips so damn cute. Her light eyelashes flutter against relaxed cheeks.

"It's cold," she says, her voice husky and sleep-roughened. "Where are the covers?"

"Shh." I kiss her shoulder. "Don't move. I'm at three hundred and fifty-four."

"What?" This shift has more heft to it. Her arm connects lightly with my face. "What are you doing?"

"Counting your freckles. There's just so many of them. I'm enraptured." Waking up with Maggie is everything. The way she's cuddled into me, her leg slung over mine, my hand on her hip, as though I've found my place in the world. Like, *here I am. Finally. Exactly where I'm supposed to be.* Sleeping alone after this will suck.

"You're annoying is what you are." She kicks her legs like a tired child. "I need covers."

I roll on top of her, wrapping her in six-foot-one inches of naked man. "I'll be your covers."

Her *ugh* quickly turns into an *ahh* as my morning wood finds his favorite place. She wiggles her hips. "Someone's excited."

"I'm always excited with you."

We shift and moan, my shaft gliding over her slickening center. The thrill of rubbing together crackles through me, knowing how good it'll be when I slide inside. I move down her body, kiss the freckles I was attempting to count, lavish her beautiful breasts and nipples with attention. I fucking love her tits, so full and lush, her pert nipples sensitive as I flick them with my tongue. She moans and clutches my head. *Fuck yeah.* I nose and kiss her belly, dipping lower to those soft red curls that need their own shrine.

I blow air against her until she squirms. "If you're cold, I can come back up there."

She digs her fingers into my hair. "Don't you dare."

I chuckle against her and give her slit a long, slow lick. Her hips jerk on a soft moan. I tease her some more, dropping wet kisses and licks to her inner thighs, getting my beard all over her, moving closer to that swollen little nub, then away.

"Lennon." She squirms and curses. "I need…" She gasps.

I lick the folds flanking all that gorgeous wetness. "What do you need, baby?"

"More."

"More what?" I bite her thigh.

She trembles against me. "Make me come."

"My fucking pleasure."

I run the flat of my tongue up her center, then go in hard, flicking her clit, sliding one then two fingers inside her. I tap that special spot that makes her clench down on me. Work her over the way I've learned she loves, getting lost in the taste of her, how responsive she is, her throaty sounds of pleasure until she cries my name and damn near rips out my hair. Then I'm up and over her, pushing in with one deep thrust. I lift her ankles to my shoulders, all of her exposed to me—the bounce of her gorgeous tits, endless freckles I'll never be able to count. One heart I'm trying my hardest to capture.

"Your pussy is so hot and tight. Fucking perfect."

"I'm tight because you're—" she gasps as I thrust deep "—*big*," she finishes. "Fuck, you feel good."

"You're about to feel better."

I circle my hips, rubbing against her most sensitive areas. I shift my attention to her face. Wait for her to open her eyes. Connect with me before we fall apart. She does, and she's gloriously unguarded. A stolen moment when her lips quiver and her eyes get bottomless, locked on mine. A river of emotion flows between us, then it's gone. She squeezes her eyes shut again, severing our connection.

Something in my chest pinches, but I'm too dismantled to dwell. An inferno gathers at the base of my spine, so fucking hot and torturous in the best way. I drag against her tight inner walls, thrusting harder, faster. When she cries my name and contracts around me, I lose control, coming in endless streams.

I splay on top of her afterward, letting my full weight hold her down. "Are you warm now?"

"I can barely breathe now. God, you're heavy." She tries to push me off.

I don't budge. "You're stuck here for the day. You're not going anywhere. Call in sick at work." I suck lightly on her neck. "We can finger paint each other."

Her throaty moan is a delicious reward, then she stiffens. "Shit. Oh fuck. *Shit, shit, shit.*"

She shoves at me, and I move this time, my satiated limbs tensing for battle. "What happened?"

"Painting—I'm supposed to meet my mother before work." She's up and moving, looking bewildered as she glances wildly around the room. "She's surprising my dad by repainting his study, and I'm supposed to help her move the furniture. I just...I don't know how I forgot."

Shit. Oh fuck. Shit, shit, shit is right. It took weeks for Maggie to build up the courage to sleep over. To trust me and trust she wouldn't get so consumed with us she'd neglect other aspects of her life. Now she's a wild woman, stumbling over herself as she snatches up her bra and underwear. It takes several tries for her to get them on.

Unsure how to stem her panic, I pull on my sweatpants and stand at a distance. "If you're a bit late, I doubt your mom will be mad."

Without glancing at me, she mumbles under her breath, then storms into the bathroom and knocks the toothpaste and her bottle of moisturizer on the floor. A few swears later, she grips the sink edge and drops her head forward.

Tentatively, I follow her trail of wreckage and run my hand down her back. "I'm sorry I kept you in bed."

She slumps. "It's not your fault. It's mine. I forget things easily and am usually on top of writing myself notes—reminders so I don't lose track of my to-do list. And I set alarms on my phone." She glances at me over her shoulder, her features tight. "My phone's downstairs in my purse and my written calendar is at home, so I'm having a freak-out. I'm sorry. I'm feeling panicky and angry at myself, and I'm taking it out on you. Just give me some space, okay?"

Her intense reaction isn't so different from my claustrophobia. Fears and freaking out when outsiders can't see the walls closing in. It's a shitty way to feel, and I hate this for her.

I nod and do as she asked—head downstairs to give her space, when all I want is to help her somehow. Last night, talking about our future goals, challenging each other, making love, and waking up to her wrapped in my arms cemented how vital Maggie has become to my life. But her fears are obviously still alive and well.

Feeling tense, I move stiffly around my kitchen, fill my

teakettle, plunk down a mug, and rummage noisily for a spoon. I hear Maggie before I see her, rushing down my stairs. I meet her by my front door, ready to haul her against my chest and give her a reassuring hug, but she doesn't look at me or pause.

She grabs her jacket and purse and calls a quick, "Talk later."

The door slams in my face.

"Thanks for sleeping over," I mutter. "I had a great time too."

I walk back into my kitchen and shove a tea bag in my mug, hating the prickly sensation at the base of my skull. The sharp stabs firing in my gut. I'm annoyed with Maggie. I feel badly that she struggles with her focus and almost missed meeting her mother, but she all but brushed me off. The irritable sensations remind me of my edginess in high school, my resentment at her dismissals.

I glance at my phone, debate calling or texting her. Explaining that she needs to consider my feelings too, but my face goes hot. A hint of anxiety pitches in my stomach. I swallow hard.

I don't want to make this about me, which must be why I feel off. Maggie asked for space. Disregarding her needs would be disrespectful. Avoiding a confrontation with her is a *kindness* on my part.

Forcing a slower breath, I settle at my kitchen table and inhale the sweet, grassy scents of my fair-trade green tea. I recall what a great night we had together. Surely the good will outweigh the bad in Maggie's mind.

My phone pings with a text, cutting through my thoughts. When I see *Nemesis*, I freeze. If she's already backpedaling, deciding being unhappy on her own is easier than being happy with me, I'm not sure how I'll return to kissing her goodnight at my door. Or even worse, to her fighting harder against our connection.

Stretching my tense jaw, I read her message.

Nemesis: Will you meet me for lunch?

I narrow my eyes and scratch my chest. She hasn't dismissed me with "Bye, Lennon," like after our first kiss. Still, there's no warmth or affection in the perfunctory text.

Me: I was planning a hunger strike, but I'll put it off. What's the dress code? Black tie?

Nemesis: No dress code. Meet me at 12.

Her lack of comeback to my jokes isn't a good sign. She's giving me no signs at all.

Me: Naked it is. See you at noon.

Dots indicate an upcoming reply, likely an irate comment, warning me not to show up naked. All I get is a thumbs-up.

I squint harder at the exchange, trying to ascertain her headspace. I get absolutely nothing. Maggie has once again become impossible for me to read. I sip my tea, forcing the hot liquid down my throat. Maybe I should wear Desmond's football gear to our lunch. Something thicker than skin and bone to protect my heart against whatever I'm about to face.

CHAPTER
Twenty-Seven

HAT AND SCARF ON, I wait for Maggie outside town hall, decidedly not hungry for lunch. Awareness of an impending Maggie meeting usually has me caught in a mix of keyed-up excitement and anticipation. All I feel today is mildly nauseous.

Townsfolk hurry by, bundled up to their chins. I hunch to ward off the cold as a halo of permed curls walks toward me. There's no other way to describe Sandra at this moment. Her scarf is tied so high around her face all I see is her tightly curled brown hair bobbing my way.

She stops in front of me and pulls down a sliver of her blue scarf, revealing her nose and mouth. "When you need my services, I'm good at sourcing information."

"Okay," I say, attempting to dissect her offer for clues. "Why, pray tell, might I need your information-sourcing services?"

"You'll know soon enough."

Her face disappears back behind her scarf, and she continues toward Main Street, leaving me leery. Sandra is ground zero for town gossip, but I have no idea what she knows.

With no clues to unravel her riddle, I resume my waiting. Maggie's late coming down from work, which doesn't help my agitation. I shift on my feet to keep warm. Any longer out here and I'll need to start doing Zumba to avoid frostbite.

Attempting distraction, I check out the revamped decor on Main Street. The bloody skeletons and beet-smeared Halloween masks are down. Bouquets of evergreen cuttings are tied to the lampposts in their places, half of them adorned with bright holly berries, the others with large blue dreidels. I think back to some of my talks with Maggie and realize Chanukah is in ten days, which happens to fall on my birthday. Maybe we can plan a combined Chanukah and thirty-first birthday bash, *if* she doesn't drop-kick our relationship to kingdom come.

"Lennon, hey."

I look up. My former pal Mizhir is only a few steps from me, blinking as though he wasn't looking where he was going. I certainly didn't notice him, and seeing him right now ratchets up my discomfort.

"Heard your adventure camp's doing well," he says.

"Littlewing has been well received, thanks." I force cheer into my tone, even though the question is a throwaway salutation. It's not like the guy cares what I'm doing. "The adult portion, Bigwing, launches in the spring and should be great. Especially the nudist aspect. Makes wearing the harnesses for the ropes courses mighty interesting."

He laughs. "I miss your jokes, man. You always cracked me up."

If he misses my jokes so much, why didn't he bother returning most of my calls after he left for college? Whatever. Time marches on, even if you've fallen out of line. "Always happy to amuse."

His next laugh comes out awkward. "Yeah, well. Gotta run." He opens his mouth again, as though to say something else, but he just waves weirdly and moves along.

I find myself scowling at his back. This brief interaction was no different from our others—surface chitchat, neither of us taking concrete steps to reconnect. A step I refuse to initiate. *Not* because I'm avoiding conflict. With our history, it's his move to make.

A flash of red catches my eye, and my annoyance reverts to unease. Maggie is on her way over, hurrying through the chill. Normally I'd open my arms to my favorite fiery woman, draw her into a hug. Whisper filthy things in her ear. Unsure where we stand and what this lunch entails, I shove my hands into my pockets.

She stops a foot away. "Thanks for coming."

I offer a stiff nod. "How was your morning?"

"Okay." She tugs her coat tighter and peers at me more intently. "You okay?"

Heat pinches the back of my throat. The urge to tell her this morning was rough on me rises, but I swallow hard. "I'm fine."

She stares at me a moment longer, a furrow denting her brow. "So, um. I kind of planned a thing."

"A thing?"

She juts her chin toward my shoulder, motioning to something behind me. I turn and see a lone tent set up in the middle of the grassy square. So stuck in my head, I hadn't noticed it. There's no one hanging out in the square, because it's a freeze-your-balls-off November day, but that looks like E's blue two-person tent. "We're camping in town with E?"

"He lent me his tent." Her arms come around me from behind, and she fits herself against my back. "I didn't handle this morning well. I wanted to make it up to you and planned a picnic lunch."

My heart thumps a relieved beat. "I'd love a picnic," I say quietly, gathering her arms more firmly around me, wanting to lock them in place.

Holy *fuck*, do I have it bad for this woman.

I don't say more about this morning, and she doesn't

embellish on her apology. She's here. She planned a special lunch for us. That sentiment is all that matters.

She grips my hand and leads me to the tent but stops outside. "I need to organize. Give me a sec."

"Okay, but if I get a better offer to eat the roadkill I passed on my way to town, I might take it. I suggest you're quick."

Mock glaring at me, she smacks my chest then disappears inside the tent.

"Okay," she says a moment later and pokes her head out. "Your picnic awaits."

Her crooked smile is too cute, equal parts nervous and excited. No longer wary or frustrated, I cram my big body inside the tent and *yeah*. There goes my heavy pulse again.

A checkered cloth is on the tent floor, as are a collection of my favorite foods: Smash Shack strawberry milkshakes, tofu tacos from the Hot Vegetarian local food truck, along with a couple of Delilah's face-sized M&M's cookies. There's even a battery-operated space heater next to Maggie's coat and gloves. The woman of the hour is sitting cross-legged at the far side, biting her lip, watching my every move. A wave of emotion pushes at my chest.

Calm the fuck down, heart. Now's not the time to get carried away.

This is just lunch. An apology. Maggie hasn't indicated she's as deep in this relationship as I am.

I shove my hat and coat against the side and sit across from her. "I can't believe you made all this yourself."

She laughs. "I at least get points for driving around and picking it up, right?"

"You get all the points," I say, my voice turning low and rough. The top two buttons of her blouse are undone, a tease of red lace peeking out. "I'm hungry for everything in here."

Her nostrils flare. My body tightens with need, but we're in a tent in the middle of town. Best if we keep things PG-13.

I lift my milkshake and hold it toward her. "A toast to you

6 CLUES YOUR NEMESIS LOVES YOU   245

and this awesome picnic." Smiling over our straws, we clink cups then sip our drinks, and *yes*, that groan I make is part lust for Maggie and part strawberry-milkshake heaven. "Tell me all about painting with your mom and your morning at work."

She takes another long sip and sighs. "Do you want the bad news first or the painful news?"

"With options like that, how's a guy supposed to decide?" I break off a piece of cookie and hold it out to her. "Let's go with bad."

Instead of taking the treat with her fingers, she leans forward and wraps those sexy lips around the cookie, sucking on my fingers before she pulls back.

PG-13

PG-13

PG-13

I blow out a measured breath. "You're cruel."

She winks. "As for the bad news, Mom knocked over the dark purple paint, which then ran through a rip in the drop cloth, and the carpet in Dad's office is oatmeal."

"Yikes." I lift my cup again in salute. "Here's to new carpeting."

"And to the fact that my father doesn't have a temper."

We clink and sip. "Hit me with the painful news before we devour these tacos."

She rubs the bridge of her nose. "The cidery has a plumbing problem. My seniors event is in five days, and the lunch was supposed to be there. As you can imagine, Shannon is not impressed with me."

"But it's not your fault."

"Sure, but it's my event. The one that needs to prove how organized and responsible I am after the last fiasco. She gave me her dreaded bland face and said, '*Fix this, Maggie.*'"

"The bland face." I shudder. "How did you survive?"

"By not going down without a fight. I've already found a

new venue. Stallard Winery offered to move around an event and fit us in, but I've basically promised them my first child."

I balk at her. "Without asking my permission first?"

She snorts out a laugh, then drops her gaze. More eye-contact avoidance, all because I couldn't resist a joke about our future children. Except I'm not really joking. I'm planning any and all of my kids to be shared with Maggie Edelstein, but joking without thinking is my kryptonite. Pushing us toward future talk, when Maggie's happy living in the moment.

"I jest," I tell her. "If your firstborn is with Hagrid—"

"*Harrison.*"

"Whatever. Giving the kid away might not be so bad."

She leans forward and punches my shoulder. "Be nice."

"I'm always nice." And horny when I'm with Maggie. "Have I told you how hot you look today?"

"Me?" She chews another piece of cookie and licks her luscious lips. "All I'm thinking about is how to get my mouth on your thick cock without getting covered in tofu tacos."

"Jesus, woman." I rub my hand over said cock as I clench and hold.

Her heavy-lidded eyes zero in on my straining fly, killing me. "Unfortunately, my boss could walk by here at any moment, and I can't return to work covered in guacamole and secret sauce. The blow job will have to wait. And I believe it's your turn to share. What's the latest on your father's tell-all? Family meeting still set for Tuesday?"

My body instantly cools. I grunt the affirmative.

Discussing anything related to my father makes me feel like I'm still lying about his latest text, which isn't a lie because that's not what she asked. As usual, the Life Wrecker does an excellent job infecting my life without even being here.

The new topic my father is intent on discussing is likely also about his book. Mom probably knows the dirt already. She didn't organize our family meeting as quickly as I expected. The delay could be linked to whatever new bomb his tell-all dropped, beyond the affair that led to his criminal activities. Or it's the affair that has her upset, and she needed time to digest that information. Or this new topic is totally unrelated, and we're about to be thrown for a whole new loop. Regardless of the outcome, I'm dreading our Bower family chat.

"I wish you could come," I say, even though our meeting is the same day as her important seniors event.

"Oh, Lennon. I'll be—"

"I know you can't," I cut in quickly. "Totally get it. Just want you to know I want you there."

She reaches over and takes my hand. "We'll hang out after, okay?"

I kiss her knuckles. "Absolutely. For now, we have more delicious food to eat while you tell me about the blow job you wish you had time to give me."

She laughs and tosses a piece of cookie at my face. We eat and talk, cozy in our tent of two, the outside world banished for a spell. Like we're at her pond, our secret place where nothing and no one can touch us.

Until I hear hushed whispers coming from outside the tent, way too close for comfort.

"Are they in there?"

"They're definitely in there."

"Are you sure?"

"I helped her set up the tent, and Sandra said she saw them go in."

E's and Delilah's voices are easy to recognize, and I tense. The only reason those two are staking out our tent picnic is if they're up to no good. Even worse, it appears as though Sandra ratted me out to my obnoxious brother.

Maggie freezes, eyeing the zipped exit. "This is not going to end well."

"I'll take care of the heathens," I tell her, then give the

shadowed side of the tent a slap. "Get the fuck away from our private luncheon."

"No can do," E says, sounding way too amused. "Delilah dared me to fart inside there, then zip it up and lock you in."

"I did *not* dare him to do that," comes Delilah's panicked voice. "Babe. You can't."

"I can and I will. This is the guy who dared me to eat a cactus."

"But you're the idiot who actually ate the cactus."

Maggie morphs into a fiery she-devil intent on razing the earth. "If he unzips this tent, I will fucking kill him."

"Not if I kill him first." I lean over our mostly finished food and cup Maggie's cheek. "If I don't make it out the other side of this alive, please build a very muscular statue of me to immortalize this battle."

She clutches her chest in rapture. A woman sending her beau off to war. "You better come back to me. But if you don't, you'll look like a bearded version of Dwayne 'the Rock' Johnson."

God, I adore this woman.

I kiss her hard on the lips, then turn as the zipper starts to slide down. As expected, E's butt pushes through—thankfully clad in jeans—and I don't wait for the moron to let one rip. I lunge forward and punch his butt cheek, sending him sprawling on his face.

He recovers quickly, running away from me. I'm hot on his heels, blasting from the tent and hitting my stride. *The asshole is going down.* E laughs while he's running, dodging left and right as I lunge for him. I grab his jacket, but he slips away. Changing tracks, he glances at me over his shoulder, heading back toward the tent. In his cockiness, he doesn't see a wayward branch on the grass. The second he stumbles, I'm on him, dragging him down, panting and growling and getting him under my control.

Unlike Des or Jake, I don't punch E in the kidneys like he

deserves. I get on top of him, hold my forearm against his throat, then shove my hand up his shirt and find his nipple.

I twist. He yowls.

I jump off him, fist punched up, and do a mini victory lap.

"I won't be able to breastfeed now," E whines from the ground.

"Serves you right." I help him up, the two of us dusting grass off our clothes. "I can't believe what a dick you are."

"Since when can't you take a joke?"

"Since every moment with Maggie is a balancing act, like I'm one wrong move from losing her."

We stand together, far enough from the girls that they can't hear us. They're having their own private gossip session, stealing glances at us while whispering to each other.

E slaps my back. "She's smitten. When women do the whisper thing with their friends, it means they have feelings. Big feelings they can't say out loud yet."

"Yeah, well. Maggie's big feelings are wrapped in bigger feelings, and those bigger feelings have feelings of their own. Suffice it to say, convincing her to trust herself with me isn't straightforward."

"And yet you're still crazy for her."

I let out a roughened grunt. There isn't much else to say.

E picks a dead leaf out of his hair and flicks it on the ground. "Are you dreading our family meeting as much as I am?"

"Nothing good will come out of the tell-all. Also…" I haven't shared the details of Dad's bank account with any of them yet. Dealing with them all at once seemed like an easier prospect than getting hit with random buckshot at different times. Except E's the most sensitive of us. He'll understand why I shut down after that reunion. Why I'm still struggling to decide whether I should use Dad's book money to buy my house.

He squints at me. "If you want to share in the sharing circle before you're faced with Desmond's wrath, I'm all ears."

"Probably the smart move," I say, suddenly antsy to unload the drama.

I give him the truncated version of the meeting with Dad and his brutal apology: Raymond S. Bower only caring about himself, the money we now have, my issues using it, and the text I haven't answered, skipping the part where he cheated on Mom. I don't have the stomach to watch E get extra angry while in the middle of an interrupted date.

He shifts on his feet and kicks at the grass. "Our father really is a piece of work."

"He's something, all right."

"As far as the money goes, I have no qualms using his cash."

"None at all?"

"You know I hate that he wrote this book. I hate that he treated you like you didn't matter. But I'm tired of being beaten down and blindsided by him. I think we deserve some fucking compensation. He didn't earn that cash. *We* earned that money through our suffering. So yeah, I think we should all use that money. *You* should use it to buy your first home."

"But I don't want to absolve him of his guilt," I say, voicing thoughts I hadn't fully realized until now. "I think that's part of what's bugging me. Accepting it will make him think he's forgiven."

"Our father is a lot of things, but stupid isn't one of them. He knows nothing can change what he did. If anything, taking it might make him feel shittier. Every time a royalty check comes in, a check he can't use, it'll remind him that his actions had repercussions."

I chew the inside of my cheek, still on the fence but slipping to the *yes* side every time I discuss the issue. Desmond doesn't know about this money, but he used his WITSEC principal without batting an eye. Maggie thinks I should use the cash. E agrees, and I really want that land. I also want to slip out of Dad's emotional hold on me. I have a feeling *not* using the money will torment me more than living in the home I'm dying to call mine.

"About the other text you haven't answered," E says, "Any thoughts on what he still wants to talk about?"

I'm about to say *the book*—another revelation to piss us off—but I dig my heel into the grass, making a deep divot. There's another possibility that makes sense, a potential reveal I've been trying to ignore. "I could be off, but I've been wondering if he's sick. It would make sense with the money. If he's dying, he won't need it. And the whole lame apology attempt might've been him setting his affairs in order."

Or maybe he'll tell us he's sick, but it'll be a lie. A way to weasel back into our lives, then *bam*. He'll be miraculously recovered, his free pass to once again be our father dripping with deceit. For some reason, my hands shake. I shove them into my pockets.

E rubs the scar on his lip, looking as edgy as I feel. "It's a possibility but could be a stretch. Whatever it is, something's off. Mom waited a long time between finishing that book and organizing the meeting."

"Yeah." That's all the wisdom I've got. There's no point guessing what our father is up to. There's only linking arms, bracing our legs, and hoping we're strong enough to withstand his next storm. "Speaking of being sick, I should tweak your nipple again. Test if multiple times still makes you nauseous like when we were kids."

E splays his hands on his chest. "No fucking way."

"You're the one who ruined my lunch. And—" I flinch away as he strikes a weird karate-type pose. "What the hell are you doing?"

"Fighting you off."

Aside from running, E was never a natural at sports or athletics or general coordination. Apparently, he still isn't. I match his asinine pose, trying to reach his chest, the two of us laughing as we swat at each other and pretend we can do karate.

"You guys know there's something wrong with you, right?" Maggie calls.

I wave at her while grabbing for E. "You can have our autographs later."

"It was WITSEC," Delilah tells Maggie loudly, making sure we hear. "Sadie and I have discussed it at length. All that time in seclusion stunted their maturity. Sorry to say, but what you see is what you get."

E and I slap and kick at each other some more, grinning and laughing.

Maggie shakes her head, watching us be assholes. "Can we apply to the government for new models?"

If that works for them, maybe I can apply for a new father too.

CHAPTER
Twenty-Eight

BLUE HAIR and dentures abound in Windfall this afternoon. Seniors shuffle about, chatting affably with townsfolk and perusing the local shops. I stand beside my truck, taking in the jovial mood and busy sidewalk, so proud of Maggie for creating another wonderful event. She even set up tables in the middle of town square with games of chess and checkers. A small crowd is gathered there, enthralled by the players. If I didn't have a Bower family meeting in thirty minutes, I'd be enjoying the scene, heckling the chess players and helping old ladies cross the street.

But I do have a meeting. And a headache. A knot in my neck kept me up most of the night. Or maybe that was my mind spinning to all the ways today is going to suck, which has contributed to the dark circles under my eyes.

Maggie's outside Sugar and Sips, leaning over a table of two older gentlemen. She smiles and laughs—her *real* smile and laugh, loose and unabashed—and the tension in my neck eases a fraction. I didn't plan to come here. I intended to drive to Desmond's and get there early. Spend time with my brothers before our worlds are turned upside down again, but I somehow wound up here, searching for my favorite shade of red.

I haven't seen Maggie since our picnic. Five days of missing her between quick texts and daily phone chats. She said she was busy with this event, getting organized and putting out last-minute fires, but I have a sinking feeling she's replaying our last morning together. How angry she was at herself for forgetting to help her mother, wondering if dating me is bringing out her most-hated traits. She may have planned that apology picnic, but I know Maggie. Setbacks sit with her.

As far as I'm concerned, there's no option but us staying together. I've never been as happy as I am when I'm with her. Ginormous Expectation Land—fairy lights twinkling above us, gorgeous hikes, karaoke ambushes, winter tent picnics, sharing our future hopes and dreams, laughing as we're tangled in the sheets. I'm pretty sure she's never had as much fun as she does with me. She's told me plainly how much I make her laugh. We support each other, push each other. We listen to each other when we need to vent. Which, I guess, is why I came here instead of going to Desmond's. I need a shot of Maggie Edelstein to soothe my nerves.

I walk across the street and wait as she finishes buttering up the gentlemen sipping their coffees and eating their baked goods.

She waves when she sees me but returns her attention to her audience. "If I ever meet April, I promise I won't tell her about the chocolate cookie."

"You better not," the man grumbles. "My daughter is a lawyer."

She pats his shoulder. "Your secret is safe with me."

The way she's bent over, her jacket hangs open and the neckline of her top dips. The man across from her wearing the fedora, who has an ample view of her cleavage, grins at her tits. "It's been a splendid day. Hope you organize it again next year."

I have no doubt this fine sir has had the time of his life. The memory of staring at Maggie's boobs will keep him happy for weeks to come. At least, that's the effect her full breasts have on me.

She straightens and swishes my way. "To what do I owe the honor?"

I kiss her cheek. "Just needed to see you."

Her face softens, but she takes my elbow and leads us to a quiet lamppost. "You're nervous about the meeting."

As always, Maggie reads my mind. "It's either that or I drank six Red Bulls without realizing it." My jittery heel bounces, proving just how strung out I am.

"Will everyone be there?"

"The whole messed-up Bower clan." Cheers come from the square, capturing our attention. Another rush of pride swamps me. "The event looks like it's a hit, as I knew it would be."

Maggie beams, taking in the clusters of seniors smiling by the bookstore. A few other pairs leave galleries and boutiques with shopping bags. "Honestly, it's been amazing. They've been having fun and spending money. I even think the winery was a better lunch venue in the end."

"Of course it was. They had to earn your firstborn." She gives her head a rueful shake. I tuck a loose strand of hair behind her ear. "You won't have to worry about seeing Shannon's bland face after this."

"I think she'll be pleased. But back to you." Maggie thrusts her shoulders back, hitting her army-general posture. "Whatever happens with your family, it'll be fine. You'll be fine. You have your brothers, and they have you. The Bowers are a force to be reckoned with."

"Will you come with me?" The question's out before I think better of the request. She's already told me she needs to be here. This event is important for her career. "Sorry," I say quickly. "Ignore me. I know you can't come."

I glance away from her, rub the back of my overheating neck. She's right. The meeting will be fine. I'll be fine. If Dad's sick, nothing changes. He's still an asshole out for himself, but my throat tightens and my eyes burn. I bite my cheek and study my shoes, unsure what the hell is wrong with me.

"I'll come." Maggie threads her fingers with mine, pulling my attention from the cobbled stones to the compassion in her searching eyes. "The event's almost over. All that's left is loading the seniors onto buses, and each bus has staff to help."

"You're sure?" I hold my breath, too relieved to believe her.

She nods. "I want to be there for you."

"God, I love you," I say on an exhale and immediately tense.

Maggie's eyes go unpleasantly wide—*shocked* wide, deer-in-the-headlights wide—and I curse myself. She's not ready for *I love you*, but I won't apologize for blurting out my true feelings. I love this woman. Real love. Not nineteen-year-old infatuation. The kind of love that grabs you by the chest and squeezes.

"I know you're not ready to say it back," I tell her softly. "The words were just too big to keep in."

She nods and touches her neck, her attention darting to my face and away. "I wasn't expecting… We're just out here, and—"

"Mags?"

She looks at me desperately, like I might hold the answer to world peace. "Yeah?"

"Do you want a lift to Des's, or will you drive yourself?"

She startles at my off-topic question, as per my plan. Distracting her with tangible issues is better than her overthinking my confession into oblivion.

"Right. Yeah." She surveys the street again, her moves jerky. "I have a couple last-minute things to do. I'll meet you there."

I pull her against me, hold her until she relaxes slightly. "I can't thank you enough for coming with me. And look out for the gramps in the fedora. He was eyeing your boobs."

She laughs, but the sound is stilted. With a quick cheek kiss, she returns to her duties.

I watch her a moment longer. Wait for her to glance at me again and give me her soft eyes. She keeps her back to me and doesn't turn once.

CHAPTER
Twenty-Nine

AN HOUR LATER, Desmond and Sadie's house is full of Bower boys, each of us antsy in our own special way. Des is wearing his resting mad-at-the-world face, alternating between gnashing his teeth and looking wistfully at the ceiling. Sadie just flew in from a stint of work in Arizona and is upstairs with Max. Des gets extra ornery when she's not in touching distance.

E and Delilah are at the kitchen counter, all over each other. Or more to the point, Delilah is rubbing E's back and whispering to him while he leans on her and destroys his cuticles. Jake is standing solo with his beefy arms crossed and face hard—the oldest brother and Bower bouncer. One wrong move, and he'll haul your ass out of here.

Then there's Cal. He's talking to Mom, nodding and smiling his congenial smile. He's the brother who sees the silver lining. The one who puts everyone before himself and probably does deals with the devil to solve our problems. If he's stressed and worried about this meeting, I don't see a hint of it.

Unlike my predictable brothers, I haven't resorted to my usual modes of self-defense. Not one joke has been uttered since I walked in here.

"Do you want water?" Maggie asks me. I wasn't sure what to expect with her since my blurted *I love you*, but she showed up as promised. She's been sweet and kind, shooting concerned glances my way, asking how she can help, but she's also felt distant.

I wrap my arm around her. "No, thanks. I'll just puke it up."

She rubs my stomach but doesn't tuck in closer like she normally would. "Are you more worried about your dad's book or telling your brothers about the money?"

"Yes," I say.

She gives my abdomen another pat. "Everything will be fine."

Before my nervous stomach folds in on itself, Mom calls us into the living room. Once inside, no one sits. I don't even call dibs on the divan-chaise-longue-*whatever*, which is incredibly comfortable but will do nothing to alleviate my building ulcer.

I really don't know which part of this meeting I'm dreading most. Talking again about my reunion with Dad will bring back the ugly feelings I've been trying to forget. Hearing what Mom learned, how upset and mad she might be, has the potential to break me or provoke my anger. Probably ruin my ability to rationally explain about Dad's guilt money.

I search for saliva in my mouth and attempt to swallow. It's a Herculean effort.

Mom surveys her boys and takes a deep breath, but I step forward and clear my throat. "You all know I recently met with Dad," I say, stealing the floor. Whatever Mom says will only make me feel worse. Better to get my announcement over with.

My brothers wait on me, faces tense and unforgiving. I look to Mom for approval. She nods her encouragement.

"So." The tension in the room balloons. Locating my saliva gets harder. "Dad dyes his hair," I blurt. "Awful dye job. Pretty sure there will be a comb-over soon."

And there we have it, my ill-timed humor resuscitated to make everything awkward.

Jake rolls his eyes.

Cal nods sagely. "Good intel."

Desmond's face is a picture of frustration. He appears to be rehearsing for a role in the classic sixties movie *This Man Must Die.*

E smirks at him. "I feel it's my duty to explain to Sadie that you look most like Dad and are heading for comb-over land. I wonder if she'll cancel the wedding."

Des sucks on his teeth. "The only thing getting canceled is your invitation."

"Lennon," Mom says, not letting her idiot sons distract her from why we're here. "It's okay. Whatever your father said or did, we won't be angry with you."

I glance at Maggie. She keeps her distance but gives me a small nod.

I forge on, the words less jammed in my dry throat. "Aside from the dye job, he wanted to apologize for what he did, but it was pretty clear he was just going through the motions. He didn't care about me or ask about any of you, which I should have expected but kind of didn't. Regardless of that unpleasantness, the main reason he wanted to meet was to give me banking information—an account he set up in my name, but the money is for all of us, and there's a fair bit of it."

"I will *not* touch his dirty money." Desmond's already blowing a gasket. "Tell him to flush it down the toilet or give it to charity. How does he even have access to that kind of cash? Is he laundering again?"

"*None* of us is touching his blood money," Jake barks, laying down the law.

Cal holds up a hand. "Can we let Lennon finish? He's not done."

"Or we can bet on how many seconds it'll take for Des to punch a wall." E taps an edgy beat on his elbow.

Des flips him the finger. Mom sighs her here-we-go-again sigh, as the rest of us start calling out numbers, guessing how soon Des will explode: *five, two, three, four-point-five.*

"Are we playing guess the number?" Sadie joins our tense family and fits herself into Desmond's side.

"Yeah," Des grumbles. "We're guessing E's IQ."

He kisses her head, and his aggressive facade melts away. Sadie is his center of gravity. Always has been, always will be. Serenity that I understand, which makes Maggie's reserved behavior all the more unnerving. I want her arms wrapped around me, holding *my* center together. But her arms are folded over her stomach and she's studying the floor, like she's lost in her own thoughts.

Swallowing my discomfort, I focus on my family. "I had the same reaction when Dad gave me the bank details, but..." I look at my brothers and Mom, these amazing people who have suffered too much and deserve the world. *I've* suffered enough and deserve to follow my dreams.

"The money isn't drug money," I say. "Not directly, at least. The account is for the book—the advance, foreign rights earnings, and any eventual royalties. It all goes in there, and it's for us. And before you all scream and punch walls, I think we should accept it. It's the least he owes us, and I'm tired of letting his actions overshadow my life. Not taking it would linger more negatively than using it. A lot of good can come from that cash."

A house for me. Financial burdens eased. Releasing some of our anger to let in hope.

"I won't." Desmond isn't as snarly, not with Sadie by his side, but his jaw looks ready to snap. "This is different from government money. I want nothing from him."

"Fine," I say, understanding exactly how he feels. "Then I'll take your portion and start an account for Max. Taking the money doesn't mean we forgive Dad."

"But that's exactly what he'll think," Des says. "If we accept that money, he'll think he's absolved."

I look at E, think about his rational thoughts on the matter. "Every time he gets a royalty check and knows he can't use the cash, it'll remind him of what he did. Of how much he hurt us. That's not forgiveness. That's a life sentence of guilt."

"Lennon's right." Jake cracks his knuckles, a popping sound that never fails to give me the shivers. "If the money is from the book, it's aboveboard, and nothing he gives us changes the past. He knows it. We know it. There's no getting back our ten years or forgiving him, but I won't let my bitterness undermine our future. If it'll help us rebuild our lives with our old names, I don't give a shit what he thinks. I vote yes." He looks to Mom. "What do you think?"

She has one arm wrapped around her stomach, her other tucked against her side with her hand covering her mouth. It's a familiar pose, one I haven't seen in a while, like she's trying to make herself small. "I think it's not my choice, but I'd love to see your financial burdens eased."

"I'm in," Cal says. "Jake and I could use it for our construction business. Better that than Dad getting the cash."

"Agreed," E says. "I'll use it to build my porn empire."

Delilah rolls her eyes.

I'm not sure when E usurped my role as Bower Jokester, but I actually laugh. "What about you, Des? Do I need to set yours aside for Max, or will you take it?"

He and Sadie lock eyes.

"It's your choice," she says quietly, "but I agree with them. Your father shouldn't have that money. It belongs to all of you."

His posture softens, and he rubs his hand up and down her arm. "Okay," he says, barely audibly.

That was easier than I expected. No walls were punched. The

furniture in the room is still intact, and I actually feel relieved. Excited to contact Mrs. Jackson and take this huge step forward in my life. Maybe Mom's news will be easier to handle too. I've probably been a nervous wreck for nothing, worrying myself over imagined drama.

I step back, giving Mom the floor.

Maggie touches my arm briefly. "You were great. I'm so glad you decided to use the money."

"It feels like the right choice." I want to lean down and kiss her cheek, but something in her angled posture stops me. "I'm also considering ditching the adventure programs and becoming a bad-news teller. People can hire me to share their horrible tidings. I obviously excel at dropping emotional bombs."

She doesn't laugh at my joke or roll her eyes. Her attention is back on the floor, like I'm not even here, and I'm done walking on these eggshells. We need to talk. I need this family meeting over stat. My "I love you" clearly freaked Maggie out, and I need to explain that we can slow down, hit pause on bigger emotions, as long as she continues showing me how much she cares.

"About your father's book," Mom says, moving things along. But she doesn't continue. She's still shrinking herself, both arms wrapped around her middle now, her shoulders hunched forward.

My worry over this impending drama claws back to life. I circle my arm around Maggie to pull her closer—my safe place, even when she's acting weird—but her phone rings.

"Shoot. Sorry." She digs her phone from her pocket and frowns at the screen. "I need to take this. Work," she says as she hurries away.

I watch her retreat to the kitchen, feeling more unmoored.

"About your father's book," Mom says again, stronger this time. "I finished it a while ago, but I needed some time to let it settle before—"

"Oh my God." Maggie's panicked voice cuts through my tension.

I move right away, jogging to her in the other room, latching on to any excuse to delay Mom's reveal. And Maggie's *oh my God* is not good. Not when she's dealing with work.

"What happened?" I ask before I reach her.

Her face is pale, her hand clutching her chest. "Are they sure? Did they double count?" She squeezes her eyes shut and mouths *Fuck.* "I'll be right there. We'll find him. He must have wandered away."

She jumps into action, rushing to her jacket at the front door, with me on her heels.

"Mags. What is it? What happened?"

"One of the seniors isn't on the bus. They thought they counted everyone and drove back to the retirement home, but one of the men is missing." She yanks her jacket from the hook and jams her hand through the arm. "What if he's hurt? What if something happened to him?"

When she starts shaking, I pull her against me. "We'll find him. We'll have the whole town searching. Or just Sandra. She's basically a clairvoyant private eye."

Maybe she *can* see the future. Maybe that's why she told me she's good at sourcing information. She foresaw that a senior would wander off.

"This isn't funny." Maggie shakes me off with an aggressive shrug. "Not everything is a fucking joke!"

"No. It's not. I'm sorry." I mean, honestly. What the hell is wrong with me? When will I quit falling back on stilted humor when I'm stressed? Now Maggie's avoiding my eyes, worse than in the living room. She's blocking me out so hard a gnawing unease floods my gut.

"We'll find him," I tell her again, grabbing my jacket. "This isn't your fault."

"Not my fault?" She rounds on me, fury staining her cheeks.

"I shouldn't have left. I knew it. I should've stayed, made sure they all got on the buses, but I did what I wanted instead of doing my job. I did what *you* wanted. So, thanks for that, and I don't want you coming."

"I didn't force you here at gunpoint."

"No. You guilted me here, because that's your thing, isn't it? You push and push for what you want, no matter how other people feel, and I can't take it anymore."

She yanks the front door open, still struggling to get her jacket on as she runs out. She doesn't glance back at me or wish me well for the rest of my family meeting. She doesn't turn and tell me she's having one of her freak-outs and needs space. She dashes to her Jeep and peels off in a screech of tires, leaving me with an ache in my chest and a growing hollow in my stomach.

CHAPTER
Thirty

I'M NOT sure how long I stare at the street where Maggie's Jeep used to be. I can't shake the pain in my chest or the dread in my bones. I never should've told her I loved her. I shouldn't have asked her to come here with me. The seniors event was important for her career and her confidence. Now both are in jeopardy, and I'm pretty sure she just broke up with me.

I finally close the door and force myself to turn. Delilah's there, her big blue eyes filled with compassion. "She didn't mean what she said."

"Yeah, she did."

And she wasn't wrong.

When I pushed Maggie to give me a chance and coaxed her to date me, wooing her with paint fights and redacted love notes, I knew she had commitment issues. Delilah blatantly told me Maggie breaks up with guys who get too serious. Regardless of her fears, I steamrolled forward, blurting out my feelings, reaching for what I wanted—*her*—even though she needed me to move slower.

I rub my stinging eyes. "She's so hard on herself. With her mom and everything. I get it, but I also don't. Nobody's perfect.

Her parents don't expect her to be a Nobel Peace Prize recipient, but I see it in her face when things go wrong, this irrational fear. Like she's destined to hurt others, and I know she's worried she'll get hurt if she gets too close to people."

As though loving someone will always end with her standing at a gas station, left behind and discarded.

I drop my head forward and massage my chest. "Don't think I ever stood a chance with her."

Delilah wraps me in a hug. "Maggie and you are meant to be. You made her realize so much about herself, including that she deserves to be happy. After they find the missing man, she'll decompress. But you need to explain how much her actions hurt you too. She needs to understand it's not just about her."

I nod as I hug Delilah, mainly to cut off her pep talk. Sniping at Maggie would only make her feel worse about herself, and it wouldn't accomplish anything. She refused to acknowledge me in public as teens and refuses to acknowledge her true feelings for me now. Sure, I might have pushed too hard, too fast with her, but I don't think she ever planned to give me a real chance.

"Mom would like to get on with her grenade launch," E says, waving at us from the end of the hallway. "Also, quit trying to make out with my girlfriend. You don't stand a chance."

I sigh but don't release Delilah. "Delilah is Team Lennon now. She realized I'm packing bigger heat." I gesture at my crotch.

Delilah pinches my side until I let her go. "Why do guys always revert to penis jokes?"

"Are there other kinds of jokes?" I ask, rubbing my side.

"Child," Delilah mutters. It's the same type of cute comment Maggie would make, gutting me all over again. "And there's only one Bower for me," she adds. "Even if he sucks at charades."

"Babe." E becomes a study in indignation. "We've talked

about this. *I'm* great at charades. You're just shit at guessing my clues."

I follow them and their sickeningly cute banter, feeling worse by the second.

Back in the living room, Mom is whispering with Jake by the TV. I resume my spot from before. Solo this time. I jam my hand through my hair and stare at an abstract painting on the wall. The haphazard strokes remind me of painting with Maggie, rolling Island Getaway green across her boobs, then watching her hold my fingertip-kiss in her palm.

I give my hair another tug.

Cal comes to my side, probably worried I'll be bald in the next few minutes. "Hope everything's okay with Maggie."

Since I'm in no mood to discuss Maggie, and the fact that I probably just lost her, I say, "Hope everything's okay with you and Jolene. Remind me again why you refuse to call your former best friend?"

His complexion pales. His eyes dart to the floor. "No reason."

No reason, my ass. I pin him with a hard look and open my mouth to finally ask what's up with them, but he slaps my back. "I prefer standing next to Mom. Be there in case she needs me."

He marches to the other side of the room and avoids my stare. That schemer has secrets. He either fought with Jolene before WITSEC or he tried to covertly help her with something and it bit him in the ass. Whatever he did, it must have been a doozy.

"Lennon," Mom says, corralling my attention, "I hope Maggie's okay and they find the man from the bus."

"Actually," Delilah cuts in, holding up her phone. "She just texted. They found the man."

Thank God. I pull my phone from my back pocket, expecting to see a text too. Maggie sharing her relief or telling me she's coming back, admitting she yelled at me in a moment of stress and worry. Nothing's there.

The ache in my chest worsens, like someone's carving it up.

"That's such a relief," Mom says, returning her focus to my brothers, while my breathing turns shallow. "Back to your father's book, there are two things you need to know—details he mentions in the chapters that will upset you. Things you should be told before you read about them yourselves or hear about them through the media."

The room goes deathly still. We're Bower boy statues, waiting for this latest sledgehammer to shatter us, and the word *sick* pops into my head. My father is for sure sick and dying, and I hate the dread that fills me at the thought, the flicker of sadness.

"First," Mom says, "I want you all to know I'm okay, but your father had an affair years ago, before he started laundering money."

"Goddamn bastard," Des growls.

A polite slur compared to Jake's, "Motherfucking, piece-of-shit *prick*."

Since this upsetting news isn't news to me, I don't join the insult party. The shots launch hard and fast. Mom talks over them, explaining that she wasn't shocked, making excuses about some rough spell they went through and how the cartel used the affair to blackmail him into laundering money. I barely hear her. I know this story, and seeing my brothers upset and furious has me wanting to hit something.

I wish I could drop a protective bubble over each one of them, shelter them from more pain. Snap my fingers and change our history. Give us a different father.

I scratch my beard, have the violent urge to shave it off. *Hot.* I'm suddenly hot and edgy, the walls feeling unpleasantly close.

"That brings me to the second thing," Mom says, her worried tone cutting through my mounting discomfort. "I want you all to know I had no idea about this. I kept in touch with your father for a couple years at the start of WITSEC, let him know how you were all doing, but I eventually needed a clean break, and he didn't push. I had the impression he was keeping in touch out of guilt, not interest. That might have been the case, but according to his tell-all, he also had other things filling his time."

I've gone from dreading the words *he's sick* to holding my breath. This reveal is not going as I expected. Cutting ties because he didn't care enough has nothing to do with having cancer or some inoperable brain tumor. My brothers look equally as confused and wary—matching expressions of Here We Go Again as we wait for the ground beneath our feet to crumble.

Mom's eyes go glassy. Her concerned gaze travels over each of us, eventually landing on me. "Your father is with someone new. I believe they got together not long after WITSEC, and he has two sons with her, which means you have two brothers. Their names are Brayden and Luke. They're seven and five. From what the book says, your father is committed to them and his new partner. I think he sees this as his second chance to get parenting right, and…"

A whir builds in my head, getting gradually louder, overtaking Mom's rational voice.

Because *what in the actual fuck*?

The father who wants nothing to do with me has another family? Two new sons? A new life? Kids he probably cares about and loves. They probably fish and hike together. He probably jokes with them and bastardizes music lyrics to make them laugh and takes them on special milkshake trips. He obviously loves them enough to be in their lives and "get parenting right," and I don't know where I fit into that picture.

I mean, I don't *want* to fit into that picture. He doesn't deserve my love, but he didn't soften once at our meeting or look interested or seem to care. He was making amends with money, so he could go to his new family with a cleaner conscience, and I'm suffocating all over again. Walls closing in. Lungs too damn tight.

Cal's beside me, his hand on my arm, but I can't. I just *can't*.

I shove him off, storm to the hallway on a mission for my coat and the front door. I grab my stuff and bust outside as Mom and E call after me. I don't turn or stop. I can't. The whirring noise is getting louder, and I don't want to break down in front of them. They have enough heartache to deal with.

I hop in my truck, fumble with the ignition, and drive off as quickly as I can.

My phone, of course, blows up.

I love that my family cares. Honestly, I do. They are the fucking best and I love the shit out of them, but now's not the time. I turn up the music, switch the stations until a rock song blares. I squeeze the steering wheel so hard I'm shocked it doesn't crack.

Maggie's *I can't take it anymore* twists with the knowledge of my new half brothers, all of it tumbling together, leaving me with one awareness—I am lacking. I'm not good enough. Even my high school friends ditched me during their college years.

The windows are down. Fresh air blasts my face, but breathing gets harder.

Pressing more firmly on the gas, I gun it to my farmhouse and park in the driveway. I grab my phone, disappointed all over again that Maggie hasn't texted me. I'm head over heels in love with her, and she can't even ask me how my family meeting went or fill me in on her work disaster. All I got were a few angry words, and *poof*, she's out of my life. Like she never really cared for me at all.

Whatever. She clearly needs something I can't give her. Turning myself inside out to make her happy has never worked for me. What I need is space and time. An escape to get over her and deal with this new shock, and there's only one place that can happen.

Agitated, I scroll through my messages and hit Cal's name. He's the most understanding of my brothers. If I message him, he'll take me at my word and not come searching for me.

Me: I'll be fine. But I need to get away for a bit. I'm heading camping. Probably a week with no internet. I'll be back for my birthday. Don't send out the National Guard. Tell Mom.

I almost power down my phone, but my thumb hovers over the name *Nemesis*. The last time I got upset over my father and disappeared, I worried her. When I went into WITSEC, she thought I'd abandoned her like her mother. I doubt she wants to hear from me, but the possibility of hurting her in this vital way is too much to pile on to my already shit-pile of a day.

I type out a quick message and read it over.

Me: As it turns out, my father has a new family. Two boys with another woman. And it's crazy how betrayed I feel. How unwanted. I know we're over and this doesn't concern you. I guess I just wanted to write it down. I'll be out of touch camping for a week. I'm sorry about work and that you couldn't truly be happy with me. But I don't regret telling you I loved you. I only regret that I just got to say it once.

On my third read, my eyes get misty.

Love, I tell ya. Cupid and his arrows should be banned from the mortal world.

I send the text and debate messaging my father the way Maggie would want. Finally yell at him about how much his dismissal hurts, but my stomach lurches. My pulse picks up. No part of me wants to speak to him, and what would be the point? Like with Maggie, pushing won't change the outcome.

I power off my phone and drag a hand down my face. My activity programs are done until the new year. Nothing is keeping me in Windfall, and I read a great blog post last month on my favorite Get Outside North Carolina website, detailing a less-traveled trail that would fit my needs perfectly. A week away from life will calm my mind. A solo trip to curse my father, find some semblance of peace where he's concerned. Time to accept that Maggie and I are over for good, even though the thought of losing her has a fault line cracking through my heart.

CHAPTER
Thirty-One

MAGGIE

I STARE out of my Jeep's windshield, unable to press the ignition or move. Blinking is a painful effort, and I'm pretty sure my heart has forgotten how to pump. Or maybe this is how it feels when you light your own heart on fire and watch it burn.

I keep replaying my abrupt departure from Lennon, unsure what the hell is wrong with me. Except I know exactly what my problem is.

Love.

I love Lennon Bower so much—turn-your-world-upside-down-and-every-which-way love—that I panicked. Ran instead of facing the undeniable truth. Now I've hurt the one person who means everything to me.

What if I've lost him for good?

Scared I messed everything up, I finally move. Shove through my purse and yank out my phone. I need to call Lennon. Apologize to him. Explain that hearing he loved me was so freaking amazing but also terrifying. Beg him to give me another chance.

When I tap the screen, my text icon displays a message. One touch shows that the text is from him, and my pulse races. If he's ending things, I don't know what I'll do.

Holding my breath, I pull up his message. By the time I get to the end, tears are sliding down my face.

> Bane of My Existence: As it turns out, my father has a new family. Two boys with another woman. And it's crazy how betrayed I feel. How unwanted. I know we're over and this doesn't concern you. I guess I just wanted to write it down. I'll be out of touch camping for a week. I'm sorry about work and that you couldn't truly be happy with me. But I don't regret telling you I loved you. I only regret that I just got to say it once.

Fuck. Shoot.

Shit, shit, shit.

I'm furious at his father for blindsiding his family like this. I'm furious at myself for not running back to be with Lennon during this tough time.

Hiccupping on a sob, I try calling him. It goes straight to voice mail. "No," I whisper hoarsely while jamming my finger on my Jeep's ignition button. "No, no, no. Goddamn it, I love you so much."

I pull out of my parking spot on Main Street and get stuck behind a slow driver taking their sweet-ass time. Nearing all-out panic, I call Delilah.

"Lennon left," she said as soon as she picks up. My best friend knows me too well.

"I fucked up."

"You did."

"He told me he loved me today."

"And you hit panic mode?"

"Self-destruction mode is more apt."

I debate honking at the slow driver, but there's no point rushing to Lennon's. He was clearly in a hurry to get away from his family and me. He'll be gone before I get there.

I dash at the tears on my face. "I should never have brushed him off like that, especially with everything he was going through. I was just so worried about the man who went missing, and my head was having a stupid fight with my heart over the fact that my boyfriend loves me." Or, more accurately, the fact that I love him and couldn't get the words out. "I am such a fucking mess. That whole meeting with his family, I was standing there trying to build the nerve to tell him how I felt, when I should've been focused on him. Then that call came, and I lost it. I think I used it as an excuse to run away."

"You're human, Mags. None of us is perfect. I kept secrets from E for so long that it hurt us both. Emotional fears are often more powerful than tangible ones."

And they do more damage. "I think I've lost him," I say, fighting another rising sob.

"Lennon was upset," Delilah says gently. "He was frustrated with you and shaken by his father's latest bomb drop. But he hasn't fallen out of love with you in the span of an hour. A week-long hike won't make a dent either. E says he's never seen Lennon as happy as he's been with you."

Another match lights under my incinerated heart. "He keeps telling me I need to talk to my parents about my issues, and I'm starting to think he's right. He deserves a woman who's all in, someone who loves him with her whole heart. I want to be that woman," I say more quietly.

"I think that sounds like a really smart idea."

I sniffle. "So do I."

To finally tell my parents I lie to them about work to impress them, like I'm still that little kid who heard them say they regretted my adoption. Explain that I can't hold a real relationship, scared I'll be hurt again. Fear of loss. Being alone, discarded. So freaking textbook it's embarrassing. Maybe finally facing the issues head on will help me handle the intensity of what Lennon makes me feel, because that man makes me feel *everything*.

"I'm going to his house," I tell Delilah, turning my Jeep toward the only place I want to be. "Just in case he hasn't left yet. But I'll call my mom too. Talk through everything with her and my dad."

"I'm here if you need me. Call me day or night."

"Love you," I say and hang up.

I'm not sure why being close with Delilah doesn't petrify me the way being close with Lennon does. Romantic love sinks deeper somehow. Grows your heart in a way that leaves it vulnerable if that portion atrophies. But after Lennon's text, it's clear there's no protecting myself with him. This heart of mine is so full of him I can barely breathe.

I won't shy away from telling him I love him again. The reality of losing him is a heck of a lot scarier than opening myself up to potential pain down the road. Which means I need to do better than a simple apology. I have to show Lennon how I feel with more than words, and I have an idea that just might work. A surprise for when he gets back.

As long as he hasn't decided I'm not worth the effort by then.

CHAPTER
Thirty-Two

DAY ONE HIKING, it pours. I am a drowned rat. I am a sad sack of a man, who is cold and shivery and bitter. Mother Nature is doing nothing but pissing on my head. A smart man might have turned around or hunkered down in his tent for a day or two. Ridden out the storm. But this hiking trip isn't about pretty scenery and the brightness of a sunny December day. This trip is a pilgrimage. My journey of reckoning and self-understanding, where I face my demons and come out the other side stronger. Or I'll slide down one of these muddy slopes and drown in the dead leaves and muck at my feet. Whichever comes first.

Day two hiking, it snows. I was smart enough to pack a hat and gloves, and I have a good supply of dehydrated meals, but in my rush to get away from it all, I forgot my long underwear. There's a chance my kneecaps will fall off. And my nuts.

I pull my pack higher and push on, head down, one foot in front of the other. No time to focus on the numbness in my lower limbs or the pain in my heart. That's the thing about facing off against nature. Survival trumps my mental stress. Moving, eating, drinking water—the basics of living—take over. I'm a body in motion, battling the elements, reminding myself that I am strong and resilient. A man who can endure, like I did eleven years ago, when my father tore me and my family from the familiarity of our lives.

Except being cold and wet sucks.

I pass an intersecting trail and trudge up a steep incline, focusing on keeping my footing secure. At the top, I take a much-needed break and rummage for my water.

The crunch of dead leaves has me stiffening.

Since moving to Windfall, I've spotted coyotes and foxes on my hikes and plenty of smaller rodents. While I haven't seen cougars or black bears, there have been enough paw prints and droppings to know they're around. The last thing I want to encounter out here alone is a cougar or a bear.

Another crunch sounds. My heart shoots into my throat.

I scan the forest around the trail, peering through the poplars and black birch. Nothing moves. There could be a person on the trail, but it's not a popular trek this time of year. If it's an animal, I need to make noise, scare off whatever's lurking in the forest.

Neck tense, I drop my pack and dive in for my metal pots, swearing when I have to pry them out from under my sleeping bag. More crunching echoes, closer this time. When my hands finally close on metal, I give my best B-movie scream and start smacking the pans together as I pull up from my pack…and I'm face-to-face with Mizhir.

"What the fuck are you doing here?" I ask through ragged breaths.

He frowns at the pans in my frantic grip. "What the fuck are you *doing*?"

A crazed laugh squeaks out of me, my adrenaline leaching as incredulity sinks in. Running into anyone out here is unlikely. Running into Mizhir? Lady Luck clearly has a bone to pick with me.

"Oh, you know," I say, dropping my pans and regaining my

equilibrium, "I'm starting a one-man band. Thought being out here in the quiet would be a good place to practice."

He snorts. "Don't quit your day job."

I sure as hell should quit trying to escape my life. I can't seem to run far enough away. "Are you doing the Klauser Loop?"

"Part of it." He shirks off his pack and drops it beside mine. "I read about Klauser on Get Outside North Carolina but wanted to be out for two weeks. It bisects Green Ridge and Lorrey Kane. Instead of doing a loop, I arranged a drop-off and pickup at each end."

We nod at each other, like we ran into each other in the town square, not in the middle of fucking nowhere. "That's why I'm here too," I say, but I flash to Maggie's sharp eyes before she tore out of Desmond's house, to Mom's worry when telling us about our new brothers. "I mean, the post isn't *why* I'm solo hiking, but Get Outside NC is a great website. The loop looked good."

"Right? The hikes they list are always spot-on."

We share more useless nodding and silent awkwardness, as I try to stop thinking about my imploded life.

Mizhir tugs down his hat. "I'm not actually out here because of the article either." He crosses his arms and shifts on his feet. Standing still in the cold is no one's friend, but there are dark circles under his eyes I hadn't noticed before. "Shit went sideways for me at work." He exhales on a sigh. "It was either split or drown."

Whenever I saw him in town, he seemed upbeat. Either his job hit a downward spiral recently, or he was putting on a brave face. "I don't actually know what you do for work, which seems strange."

"It feels shitty, is what it feels like." His dark eyes flick up to mine. "I hate the strain between us."

"Yeah," is all I say. *Shitty* and *strained* are the best ways to describe how seeing Mizhir always feels.

He kicks at a patch of snow. "I should've reached out to you properly after you got back, but I didn't want to talk about how bad things were for me at work. Kind of like why I ditched you when I went to college."

A cold wind makes me shiver, but I don't move to keep warm. Trying to compute what he's saying is taking all my concentration. "What was going on when you went to college?"

"My dad lost his job, and my folks split for a while. Everyone was going out to parties while I sat on the phone and listened to them bitch about each other. My grades tanked, and I get bad insomnia when things are stressful. It was a rough time, and talking to friends when things are bad isn't my forte. I get kind of embarrassed about my life, I think. It's easier pretending things are fine…until it's not easier. Like now."

I blink at him, taken aback. When he quit calling me from college, I never once asked Mizhir if he was okay. I assumed he was out having a blast, making new friends, leaving me for bigger and better things. Talk about being oblivious.

"I had no clue, man. To be honest, I wasn't in a great place either back then. Felt like I'd been left behind by you, which seems pretty insular and immature now that I think about it."

He smirks. "We *were* immature. Remember when we'd play video games with our feet while tossing spitballs at each other?"

"Okay, yeah." I smile at the memory, the two of us being jackasses for a laugh. "We were immature, but it's no excuse. I should've called more, visited when I didn't hear back."

"And I shouldn't have pushed you away."

We nod at each other again, awareness in the slow movement this time, both of us understanding each other a bit better.

"I was sick when I heard about witness protection," Mizhir goes on. "Can't imagine what you went through. Then you came back, and I was struggling with work. I should've done more to connect."

"Guess it's a good thing we ran into each other out here." And I should quit assuming I'm the only one with problems.

People's insides don't usually match their outward image. I mean, I tell jokes when I'm uncomfortable. I should know better.

Mizhir gestures to the trail, his face brighter. "I'm on the Klauser Loop for a day and a half before it splits into Lorrey Kane. If you don't mind company, is it cool if we do it together?"

It's freezing outside, but warmth spreads through my chest. "That would be awesome."

We pull on our packs and head out, hiking and talking like we didn't lose eleven years of friendship. I catch up on Mizhir's work woes—the main investor for his Rate Your Date app disappeared, and he hasn't found a replacement, but his parents' marriage has thankfully been strong since their short split. We laugh about stupid shit we did growing up, and he asks about WITSEC and gets furious at my father for ruining our lives.

During lulls, my mind slides to Maggie. I picture us laughing together, walking hand in hand behind the Yard Goat Gallery. More dangerous fantasies hit too—her naked over me, moving her hips, taking me deep. I have to bite my cheek to kill the memories. The speed with which our relationship ended still grates on me, but I'm sad more than anything. Fucking devastated that she won't be in the future I imagined for us.

At least Mizhir and I have started to reconcile.

"If I saw your father now," he says, scowling as we discuss my sojourn in WITSEC, "I'd probably slash his tires."

We're at our campsite, huddled under a hung tarp, cooking food on my small camp stove.

He passes me his flask of bourbon.

I take a healthy pull. "Turns out he also has another family. Two boys he apparently loves and dotes on."

I still don't understand why I care so much. Nothing he does should affect me, but I find myself curious if his boys are obnoxious like me or volatile like Des. If they're creative like E, bossy like Jake, or congenial like Cal. I don't know if we got our traits more from Mom or from Dad. Maybe neither. Maybe we're just us, and they're just them. Half brothers who might need a collection of Bower boys to back them up if their father resumes his role of Life Wrecker Extraordinaire.

I rub my eyes. "My father is such a dick."

Mizhir flings a stray branch into the darkness. "Fuck him."

"You can say that again."

He looks at me dead on and says, "*Fuck him*," harder.

I pull in a lungful of cold air, resentment frothing hotter in my gut. "Fuck him," I mutter, wanting to taste the words for myself. Feel their power. "Fuck him," I say louder.

"Fuck him!" Mizhir shouts, his head tipped back.

"Fuck him!" I scream, picturing my unemotional father at the diner, his dyed hair a brown stain on his scalp. "You're a motherfucking asshole shitbag prick!"

I clamp my mouth shut, worried a family might be camping somewhere on this trail. But damn, that felt good. So good and liberating I can't help wondering if Maggie was right about my confrontation issues.

Maybe all this angst *did* fester because I didn't yell at my father and tell him how I truly felt, relying on trusted jokes instead. If I'd yelled at the diner, Dad wouldn't have sat there silently. He would've replied with a rebuttal, and I would've had to take it. Faced whatever he might have said in return, even if that "whatever" was hurtful and insulting —a possibility that has my heart racing. The erratic beat pounds so hard it gets tough to breathe, like that's the issue I've been battling. Fear of rejection more than fear of fighting.

I certainly never asked Mizhir why he quit keeping in touch when he went off to college. I never pushed with Maggie, demanding to know why she wouldn't talk to me at school. I assumed she was obsessed with her public image and Mizhir was happier without me, both conclusions dead wrong. Maybe self-doubt kept me quiet back then. Fear that Maggie would say I wasn't jock enough or popular enough or cool enough to associate with her. That I'd never be good enough.

Everything back then was Dad's fault and Mizhir's fault and Maggie's fault. I was the good guy who forgave and forgot. But I didn't forget, did I?

Like I can't forget Maggie now.

CHAPTER
Thirty-Three

THE NEXT DAY is cold but dry. The sky is blue. The mud-caked ground is firm from the chill, my steps surer and steady. I lift my head as I walk, easy strides with Mizhir at my side. We hike and talk, taking in the sentry of trees around us, some branches naked and resolute, the evergreens obstinate and spiky, undisturbed by winter's hand.

Eventually, we arrive at a lookout—our last stop before our trails split apart.

"My dad isn't fully why I bolted on this camping trip," I say on an exhale.

"Maggie" is his reply.

Goddamn Maggie Edelstein. "How'd you know?"

"Windfall is the size of a Petri dish."

I laugh. Isn't that the truth. "We had a fight, and I didn't speak my mind. Barely pushed back, kind of like the way I dealt with you as teens. I mean, a lot was going on. She had to rush off, and I had my family meeting. But when she lashed out, I assumed she was ending things with us, which seems to be a pattern of mine—making assumptions without all the facts.

Except maybe she wasn't breaking up with me. Maybe she just needed space before we talked things out."

I should've waited before taking off, spoken to her after the dust settled, been more honest about how her abruptness had hurt. Insisted we talk things through.

I should've fought like hell for the woman I love.

Mizhir stands beside me, the two of us watching an eagle soar on the wind. "Sounds like you two have unfinished business."

"I miss her like crazy."

Mizhir cups my shoulder. "You need to be honest with her, man. Talk out whatever went down, and don't shy away from the tough stuff."

"She probably won't give me the time of day. Last time I had an issue with my father, I disappeared on her and she freaked out—told me to never take off like that again. I texted her I was going away this time, but leaving Maggie is a huge insecurity for her."

"Then I guess you should start hiking pretty fucking fast. The longer you're away, the more she'll stew."

I drop my head back and growl at the sky. "Why didn't I just drive to Maggie's instead of taking off?"

Chuckling, he shakes his head. "If you're anything like my father, it's because you're not good at noticing when you're lost. That's why men don't ask for directions. Half the time, they cluelessly think they're on the right trail. We need bigger road signs."

I need a fifty-foot sign that reads: Quit Running from Your Problems. "I hate that we took so long to reconnect, but I'm really happy I ran into you out here."

"Feeling's mutual, man. Now get going and get your woman back."

After a bro-pound half-hug with our awkward backpacks, Mizhir and I make plans to meet up in Windfall. I set off at a quick pace, my mind spinning over all I need to do at home— call my father again, tell him exactly how much his choices hurt me, talk to my family about our new brothers and what that means. Then there's Maggie.

This trip has reminded me I'm a survivor. I'm strong enough to endure in the wilderness on my own, which means I'm strong enough to survive without Maggie. Except I don't want to. I want Maggie in my life, my home, my bed, sassing me and giving me hell and loving me with her whole heart. I have to tell her she hurt me, but I also have to apologize for walking away without fighting for us. After which, we better be getting back together.

As I hike, I make a mental list to manifest the future I want. I've called it "6 Clues My Nemesis Loves Me."

1. Maggie shared her painful history with me at her pond.
2. When I was out of reach after my Fun Father Reunion, she was visibly upset.
3. Although my humor annoys her at times, she still laughs at my jokes.
4. She planned a romantic picnic with my favorite foods.
5. Even though I blindsided her with my reckless *I love you*, she left her event early to support me.
6. She pushed herself out of her comfort zone because her feelings for me were too big to ignore.

I need to do the same for her. Be uncomfortable. Tell her exactly what I'm feeling instead of doing my usual duck and run. Prove to her I want to change and be a better partner.

So, yeah. The second I'm done this trip I'll drive straight to Maggie's (after I shower off the stink from a week of wilderness) and show her I'm ready to be the man she deserves.

CHAPTER
Thirty~Four

I SPEND the two-hour drive to my farm thinking about all the things I need to say to Maggie. I also get hot and bothered thinking of all the things I want to *do* to her. Today is the first night of Chanukah. She'll be with her family later this evening, lighting their menorah and celebrating together. I have to head her off before that happens. Which means I need to drive faster than is safe and take the quickest shower in the history of showers to delouse myself.

If she refuses to let me into her home, I'll remind her it's my birthday. She can't turn me away on my birthday. The only person I want to ring in my new year with is her.

The second I hit the entrance to my driveway, I unclick my seat belt, ready to jump out as soon as I park...but I see a Jeep. A glowing white beacon telling me my favorite person is here. She must love me too, as my list predicted. She must be as desperate as I am to make things right. Or she's here to kick me in the nuts for taking off the way I did.

I turn off my ignition, drag my wrist across my clammy forehead. She doesn't pop out of my house or appear through the curtained windows. She could be in there, gathering my clothes to set them on fire. She might be writing "we're done" in blood-red lipstick on my mirrors, like a creepy B-movie murderer. Options I'd get behind if they work off enough of her frustration that she gives me another chance.

Unable to delay any longer, I push out of my truck and head for my door, quick strides eating up the mowed grass. A white paper taped to my screen door stops me in my tracks. It looks like the type of note I left on Maggie's windshield, and a slow smile spreads over my face. If she was plotting my demise, she wouldn't leave me a note. She wouldn't play cute games with me.

I take my front steps two at a time, peel the paper off my door, expecting several lines. I get one word:

[REDACTED]

Tipping my head back, I bark out a laugh.

Fuck, do I love this woman. No longer worried she'll yell at me without giving me a chance to talk, I shove open my front door, searching the entryway and narrow hall. There's no Maggie in sight, but there's another note on my living room coffee table. I have it in my hands in seconds. I flip it open, only to laugh again.

[REDACTED]

A rectangle of white catches my eye, another note on my dining table up ahead. I strut for it, knowing what it'll say, smiling as I open it.

[REDACTED]

Straight ahead is my small farm-style kitchen. I'm jogging now, scouring my house for my wildfire woman. I don't find Maggie, but there's another note affixed to my back door. I tear it off, expecting another [REDACTED]. What I get has me laughing harder.

IF YOU SMELL AS BAD AS I THINK YOU DO,
SHOWER BEFORE YOU LOOK FOR THE NEXT NOTE.

I don't waste a millisecond. I dash down the hall and up my stairs, turning on the shower and stripping so fast the water's still cold when I get in. I don't care. I shiver and scrub myself raw and shampoo my hair, skipping the conditioner because who has time to condition when Maggie Edelstein is playing games with their heart. I rush out so fast I almost bite it, recovering quickly while vaguely toweling myself off.

Half a minute later, I'm wearing sweats and my Ironic T-shirt. I tear a path down my stairs, grab a jacket, then jog out my back door.

I scan my yard, pulse racing, lungs pumping. It takes an impatient moment to find the next note—a paper tacked to the large oak delineating my property line. I rush toward it, expecting another one-word winner. I get something more.

LENNON. I DON'T KNOW WHERE TO START, SO I'LL START AT
THE END.
I LOVE YOU.

I close my eyes and press my hand to my pounding heart. I wasn't sure I'd ever get past Maggie's tough exterior to the soft center of her, ever experience the joy of hearing those words. Her lips may not be forming the sounds, but I see her in the letters that wobble slightly. Her vulnerability. Words that have the power to heal and hurt. Love is cruel like that. Lifting you up if requited, lashing you if not.

I lean into the tree for support as I read the rest.

EVERYTHING ELSE LEADS HERE, TO THIS FEELING THAT'S SO BIG
AND BRIGHT I CAN BARELY BREATHE AT TIMES. I OWE YOU
MORE THAN A SIMPLE NOTE. I OWE YOU AN EXPLANATION AND
AN APOLOGY. ALL THE "REDACTEDS" SO YOU UNDERSTAND
HOW SORRY I AM. I MADE YOU FEEL UNWORTHY AND
UNLOVED, AND I'M ASHAMED OF MYSELF FOR THAT. YOU,
LENNON BOWER, ARE EVERYTHING. I'M AT YOUR FAIRY TREE.
PLEASE COME FIND ME. I WANT TO EXPLAIN IN PERSON.

PS: I SERIOUSLY HOPE YOU SHOWERED. PLEASE GO SHOWER.
LIKE, DON'T COME IF YOU HAVEN'T SHOWERED, BUT I REALLY
HOPE YOU COME AND DON'T YOU DARE SHAVE THAT BEARD.

I press my nose to the note, hoping to catch her strawberry-milkshake scent. I don't, but I grin and break into a jog, dodging rocks and strewn branches, cool air rushing my face. The few clouds above play hide-and-seek with the sun. I jog down my cut path, past the dilapidated barn and its sunken roof, wild grasses charting my course as I round the corner and come to a stuttered stop.

Red coat.

Red gloves.

Red hair the color of fire.

Red lips breaking into a smile.

And a blue tent I wasn't expecting, which looks like the same tent Maggie used for our picnic lunch.

My lungs crowd my chest, and I sprint, on a collision course with my nemesis. I rush toward her as she rushes toward me, her little hop-steps making her look adorable. The second we meet, I crush her to me, lift her up, and spin her around. I put my mouth on hers and kiss her hard, my hands in that scarlet hair, my tongue seeking hers. She whimpers and softens. I think I taste salt, a tear sliding between us, and I thank my sleepless nights as a moody teen for sending me on a midnight walk and stumbling on to Maggie.

"I love you," I whisper to the gentle curve of her ear. "I'm sorry I left so suddenly. It wasn't because of you. Not really. It was because of me."

Sighing, she rubs her cheek against my beard. "I know. I love you so much. I'm so sorry I hurt you."

Right. *She hurt me.* The uncomfortable confrontation I promised myself I'd have, honoring myself and showing Maggie I'll be a more honest partner moving forward.

I create space between us and cross my arms, attempting a serious expression, but I'm grinning. "Above everything else, I *am* very sorry I took off without talking to you, but I'm also upset with you."

She bites her lip—God, I love when she bites that plump lip —and does an equally crap job of looking somber. "I know. You should be."

"I hated how you treated me in high school," I go on, and *yes*, I'm half grinning, too fucking happy right now to bring the full heat, because this is who I am. A man who speaks softer, taking longer to get out his true feelings. "You made me feel like a second-class citizen back then. I know I didn't have my shit together, flunked classes, and was on a first-name basis with our principal, but the way you ignored me in public sucked."

She nods quickly. "I know. I was awful."

"You were, and I get it now. I know you thought I was your gateway drug, the always-in-trouble kid who would unleash your wildest side, but it hurt then, and your distance hurts now."

I'm no longer smiling. I pass my hand over my mouth, trying to find the right words, fighting the nervous energy confrontation conjures.

"Mags." I meet her eyes. Her face gentles, and she doesn't glance away. "I love you. I don't expect our relationship to be all laughs and love notes and paint fights, but I do expect mutual respect, because I have my own insecurities. When you put up emotional walls or leave the way you did at Des's house, blowing me off, I take it personally, even if it isn't personal. I did that with my father too. Took everything more personally than it was intended, when his choices were always about himself. It'll take me a while to figure out that part of myself, so even if your actions come from *your* vulnerability, they sucker-punch me. I promise to do better being honest with you, speaking up if I'm upset, and I need you to promise me the same."

"I promise." Eyes brimming, she nods and cups my cheeks. "I promise. I'm so sorry. After everything settled from work—"

"How pissed was Shannon?" I can't help but interrupt. My first concern will always be Maggie.

"She was *not* happy, to say the least. The bland face made an appearance, but she also sat me down and told me not to be so hard on myself. Reminded me I can't be everywhere at once when running events. All I can do is plan and put people in place, which I did. She was actually impressed I found Mr. Sorenson so quickly."

"You used Sandra, didn't you?"

"Of course I used Sandra." She lets out a watery laugh. "Sandra also told me she has the address for your half brothers."

Honestly, Sandra is a national treasure. Her cryptic words about being good at sourcing information make more sense now. Somehow, she must have gotten hold of an early copy of my father's tell-all and went in search of his family.

"How are you doing with all that stuff?" Maggie asks softly. "With your dad and his other sons? Are you okay?"

"I actually think I want to meet them." My first concrete feelings on the matter. Growing my family, despite my father's failings. "I also need to call my dad and finally confront him, but that can wait. I believe we've gotten off track." I bat my lashes at her. "You were in the middle of apologizing to me."

She huffs out an amused breath and holds my hands. "The reason I didn't come back after we found Mr. Sorenson, or text you about it, was shame. I was *ashamed* of how I treated you. Yelling at you and blaming you for my choice to leave the event wasn't okay. I was stressed and overwhelmed and lashed out when I shouldn't have, especially with what you had going on. I was also upset I didn't have the guts to tell you I loved you too. Then I read your text, that you were leaving, and I..."

Her lips tremble, her sad sniffle slaying me. "I lost it. Drove here, terrified to lose you, hoping to catch you before you left. When it was clear I missed you, I got E's spare key and slept here the first couple nights, praying the bad weather would bring you home. You obviously didn't show, but I also realized you were right."

I run my knuckles down her cool cheek. "I'm always right, Gingersnap."

She laughs, twining her arms around my neck. "I will ignore all parts of that horrible sentence, but you were right about my parents—about me needing to open up to them, talk about the uncomfortable feelings I've avoided all these years."

"You spoke to them?"

She nods. "It was tough. There were tears all around. They knew I overheard them questioning if adopting me was a bad choice, but they didn't know how deeply that rejection hurt. How it all festered with my mother abandoning me at the gas station."

"I bet they felt awful."

"I've never seen my dad like that. He hugged me so hard I couldn't breathe, told me over and over they love and support me no matter what. Explained how hard that time was on them, trying to do right by me. And Mom was a mess. Admitted how scared she was for me back then, and that she had her own issues feeding that fear—worry about losing me the way she lost her sister. It was a hugging, snotty mess, and when I told them how I pushed you away because I was scared, they got mad."

I frown. "At you?"

"More at themselves, I think. Like they failed me. Mom and I stayed up late talking about hard times she and my father went through, how scary and wonderful relationships are. That my constant striving for perfection and holding myself to an impossible gold standard is so damaging. That real love means loving someone for their strengths and their faults. She even admitted she disliked Harrison and thought he was wrong for me."

I curl my lip. "She must've shaken his hand."

"You can't still be jealous of Harrison."

"I will always be jealous of Harold and every other loser you dated. Those were years I missed with you."

She drags her nails over my scalp, making me sigh. "If you forgive me for hurting you, you won't miss any more. When you told me you loved me, I freaked out because I knew I loved you too, and that scared the hell out of me. But I'm not scared anymore. I promise to do my best going forward, to talk more openly about what I'm feeling, with you and with my parents. I'm so sorry I wasn't there for you at your family meeting."

"It's okay." I tuck a flyaway hair behind her ear. "We're okay."

She gives me a tender smile, then glances at the sky. "I know we have more talking to do, but can we do it later? You got home later than I expected, and we're actually on a schedule. We have your birthday to celebrate and my family's Chanukah party to attend, if you're up for it all."

I wrap my arms around her and pull my favorite nemesis against me. "I'm up for whatever you have planned. And since we have the rest of our lives to talk, let's get this party started."

She doesn't freeze up at my mention of a future together. She pulls my head down, kisses me soundly, then whispers, "Our whole lives. Now get in this tent before I freeze."

CHAPTER
Thirty-Five

LIKE AT HER TENT PICNIC, Maggie has a small heater inside to warm the cozy space. Unlike our tent picnic, there's a small towel, a thick blanket, and two wrapped packages tied with bows.

"Is it someone's birthday?" I ask, touched she planned this intimate setup.

She crawls in after me, the two of us on our knees as she hands me the smaller of the two gifts. "You're officially *in* your thirties now. Celebration is required."

"The only gift I need is you."

"I'm pretty sure you'll like these." But her chin dips, and she fidgets with her jacket cuff. Self-conscious moves I don't associate with Maggie.

I lift the gift and shake it by my ear. Nothing rattles. "Is it a stink bomb to toss in E's apartment?"

"Nope. He helped me set up his tent for the picnic and again today, so I owe him."

"Maggie." I huff out a dramatic grunt. "He'll probably show up again with another of his obnoxious ambushes, and owing E leads to horrible favors like unclogging his toilet or doing his laundry for a month."

"He promised he wouldn't crash my plans, and the favor isn't anything bad. I just agreed to call you a hipster at least three times this week." Her full-teeth smile is adorable.

I try to scowl, but the effort is useless. Maggie can call me whatever she wants. "You know what, it's fine. I don't care anymore. I like craft beer, I like my beard, and I like wearing skinny jeans and fitted T-shirts to show off my svelte body."

"I love you in whatever you wear," she says, her voice turning intimate.

I inch forward on my knees and grab her by the waist. "I love you. Period. End of story."

We kiss softly, the hum of the heater and rustle of the wind joining our heavier breaths. "I also love presents," I say. "And less clothing."

We toss our jackets aside, and I grab the smaller gift again. Maggie scrunches her nose, waiting on me as I draw out the moment and turn the package over in my hands. Interest piqued, I untie the red bow—my favorite color—then shred the paper, to reveal a purple box with the words "long-lasting" and "slippery" written on it.

Honestly, I have the best girlfriend in the world. "You bought me lube."

Her cheeks are mottled, her tongue sneaking out to wet her lips. "I dare you to touch yourself," she says, brazen. "Here, in front of me," she adds.

She's stealing my lines—the exact words *I* used our last night at the pond. An evening I've replayed a million times over: everything we said, her frayed jean shorts sliding down her legs, her yellow tank top pulling up over her fire-red hair.

Since her hesitant request to recreate that night, I haven't broached the subject or set up a sexy scene with candles and rose petals. I thought I was waiting for the perfect night. Truth is, I was wary. Maggie often uses sex to create emotional distance. Aside from erotic, recreating that life-changing moment would be intensely emotional. If we'd gotten naked and relived that memory, and she refused to give me her eyes and trust, it would've hurt.

But she's swapping our roles for our reenactment, showing me her vulnerability.

"That's a bold dare," I say, repeating our exchange verbatim, my heart beating faster.

"You can say no." Her voice turns husky. "You can always say no."

Like that's a possibility. "Dare accepted, but I dare you to do the same."

"Yeah." Her open expression is everything. "I'll accept your dare."

"You can't touch me though," I add. If we're reenacting our mutual masturbation, we're doing this right. Plus, it's not her hands I want this time. It's her eyes. "You can only look."

Without breaking eye contact, she slowly unbuttons her cream blouse, revealing sexy white lace. I groan and grab my T-shirt by the back of my neck and yank it off over my damp hair. Her bra goes next, but she doesn't make this easy. She palms her breasts, squeezes all that lushness, circling her nipples and giving them a pinch. Her throaty moan fucking undoes me.

"You're a goddess." I drag my hand over my aching cock, rubbing the rigid length through my sweats. It's not enough. Unceremoniously, I fall to my back and drag off my sweats and briefs and socks in an awkward tug and shimmy. By the time my clothes are tossed to the side and I face Maggie, she's naked on her back, tracing circles on her pale belly.

My ravenous grunt is pure caveman. "Maybe we should allow touching. No touching is so yesterday."

She smiles and moves her hand to those tight red curls. "Don't break the rules, babe."

Fuck, I love it when she calls me babe. I love seeing her like this, exploring herself, looking at me with so much *want* and trust I'm in danger of coming too soon. I grip my shaft, give it a squeeze. Nestle my knees between her spread thighs. *So fucking hot.*

I open my incredibly thoughtful gift and squeeze a few cool drops on my stiff length, then some on her glistening pussy. My first stroke down my shaft has her eyelids falling heavier. A pant of bated breath escapes her. Her hips shift and rock. I run my left hand down lower, cupping my balls as I pump myself in long, slow pulls. She spreads her legs wider, pushes her hips higher, chasing her pleasure with her fingers.

We don't talk. Just look our fill. My pulse kicks up with each sexy move, and when she dips two digits inside herself, moving her wetness around, lightning shoots through me. She's not rubbing herself hard yet. She's drawing out her pleasure, circling, breaking her rhythm to slow herself down, returning to that swollen nub I love flicking with my tongue.

"Fuck, Mags. I can't wait." I stroke harder, faster, my thighs starting their telltale burn. The tingling at the base of my spine expands upward. "You're so fucking hot."

Her panting grows louder, her free hand squeezing her breast as she works herself over. I find myself holding my breath, watching her face, expecting her to close her eyes at any moment. Cut the intensity of our connection. Instead, I'm gifted with the best present of my life.

Her eyes fill with affection, and a tear spills over.

"I love you so much." Her whispered words are ragged and gasped, her lips trembling and hips rocking as she hits her peak and cries out her pleasure.

"So fucking much" is all I manage, then I'm coming, my dick pulsing in my hand, my release streaking her stomach and breasts until I'm spent.

We stare at her body, the evidence of what we've done filling the tent with the scents of sex and trust and something deeper. I'm not wondering if Maggie likes me as much as I like her. I'm not worried she'll ignore me tomorrow or freak-out if I blurt my feelings. Finally, we're on the same page.

She touches a streak of my come and moves it around her belly. "God, that was hot."

"Consider my mind blown, but I'm done with the no touching." I grab the small towel she brought and clean her up, then lie beside her, gathering her naked body close. "You're amazing."

"We're amazing," she says, tracing circles over my heart and playing with my chest hair.

I practically purr. "Can we postpone Chanukah? I don't want to leave our love nest."

"Sadly, we cannot. But we have forever to nest, and you have another gift to open."

She passes me the larger box.

With one arm under her neck, I give it a shake. Once again, nothing rattles. "Assuming there's a theme, are these anal beads?"

She rolls her eyes. "No."

"Is it a dildo I get to use on you?"

"Still no."

"One of those blow-job-stroker things you get to use on me?"

Laughing, she pinches my hip. "Would you just open it already?"

"So impatient," I mumble as I awkwardly unwrap it with one arm behind her neck. The white box under the paper has no writing to give me clues. Curious, I open the flap and pull out a picture frame. One look at the photo inside and I crack up, stuffing my face in her hair, shaking us both. "I can't believe you did this."

"You seemed to really want it."

I lock my leg over her and kiss her head, then look at the

picture again—Maggie in her hot-dog costume, looking adorkulous. "I can't wait for Halloween next year. We'll be Mr. and Mrs. Hot Dog."

Her hand becomes a threatening lobster claw at my hip. "No, we most certainly will not."

"But you'll have mustard up your middle. I'll do ketchup. It'll be great."

"It's not happening, Lennon."

"It's definitely happening, *Gingersnap*."

She growls and shoves me off her, pretending she doesn't love the idea, but there's a glint in her eye. "Race you to the house. Last one there has to clean up the tent later tonight."

She's out before I'm on my knees, practically stepping on my head for leverage. She streaks naked across the property in the freezing fucking cold, laughing and hollering while I race after her. Honestly, best birthday in the history of birthdays.

CHAPTER
Thirty-Six

BY THE TIME we're cleaned up and parked in her parents' driveway, my bubble of happiness is less bright. I'm beyond in love, excited to spend time with Maggie and her family, but I still have unfinished family business of my own.

"Do you mind if I don't go in right away?" Still gripping the wheel, I glance at Maggie. "I think I need to call my father."

She angles toward me and presses her hand to my thigh. "Of course. I'll wait outside the truck. If you need me, holler."

A quick kiss later, I'm alone with my renewed anxiety, but I don't hesitate. I thumb to my father's last text.

> Life Wrecker: I know you don't want to hear from me, but you left before I finished. There's something else you need to know.

That "something" sure was something in the end. Not a deadly disease as I thought, but I still feel as though I've lost him. My imagined version of him, that is. The man who I thought loved me and missed me in his life.

Swallowing roughly, I call him. The second the phone rings, my stomach churns. I debate hanging up, but I need to do this. Say the things I never said. Be the guy who can push through tough hiking conditions, face losing the love of his life, and come out the other side stronger.

Two rings later, the line clicks over. "Hello?"

"Hi." I clench my teeth, probably ruining thousands in orthodonture work. "It's me. It's Lennon," I add, when I realize he probably doesn't recognize his own son's voice.

"Oh, Lennon." A pause follows, along with an annoyed jab of my heart at his hesitant tone. The sound of splashing water and laughter rings out. "Now's actually not a great time. Can I call you back?"

Can he call me back? Can the asshole who ruined our lives go have a pool party while the rest of us still struggle to come to terms with our lives?

Growling, I glance through the windshield. Maggie's watching me intently. She mouths *I love you*. Or maybe *Elephant shoe*. The sight of her compassionate face strengthens my resolve.

"Sorry, no can do. We're talking now."

"Sure, okay. Give me a sec." His words are rushed, and a distant *Dad, look at me* carries through the line. Another splash. More laughs—evidence of his happy new life and happy new family—but the hurt and anger I expect don't come. A new awareness sinks in. Understanding that his feelings about me no longer affect my feelings about myself. *I am man, hear me roar.* I don't care how this call ends. I only care that it happens.

"Sorry about that." He sounds exhausted. Probably got tired while dyeing his hair. "Thanks for calling. I know it's not easy for you."

"Actually, you don't know anything about me. Or any of your kids. Although that's probably not accurate. I bet you know plenty about your new sons. I assume that's why you wanted to talk?"

"You got a hold of the book, then?"

"Mom read your tabloid trash, so thanks for putting her through the wringer again."

"Look, Lennon. I know you're mad. You have every right to be, but I wanted you to learn about your brothers from me. You and I—we were close. I've wanted to reach out so many times. I just didn't feel it was my right. Losing you and your brothers was my penance," he drones on, like he's reading cue cards. "I've had to live with that. I'm not sure if you want to meet my boys. I'll leave it up to you. All I can hope is that you and your brothers are happy. That you've made something of yourselves, despite me."

His tone is so neutral and pragmatic it's almost shocking, but I know better than to be surprised. This is more of the same, him saying appropriate words to ease his guilt, and I'm done hoping he's something he's not.

"I'm not sure if your therapist buys that penance bullshit, but true penance is supposed to be hard. It's the tough stuff of facing your mistakes, not walking away and ignoring us while you move on with your life. That was the easy way out. The same way you got out of jail time with the Feds, when every part of what you did was *illegal* and *destructive* and *narcissistic*, from the affair to working with the cartel, to pretending we didn't exist after the fact. I don't know if you're more honest with your new kids, but I know I want you to do better with them. Raise them well and show them consistent love, if you can manage that.

"As far as we're concerned," I go on, my words stern but steady, "I hate you for what you did. You have no idea the damage you caused, how many lives you ruptured." I almost tell him about Des and Sadie, that she was pregnant when we left and Des lost ten years with Max, but he doesn't deserve our secrets. "I only called to say that you hurt me more deeply than I ever realized, and I'm still working my way through it. *Despite you*, as you so nicely said. If you need forgiveness, you can take it. But I want you to understand you didn't earn it."

I haven't raised my voice and yelled, but I don't need to. Maggie is a yeller when she's upset. Fiery and passionate to the core. Des and Jake are known for letting their inner cavemen roar, but we're not all built for shouts and outbursts. As I sit in my truck, shaking slightly, awaiting my father's reply, I realize it's okay to be me too. Forthright and stern when needed, but quieter. Internalizing as much as I'm saying. If we all lashed out when stressed, the world would be a pretty volatile place.

"That's fair," he finally says, more sadness in his voice than I expect. "And I really need to go. Good luck with everything."

He hangs up. Doesn't offer another apology or tell me he loves me. He doesn't even wish me happy birthday.

I stare out my windshield, waiting for residual anger to surface or numbness to take over. Neither happens. Our talk didn't change what he did or fix anything specific, but I'm okay. This was a reminder that nothing with my father has been personal, as I believed. He didn't ruin our lives because I wasn't enough for him or because I failed classes or because he didn't love me. He laundered money to serve his best interests, and I'm better off without him in my life.

The second I'm out of my truck, Maggie curls herself around me. "Was it awful?"

"It wasn't awesome, but it was necessary. As far as I can tell, his new family is his do-over. His chance to see if he can be different. At least, I hope he's serious about that, for my half brothers."

She pulls my face down to hers. "I'm so proud of you for confronting him."

"Thanks for pushing me to do it," I whisper against her lips.

I kiss her, tender at first, but tender only lasts so long with

Maggie. I haul her closer, kiss her deeper, reveling in the security of our feelings for each other.

"I love you," I murmur between swipes of my tongue.

She nips my lip. "I love you more."

It's a competition now. Who can love whom hardest, everything with my nemesis a strategy and a game. You better believe I'll win.

"Can you two get in here before you're arrested for indecent exposure?" Maggie's sister, Emma, flutters her fingers from the door.

"This property is secluded," I say. "No cops in sight. We can grope all we want."

Emma hooks her thumb to the side. "Our uncle's a cop and viciously overprotective, so we'll see how that goes."

A large man is standing at the window, his massive arms crossed, scowling at me.

"You didn't tell me your uncle's an overprotective cop," I whisper-hiss to Maggie.

She pats my cheek. "He's a bigger, beefier version of my father. Huge guns." She flexes her arms in the universal tough-guy pose. "As in biceps, but he also has an impressive gun collection."

Now she tells me. "If I'd known, I would've worn the football gear and protective cup."

"And not grace us with your latest in hipster fashion?" She gestures to my skinny jeans and moves out of grabbing distance. "That would be criminal."

I don't give her hell for teasing me, but I do plot ways I'll make E regret this latest blackmail, which will involve his fear of snails. "My hipster clothes and I would like to go inside now, if you and your obnoxious humor don't mind."

She bats her long lashes at me. "We don't mind at all. Also…" She rushes in for a cheek kiss. "I love you."

My grin verges on ferocious. "I love you more."

Once inside, we're bombarded by Edelsteins. Hugs and kisses are passed around the rowdy group, scents of frying potato and roasting meat filling the air.

The big cop, Uncle Matt, shakes my hand, nearly crushing my fingers. "Maggie and Emma are like daughters to me," he says, dragging me closer. "Any man who hurts them, hurts me."

"Ha-ha," I say, unsure why I'm fake laughing. "I would never knowingly hurt Maggie. Or you. Or anyone whose number is on your speed dial. There will be no hurting if I can help it."

"Ignore Matt," Mrs. Edelstein says, saving the bones in my hand by pulling me in for a Mom Hug. I've always loved Mom Hugs. The feeling of being cocooned in kindness and grace. "Thank you for being patient with Maggie," she says softly. "She puts up a strong front, but inside, she's vulnerable. And incredibly special. I've never seen her as happy as I have when she's been with you."

I inhale her kind words and overwhelming warmth. "Thank you for raising her. She's an amazing woman. I can't believe I'm lucky enough to be with her."

She sniffles and nods, then pats my back and leads us into the living room for drinks and general mayhem. Aside from overprotective cop Matt, Mr. Edelstein has a sister, and both siblings have three kids, each one funnier than the next. Three of Maggie's grandparents are still alive, and the family loves teasing their matriarch for keeping the items in her fridge lined in perfect rows. There are jokes about one person's poor parking skills and another's shoe obsession. No one takes the ribbing personally or gets annoyed.

The atmosphere reminds me of my family now, in the aftermath of WITSEC, all of us showing love through good-natured taunts and friendly insults. I brace for the absence of Maggie's birth mother to infect the mood. The shape of her shadow hanging over the jovial room. Except it's not here. Maggie's smiling her biggest smile—open, loose, carefree—

laughing so hard at something her cousin says she wipes tears from her eyes, and a deeper awareness settles. We don't need to reconcile with our parents or relatives who've hurt us to be happy. We have to reconcile with ourselves. Confront or not confront as the situation dictates, then embrace the people who lift us up and hold them close.

When the sun dips below the horizon, Mr. Edelstein clinks his glass with a spoon and places their menorah on the wooden hutch.

"We light the shamash first," Maggie whispers to me as her father lights the tallest center candle. "Then we use that to light the others. Mom called it the 'helper' candle growing up. Told us we should be like the shamash, always helping others shine."

The group chants, "Baruch Atah Adonai Eloheinu Melech Ha'olam…" A whir of Hebrew I don't understand, but I love the rolled Rs and guttural inflections and Maggie's strong voice at my side. I love being welcomed into her family's traditions, learning more about the shark girl who swam circles around an insecure nineteen-year-old boy.

Two more blessings follow, then Maggie bends toward my ear. "We only light one other candle tonight, the first night of Chanukah, always starting with the candle at the left, adding a new candle on each of the eight nights."

"The Festival of Lights," I say, remembering the term.

She nods and squeezes my hand.

The first candle is lit in quiet contemplation, the shamash replaced in its center home, then happy chatter breaks out as Maggie's father calls everyone to the dining room.

I tug her closer, inhale her strawberry-almond scent. "Thanks for inviting me tonight."

She fits herself snugly into my side. "I love having you here."

"I love being here more."

"I love it most," she murmurs and kisses my lips.

CHAPTER
Thirty-Seven

"JUST JUMP ALREADY," I call from the ground. "If you fall, I swear I'll catch you."

Maggie is thirty feet above me, clutching the rope attached to her harness in a death grip. "No, you won't. I saw you drop E."

"Of course I dropped E, but I didn't let him hit the ground. I just made sure his life flashed before his eyes."

Bastard deserved it. It's been four months since we learned about our half brothers, and E loves riling me around them.

The second Callahan showed up with them today, E said, "Not sure if you remember your hipster brother, Lennon. He's famous for kissing Farrah Khatri the day after he got his braces, and his braces locked with her braces, and the lunch duty teacher had to call 9-1-1."

First, no one called 9-1-1, but E loves to exaggerate my humiliation.

Second, the locking only lasted, like, five seconds, but Lana Young was there and broken telephone happened, so by the time the rest of the school heard, Farrah and I were locked together for hours and the cops needed to use the Jaws of Life to separate our faces.

"I won't let *you* fall," I shout to Maggie. "What good would I be without you in my life?"

She eyes the row of planks ahead of her. This is one of the harder ropes courses, with a row of six wood planks, each hanging by a set of ropes and spaced apart. She'll have to jump from one plank to the next and find her balance each time, before moving on to the next challenge.

As expected, Maggie's glaring at me like I've strapped her to a bomb. "I can't believe you're making me do this. And of course you'd be useless without me in your life."

Truer words were never spoken. "Exactly. I've got you."

"No, he doesn't," E pipes in, still pissed I half dropped him.

"I don't think he's strong enough." This from a smirking Desmond.

"His upper body is kind of scrawny." Jake snickers at his own moronic joke.

"He's lean but strong," Cal says. My new favorite brother. "Hipster strong," he adds.

Nope. They all suck.

"He won't drop you," Max shouts, earning his award of Best Nephew Ever. "It looks scarier than it is. Don't think so long about it."

"You can do it," Brayden adds, cupping his hands around his mouth.

"Yeah!" Luke chimes in with a little jump, his high-pitched voice not yet plagued by puberty.

I'm not sure how Brayden and Luke turned out so well. Not only are my new brothers fun and nice, they seem happy. Brayden has brown hair like the rest of us, but his face is longer and he has blue eyes. Luke has blond hair, those same baby blues, and bigger ears his brother teases. They don't look much like my brothers and me, but there's familiarity in their wide-set mouths. Bower DNA scrambling to the surface.

Callahan volunteered to be our intermediary where they're

concerned. He doesn't speak to Dad, but he used Sandra's intel to communicate with their mother. He arranged our first introduction in Houston, where they live, and this trip to Windfall. It's only our second time with them, and I doubt we'll see them often, but having them here for this inaugural testing of our ropes course feels right. Even better, they've learned they have five brothers to count on, no matter what curve balls life tosses their way.

"If you jump," I tell Maggie, "you can have control over the remote for a month."

It's been a battle since she moved in to my place. She has a love for cheesy Netflix shows, but I'll take TV torture if it comes with Maggie. Owning that property and sharing it with her is the definition of having the roots I've craved for so long.

She stares down at me. "Seriously? A month of TV control?"

"Seriously."

"Okay, okay, okay," she chants to herself, bending her knees in preparation. "I can do this. *Netflix. Netflix. Netflix.*" She stiffens, seems to rethink the jump, then she firms her jaw and launches herself forward, arms outstretched to catch the next set of ropes.

I tense my arms as she lands, making sure the rope hooked to her is taut. The plank sways. She slips and almost bites it, but she finds her footing and leans forward with a victory shout.

She beams down at me. "I get all the Netflix!"

I grin at the harness hiking up her shorts. "I can see your underwear."

She gives me the finger. I retaliate with an air kiss.

An hour later, we're outside the cabin Maggie and I painted Island Getaway green, enjoying a potluck barbeque, complete with Delilah's famous baked goods. Her and E's dogs chase sticks and make everyone smile. Mom spends time with Brayden and Luke, then she sits with Max while he shows off his latest drawings. That kid never leaves the house without a sketchbook.

313 CLUES YOUR NEMESIS LOVES YOU

Everyone's relaxed and happy, except Cal, who seems more subdued than usual. He's standing with Jake, staring off at the forest while Jake talks about something.

Before I can head over and see what's up, Ricky and Aaron arrive to join the festivities, along with Mizhir.

I meet them and pull Mizhir into a one-armed back-pound. "Glad you made it."

He holds up a foil-covered bowl. "Wouldn't have been the same without my chickpea salad."

"Or your bad jokes. Let's get you fed."

We grab plates of food and shoot the shit, reminiscing about the time I egged him on to hide a dead rat in Mrs. Klassen's desk.

"You were such a dick back then," he says around a mouthful of potato salad. "You totally knew I couldn't say no to your harebrained schemes."

"They were *great* harebrained schemes."

"Because you weren't the one touching the dead rat."

I really was an evil genius. We eat and laugh as my friends and family enjoy the afternoon, while Maggie and I steal tender glances at each other.

"Can't believe it's ready," Des says, coming to my side as Mizhir goes for another helping of food. Des surveys the low ropes course for the younger kids. "I tested the swinging tire again with Cal. The thicker rope works great."

"We should've let E on it before he fixed it."

Des smirks. "Not sure how I dropped the ball on that one."

"Thanks," I say, no longer joking. "For pushing me to come to Windfall and for joining my business. I wouldn't have any of this without you."

A growing brand. Greater success on the horizon. Maggie, most of all.

He shrugs a shoulder. "I owed you. You're the one who pushed me to face Sadie."

"I was, wasn't I?" I tap my chin. "Come to think of it, you're the one who should be thanking *me*. Or at least offering to clean the cabin bathroom for a month."

He flattens his lips. "Sure, I'll offer that. Right after I blow up a picture of you with your braces and plaster it on the wall."

Sweat slicks my brow. I step closer, getting up in his face. "You better fucking not."

He smirks. "You better fucking not piss me off."

The crunch of churning gravel interrupts our stare-off, drawing our attention to the parking lot.

"Sorry I'm late!" Jolene calls as she gets out of her car—a newcomer I wasn't expecting.

I'm not sure who invited her. Maybe Delilah or Sadie...or possibly Jake. They may be exes, but they've hung out a few times since he's moved back to town. Or maybe she and Cal have finally patched up whatever fight they had over a decade ago, and she's here to see her former best friend.

Des leaves me to join Sadie and Max. I glance at my other brothers. Jake brightens and waves to Jo, striding to her with purpose, but Cal does the least Cal thing I've ever seen and actually *curses* under his breath. Abruptly, he marches away, disappearing behind the cabin.

The move reminds me of my early days hiding from Maggie.

Speaking of the love of my life, my favorite woman swish-sway-saunters toward me. "Why aren't you smiling?" She pushes to her toes and kisses my ear. "Is it the loss of the Netflix?"

I groan and run my hand down her side. "A bet's a bet. I'll happily watch whatever horrible show you want, although there might be some heckling."

"I'm counting on it."

I nose her neck and kiss her freckled skin, but my attention slides to Jake.

He's talking close with Jolene, his hands tucked into his

shorts pockets. Nothing about them talking is odd, except his head is tipped forward as though he's *bashful*—a state of being I don't associate with Jake—and Cal is still disappeared behind the cabin. "Something's up with Jake and Jolene. Or maybe Cal and Jolene."

"Yes on both fronts." Maggie turns to people watch with me. "I think Jake is still into her. And every time her name comes up around Cal, he looks like you when you're stuck in an elevator. Delilah and I can't figure out why."

"Are Jake and Jo getting back together?"

She studies the duo. "From what I've gathered, they're just friends. But even if he wants more, I doubt she'd go for it. Didn't he cheat on her before WITSEC?"

Right. That idiotic rumor about him and Larkin Gray hooking up after a party. "No way Jake cheated. Not his style, but the rumors were intense."

"Whatever happened," Maggie says, "I'm not sure Jolene feels that way about him anymore."

So Jake is maybe trying to rekindle things with Jo, and Cal is being a weirdo, avoiding her at all costs. I smell trouble.

I kiss Maggie's luscious lips. "Excuse me while I investigate."

She squeezes my ass covertly. "When everyone's out of here, we're getting naked in the grass."

A throb of desire floods me. It never takes much with her. "If we must."

I slap her hip and head for the other side of the cabin, where I find unflappable Callahan scrubbing his hand over his face as though he's just been told he has a month to live.

"What's up with you and Jolene?" I say, not beating around this thorny bush.

He startles and blanches, like I've caught him jacking off in Mom's favorite oven mitt. (*Yes*, that actually happened. And *yes*, I used the intel to bribe him into dares.)

"Nothing's up," he says way too fast. "I just needed some shade. Sun was hot."

Nope. The man does nothing but evade these days. "Why don't we try this again? You've been weird for months. I've barely seen you talk to Jo since you've moved back. She was your best friend for nine years. Whatever fight you had or whatever happened before WITSEC doesn't matter now. It's not like you two were hooking up."

His skin flushes, and his eyes dart to the grass. Just a second, but oh my God.

Oh my fucking God.

I grip the front of his shirt. "You *slept* with her?" His brother's girlfriend. Or ex-girlfriend, depending on the timing. Not that the timing matters.

"*No*," he whisper-hisses, slapping my hands away. "I've never touched Jo. I'd never do that to Jake."

"So, what? You just secretly have the hots for her?"

His cheeks burn redder than Maggie's hair. "Shut up. It's not like that."

"I can't shut up." Because holy fucking shit. Cal is lying his face off. "Are you telling me you covet your brother's ex? Or current crush, considering he's still into her and obviously invited her here."

The only way to describe Cal's expression is *terrified*. "If he wants her, that's great. Really great for him, because nothing happened with Jo and me. We just drifted as friends do, so quit being such a pest." He glares at me and storms off in a huff.

I stare after him, bewildered. Cal doesn't glare or storm. He doesn't hide from his family or get this defensive. He fixes *our* problems, which means he might actually have it bad for Jo. Nowhere on my Bower Boys Disasters Bingo Card did I have *Cal Falls for His Brother's Ex-Girlfriend*.

Maggie comes around the corner and wraps her arms around my neck. "Cal left early. Said he wasn't feeling well."

I press my forehead to hers. "This might be bad. Like, really bad."

"Does Cal like Jo?"

"It's a possibility." I'm not sure why I never considered this. Maybe I was in denial, didn't want to see either of my brothers hurt. But this is something Cal would do—our secret vigilante, putting everyone before himself, hiding whatever he's been feeling to make sure Jake's happy. The man will let himself be flayed to ribbons before he does a thing to upset our family balance, when he deserves to be as happy as me.

"Are you sure Jolene isn't into Jake?" I ask, holding Maggie tight.

She runs her hands through the curly ends of my hair. "Not for sure. Just a sense. But you can't meddle. They have to figure this out on their own."

I groan and hug her fiercely. My life preserver for weathering all Bower storms. "You're not allowed to fall for any of my brothers."

"You're the only Bower for me." She pushes my head up, brushes her lips against mine, deepening the kiss with a sweep of her tongue. "I can't wait," she whispers against my mouth, "to watch all the romances on Netflix this month."

Laughing, I grab her hand and spin her into an impromptu dance, catching and dipping her back the way I sometimes do. "It's fine. I'll just stare at you the whole time while I plan our hot-dog costumes."

Epilogue

Callahan

All I've ever wanted is to give my brothers the happiness they deserve. There's nothing more important than ensuring they find love and success in life, but I've encountered a problem. A troublesome hitch I can't control. Specifically, the fact that every fiber of my being is highly attuned to my former best friend: Jolene Daniels, Ruiner of My Serenity.

I sense her the second she's near, like this precise moment. It's not just the telltale tingling up my neck when she enters the art gallery or my knee-jerk instinct to flee. My oldest brother's sharp intake of breath is a dead giveaway to her presence, followed by his I-want-my-ex-girlfriend-back sigh.

"Jolene's here," Jake says, like I don't know. "She brought drinks."

I keep my back to her. Pretend my heart hasn't turned into a jackhammer. I carefully lift another painting off the wall and lean it with the others.

Her appearance here isn't odd. A number of townsfolk

turned up to help the Yard Goat Gallery owners clean up after last night's spring storm. It was a doozy, blowing through Windfall with a decisive hand, but the Yard Goat sustained the only real damage. An old tree came down on the train-station-turned-artist co-op, shattering windows and puncturing the roof. Some art was damaged beyond repair. Water seeped in, which means new floors are needed, along with new windows and drywall and a fresh coat of paint.

Since Jake and I run our own construction business, and I'm friends with one of the artists, we volunteered our help. Everyone else is here because this is Windfall. A close-knit community that helps when others are in need, sweeping, lugging, gossiping, arguing good-naturedly over what should be done next, or, in Jolene's case, bringing refreshments.

"I should go talk to her," Jake says, but my oldest brother doesn't move. "I still can't get over how great she looks. Even more beautiful than when she was younger, don't you think?"

I clench my jaw. If I don't turn around and participate in this painful conversation, Jake will wonder why I'm acting weird. He won't know *why* I'd like to demo the brick wall in front of me and sprint through the wreckage, but the wondering is just as bad. Wondering leads to questions. Questions lead to uncertainty, which eventually leads to mistrust. For twelve years, I've successfully hidden my role in his breakup with his ex-girlfriend, who happens to be my ex-best friend. Neither of them knows what I did, and I plan to keep it that way.

Unfortunately, there's no avoiding Jolene in this shoebox town.

Steeling my nerves, I turn around and, *Christ*. There goes my body again—*reacting*—like last night's storm is blowing through my chest.

Jo may appear innocent enough, with her country-girl charm, flirty brown hair, and warm chestnut eyes, but the beauty mark on her right cheek is the first clue she'll mesmerize—a dash of sensual mixed with sweet purity. Dangerous without even trying. All this time later, my insides go chaotic around her. I still sense when she's in a room. She was my best friend for nine years, two of which she spent dating my oldest brother. We've been apart for twelve years since then, but my forced absence hasn't changed the facts—what I did to her and Jake was *bad* and *wrong*, and the guilt is even worse now.

"She does look great," I tell Jake, forcing a placid expression. "Have you asked her out yet?"

"Not on a proper date. The way things ended with us was messy."

Because I'm an asshole, and Jolene thinks Jake cheated, when he did no such thing. "That was just the town rumor mill."

"I know. I think she knows it too. When it all went down, she said that wasn't why she wanted to break up. But I'm not sure that was true, and doubts can linger."

Forget asshole. Just label me traitor and toss me to the wolves. "Give it time. You two were meant to be together."

Townsfolk are busy, moving easels and art supplies, carefully navigating the glass on the floor. Jake leans on his broom and shrugs. "I know she's happy I'm back. We've hung out at her bar a few times, but people are always around, and I get weird vibes from her."

"Well, we did vanish for over a decade."

He smirks. "I survived witness protection, and all I got was this lousy life?"

"We should make T-shirts."

"Or kill our father," he grumbles.

"There will be no killing." I refuse to let anything bad happen to my brothers, even if murdering Raymond S. Bower would be justice served.

"Hey, you two!" Jolene grabs a couple of sodas and brings them our way.

She's wearing cowboy boots and a jean skirt that shows off

her shapely legs. Her fitted blue T-shirt reads *Fishing for Trouble*. Isn't that the God's honest truth? This woman never fails to inspire anarchy.

I accept her drink and nod at my brother. "Jake was just saying how great it is to have you back in his life."

For a second, her gaze seems to slide down my body. The perusal isn't interest. Jolene never looked at me the way she looked at Jake. She's likely surprised by my bulk now that I hit the gym daily on top of my construction work, but I instantly feel flushed.

Expectedly, she blinks and looks at Jake. "It has been great having your family back. I missed you *both* a lot." Her attention flicks back to me. "I've tried calling you a few times, Cal. You're never around."

"I've been busy," I say. Mainly avoiding her.

"What he's doing," Jake says, his tone hard, "is taking on extra work he doesn't need to do."

I crack open my can and take a long gulp of fizzy lemon soda. Anything to cool me down when around Jo. Unfortunately, nothing douses the fond memories she inspires—us competing in Monopoly or Sorry until the person losing upended the board in a dramatic fury. Playing touch football after a hard rain, diving into mud puddles, cracking up as muck covered us head to toe. We studied together, often ate dinner at each other's houses. Helped each other when needed, like the time she broke her arm jumping out of her tree house.

I was at her house daily while she was healing, writing her assignments, even brushing her hair and helping her get dressed. I could barely breathe those days, holding out her jeans, feeling the drag of my thumbs up her thighs, the sharp dig of her fingers into my shoulders as she used me for balance. Teenage hormones were not my friends back.

Adult hormones aren't much kinder.

"There's nothing wrong with helping townsfolk," I tell Jake, forcing my focus on him. "Mr. Elroy needs a new back deck. The Liangs need a fence for their puppy."

His nostrils flare. "You're doing too much."

This is typical Jake. Our stand-in dad who kept us together when our worlds fell apart. I love that he cares so much, except his thoughtfulness enflames my guilt. "After being gone so long, it feels important to help where I can and reconnect with people. Like you two are reconnecting," I say emphatically.

Jolene glances at her cowboy boots. Jake scratches his chest, his intense focus shifting to her beautiful face. Their reconnection might take time, but I'm a patient man. I'll do my damnedest to give Jake everything he deserves. Namely, Jolene.

"What you're doing," he says to me, back on my case, "is working yourself into an early grave."

"The only person going into an early grave is our father," Lennon says, joining us.

"Again, no one's being killed." It's amazing how many times I've uttered that sentence in my life.

"Death is a natural part of existence," Lennon says, smirking through his hipster beard. "Speeding it up is simply helping evolution." His smug expression passes over our awkward group, then settles on me. He raises an eyebrow brimming with know-it-all condescension. "How is everything these days, dear brother?"

I clack my teeth together. "Great, thank you."

"Like, *really* great?"

"As great as great gets."

"So you're *great*?"

"Absolutely," I say with a forced smile, refusing to look at Jo.

Here's the thing with Lennon. My meddling brother thinks he knows my secret. He thinks I'm as far from great as great gets because I'm in *love* with Jolene. I may be guilt-ridden over what I did—and there's no denying I'm still attracted to her sensual-innocent-siren self—but that's pure chemistry. I haven't spent time with Jolene in twelve long years. I no longer obsess over her, dream about her, wish we could be together. As long as I keep our friendship minimized, I won't revert to my old pining ways. Plus, I have a plan to reunite her with Jake and fix the mistakes I made.

"If you'll all excuse me," I say as I inch away from the group, "I think they need help with the tree carnage outside."

This is my life these days. Making quick exits from coffee shops, family gatherings, bars, get-togethers. Anything to avoid Jolene and keep my family from learning too much.

I make haste and march toward the exit, but I feel Jo's attention on me as I move. She's probably confused as to why her former best friend is avoiding her like it's his job.

Once outside, I spot Ben standing over the fallen tree. He squints at its girth and rubs a hand over his shaved head.

"We'll need an arborist for that," I say, strutting toward him. A much easier task to focus on than righting my wrongs. "They can cut it up and turn it into wood chips."

"Sure, but…" Ben gets a hazy look in his dark eyes. "It's a great shape—the way it protrudes in sections. I could carve a bear in the top half."

"Or just a portrait of me."

His lips quirk. Ben is a built Black man who would look at home on a sports field, but he's a sculptor who started this artist co-op with other like-minded creators. "Too bad the gallery has investors, and I promised them we wouldn't create anything terrifying."

I attempt not to grin too wide.

At the start of WITSEC, I dwelled on what my old friends were doing, worried our disappearance knocked them for a loop. I obsessed over Jolene plenty, even though we were estranged by then, unsure if losing Jake and me in one night devastated her. Eventually, I decided worrying was for the weak.

I'm good with money and investing. Over the years, I built

my savings, made discreet contacts in Houston. Found ways to keep tabs on the people I love. Ben has no idea I'm the silent partner financing his art gallery. My family doesn't know I hired a woman living in Windfall to do my bidding as needed. Why stress over the happiness of those you love when you can use a spy to ensure their success?

"I'm glad your investors are keeping you on your toes," I tell Ben, pleased my shell company has helped him realize his dreams. "Plus, people love a good story. When this is carved, tell prospective buyers the tree was about to crash down and you saved a child stuck in the branches before it fell. It'll cause a bidding war."

"That would be lying."

"Or just a creator creating."

"Or lying," he says on a laugh and slaps my back. "If I haven't said it enough, it's great having you home."

Being home is certainly better than I expected. The Rough Ridge Mountains in the distance center me in a way Houston's cityscape never did, but it's not just the rugged landscape and quaintness of Windfall that gives me this sense of peace I haven't felt in twelve years. It's watching Lennon, who's outside now with Maggie, the two of them laughing as they toss broken branches at each other. E has shown up with Delilah, and I swear I never thought I'd see him smile this wide again. Even Desmond is here. He's still snarly and grumbly, but the spark of affection in his eyes as he tosses his son over his shoulder and holds Sadie's hand like he can't live without her...well, I'm downright moved.

This is my purpose—securing my family's happiness. This is why I don't leave life to chance.

"Javier's moving later this week." Ben grabs lopping shears to cut a longer branch. "If you're free, we could use another hand."

I mentally review my commitments—building Mr. Elroy's

new deck, the Liang fence, renovating the Rosen kitchen with Jake, adding a garage and granny suite for the Whites with him. There won't be much sleep in my future, but Javier was part of our posse back in the day. I haven't seen much of him since my return. "Count me in."

"Sweet. I should see if Jolene can come too."

"Nope," I blurt and launch a branch sideways.

Dammit.

Ben straightens and leans on his shears. "You don't want Jolene there, or Jolene's busy?"

"The latter, I assume. She's busy running her bar."

"Why do you assume?"

"Because it makes an ass out of U and Me?"

He huffs out an I'm-not-buying-what-you're-selling laugh. "Amusing, but you two used to be inseparable. I *assumed* you picked up where you left off."

We left off with me shutting Jolene out for no fault of her own. So, he's not wrong. Things are as uncomfortable as ever. "We're fine. Some friendships just don't last the test of time. Not that we're *not* friends. We just aren't as close as we were."

He stares at me like I'm that tree trunk, my true form hidden under layers of gnarled bark.

When his unwavering attention gets too much, I punch his shoulder. "I should check on the other helpers. Send me Javier's moving details."

I swivel before he replies, unsure where it's safe to work. I need a Jolene-free zone. Somewhere I can focus without everyone getting in my business. I spot a couple of old ladies attempting to pick up the heavy Yard Goat Gallery sign and march toward them.

But Jolene Daniels, Ruiner of My Serenity, steps in my way.

"You're avoiding me," she says pointedly and blows a wayward strand of hair from her eyes. She was never one to beat around the bush.

Unlike me, who excels at evading. "Like Jake said, I've been busy."

"Too busy for me?"

"Nope. Just"—I wave a vague hand around—"life. Work. It's not easy starting fresh somewhere."

"Exactly." Her brown eyes go soft. "I totally get it. At least, I want to try to get it. I know things were strained between us before you left. I'm not really sure why, not that it matters. You're home now, and I want to help you adjust. I want my best friend back," she says more quietly.

My heart feels like it's in a vise clamp, pressure slowly squeezing the uncooperative organ.

There was a time I wouldn't hesitate to open my arms. Beckon her in. Hug and console this woman who used to be my other half. But the urge to run my nose up her ear strikes, to splay my hand on her lower back, feel her soft body molded to mine, my thigh pushing between hers as I—

"We'll go for drinks soon," I say and stalk away.

We won't. I don't trust myself around Jolene. I have no clue why, all these years later, she still makes me feel ravenous yet tender. Discombobulated. Having one-on-one time with her won't help my plan to reunite her and Jake. Which is fine. Operation Jake Wins Back Jolene goes into high gear tomorrow. Once they're in love and happy, my body will remember where it belongs—far away from my former best friend.

———

What happens when Cal gets stuck rooming with Jolene while he furtively tries to deny his feelings for her? Find out in Book Four, **4 Hints You Love Your Best Friend.**

Author's Note

I had a blast while writing this book, but I also had reservations.

Hard fact: readers are way harder on heroines than on heroes. This is something that's always upset me, because it's reflected in our daily lives. Too often, people criticize women more harshly than we criticize men. Men are celebrated for hooking up. Women are vilified. Men are told they get more attractive as they age. Women often become invisible or are judged for looking old.

There are so many layers to unpack why, as a culture, we hold women to more damaging standards, and I hate that these behaviors trickle into our views of romance novels. Heroes can bully, be rude, act aggressive, refuse to share feelings, and we fall in love with them.

If a heroine shows those attributes, before they grow into their better selves—that uplifting journey throughout the book— readers often sharpen their pitchforks and call them "unlikeable."

When I started writing Maggie, I realized pretty quickly that she was on the prickly side of sassy. She might piss off some readers for being closed off at times, or for keeping Lennon at arm's length when she wasn't coping emotionally, or for lashing out when she was stressed or upset.

I debated curbing those behaviors of hers to appeal to the masses, but I pride myself on writing relatable characters (with a dash of wish fulfillment), especially as my books have progressed. And Maggie, for me, is exactly that—not perfect and relatable.

Personally, I'm notorious for internalizing when I'm upset and can't for the life of me say The Thing I need to say. I get closed off in those moments and shut down. I'm also kind of like Lennon, who avoids confrontations. I see some of myself in both of these fallible characters. Maybe you see some of yourself too, or maybe you know people like them.

Either way, I hope you appreciated their struggles to grow emotionally, without being too hard on Maggie. I hope my books lift you up by showing that change and betterment are always possible, but it's also okay to get there more slowly.

Here's to many more happily ever afters with my perfectly imperfect Bower boys crew!

xox Kelly

Also by Kelly Siskind

Bower Boys Series:

50 Ways to Win Back Your Lover

10 Signs You Need to Grovel

6 Clues Your Nemesis Loves You

4 Hints You Love Your Best Friend

More to come!

One Wild Wish Series:

He's Going Down

Off-Limits Crush

36 Hour Date

Showmen Series:

New Orleans Rush

Don't Go Stealing My Heart

The Beat Match

The Knockout Rule

Over the Top Series:

My Perfect Mistake

A Fine Mess

Hooked on Trouble

Stand-Alone: Chasing Crazy

Visit Kelly's website and join her newsletter for great giveaways and never miss an update!

www.kellysiskind.com

About the Author

Kelly lives in charming northern Ontario, where she alternatively frolics in and suffers through the never-ending winters. When she's not out hiking or home devouring books, you can find her, notepad in hand, scribbling down one of the many plot bunnies bouncing around in her head. Kelly's novels have been published internationally, and she has been featured on the Apple Books Best Books of the Month list.

Sign up for Kelly's newsletter at www.kellysiskind.com and never miss a giveaway, a free bonus scene, or the latest news on her books. And connect with her on Twitter and Instagram (@kellysiskind) or on Facebook (@authorkellysiskind).

For giveaways and early peeks at new work, join Kelly's newsletter: www.kellysiskind.com

If you like to laugh and chat about books, join Kelly in her Facebook group, KELLY'S GANG.

Connect with Kelly on social media:
Twitter/KellySiskind
facebook/authorKellySiskind
Instagram/kellysiskind